We  Ku... dren

A tale from Ragaris

by

Penelope Wallace

A Mightier Than the Sword UK Publication

We Do Not Kill Children

The Tales from Ragaris

By Penelope Wallace

A Mightier Than the Sword UK Publication

Paperback Edition

Copyright © Penelope Wallace 2016

Map of Marod by Stephen Hall

Cover Illustration by Ian Storer

Cover Design by C.S. Woolley

ISBN 978 153 983 779 4

"I will sing of loyalty and justice; to Thee, O Lord, I will sing."

(Psalm 101:1)

To the memory of my parents

John Cecil Hall, philosopher, Liberal and

singer, 1930-88

and

Ursula Eunice Hall née Ewins, historian and

socialist, 1926-2015

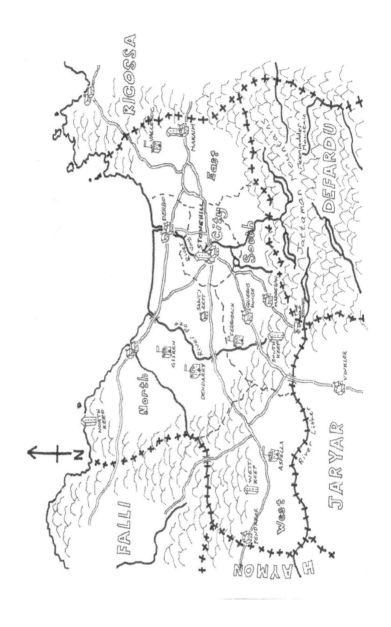

Characters

Based at Stonehill:

Royal family of Marod

King Arrion of the Marodi

Queen Malouri, his wife

Their children: Prince Jendon, aged 19

Princess Daretti, aged 17

The King's aunt, Lady Sada, Warden of the Kingslands

The King's Thirty

Southern Six: Gemara Kingsister

Dorac Kingsbrother

Kremdar Kingsbrother

Tommid, Kremdar's squire, aged 13

Hassdan Kingsbrother

Meril, Hassdan's squire, aged 14

Kai Kingsbrother

Soumaki Kingsister

Western Six: Gardai Kingsbrother

Torio Kingsbrother

Northern Six: Mayeel Kingsister

City Six: Sheru Kingsister

<u>Other</u>

Lord Vrenas, Marshal of the Kingdom

Abigail Anni, Bishop of Stonehill

Lady Karnall of Aspella

Herion of Maint, her nephew

Ralia, her grand-daughter

Attar, Herion's steward

Sil, a woman in Herion's service

Captain Renatar of the Castle guard

Sister Susanna, King's priest

Lady Kara of Meriot, King's Questioner

Saysh, later Saysh Kingsbrother

Alida, a painter, Hassdan Kingsbrother's wife

Lilli, their steward

Shoran, an apothecary, Soumaki Kingsister's husband

Chief Secretary Andros

Makkam, a senior secretary

Marrach of Drumcree, a visiting landowner

      Gormad, Marrach's squire, aged 10

Jamis and Hanos, squires

Arvill, Laida, Braf and Morvan, soldiers in the army of the Kingslands

Mritta, a tailor, and her son Edric

Karila, a trader in wooden crafts

At Ferrodach:

Gahran, Lord of Ferrodach

His children: Ilda, aged 12, Gaskor, aged 9, Filana, aged 5

Hagouna, his steward

Dav, a member of his household

Captain Rabellit, an officer in the army of the Kingslands

Anni and Josper, soldiers

Finya, a poor woman in a village on Ferrodach lands

At Dendarry:

Ramahdis, Lord of Dendarry, and Farili, Lady of Dendarry
(parents of Gormad)

Their other children: Kammer, aged 8, Beta, aged 6, Kiri
aged 2

At Gisren:

Praja, wife of Kremdar Kingsbrother

Their daughter Yaina, aged 3

Lukor, their steward

At Aspella:

Lady Rakall of Aspella (Lady Karnall's daughter)

Lord Jovian, her husband

In Jaryar:

King Rajas II

Lord Ramos of Marithon

Lady Igalla of Arabay

Sali and Artos, proprietors of The Hanged Man inn in
Vinkler town

Melina, a woman of Vinkler

And other soldiers, nobles and people of Marod and Jaryar

Part One – The Stones

1 October 570 After Landing

FIRST DAY OF EXILE

Five days after the murders, the trial.

Dorac had always hated being stared at. He stood, flanked by guards, in the centre of the White Hall in Stonehill Castle. Around three sides were crammed men, women and children. Most, though not all, he knew, and every eye was fixed on him.

Fifteen years ago, he had sworn his oath to King Arrion's mother in this hall. Since then, he had received orders here, and delivered reports, and greeted new brothers and sisters. It was the centre of the life of the King's Thirty.

The long white walls glared in on him.

Before him on the left was a table with the holy gospel, on which the witnesses swore. The priest, a short scowling woman, stood beside it, and the King's Questioner, Lady Kara. On the right, another table with that cloak, *his* cloak, stiff with blood. The witnesses sat behind. Kremdar looked troubled, Arvill looked distraught, and Braf looked like nothing.

The eyes burned into him, and raised sweat.

He answered what turned out to be the last question, and was told to step forward and take the oath. With his right hand on the open book, hearing himself stumble over the words, he swore that the evidence he had given was true. He knew that no one believed him.

The eyes shifted away, and he was cold. Everyone looked – Dorac looked – at the man sitting on the dais at the north end of the hall. King Arrion, his lord for nine years. His lord, his friend, his brother. Everyone else had been staring at him because they believed him guilty. The King looked away for the same reason.

"Your Grace, do you wish to retire to consider?" asked Lady Kara.

"No. But he may sit down." So someone brought him a stool, but he ignored it. He waited. Fought the knowledge of doom coming. All around the walls there was a hiss of talk. Dorac could not hear the words. But he could guess.

"He murdered three children, and thought the King would approve. One of the Thirty! Why is it taking so long? What is there to decide?"

The King stood up. Silence beyond imagining.

"Dorac Kingsbrother, I find you guilty of the murders of Ilda aged twelve years, Gaskor aged nine years, and Filana aged five years."

It still seemed impossible.

Hands pressed on his shoulders, pushing him to his knees. Blood pounded behind his face. Possible and actual. At least he would soon be dead.

"You have served my mother and me and this land with great loyalty for many years. I do not doubt that you thought what you did was for the best. Words were spoken at Council that may have helped you to believe this. But whatever your motives, it was an abominable act.

14

"From this day, and forever, you are exiled from this land, and from the fellowship of the Thirty. If you are still within the realm one week from today, or if you ever return without the King's word, I will have your life.

"I take back your companionship, I take back your land and your gold to comfort the bereaved, I take back your horse and your armour." He paused. "Your sword you may retain. Go from here, make a better life, and may God forgive you."

That was all. He barely noticed the eyes now. As he stood up, he overbalanced and had to steady himself on the floor. Someone almost laughed. He bowed to the King, turned, met Kremdar's eyes one last time and walked out of the Hall.

So his life ended.

*

But still he walked and breathed, and had to decide what to do.

In fact he went to his cell, packed his satchel as if for a normal journey, handed over the gold in his pouch and even spoke a few words to one of the guards. Yet also it seemed that he walked in a straight line from the Hall to the Castle gate without looking back. *They believed Kremdar. He believed Kremdar.*

The King said, "I find you guilty." Kremdar said, "I did not want to believe it, it was so horrible."

His brother's lies, his lord's condemnation carried him on as he strode through the familiar streets. More and more eyes. Soldiers and beggars. Shopkeepers and apprentices. Even dogs. More and more whispers. "Only exile! Why is he still alive?"

The news was spreading through all the city of Stonehill.

15

Gemara and the others would be returning soon, would hear and would curse him. In a month his crime would be known everywhere. His steward would hear it at Valleroc; his cousin in the north; Tor's sister, whatever her name was, in the east. His father would hear it, if he were still alive, and sober enough to listen. The reputation of the Thirty's Southern Six would be damaged forever.

Dorac the Childkiller. A good name for a story.

"Once there was an evil man. Once, and not so long ago -" And the story would end with a warning to be good, or else that man would creep into the house at night, and do to you what he did to those children at Ferrodach.

"Please."

A small pant, almost too quiet to hear.

"Please!"

He glanced down. The boy was running to keep up. "Please don't walk so fast."

Dorac grunted.

"Please."

He stopped and stared down at the gasping child. Somebody's squire, very young.

"What are you doing?"

"I wanted to -"

The confused pity in the face and voice was unbearable. Dorac drew his sword, and held it to the boy's throat. "Go back," he said, "or I will kill you."

There were gasps from the whisperers. No one dared to intervene.

"You – you wouldn't -"

He wouldn't. Kremdar and Arvill's Dorac, the monster with his name – *he* would.

"Go back," he repeated, "or I will make you wish you had."

But he needed no threats. His legs were long enough to outwalk young Gormad.

He turned again, and went on faster. Alleyways, churches, shops. No one spoke to him at the gate.

Away out of the city, south, anywhere.

*

Gormad trailed tiredly back up the hill to the Castle. The other squires were standing in clumps, arguing about what they would have done to the murderer, had they been the King. They stared at him, surprised or sniggering.

Why had he gone chasing after the exile? *Why?*

He avoided even his friend Jamis, and wandered out to his favourite place in the gardens, the hidey-hole under the bushes. He wished Meril were here to talk to, but she was away dealing with raiders with her lord.

He had no tasks now that Marrach was dead. He was a squire without a master. He would have to apply to the King for a new lord or lady. Or go home to Dendarry.

Gormad had gone to the trial because everyone else was going, because he needed something to fill the unreal emptiness, and because of his lord's mysterious words.

All the long days, while Marrach was "ill", and then "not getting better", and at last openly "dying", Gormad had sat beside him, and waited on him, occasionally sung to him, held a bowl for him to cough blood into, and wondered if he would ever have a normal life again, one that was not drenched in confusion and worry.

He had worried stomach-crawlingly about his lord. He had wondered, with some guilt, what would happen to *him* if - when -

And sometimes he was distracted by worrying about Meril. They were fighting at the northwest border. She might not come back. When he dared to voice this terror, Marrach said that fourteen-year-old squires did not actually fight. But the Haymonese and the Jaryari were the evil enemy, and perhaps they wouldn't keep the rules.

And all this worry was quite boring, and made him want to scream.

He had paid little attention to mutterings about treason at Ferrodach, wherever Ferrodach was. Then one dark evening, when the physicians were looking even gloomier, the room reeked of illness and the walls were closing in, Jamis pounded up the stairs with news too strange and gruesome not to be told at once.

"D'you remember they sent the Kingsbrothers to Ferrodach?"

"No."

"Dorac and Kremdar of the Southern Six went to arrest Lord Gahran – the Council's just learned he's a traitor – scheming with the bloody King of Jaryar – they were sent to arrest him or chop his head off, or whatever, and what d'you think Master Dorac did?"

"What?"

"Lord Gahran poisoned himself, and Dorac went straight away and murdered his children."

"Whose children?"

"Lord Gahran's, you idiot, three or four children. He cut them into *pieces*. The youngest one was *five*. Some people say that Lady Sada had said at Council that they should be killed, because they're traitor's blood, but the King had said not to. But anyway, he did, and he's been arrested by his own brother, and is being brought back for trial here. Everyone's going to go. A Kingsbrother on trial for murder!"

Marrach murmured weakly, "What did you say?"

Jamis explained it all again, a little more slowly.

"Dorac Kingsbrother would never kill children."

They asked him what he meant, and did not understand his answer, and that was almost the last thing he said to Gormad. The physician and the priest turned him out, and Marrach died that evening.

So Gormad went to the trial. *Cut to pieces*, Jamis had said. *Exaggerating*, thought Gormad sensibly, but he was wrong. Dorac Kingsbrother stood in the Hall, face bruised because he'd fought with the soldiers arresting him, and insisted that everyone else was lying. *Like in a story.* He looked innocent to Gormad. But the King, who ought to know everything, and who had chosen the Thirty, every member of every Six, and loved all of them as brothers and sisters – the King had condemned him. Suddenly Master Dorac looked as empty and lost as Gormad felt. And he walked out, and after a while Gormad followed him.

Why *had* he done that? "I wanted to -" He wasn't even sure how he would have finished the sentence. Gormad sat under the bushes, hugging his knees, haunted by the death of one man, and the face of another. And tomorrow was his lord's funeral. More emptiness, more nothing.

Hunger drove him out, and he ate supper with the others –
"What did the childkiller say to you, Gormad?" – and attended chapel,
and went to bed. He lay, still haunted, in the dark. The funeral was
tomorrow. The King would write to his parents. And his father would
say, "You are no longer a squire. Come home." *After all his struggle to get
away. How Kammer would laugh.*

Where could an exile go? How far had he got? South was the
enemy land of Jaryar, whose kings claimed that all of the north and west
should be theirs, and had plotted with Gahran the traitor. East was
Ricossa, where everyone was fighting each other. Southeast were the
mountains. Master Dorac had seven days, six now, to reach a border.
How long would it take him, if he walked all the way?

Walked all the way.

Gormad had not realised he had been asleep, but suddenly he
was awake, and it was the middle of the night, and he had the
beginnings of the most stupendous idea. *Yes.* It pieced itself together
logically in his buzzing head. Very quietly, he slipped out of bed,
fumbled for his secret horde of money and crept out to the stables in
the dark.

*

Few people were heading towards the city. Dorac strode past those
who were leaving, ignoring their stares. A troop of soldiers passed, sent
to reinforce the southern border with Jaryar, and for them he stepped
aside. But after a while he was alone on the road, fields to right and left,
and an occasional farmhouse – wood or more rarely stone – or an
autumn-gold tree. The October breeze flapped his cloak. Above, dirty
white clouds were bottomed with dark grey. Slowly the light faded. He

walked on until it was fully dark.

On the edge of Harro's tidy fields, there was space to sit under an elm. He drank, and ate already stale bread. He prayed, but emptily – for what can a dead man say to God? Then he wrapped himself in his blanket and lay down. As so often before, but rarely without companions.

Tomorrow he would need to find or buy more food.

Tomorrow.

All through the hours of praying and shouting and battering the walls in Ferrodach, through the journey back under guard and more hours imprisoned in the Castle, he had supposed he must be either believed, or executed. He had given no thought at all to anything else. To having to live on, without life.

But the King had been merciful.

As never before, he was aware of the cold, and the hard earth, and the impossibility of sleep.

But not impossible in fact, for the sound of hooves woke him. Dorac tensed, rolled over and gripped his sword. The roads were never safe. Two horses, one with a rider, picking their way in the dark. But then the riderless horse ambled across, sniffing.

It was Derry.

He stood to allow the beloved stallion to nuzzle his face, his heart breaking again.

"Please."

That voice! He swung round in fury. The child's small figure was looking down at him from the height of a saddle.

"My lord is dead, sir. I need a new lord."

21

This made no sense. He dragged his mind to something that did.

"You make me a horse-thief as well as a murderer?" Perhaps he *would* have to kill him.

"No! I -"

"This is the King's horse now."

"I bought him! I did!"

It still made no sense. The boy went on talking, but he could not listen. There was a blackness in his head, but eventually he put himself on Derry's back, and rode away in the dark.

He was so tired, and that must have helped the blackness, for he thought of nothing at all. He rode, not fast, along the road under the autumn stars, until at last the grey came, and he reached the crest of a low hill where the road twisted slightly east. The sun was rising. So beautiful, the sky so threaded with gold and pink, that he woke up again.

The unbearable tomorrow.

2 October 570

Gormad saw the man bend his head, and then slowly dismount. He stared blankly at the boy for a moment, before turning away to rub down his horse. Gormad copied him, hoping this would not annoy. You never knew with grown-ups. Then Master Dorac sat down against a tree, unbuckling his sword and laying it at his side, and took some bread out of his satchel. After a little, he tossed a chunk in Gormad's direction.

"Th-thank you, sir." His voice sounded loud. There was no answer. He realised that he was both rather frightened and very tired. He opened his eyes as wide as he could, and tried not to yawn.

Dorac sat staring ahead after finishing his bread. Then he got up and stretched. He bent down and collected some small objects from the ground. Sitting down again cross-legged, he placed a small pebble in front of him. Then another, and another: five in all, wasn't it? He sat staring at them. Gormad wondered, and dared say nothing.

Elbows on knees, chin on hands, Master Dorac sat in the company of his little stones for a long time. He picked up one and tossed it away, and then a second. Gormad itched in the stillness. Birds sang. The sun had risen, but the breeze was cold.

At last there was only one pebble left. Dorac shut his eyes and spoke silently. Then he crossed himself, scooped up the stone and scrambled to his feet. "Amen." He threw it into the air, and bent to retrieve his sword.

For the first time, he looked at Gormad, from very high up, and not as if he were pleased to see him. Slowly and heavily, he said,

"Gormad, son of - Ramahdis. You said you bought my horse?"

"Y-yes."

"In the middle of the night?"

"I - went to the stables and there was no one there. I left some money, and a letter."

"How did you know which one?"

"Err - He's very distinctive." ("The ugliest piebald in the King's stables," someone had said.)

"How much?"

"Seven gold."

"A squire has seven gold pieces to give away?"

"My father gave it to me."

At the look on Dorac's face, Gormad scrambled up and stepped backwards.

"The truth."

"It is the truth! I swear! My father's rich. He gave me the gold, and told me to keep it secret, but said I might need it for the honour and respect of the family."

The man paused, and then shrugged.

"Some day I shall repay you - Thank you. Now go home."

Say it. "I want to go with you."

"I am going to the Old Stones."

Gormad gasped in horror. "No! You can't!"

The man turned away.

"You *can't!*"

And he whirled back, and his anger was terrifying, and his hand was on his sword. Then Gormad remembered what he was supposed to have done.

"The bodies were all hacked apart," the soldier Arvill had sworn, almost crying. "Our feet were slipping in the blood."

Several gasps of time passed. *Steel at his throat yesterday.*

The man turned away, and reached for his horse's bridle. "Go home."

Go home. But –

"Please! I don't want to go home."

There was a short pause.

"I am going to the Old Stones," said Dorac. He swung himself into the saddle, and rode off.

Gormad found he had pissed himself, and went cold with shame. But it was a kind of permission.

*

After hours and hours of riding silently just behind, he dared to ask, "Can I ride beside you?"

The man barely glanced at him. "Ride where you like." So they went on, side by side, through the morning, past a few farms and a lake. Here they stopped for the horses to drink. Dorac stared at the water for a long time, for no reason that the boy could tell. It was just a lake, that his tutor would have called "a wonder of God's creation", and his lord would have called "beautiful, isn't it beautiful?" After this the road divided, and they took the narrower way, with more trees, and barely enough room for two. They disturbed more rabbits and pigeons than before.

And on, with a dark *Do Not Talk To Me* cloud that you could almost see surrounding the man. Gormad told himself a hundred times to be patient. He hadn't realised yesterday that the company of someone who had lost everything would be so – not dull, he was too scary to be dull, but - depressing.

Gormad had not been to Stonehill before arriving with his lord eight weeks ago. In any case, the King's Thirty came and went on their exciting missions, and were rarely in one place for long. He'd barely been aware of Master Dorac before Jamis's news. But kindly Meril, four years older, had befriended him, and he did remember that her lord, Master Hassdan, was in the same Six. To be the squire of a Kingsbrother or Kingsister was high glory, and he'd wanted to hear everything she had to tell. He couldn't remember her saying anything good or bad about Dorac – she liked Kremdar, and was nervous of Gemara, and of course Hassdan was wonderful. (Meril was a little boring on the subject of Hassdan.) Nothing about Dorac.

But he was a Kingsbrother, and so he must be a mighty and noble warrior. They all were; that was what they were for. Although he didn't look it. Marrach of Drumcree had been disfigured by losing an ear in some fight, but before his illness he had otherwise looked the part of a lord, or even a hero. But Dorac -

Gormad rarely studied people's appearance, but now he had nothing else to do. Like most people, Dorac was brown-skinned and black-haired. But he must be forty years old at least. The longish hair was going grey. His chin was roughly pock-marked, and when he showed his teeth (which was rarely) some were missing. He was broad-shouldered, but not impressively tall.

And he had rather small eyes. Jamis said you couldn't trust a man with small eyes.

They stopped again for more silent bread and water. Dorac said, "Rub down the horses, and watch them", and disappeared into the bushes. Gormad was not sorry to dismount, stretch his legs and relieve himself. Obediently he rubbed down the piebald and then his own friendly Champion. "Wish me luck," he whispered to Champion's nose.

Dorac was gone a long time, and being alone became even worse than being with an angry perhaps-murderer. When he came back, however, he was carrying a few fish, and some green stuff that was not grass. He gave Gormad a not quite unfriendly nod, and they mounted again, Gormad with some difficulty. He wished he were taller.

At last he could bear it no longer. "Your pardon, Master Dorac," he said very politely. "Why do you want to go to the Old Stones?"

Slowly, without looking at him, "That's my concern."

"But you can't go there! You can't just die!"

"That's my concern."

Gormad could hear the adult threat, but he could not stop himself.

"But you're only an exile! You could go anywhere -" His voice faded. Abruptly, Dorac had swung down from his horse. He drew his knife, cut a stick from a nearby tree and began to strip the bark.

Not looking up, he asked, "Does your father beat you?"

"N-no."

A faint look of surprise. "Your mother, or your lord?"

"Once."

The stick was bare. The man swished it through the air once or twice, and turned to stare into Gormad's eyes. "*I* will beat you, if you tell me again what I can't do." He tucked the stick behind his saddle, and mounted. They rode on.

After a little, to his huge shame, Gormad began to cry. He cried as secretly as he could, but he knew the man was aware of it. Miserably he waited to be told, with blows, that the solution to his snivelling was to turn around and go back.

But Dorac said nothing, and in time the fit passed. He wiped his nose on his sleeve, and snorted up snot as quietly as he could.

It seemed a very long time before they stopped again. The sky was beginning to darken, and they watered the horses, and then led them off the road to a small clearing that Dorac seemed to know. He said, "Can you clean a fish?"

Gormad spent a frantic moment choosing between "I'm ready to learn", "No", and "I'll try", before choosing the most straightforward. "No."

"Can you make a fire?"

"Yes."

"Do that, then."

He was going to have to prepare the space, gather the kindling and light it, under the eyes of Dorac Kingsbrother.

"Don't look doubtful," his lord said in his memory. "You will learn as you do it, not as you don't."

*

"It still seems incredible," Kremdar finished. "But they were alive when he walked in, and there was nowhere to hide in the room, and no one else went in or out. It had to be him. I'm sure he hated doing it. Perhaps that's why he was so - wild. Like a madman." He shuddered, and lifted his lean face to look at his four remaining siblings of the Southern Six, gathered to listen to him in the small room. Dust danced in the afternoon sunlight streaming through the open window.

The almost unbelievable news had met them as they returned to Stonehill with the troops from the border skirmish at Kerrytown. Those from the other Sixes drew away a little, to allow the Southern to absorb the shock. They reported back to the Lord Marshal, and sought out Kremdar.

Gemara, the leader of the Six, had been pacing up and down throughout Kremdar's narrative. She was almost a quarter of a century older than anyone else present, which perhaps made her the wisest. She was tall and gaunt and dark-skinned, her grey hair tied in an unfashionable knot on top of her head, making her look even taller. Her arms crossed her body tightly, binding her together as if the emotions she always controlled were about to burst out.

Hassdan stood silently in the corner, staring fixedly at Kremdar. His tall frame, pale skin and hair, and plain intelligent face made him a distinctive figure, even without the accent that marked him out as Jaryari-born.

Kai and Soumaki sat at the table opposite Kremdar, neither concealing their shock. Kai was weeping unashamedly, tears trickling down his handsome face and into his neat dark beard. He could not keep his hands still; they scrunched his thick hair; they flattened themselves on the table; they clenched against his cheeks.

Soumaki, the youngest at twenty-six, held herself contrastingly still. Soumaki was chubby-faced and stocky, with the muscular upper body that came of constant archery practice from the age of ten, yet somehow she always managed to look fragile and delicate. Now she gave little concerned gasps at appropriate moments, but said nothing.

Kremdar's face, scarred on one cheek from a long-past battle, was in shadow as he leaned forward, staring at his thin fingers laced tightly together. He had obviously had to go through this account many times. "If he'd only admitted it, the trial might have ended differently," he said now. "It would have been more honourable. His motives were loyal, and I think the King might have forgiven him."

"I would not have done," said Gemara. "Five years old."

There was a short silence.

"I still can't believe it," said Kai heavily. "Dorac wouldn't do something like that."

"Dorac has killed many people. He is not gentle," said Gemara.

"In battle! He never did anything like this! I can't believe it!"

Soumaki said unwillingly, "He must have thought it was necessary."

"*I* can barely believe it," said Kremdar. "It's not like him. And I can tell you, he didn't do it lightly. His face, when he came out of the room -" He shook his head, as if turning away from the sight. "It haunts me almost more than - having to bury them."

"They *would* have grown up," murmured Soumaki, tears sliding down her face.

"Where will he go?" asked Kai. "Seven days - To Valleroc?" They all knew how much the grant of the estate had meant to him eighteen months before, his childlike joy.

"Don't be absurd. He's lost his lands," said Gemara, frowning.

"What matters," said Hassdan, "is not where he goes, but what he does. We now know he's a childkiller. Is he anything else? Is he a danger to the King?"

"Dorac would never harm the King!" Kai exclaimed predictably.

"We don't know anything any more," said Hassdan, and exchanged a glance with Gemara.

They talked on for a little, and then separated. Kremdar had a spell of guard duty to finish. Hassdan and Soumaki had houses in the town, where Hassdan had a wife, and Soumaki a husband and children. Kai wanted a drink (of course), but found Gemara jerking him back into the room.

"We allow you to judge cases. We must be mad. Have you any wits at all, Kai, or are they pickled in ale?"

Kai was not in the mood for this. "Bring out the crap you're thinking, then."

"Stop saying you 'can't believe it'. Stop saying it, and think."

He looked at her.

"Dorac told the court he went into the room saying 'they have to be told', informed the children their father was dead, and left."

"Uh-huh."

"Kremdar told the court that Dorac went in saying what sounded like 'they have to be *killed*', and came out looking haunted and blood-stained, and then he and Arvill and the other soldier went in -"

"I follow you," said Kai. "So that means -"

So if Dorac was telling the truth, Kremdar was lying. So if Dorac didn't kill the children -

"You don't know which of them to believe. Neither do I. But for today the truth is Kremdar's truth. For today we don't deny or doubt that. Do you understand now?"

But Kremdar would never -

There was a pause. Kai asked in a low voice, "Is that going to change?"

"Meet me in the east stables during evening chapel."

And she stalked out.

*

Kai's favourite remedies for pain were the love of a woman, and alcohol. But on Sundays Karila was holy and virtuous, and joined her parents and grandparents after church, and few of these people approved of Kai's part in her life. He disliked drinking alone, so he went to the Great Hall of the Castle, where there was always ale for the King's siblings.

No one was talking about anything but Ferrodach.

Gemara's words beating a drum in his brain, he repeated over and over, "It's a terrible thing", and "I had no idea he would act like that", like a child memorising its lesson, and sat down at a table with his mug. The huge Hall felt grotesque, an alien cavern, and the people, from the unfortunate serving girl being cuffed for slowness to lovely Ralia flirting with the King's son, were remote strangers. All around him, people were saying that they had always suspected something about Dorac.

"I'd never have guessed *children* - but he does have a nasty streak."

"D'you remember what he did to Marrach years ago? He

should have been stopped right there."

"Have you seen him after a fight? Blood everywhere, eyes wild, laughing - You could see how he loved the slaughter."

That's a lie. Dorac doesn't know how to laugh.

"They were ripped apart in a frenzy, Arvill said. Five years old, the youngest. Five years old!"

"King Arrion always favoured Dorac. And, ah, he's not getting any younger, maybe he thought the King would be grateful, without saying so, and in a few years, he could retire and be heaped with wealth. Didn't work, though. Serve him right."

And worst of all -

"I can't believe it of him."

"Of Dorac?"

"No, of Lord Gahran. Dorac was not a man I'd ever trust."

*

Gemara allowed Soumaki and Hassdan a little time for their conjugal reunions, while she made some enquiries about the trial and its aftermath. Then she made her way thoughtfully to the apothecary business run by Soumaki's husband Shoran and his brother.

"Mistress Gemara, welcome. She is upstairs."

"I thank you."

Soumaki was playing soldiers with her two little sons. The older boy stood and bowed politely to the visitor, and his mother's smile faded. Gemara sat down cross-legged on the floor, and slowly began to balance the little wooden men on top of each other. The boys were silent, already knowing better than to speak.

"It will be hardest for you," said Soumaki, with her usual

33

conventional sympathy. "Knowing him longest. There are excuses. What Lady Sada said - perhaps she was right." She grimaced, looking up at the ceiling. "Now we have to forget him, if we can. When we can."

"Do *you* think he was right to do it?" asked Gemara cautiously.

"No. I only said Lady Sada might be. I don't want to think so badly of Dorac. Because – I think I ought to respect his courage. To do something like that – something he knew he would be reviled for – to do it for his king – that takes loyalty. I don't think I could do it. But -" Very lightly, she stroked her younger son's hair. "But I don't feel that. I just feel sick that I let a man like that hold my baby."

*

Hassdan's household was larger, and Gemara had to give her name to a servant. Then she waited in the back kitchen, tapping her fingers impatiently until he came downstairs. She smelt mint from the tiny herb garden outside the window.

"I was anticipating a visit," he said, sitting down opposite her, and meeting her gaze.

"You asked what more we didn't know. What did you mean?"

Hassdan shrugged. "Whether he did it."

Relief flooded her. She respected Hassdan's judgment, as she did not respect Kai's. "You think he's innocent?"

"I do not know. I do not like not knowing." He leaned his forearms on the table and placed his fingers together in a steeple. "Dorac killed them and lied; or Kremdar and two other people killed them and lied." He frowned at the fingers. "Either seems unlikely. Either is possible. Dorac is more brutal. Kremdar is less honest. I think you are believing Dorac, and that is why you are here. I am not knowing which of my brothers to believe, and I do not like that at all."

"No."

"We have to discover the truth, if we can." He paused and then added, "The truth may not be what you want it to be."

"Meet me and Kai in the east stables during chapel." She got up. "I thought Kai would prefer the excitement of midnight, but we all need our sleep."

"How you do patronise him, Mother Gemara - I'll be there."

*

Gemara walked into the Small Chamber, and bowed low.

King Arrion and Queen Malouri were studying maps of the west at a table, deep in discussion with one of their commanders. Torio Kingsbrother, the skilled but unbearably conceited youngster in the Western Six, waited with a guard by the door, and a black-clad secretary stood beside the King, ready to take notes.

"Mistress Gemara?"

"Your Grace. This is the worst news in fifteen years."

"So Makkam was saying a little while ago," he replied soberly. Secretary Makkam, who had presumably said nothing of the sort, blinked in surprise. *Learn some control, young woman,* thought Gemara crossly, before addressing the King.

"All the Southern Six crave your forgiveness."

The King said, "You and the others are not responsible for Dorac's crime. You have done well in the west. Do you have anything else for us to hear?"

"Only to ask who is to replace him."

"We haven't yet decided. Have you a suggestion?"

"No. Only – Your Graces should choose absolute loyalty."

"I thought we had," said the King bleakly. "Will that be all?"

"Yes, Your Grace."

She withdrew to her neat cell in the Court of the Thirty. About an hour later Secretary Makkam came to the door, and said politely, "You may attend His Grace in the Willow Chamber in a few minutes, Mistress Gemara."

There was only one guard outside the door, and none within. The King was pretending to play chess with Makkam, the table angled so that he was facing the door. He looked enquiringly at Gemara as she bowed. She had served and honoured King Arrion and his parents for thirty years, yet her shoulders went suddenly cold with nervousness.

"Your Grace. May I speak frankly?"

"You sought a secret audience," he said with asperity. "I assumed you would speak frankly."

Ah. Yes.

"I – some of your siblings in the Southern Six wish to make a more careful enquiry into the deaths of Lord Gahran's children." Nothing could take back those words; the dice had been thrown onto the board.

The King was very still. "Why?"

"We think there may be some doubt."

"Who thinks?"

"Myself, and Kai and Hassdan."

"You were not at the trial. I was. The evidence seemed quite clear, and I decided accordingly. You think our brother Kremdar and two other independent witnesses are lying?"

"It is possible."

"Gemara! Almost anything is possible! You want to undermine my judgment and sentence. You are slandering Kremdar. Have you no better reason than 'It is *possible*'?"

"Your Grace," said Gemara, flushing beneath her dark skin but still looking him in the eyes, "if you had asked me a week ago which of the two I trusted, I would have said both. If you had pressed me hard, I would have said Dorac. Every time. If you had asked me a week ago if Dorac could kill three children – legally blameless children – kill them and lie about it – lie to *you* – I would have sworn on my husband's grave that it could not be true. I would have believed it of almost anyone sooner. I would almost have believed it of myself." With an effort she kept her voice calm and level. "I know he may be guilty. But it seems so strange. And if he is not, then Kremdar is lying, and should not be allowed close to you or anyone dear to you."

The King stood up abruptly and walked over to the fire. There was a pause. Gemara had time to see Kremdar's amiable serious face in her memory, to watch again as it broke apart in horror and grief.

King Arrion turned back and shrugged. "I agree that it seemed almost incredible. But stranger things have been known. You have no evidence."

"No. We wish to see if there is evidence. A fuller enquiry, in secret."

"Kai and Hassdan, you say? Not Soumaki?"

"She seems to accept it."

"You want to try to find some – some fact that would show

that Kremdar is lying? What sort of fact? Do you want to torture him? Am I to authorise my sister to put our brother on the rack?"

She flushed again.

"And if you find something, what then? He's been condemned. You want to ask me to change a trial judgment? Can I do that?"

"I am no expert in law, Your Grace."

Both turned their eyes to Makkam, and the King nodded permission for her to speak.

"I do not remember. But I will see what I can find in the books, if it pleases Your Grace."

He nodded again, and looked away. "It wasn't just the cloak, and what Kremdar and the others saw, you know. His manner when he took the oath - He looked at the gospel, and he *shuddered*. Everyone noticed. He stared at it, and then he kept fumbling over the words. He's taken oaths from people for years. It didn't look right.

"What do you want, Gemara?"

"When you appoint a replacement for Dorac, have that person posted to guard duty. Appoint Kremdar to magistrate work with one of us. Allow me or Hassdan an errand that will allow us to investigate - and send Kai secretly to find Dorac. Before he does something irrevocable."

"To investigate at Ferrodach?"

"Yes."

"Do the other two know you're here?"

"I said I would meet them tonight. I didn't tell them I was coming to you. Hassdan may guess."

There was a short silence.

"Kai to find Dorac? You think that's the easier task. I've always thought you underestimate Kai." He looked up at the painted ceiling (willow branches, dappled leaves). "So. You may tell him to set out as soon as he likes. I will find an excuse. Possibly a dying mother."

"His mother is -"

He stopped her with a glance. "Dorac may have a boy with him, I hear. I want him back safely.

"I'll make the other announcements tomorrow. Makkam, arrange for Mistress Gemara to have three seals of the Thirty to take away."

"Yes, Your Grace."

"*Thank* you, Your Grace."

"Gemara." His voice was cold. "Dorac is one man. We have other things to think about. I cannot afford to have half the Southern Six chasing and worrying at the other. You have one month – no, forty days, since you will have other duties. If there is nothing, you will forget Dorac, and embrace Kremdar with love."

"Yes, Your Grace." She bowed.

"Makkam, leave us."

The secretary looked startled, but left obediently. The King wandered towards the corner window alcove, which protruded from the main room. Here they could not be overheard. He beckoned Gemara with a jerk of his head, as was his way.

"What I tell you now, you will never repeat."

She nodded.

King Arrion was smiling a little. "A long time ago - twenty

years ago - more than twenty, perhaps - for a few months one summer I loved Dorac more than any other human being."

Gemara hid her astonishment, which was great.

"Now you tell me I may have exiled him unjustly. If this is true, if anyone bore false witness against him, I want that person alive. I want them kneeling before me, and begging for a quick death. And they will not get one."

After a few heartbeats, "You can go."

*

As the day wore on, there were formalities for the dead.

Lord Gahran, who had crowned treason with suicide, was entitled only to the briefest of holy words from Sister Susanna, a ceremony to which almost no one came. His body was then burned in the inner courtyard.

But many people gathered as Marrach of Drumcree's coffin left the city, on a hearse pulled by four handsome horses. He was accompanied by his younger brother and heir, his steward and other servants.

By this time, of course, the absence of his squire had been noticed.

*

King Arrion had just finished dictating a letter to Secretary Makkam, and was walking towards the door, when Lady Sada entered. "Your Grace," she said, curtseying low and magnificently, a sure sign of irritation. That made two of them. However, she was the Warden of the Kingslands, and he inclined his head politely.

"Lady Sada."

"May I speak to you?"

"I have been sitting about all day, and am about to take a short ride."

"Can that be delayed?"

"No. If your business won't wait, you may accompany me. If you don't wish to lose so much time, or feel you aren't dressed for riding -" he glanced at her fashionably-full blue over-gown and embroidered sleeves, "you may walk with me to the stables."

"I would be honoured."

"Brother, I will take the back way. Give us six paces." He swung briskly around and made for the quieter route. Torio Kingsbrother and the other guard obediently arranged themselves six paces in front of, or behind, the Warden, who was one of the King's highest advisers – and also his aunt. Small, aged, famed for her love of fine clothing and her withering tongue.

"Yesterday's trial," she began. "Tcha. What a disaster."

"Is it so?" the King asked sourly. "Ferrodach was taken, and the children will not grow up to be traitors. That was what you wanted, I believe."

They were passing through an empty room, and the door to the spiral stair had been opened for them. Lady Sada's gown was almost too wide for it.

"I didn't want a mess like this. There should have been no deaths. First, they let Gahran kill himself. Then the open murder. That was not what I recommended. There could have been a quiet word in Dorac's and Kremdar's ears before they left, saying, 'Despite what you heard in Council, if you take Lord Gahran alive, keep the children safe, to exert gentle pressure on him. But if he dies, and only if he dies, arrange that they die too, in a scuffle or something similar. Better three dead now than insurrection later.' They were loyal. They would have listened." She paused. "Or did you in fact tell them to do that? And Dorac was too stupid to do it discreetly?"

He turned to meet her eyes, and his voice was angry. "You have no right whatever to ask that question, my lady. As it so happens, I did not. Did *you* have a quiet word with them, then? Is that what's annoying you?"

"As it so happens, I did not. But I see no reason to change my advice." They both paused on the stair, the King two steps lower, looking up at her. "Arrion, do you remember the story of Absalom, in one of the books of Samuel?"

"I have priests to supply that kind of information," said her nephew. He frowned, and said, "Absalom was the son of the great King David of Israel, who had the first thirty mighty men. He rebelled against his father."

"Yes, and the King told his soldiers to be gentle with his son, even in putting down the rebellion, because he still loved him. But David's commander Joab and his men attacked Absalom and killed him, while he was hanging in a tree by his hair. The way the priests tell it, the meaning of the story is King David's grief. 'O Absalom my son!' But Joab was right. Absalom had to die. It is sometimes necessary to do what seems harsh or wrong, and take the risk that it is sin."

King Arrion was silent for a moment. Then he said, "I'm not accustomed to hearing you quote the Scriptures at me, Aunt. Especially not in praise of murder. Absalom was a grown man, and a rebel."

"I didn't say the cases were the same. But still, Joab was right, and the King was wrong."

The afternoon was fading, and the torches were separated from them by a turn of the stair. Neither could see the other's face clearly as the King said, "Do you mean yourself as Joab, or Dorac? So. Should I have pardoned and rewarded him? Is that what you think?"

"*Pardoned?* You should have hanged him. Whatever the right decision, he had his orders, and he disobeyed them. The Thirty are obedient and trustworthy, or they are useless. And what were you thinking of, to let him keep his sword? He's already attacked Kremdar once."

"Kremdar is surrounded by friends, and can take care of himself," said the King, but his voice was not happy.

Lady Sada pounced. "A child ran off after him, did you know? Can he take care of himself?"

"Do you know which child?"

"No."

"Gormad, son of Ramahdis."

"Ah."

"I have just written to his parents, to tell them that their eldest child and presumably heir is wandering the country with a murderer. Renatar has sent people after them, but if Dorac doesn't want to be found, he won't be."

In a voice that was half a tone gentler than before, Lady Sada said, "There's no reason to think he would harm the boy."

"Until last Wednesday, there was no reason to think Dorac would harm any child, other than cuffing them if they got in his way. I would have trusted him with my life, or my children's lives, without a thought. Now - I have *no idea* what he is likely to do."

He continued down. The lack of light, the triangular stairs, and the width of her skirts made the descent difficult for her. Possibly he had chosen the route on purpose.

"About the trial - I am not happy that Kara allowed so much emphasis on my words. 'Lady Sada, who recommends the killing of children.' It was quite beside the point."

"I don't agree," he said, stopping again. "When a man is on trial for his life, his reasons or excuses are very much to the point. Although of course he denied it anyway - I thought Kara was rather harsh with him. There was no need to remind everyone of the business with Marrach, especially as no one knows what happened. Unless you do – you who know everything."

"I do not know that."

They emerged blinking into the arcade surrounding the inner courtyard. The King whistled, and the two wolfhounds Tyre and Sidon dashed eagerly up to have their noses and thrashing tails fondled. Accompanied by the dogs, the two proceeded in silence. When they were almost at the door, she said, "Arrion. This is a mess, and the boy is an unfortunate complication. But you mustn't let it distract you from what is important. The Kerrytown raid."

"There are always raids."

"The raids from Haymon, which are commanded almost of a certainty from Jaryar. And at the same time we discover that King Rajas is conspiring with one of your lords for the throne. These things are not chance. Let us hope that we have put a stop to Gahran -"

"There is more to find out at Ferrodach, I think."

"Yes, there will be. Rajas wants Marod, he wants all of the north. How many more traitors is he corresponding with? The next war may come at any time."

"I think that's a little pessimistic. But perhaps not, looking at the last three weeks. Yes. Some of the Thirty need to look into these matters."

"They have no Thirty in Jaryar," said Lady Sada. "No Kingsbrothers and Kingsisters, no People's Meetings. No true link between king and people, except what the priests provide." She snorted; she had no great opinion of priests. "What they have is great families scheming against each other, seeking the royal favour, and pushing each other out of the way."

"You think we have none of that here?"

"We have more than enough. But the trust of the Thirty and the King holds it back, because the Thirty are not themselves lords of estates. 'The king trusts the Thirty, and the Thirty trust the king. The people trust the Thirty, and the Thirty listen to the people.'"

"'And all listen to God', " the King finished the quotation. "So —"

"So perhaps that is why you should have hanged him. What he did endangers that trust."

"Perhaps. Aunt Sada, I need to name a replacement to the Southern Six."

"This is a chance at last for Ralia," she began, but he cut her off.

"Bring me some names this evening. Four, I think."

"*Four?*"

"Yes. I want to compare them with Gemara's thoughts."

"Gemara has a lot of sense."

"Yes." They were at the back doors now, almost at the stables. Suddenly the King said in a different tone, "You asked me why I let him keep his sword. It was because I could not imagine him without it, the sword my mother gave him. If it had been Gemara, I would have let her keep her horses. If it had been you - I would have let you keep your gowns."

"I am answered," she said, almost seriously, and curtsied, and left him.

*

Kremdar came off duty, and was heading into the courtyard when Hassdan accosted him.

"Shall we find a drink in town, brother?"

"What an excellent fellow you are. I shall pay." As they headed out of the gate, the bells for Vespers ringing out from the city churches around, Kremdar asked, "Where are the others?"

"Come now, don't insult us both. Soumaki is with her children, as you would expect. Kai is getting drunk, as you would expect. I have been at home with Alida, as you would expect. Mother Gemara is the only one who ever does anything unpredictable. Where she is, I have no idea." Kremdar chuckled.

When they were sitting in an obscure and almost empty tavern with mugs in front of them, Hassdan said, "I am not going to ask you to talk about it again. It must have been terrible for you."

"Thank you. It was."

"Just one thing. How is Tommid?" Tommid was Kremdar's squire.

"He is well, I think. I managed to keep him away from the bodies. He *really* doesn't want to talk about it."

"Surely. Do you want to know how we fared?"

"Yes, of course. I heard it was moderately straightforward."

"In the annals it will be. I'll forget the details before Christmas. But at this day, it still feels important. We all got a few nasty slashes, several good people died, including young Vilma-" Kremdar made an appropriate grimace, "and Kerrytown was burned. Not all of it, but too much, along with some livestock and several fields-worth of grain."

"But you got rid of them?"

"For now, according to the scouts, and burned some of their land, and so it goes. I hope Lord Gahran had no hand in planning it. If he had -" Hassdan scowled, thinking of the bodies he had helped to bury. "Did you see anything at Ferrodach that might connect with the raid?"

"I don't think so. How did your girl Meril do?"

"She was useful with the wounded. She tracks better than I do. And for all she's so quiet, she's surprisingly sharp. You may wish to know that there's a measles outbreak in Kerrytown. Do not tell Soumaki." *Never give Soumaki an opportunity to worry about her children,* was the rule.

They talked on for a while, and nothing was said about the murders until the end. Then Hassdan drained his mug, and said, "Thank you. That helped to take the taste of your news away."

"Yes." Kremdar stared at the table. "I went to him that night, after the funeral, and begged him to tell the truth. If only he could have explained - He didn't like being asked. He promised to pull my fucking head off. And once he was a good brother to us."

"To you. Not so much to me. But yes. The thought of it makes me sick."

Kremdar nodded.

*

His duties finished for the day, Torio Kingsbrother wandered through the evening streets until he came to an undistinguished and tidy alley opposite a fairly respectable tavern. And shortly afterwards a small pale-skinned man in matching green hat and knee-length gown strolled out and greeted him politely.

Torio did not much care for the steward Attar, and he wasted no time on pleasantries. "Your master may like to know that the rest of the Southern came back today. I haven't seen Hassdan or Soumaki, but Kai was drinking in the Great Hall, looking gloomy and shocked. Lady Sada has been grumbling that Dorac should have been hanged, and that her name was besmirched at the trial. And *Gemara* went to the King when I was with him, and arranged to see him in secret."

"Ah. Thank you. He wondered if she might do something of the sort. If Mistress Gemara was - dissatisfied - in any way with the verdict, do you think the King would listen to her?"

"Perhaps. She's been in the Thirty forever, and she's tough-boned enough to tell even King Arrion that he's wrong. She certainly has no reluctance about telling anybody else." Torio ended with some bitterness.

"He wasn't wrong in this case, of course. But, yes, I think my master will find this interesting, and will be grateful for more information. We don't want any trouble. Thank you again, sir. I may have a message for you shortly. God give you good night."

*

Gormad had made a fire. Dorac had scaled and gutted the fish, wrapped them in clay and baked them, and boiled up the nameless and bitter green stuff in a pan he had brought. Only the flames gave any light as they ate. They sat then, listening to the horses tearing at the grass, and the purr and occasional snap of the fire. A scream from somewhere – only a small animal being eaten by a larger animal, Gormad supposed and hoped. He had said, "I thank you, sir", for the food, and then nothing more. Children should be silent when not addressed. He felt sleepy. He felt scared. He felt sleepy again.

Dorac's face was hidden as he leaned back against a tree, staring above him. At last, however, he sighed and fixed Gormad with a stern stare. "Why are you here?"

Gormad was conscious of the stick. "I want to be your squire."

"I am an exile. I have no use for a squire. And I do not like children."

There was no answer to that.

"What happened to your lord?"

"He died. Of the coughing disease. Two days ago."

"Who was he?"

"Marrach of Drumcree."

Dorac made a sound between a grunt and a snort that did not

sound very sad.

Gormad's eyes suddenly stung.

"When did you swear to him?" asked Dorac.

"In March. Six months ago."

"Did he throw you out before he died?"

"No!"

"Then the King and Queen will find you a new lord." His voice was grating and slow.

"Maybe. But- I- the King would write to my family, they told me, and they might - my father might say I had to go home."

"Did you run away from him to be a squire?"

"No. But he - my father agreed in the end, but he didn't like me coming away. He might call me home, and King Arrion would say I had to go."

Pause. "Why shouldn't you go home?"

"I don't want to."

"What you want matters little in this world. If you think otherwise, you've been very spoilt. You don't want to go home, so you chase after a murderer?"

"You're not a murderer. My lord said you would never have–"

"*Marrach* said that? -You're lying."

"I'm not lying!"

Pause. "What did Marrach say? Exactly." The man picked up his sword in its sheath, and stroked it gently. "Or you're going home."

Gormad's blood was pounding between his ears, and his face burned. "He- ummm-"

"*Exactly.*" A hiss.

"He said, 'Dorac Kingsbrother would never kill children', and Jamis said, 'Everyone says he did', and my lord said, 'Then everyone is lying', and I said, 'How do you know?' and he said, 'That self-righteous bastard would never sully his hands with child-slaying. Not even for the king whose boots he licks. He'd never take a moral risk.'" Gormad gulped, and added, "I didn't understand all that he said."

"Which part?" Still soft.

"I – I don't know what a moral risk is."

It was very quiet for what seemed a long time. The air was growing colder, and Gormad hunched his shoulders, and rubbed his hands together for a little warmth, and the comfort of motion.

"What did you bring with you apart from the horses?"

"N-not much."

"Show me."

He pulled open his satchel, and stumbled over with it. Dorac rummaged, and Gormad tried to remember his hasty packing in the dark.

"A little bread. I'll take that. A water bottle, good. A few coins, which I'll take if I need them. A – something." Maybe that was his straw doll. Gormad's face was hot as he waited for comment. "Is this all?"

"Y-yes."

"No blankets or clothes. Weapons?"

"I have a knife."

Dorac passed it all back, without the bread. He stood up and stretched. Then from his own satchel he took a small trowel.

"Go and have a shit, or whatever you need to do, and cover it up, and come back."

Gormad did not go far. When he returned, the man had laid his cloak on the ground near the embers, and was sitting on it. He was only a shape, but the shape moved its head, beckoning the boy over.

It was very dark, and a long way from anywhere. Gormad clutched his bag for comfort. It was *very* dark. They said he had cut the children into pieces, and he was big and strong, and had a sword. People also said there were other things that some men liked to do to boys at night.

"Come on." Crossly.

Realising fully just how stupid and reckless he had been, Gormad walked over to the man sitting on the cloak.

"Lie down." As he obeyed, "Back to back is warmer."

He lay on his side, facing the dying fire, and Dorac pulled a blanket over both of them. They said nothing more, and waited for sleep to come. And in time it did.

*

Dorac slept badly, as no one had ever taught the brat not to fidget. And tomorrow there would be more chatter.

Towards dawn he woke, and lay listening to the blackbirds. He would never see Gemara, Kai, Hassdan or Soumaki again.

3 October 570

Trying to be wise and prudent, qualities no one normally connected with him, Kai had made time to sleep, and to read the transcript of the trial, so it was after sunrise that he rode out the next morning. He also stopped at the Wide Gate to confirm that yes, Dorac had passed through on foot two days before; yes, a young squire with two horses had left very early the following morning; yes, Captain Renatar had sent soldiers to bring the boy back; no, none of these people had returned.

He hoped to make up time by riding fast. As he did so, with part of his mind alert to register possible oddities and opportunities along the way, as the Thirty were trained to do, Kai being less skilled than some, he could not feel entirely unhappy. The sun shone cheerfully on him, the satisfaction of good work at Kerrytown was not completely gone, and his mind turned frequently – more frequently than perhaps it should – to pleasant thoughts of Karila, especially Karila lying naked in his arms.

But. One of his brothers was a murderer.

Dorac would never do that, he had said and thought, and so he believed. Dorac was a decent man, a man who kept the rules, and who did not take pleasure in cruelty. *And he is my sworn brother.*

But Kremdar was also a decent man, a generous and affable man, who killed – when necessary – neatly and precisely, who liked children, and doted on his own daughter. Kai had danced at his wedding – as merry a day as he could remember, sunshine in every face. *And he also is my sworn brother.*

Dorac would never - He had said that first – did that make it

53

irrevocable?

Dorac was his brother, but they were very different. One who was slapdash and untidy; one who was methodical and neat. One who laughed and cried and sang; one who thought for half an hour before opening his mouth. One who liked women, a lot, and was endlessly grateful that they seemed to like him; one who treated them with the courtesy of indifference. One to whom people poured out their sorrows; one who never told secrets perhaps because no one gave him any to keep. One who kept out of churches as much as possible; one who was seriously devout.

As the baby of four children, Kai had never expected to inherit great wealth, and he had been happy enough to join the Queenslands soldiery at the age of seventeen. A few years later, he was transferred to the garrison at South Keep, the dreich and isolated stone box that served the Southern Six – a transfer finagled, he'd always assumed, to stop him raising his eyes to Lady Maina's lovely daughter Rola. Dorac and the other members of the Six visited the Keep, and organised People's Meetings there, and issued brusque orders, and handed out severe criticisms.

Then, seven years ago, came the War from the Sea. Every Six lost members. The Southern Six lost three – and to his astonishment Kai, now Captain of the Keep, was named to replace Galla Kingsister, who had lasted only five years. He and Kremdar and Hassdan had sworn the oath and been named brothers of the new youngish king, and of the remaining three, Stimmon, Gemara and Dorac, but true brotherhood had taken time. Perhaps not for nine months, when he and Dorac and Stimmon were clearing rubble and searching for survivors after the earthquake in Bis, did he truly feel accepted. For Hassdan, born a Jaryari and an enemy, it had taken longer still. But they had all fought together and endured the worry over Stimmon's illness and collapse and enforced retirement, and then Soumaki had been the newcomer.

He and Dorac had fought back to back against the brigands of Noller. Dorac had dragged him out of a burning house. Kremdar had speared a woman who was swinging an axe at him. Only Hassdan and Soumaki bothered to say "thank you" for such things.

Kai was very conscious that Gemara had given him this task as the easiest. Perhaps she was right, but he did not think it easy. Dorac had seven days – now five – to get out of the kingdom, or to drop out of sight within it. He might go anywhere. He knew the lands of the south better than any other of the Six, and much better than Kai.

Of course, the child was an unknown factor. The boy had not returned, so that might well mean they were indeed travelling together, and therefore on horseback.

Unless Dorac had killed him as well. He pictured his brother standing over a small corpse by the road, and that froze his stomach more coldly than the reports of the trial. *No, no, no. But he would have had very little to lose.*

Stopping to let his chestnut, Diana, rest and drink, he wandered restlessly up and down, wondering what Dorac would do, and trying to find a logical reason – he wanted a logical reason – why one man, or the other, would not have committed this murder. He pictured his friends – Dorac, Kremdar, Arvill (*Arvill! Was she lying too? About something like that?*) leaving the dead traitor on his bed with the other soldier (Laida?) and filing out. Was Dorac already planning the killing? Would he not have done his curious little ritual with the stones, before making such a decision? No one had mentioned it - As an argument for his innocence, it was feather-frail.

Dorac's stones - Hassdan found them quaint. Kremdar gently mocked them. Kai (and, he suspected, Soumaki) had secretly experimented with the idea. But if Dorac was at any crossroads in his life, he picked up pebbles; and now, as never before, he was truly at a crossroads.

It was worth a try. Kai gathered a number of tiny stones, wasting the time he had saved, and sat down by the road. He caught Diana's eye, the horse eyeing him as disdainfully as Lady Sada might have done, and wondered at himself. Presumably prayer was involved, so he muttered the Our Father in hopes that would help, and settled down to consider the possibilities that would have occurred to his brother.

He had been ordered to leave, and Dorac was very obedient. He would remember that if he outstayed the week, it was every citizen's right, and indeed possibly duty, to kill him if they could. The journeys east to Ricossa, where the wars were, or north, to the coast, were surely too long. And he had set off south.

South – southwest meant Jaryar, the traditional enemy. It would only be a day or two riding, rather longer walking. In Jaryar there would surely be opportunities for a skilled, perhaps even famous, swordsman. There were wonders to be seen. Not so very far south was the capital, the Green City of Makkera itself, with its Cathedral and palaces and statues, famed in history and tale.

Kai laid down the first stone. His own desire to see the Green City was so strong that he was tempted to allow this stone to win by default. But Dorac was not him.

Southeast were the mountains, claimed by the southern kingdoms, but forbidding, almost uninhabited and deadly. What could a man do there – what would he find to eat? It was a possibility. He put down another stone.

Could Dorac be planning to return the child Gormad to his home? Kai placed another stone, but immediately rejected it. If necessary, he would have dropped the boy off at a monastery, and continued on.

There seemed something wrong with all these thoughts. Dorac was a dull fellow (Kremdar had once said) with no desire to travel, to explore, to *see*. He looked at his duty and his psalms, and no further. Surely he would be less likely to *go*, than to *do?*

Do what?

Kai had read the evidence, and the accused's cries of "He is lying! Your Grace, they are lying!" He knew what his own choice would have been. Vengeance. Vengeance on Kremdar was what Dorac had threatened, but he was riding in the wrong direction. Kai put down a third stone.

It might not only be Kremdar he would want revenge on. To go to the Jaryari, to their king, not just as a wandering soldier, but with all his skills, all his knowledge, a gift for the war that people said might be coming - Fifteen years in the Thirty: what use could King Rajas make of that? Kai turned cold again. *Dorac would never* - Slowly he put down another stone.

There was always the dark choice. For some people, Kai knew, the light went out, and life became unbearable. And they dared to take a knife or a rope, or find a cliff, and throw themselves out of it. To lose home, work, friends, reputation, to lose your name - forever - that might indeed be unbearable. Although the priests would disapprove, which meant God might, and Dorac talked a lot to God. He put down another stone.

He had five stones now, and he had to remind himself of what they all meant. And then, trying to think as Dorac, he had to reject them one by one.

He could *not* see Dorac offering to serve a Jaryari king, so he tossed that one away, and was down to four.

Jaryar. The mountains. Killing Kremdar – and being killed afterwards, presumably. Suicide.

Yes, somehow he felt Dorac's choice would involve death, for himself or for someone else. Death rather than travel. So he was, perhaps, travelling towards death? Kai looked up at the vague grey peaks of the Jattaman Mountains, and suddenly he guessed.

He could not be sure. But the thought fit, and settled implacably in his brain – and it was the most urgent. If Dorac planned to kill himself, he could do it anytime and anywhere, and only preposterous fortune could bring Kai there to prevent him. If he crossed a border, he could eventually be tracked beyond it.

But you went to the Old Stones, and when you got there, you died. Kai had to arrive first.

*

Long ago, his sister Ebbi's stories -

"Far far away," she chanted, hugging her knees and staring into the firelight, "far to the south are the Jattaman Mountains. They are full of trees and chasms and wolves. Their peaks reach up to the stars."

"Go on," urged Kai, seven years old.

"So the man with no hope travelled over the moors, through the city with its thieves, across the rivers deep and cold, and came to the mountains. And he climbed, alone. And he came to three villages, each smaller than the last. The first village is called Dayspassing. The second is called Daysend. The third has no name.

"In the last village, they warned him to go no further, but his heart was stone, and he went on. At last he came to the Place. A ring of great stones, taller than a house, put there by long-ago people. He said, 'I have come here to die', and stepped into the circle under the moon. And he died."

"Why? What killed him?"

"The Old Stones killed him. It is the Place to Die. The place killed him, and his despair."

The Place to Die. Many times Kai had pictured the quiet circle, the standing stones, the moonlight. (Did it have to be a full moon? Ebbi had said no. Their father had struck in with, "After all that travel, you think the man should be made to wait around for a full moon, do you?") And what about the villages? What would it be like to live in such a village, watching people pass through, only in one direction? Would they try to stop them? Would they give them a farewell?

"You mean whorehouses and gaming-halls?" asked Ebbi,

grinning, a few years later. By now they both knew that if the place was a story, it was one that everyone knew, and that people did indeed disappear to.

"Not gaming-halls. There'd be no point winning money. Whorehouses and taverns, why not?"

He had wondered, now and again over the years, about the villages.

*

The stiffness, and the wet cold on his skin, told Gormad even before he was properly awake that he was not in Marrach's room at the Castle, waiting while his lord coughed his life away, nor in the squires' dormitory, full of giggles and heroic oaths. He woke up to realise that he had not been killed in the night, and his adventure was continuing, which was cheery. He rubbed his face vigorously to get rid of sleep and dew, and stretched.

Master Dorac was praying silently. He then led the horses to a nearby stream, and Gormad followed. Champion and Derry drank, and Dorac ducked his head underwater, but happily he did not insist on Gormad doing so. He handed out what was perhaps the last of the bread, and some root-y thing to chew, and they headed back to the road. Although he had not yet spoken a word, at least he did not seem to be early-morning snappish, like Marrach. So Gormad's spirits rose further, and he became what his mother called "chirpy-birdy". Like most adults, she did not approve of this, but even an adult could not expect to ride all day in silence.

"Sir," he asked politely, "how long were you in the King's Thirty?"

Master Dorac dragged his face around to look at him, and seemed also to be dragging his mind from somewhere else to answer the question.

"Fifteen years," he said at last.

Gormad counted back hastily on his fingers. "Did you fight in the War from the Sea?" He could just remember the terrifying stories of the boat-raiders from the west along the north Marodi coast. And the thankfulness when it was over.

"Yes."

"Was it exciting?"

"*Exciting.*" The man stilled his horse, and stared at him. "Did Marrach of Drumcree tell you war was exciting?" he asked with contempt.

"N-no."

"'Exciting' is children at a fair." He put his hand on the hilt as if to draw his sword; but then seemed to change his mind and grunted, and the silence returned.

A little later, and slightly less cheerily, "Did you know my lord?"

"Not well."

"Did you like him?"

"No."

"Why not?"

"We quarrelled. Many years ago."

"Oh. Why?"

"That is not your concern. Are you able to hold your tongue, Gormad, son of Ramahdis?"

"Yes, sir."

"Then do."

Perhaps they were both in love with the same woman? That was what happened to grown-ups sometimes. Gormad peered curiously at Dorac, trying to imagine him much younger, and *kissing* someone, but found it difficult.

Later, without warning, Dorac dismounted and led them off the road to where a stream collected itself into a little pool. He took off his cloak and undid his belt. Gormad stared.

"We need to wash." *Wash!* "We need to buy food and other things in the market at Madderan." *A market!* "And we are not clean enough for a market. Look at yourself. *Smell* yourself. I stink of blood and fish guts and smoke, and you stink of piss" (Gormad's face burned), "and our clothes are muddy." And it seemed that he had a brush and soap in his satchel. Gormad was beginning to regard that satchel with awe.

But laundry is for servants -

*

Although a fire burned in the great hearth, there was also a brazier of hot coals and a table before the dais. Everyone buzzed with excitement, and (if tender-hearted) apprehension.

For the space in the Thirty was about to be filled. *To drink and talk with the King and call him your brother; to judge criminals and lead soldiers into battle; to carry out dangerous missions and win glory* - that was the life of the Thirty, respected and obeyed throughout the realm, and surely beyond. The White Hall was full long before the King and Queen entered for the Monday audience. They walked through to the dais from the ever-open door preceded by two guards and by Brinnon of the Eastern Six and Kremdar of the Southern, and followed by the Elder Advisers, Lady Sada the Warden, and Lord Vrenas the Marshal. King Arrion was dressed resplendently in a deep red gown trimmed with white fur, and Queen Malouri in a white over-gown with blue beneath, but their demeanour was solemn.

When they were seated, and everyone had bowed, the herald called, "Silence for the King."

The silence was instant and complete.

"In the last week, my friends," said King Arrion, "there has been something to celebrate, and more to mourn." A little sigh spread through the room. "Gahran of Ferrodach has been proved a traitor by his own hand. He is dead, also by his own hand, as witnessed by Kremdar Kingsbrother and the soldiers we sent to arrest him. His children are also dead, but if they were not, it would make no difference. His body has been burned, and his lands are forfeited. We will consider the gifting of Ferrodach in the next days."

He paused, and the six or seven people hoping for some part in that gift kept their faces impassive.

"Second, an attack in the west from Haymon has been repulsed by our soldiers and members of the Thirty, led by Captain Garas." The King thanked Garas appropriately, and went on.

"Third, Dorac of the Southern Six has been found guilty of the crime of murder, and exiled. His lands at Valleroc are also forfeited, and his place in the Thirty is empty. So. This is the first matter for today. The Southern Six, approach."

Gemara, Kremdar, Hassdan and Soumaki knelt. "And Kai?

No – he sought leave, I remember.

"Mistress Gemara has expressed her own sorrow, and that of her siblings. We appreciate their feelings, but no apology is necessary. Dorac's dishonour is his own. No blame is laid to any of the rest."

"Thank you, Your Grace." They rose. So did the King and Queen.

"Having consulted, the Queen and I name to the Thirty Saysh, son of Adshan." There was a murmur of surprise, even of disapproval. *Saysh? Really?*

Saysh, brawny and solemn, twenty-three years old, approached nervously. He had been informed the night before of the choice and the honour before him, and had prayed and prepared – at least in theory. Now he drew his sword and presented it to the King. The King's priest Sister Susanna held out the gospel, last used at the trial two days before. Saysh placed his right hand on the open book.

"Saysh, son of Adshan, King Arrion and Queen Malouri have named you to the King's Thirty. Will you accept this calling and enter this fellowship?"

"I will."

"Will you guard the King and Queen with your body, your life and your word?"

"I will."

"Will you give justice to all, listening to all, taking no bribes and fearing no threats?"

"I will."

"Will you obey all lawful commands and carry out all honourable tasks laid on you by the King and Queen?"

"I will."

"Will you welcome all the Kingsbrothers and Kingsisters as your own?"

"I will."

"From this day, do you renounce all allegiance save to God, to the kingdom, to the King and Queen and to the Thirty?"

"I renounce them. I will swear my sword to no one else."

"Will you keep this oath though it cost you your life?"

"With the help of God, I will."

Saysh bowed. Then he bared his right arm, and the ceremony continued with the branding – the smell and sizzle of burned flesh, and the flinching of everyone present. There was no shame in accepting a block of wood to bite on, as Saysh did, so as not to scream. There would have been no shame in screaming either. Few people managed without either. Kremdar had been one of the exceptions, seven years ago.

"Be welcome to our company, brother," said the King. Saysh stepped shyly into the formal embrace, and was successively embraced with the same words by the Queen, Gemara, Hassdan, Kremdar and Soumaki. The Hall echoed to ritual cheers, as those of other Sixes moved in to welcome him also.

"And Kai will greet you soon. Once he has returned from celebrating a different happy event. A girl this time, I understand."

A relaxing grin spread round the room. Kai had two children already, one in the north and one in the city. Since he had not married the mothers, most of what he might have inherited was tied up in legal provision for them. *Another one. How like Kai.*

The new Six (minus one) retreated, Kremdar up to his guard post, and the others into the crowd. Saysh stayed by Soumaki, the newest member before him, and tried to concentrate on something other than the pain in his arm.

*

Gormad's hose and braies were swinging in the breeze, and jackets and cloaks had been brushed half-clean. His shirt could not be scrubbed, as he had no spare. It was all a bit embarrassing. They had stripped and washed as quickly as they could, and Dorac had shaved. There were scars striping his back like a ladder — *had he ever been a prisoner, or a criminal?*

"Watch the clothes - warm yourself - play." The last word, as he disappeared into the undergrowth, sounded almost surprised. Gormad turned his mind to his shivering body and numb hands. One of the trees looked climbable – but he was supposed to stay clean. So he played hopscotch on the shore and practised handstands until Dorac returned with a bag full of mushrooms. The hose were not properly dry, but both were tired of waiting about.

Madderan was the dullest village Gormad had seen in all his years. It had nothing colourful in it. It was just a few houses along the road, with a church and a space in front with a few stalls. None of them looked enticing, but people were gathered gossiping around them anyway. Dorac left him by the church door. "Look after the horses. Don't talk to anyone." Gormad watched him walk up and down, eyeing what there was, and then approach a woman. It did not seem that he liked markets – he did not bargain much, or banter, or wave his hands about as he talked, as normal folk did at stalls. People were staring at him, perhaps because he didn't live in their village, and they were curious about anyone new.

Gormad didn't live there either. After pointing and giggling a bit, three children sidled up to him. Two boys, and a girl with long fair plaits.

"What's your name?"

Gormad shrugged, as his brother Kammer tended to do. It annoyed the children, just as Kammer annoyed him.

"What's your name, stupid?"

"Gormad, stupider."

"Are you with him?"

"Yes."

"Is he your father?"

"No."

"Who is he, then?"

"I'm his squire." This impressed them slightly.

"Are you servants of Lady Yenilda?"

"Don't know who she is."

Giggling more than ever, "Are you on a mission for the King?"

"Maybe."

"A brat like you? Don't believe it."

Maybe he was getting into a fight, Gormad thought suddenly, not sure whether or not this was a good thing – but fortunately at this point Dorac marched over, ready to leave, and scowling at the children. They ran off, giggling. As he and his master led their horses down the street, if you could call it that, Gormad looked around at the bustle and chatter, half wanting to stay – yes, it was dull, but it was normal life – and he noticed that a lot of the people were watching them, and whispering. Perhaps it was not only that they were strangers.

"Master Dorac!" A stout man in an apron stepped forward from his forge and bowed, smiling. "Master Dorac Kingsbrother, I believe. God be with you. I was certain the tale was wrong. This is an honour."

A pause. "That is no longer my name."

Those within earshot were silent at once.

"I don't understand, Master Dorac. How -"

"The King exiled me three days ago. If that is the tale you have heard, it is true."

Now surely the whole village was listening.

"Exiled," murmured the man in astonishment. "For – for what crime?"

Dorac took a breath. "For the murder of Lord Gahran's three children."

Gormad's gasp was lost in the general sensation. "But he didn't do it!" he squeaked.

Dorac nodded politely but without smiling to the blacksmith, and walked on. Behind them the buzz grew and grew. People's eyes were burning the back of Gormad's neck and ears. He and Dorac left the market patch and continued along the path, with small houses, stables and pigpens on each side.

And just as they reached the last few hovels, they found their way blocked. The path was narrowing, and four people stood facing them – two men and two women; two swords, a long knife, and an axe.

Getting into a fight.

They stopped. After the pause that seemed to begin his every sentence, Dorac said, "Please let us pass."

"Still giving orders?" asked the young man with the axe, leaning against the wall, pretending not to be a bully, like Hanos at the Castle. "Not so grand any more, I think. No more looking down your nose at ordinary folk, and sending them off to be whipped or hanged."

"Your face is familiar," said Dorac. "Was it pickpocketing, or attempted rape?" He looked at the woman with the knife in the centre of the path, and said again, "Please let us pass."

"You're not a great man any more, and we don't have to obey you. What are you doing with that boy?"

Me?

Dorac looked calmly all round him, up and down. "I do not see that that's any concern of yours."

"If you're a child-murderer, it is. Leave him alone. He can stay here, where he's safe."

Dorac turned to Gormad. "They are afraid I will kill you. You can stay here, where you're safe."

"It's all right, lad," said the stocky man with the sword. "We'll get you back to your home – or send you to Lady Yenilda, or the monastery. They'll look after you."

Be brave.

"I don't want to stay. Or see Lady Yenilda. He didn't kill those children."

"That's what he's told you, is it?" sneered the axe man.

"He can stay here if he wishes," said Dorac.

"I don't wish to!"

Dorac shrugged. "Then please let us pass."

"You can pass, Master Exile," said the woman. "But not the boy."

"I don't see anyone here with the right to command him. He chooses to leave."

"He is not leaving with you!"

"I wonder," said Dorac, "how much of your concern is for him, and how much for the price his horse would fetch?"

One of the men looked embarrassed, but the young horrible one stroked his axe, slowly, but in a way that made everyone look at him, and then raised his face to say, "There are four of us, and one of you. Leave now, without the boy, and you'll live. Try to take him away, and you'll die, and the world will be well rid of you. You're not in the King's Thirty any more. No one will mourn."

"You're right," Dorac replied. Gormad was suddenly cold and terrified. Dorac let his eyes sweep all round again, and casually handed the boy his reins. "There are four of you and one of me. I have served in the King's Thirty for fifteen years, and before that in Queen Darisha's armies for twelve years. I will die, but unless you've already placed your archers, at least two of you will die also."

He drew his sword and marched calmly towards the woman in the middle. And a heartbeat later, the four had all scattered except the axe man. He merely shrank against the wall, looking as scared as all bullies ought to be made to look. Dorac continued to walk forward, and Gormad hastily followed. He was so thrilled he almost choked, and his stomach fizzed with painful delight.

"*Thank* you," he breathed. Dorac said nothing. They were out of the village, and they kept walking. There were fields on one side, and the wood on the other. Gormad peered behind occasionally, to see if anyone was following them.

About half a mile further on, the path curved, and Dorac stopped. He took the reins back, and then slapped Gormad's cheek hard.

"That is for contradicting me."

He slapped the other side. "And that is for causing trouble."

Gormad had of course known worse blows, and Kammer had known much worse. But - *ow*.

"How did I cause trouble?" he protested.

Dorac mounted. "If those idiots who wanted to be heroes had not also been cowards, at least one person would be dead now. Because you don't want to go home." He rode off, and Gormad, tears pricking, followed.

Thinking it all over, he had a nastier thought, and his stomach grew heavy.

*

"You will set out for Haymon tomorrow. Lady Sada and I will speak to you privately as to the details." Two members of the Western Six bowed. The King turned to those remaining before him.

"The Southern Six. Gemara and Kremdar, you will ride to Lenchen tomorrow, for their October trials. Hassdan and Soumaki, you will leave for Ferrodach today. We need to know how active Gahran's treason was, and how widespread. Take whatever time you need, up to one month, and report regularly. Saysh, you will serve in the guard here.

71

And when Kai returns, we will find a task for him."

As they left the hall, Hassdan Kingsbrother turned to his squire and said, "Pack up quickly. We'll be leaving the city in half an hour." This was probably one of his jokes, Meril guessed. Packing and saddling the horses did not take long, but they had to wait while Soumaki delivered her boys to one of the city's childpens, and said her interminable affectionate farewells. But at last, mid-afternoon, Master Hassdan, Mistress Soumaki, Meril, and a half troop of soldiers were riding west, towards Ferrodach.

Two years before, Meril and her siblings and cousins had been told that Aunt Alida was marrying Hassdan who had been courting her for so long, and although he was a foreigner, he was quite an acceptable one, and he had agreed to take a family member as a squire, which was a great honour and an excellent start in life. He was coming to visit the estate to choose. Of the six children of about the right age, Meril was the clumsiest, the plainest, the least skilled with weaponry, by far the worst rider, and the third worst even at book-learning – and certainly the least useful. Her parents never shrank from their painful duty of telling her these things. Neither did she distinguish herself during Master Hassdan's visit, as far as anyone could tell. So when he named her as his choice, Meril was probably not the only member of the household to suppose that he must have made a mistake with the name: one that he was too proud, or too kind, to correct.

But anyway it was Meril who had ridden away from her childhood home with her aunt and her new uncle, praying desperately that she would not let him down, and be returned in – and *to* – unspeakable disgrace. Two years later, and despite the unpleasantness of what she had to witness among the wounded at Kerrytown and elsewhere, she was happier than she had ever been.

Now, as they approached a noisy watermill (clackety-splash, clackety-splash), he suddenly said, "No need to waste a day. Meril, ride beside me, and we'll see what you've learned." When he had created a little space between the two of them and the others, he went on, "If anyone should make enquiries, I am testing your knowledge of history and geography, which is deplorable. Name the nine provinces of Jaryar."

After she had struggled through this task, "If *anyone* enquires, I said. We have been sent by the King to look further into Lord Gahran's treason, and ascertain how far it is supported in his household, and among his neighbours. As you know. But you and I are also looking into something else. Dorac claimed he was innocent of the childkilling. That seems most improbable, but the King wishes us to make sure, if we can."

Meril was puzzled. He let her ask questions, so –

"Why does the King think that – that he might be innocent?"

"His Grace has not shared his thoughts with me. Only his orders, with Mistress Gemara and Master Kai. Not the others," he added with emphasis.

The world seemed to tremble. He was telling her to keep a secret from Soumaki and Kremdar!

"No, that is incorrect," he said loudly, and tweaked her ear. "How can you be discreet with that look on your face? You are learning history, remember.

"Meril, sometimes it is a duty to report gossip. The squires do nothing but gossip. Were you surprised to learn that Dorac had committed this crime?"

"I suppose so, sir. It seems such a terrible thing for anyone to do. I don't – I don't know Master Dorac very well. He never pays any attention to the squires. If it were anyone, he seems the most likely."

"You don't like him? Has he hurt you in any way?"

"Oh, no."

"You would have reported it to me?"

"Yes, sir."

"Has he hurt any of the others, to your knowledge?"

"No. As I said, he ignores us. He glares at us if we're making too much noise."

"We all do that. But you don't like him? Why not?"

Meril fidgeted, cheeks hot.

"Why not?"

"He - they said when you joined the Thirty, he-"

"Oh, Meril. How loyal of you." He was trying not to laugh. "You are not required to keep my grudges alive for me. Dorac took eighteen months to acknowledge that someone born and brought up in Jaryar could be truly loyal to the King of Marod, and he made his opinion very clear. But we moved along the road from there long ago. Otherwise, do you know any reason to distrust him?"

"No," she admitted. "Once he showed me how to take a stone out of Damson's hoof." And, unlike Gemara, he had not scorned her for not knowing.

"What do the squires think of Kremdar?"

"We like him," answered Meril promptly. "He gave a prize

once to the squire who could run the fastest mile. And he used to carry his little girl – I don't remember her name – around, and let us girls play with her. He jokes with us sometimes, like Master Kai does. Sir, Master Kremdar *likes* children."

"Indeed. And he hates mess. And whoever did this was very messy. What about Arvill, daughter of Eve? Do you know her?"

"I know who she is. I have seen her among the soldiers from the Kingslands."

"Is there any gossip about her?"

"She - well, she - I don't mean to be impertinent – or – she's not married, but she - I mean she has lovers sometimes."

"Other than Kai, you mean? That's been past for a while. Yes, I do remember hearing something about her and – was it Garas?"

"Yes, a few months ago. And someone said she was once with one of Captain Renatar's sons."

"Indeed. You don't know any other name linked to her? Or who she's favouring at the moment, if anyone?"

"No."

"Or anything else about her?"

"No, she's just a soldier."

"What about Braf, son of Arro?"

"I don't know him."

They rode on for some minutes. Then Meril ventured, "What are we going to do?"

"At Ferrodach? I have official questions to ask. No one there is going to like me, so I shall make sure to cuff and curse you, and you may attract pity. Try to make friends with the servants, but not too obviously. And I want one of your map-pictures of the house. Show the doors and windows and passages."

"Yes, Master."

"And find out something about the local priest. I assume Gahran had a chaplain, but I'm more interested in the village man or woman. We may need prayers said over a grave, and a sworn affidavit afterwards."

Meril looked at him, wondering, but he did not explain. After a little, "Sir," she said, looking down and fiddling with her gloves, "I don't understand about Lord Gahran. What did he do?"

He smiled at her. "History, Meril. The War of the Royal Siblings, in 510. The wicked and tyrannical Queen Arrabetta – surely you remember?"

"Y-yes. The country could not endure her crimes, so the Thirty and the soldiers and everyone offered the throne to her brother King Lukor."

"That is right. The only time the Thirty has turned against their Queen. And it was not 'everyone'. There was fighting. That is why it is called a war.

"The Council and the Thirty and the King's Gathering were not only deposing Queen Arrabetta, and imprisoning her at Ferrodach. They were afraid that her whole line might be tainted, so they disinherited her descendants also. So King Lukor was succeeded by his daughter Queen Darisha, and she was succeeded by King Arrion. His mother married him to one of Arrabetta's descendants, perhaps to try to heal the wounds. But Gahran was Arrabetta's most direct heir.

"He lived quietly at Ferrodach, but perhaps he'd been

resenting not being King all these years. And perhaps others were resenting it on his behalf. And then this summer someone discovered a letter he'd written to the King of Jaryar."

Meril stared.

"It seems King Rajas was suggesting a conspiracy – someone would murder the King, and put Gahran on the throne as the rightful heir."

"Murder King Arrion!"

"Lord Gahran did not use that word in his gracious acceptance of the plan, but it was plain what he meant. But from Kremdar's reports, he did very little to make it happen. Treacherous but lazy. Or so we are hoping."

*

Just before nightfall, Dorac dismounted again, watered the horses and led them between two trees and into the undergrowth. There was no path, and it was not easy going. When he stopped, it was not in a glade. The ground, between tall trees, was fairly flat, but that was all that could be said. Gormad felt very puzzled.

"No fire tonight."

"Wh-why not?"

"They may come after us. If they have nothing better to do."

"Oh."

Gormad had almost forgotten the purpose of the marketing. Dorac had bought oats and apples for the horses, which they appreciated. After they had been fed, he tossed over a bundle of cloth that turned out to be a shirt and hose.

"Next time you run away, pack a change of clothes."

"Thank you, sir." (He still did not know what to call him. A former Kingsbrother.) "I didn't see anyone selling clothes in the village."

"No. But you saw children *wearing* clothes, and some of their parents wanted money."

Gormad felt rather less grateful for knowing this, and the hose did not look like a good fit. But supper, although uncooked, was good – there was bread baked only that morning, and onion and apple, and better still, smoked bacon, and finally a raisin cake. He almost felt full. But cold.

They sat in the dark. There were night noises again that he couldn't identify.

"So. Why don't you want to go home?"

Gormad's mind went blank.

"Is home not exciting enough for you?"

"No!" It was partly true. He blushed.

"Then why?"

"It - it's my father." He couldn't think how to explain.

"You said he doesn't beat you."

"No."

"Does he starve you?"

"No."

"Does he shut you in a dark hole with rats?"

"No."

"Does he ill-treat your mother?"

"No."

Pause. "Does he fuck you?"

"No!"

"Doesn't sound like a bad father."

"I don't – I can't explain."

"Try." The impatient tone said *last chance*.

Gormad shut his eyes, and opened them again, and tried.

"He is always kind – but it's the opposite of what you said. He favours me and not the others, and I don't know why. I'm the oldest, and there are three more, and they're always being punished or scolded, and never me, and there's no reason. Specially Kammer – he's eight. Kammer is always being beaten or having to miss supper, whatever he does, and they never do that to me. There was one time – we went out riding with the dogs, and we worried some of a farmer's sheep, and broke his fence, and he complained, and Kammer -" He screwed up his face at the cruel memory. "But they did nothing to me except say 'Do not act in this way again' – *nothing*, and I was older, and it was more my fault. So Kammer hates me, and the girls are nasty to me and sorry for him, and when I ask why, they – my father and mother and tutor – say I'm imagining it, and I'm *not*.

"And I get taught more – courtesy and dancing and geography – and Kammer just has simple books and weapons training."

"The eldest is the heir and is better educated."

"But my tutor offered to teach Kammer as well, and my father said no. And Kammer wanted to learn – he likes all that. He loves reading books." He went back to the point. "So then I said could I go and be a squire for somebody, and my father said no. But lots of heirs are, even my mother and uncle said so. They argued, and I kept asking, and at last he agreed. And he sent a letter to my lord saying -" his face was hot at the memory -"I was to be treated gently and not allowed to come to harm."

"Were you?"

"My lord passed the letter to Captain Renatar, but he said he taught no pampered favourites." The memory of the other squires' reaction was too awful to touch, and he hurried on.

"And he looks at me – always kind and always calm, but something strange about it -" His voice trailed off.

Dorac thought, and then asked, "Do you look alike, you and your brother? And your father?"

"I – I don't know, sir. We've all got curly hair. All our family has, except my mother." He pulled at one of the longer spirals. 'I'm a bit darker, I suppose. But the oddest thing is, I feel he really likes Kammer and Beta better than me. He punishes them, but he jokes with them sometimes. He just looks at me."

He'd never said all that before, not even to Marrach or Meril, and it felt odd to have brought it all up – almost like being sick, with the relief afterwards. Relief, but also fear – but at least Dorac didn't laugh, or tell him he was talking nonsense - or say again "what you want matters little". He might have been thinking it though.

When the silence had lasted so long it was plain the conversation was over, Gormad asked timidly, "Can I ask you a question?"

With adult weariness, "Ask."

"You – at your trial you swore you didn't kill those children."

"I didn't."

"But you said I contradicted – he asked why you were exiled -

"

"That was the King's reason. He asked a question, and I answered it."

Swept with relief, Gormad confirmed, "So you didn't -"

Dorac banged his fist on the ground, so hard that the boy jumped. Then he was on his feet, and had disappeared into the dark.

Once again, there was nothing for Gormad to do but wait, and assume he would come back. He went over and stroked Champion, his only friend now, and then he sat down and opened his satchel. Underneath his new clothes were his special things, and he fingered them fondly. The straw doll his mother had made; his lucky green pebble; his string of beads, including Beta's spiky one; and the scroll of the Lord's Prayer that his tutor had given him. Dorac hadn't laughed at those either.

It was really getting very cold.

There was someone in the trees - He was back, and they settled down to sleep.

Towards dawn, it began to rain.

4 October 570

The next day everything changed, not just the weather. Dorac poked him with a foot, not gently. "Up. Now. Wring out the blanket, and saddle the horses."

Gormad was wet and shivering, but he still didn't want to move. As they ate raw mushrooms and more apple, and drank water, sheltering under trees as best they could, Dorac said suddenly, "Show me your knife." Gormad passed it.

"There is rust here. And it's blunt. Who can you kill with that?" He rummaged in his own satchel for oil, cloth and whetstone. "Clean it. Sharpen it." A short time later, "That'll do for now." As they set off, leading the horses, "Look around you. Notice what you could eat. Or what you could eat at a different season. Tell me when we come to the road."

As they struggled pathless through the drizzle, Gormad decided they were not going back the way they had come in. More than an hour later, they came to a path just wide and open enough to allow them to ride. Now he was sure. "Get up." Dorac walked all round him once he was mounted. It was obvious that he was looking for something to criticise, and equally obvious that he could find nothing. Gormad felt a little smug. When they set off, "What food did you see?"

"Umm - a bramble bush. And a squirrel. We could have eaten that."

"If we could catch or trap it. What else?"

The list of what he had missed, starting with more of the morning's mushrooms, took a long time. Apparently they were called "chanterelle", a pretty name for a mushroom. They rode on, the horses snorting and miserable. The path began to rise, and he noticed that they were heading towards hills. There were three days before Dorac had to be out of the kingdom. But the Old Stones might be a lot nearer than that.

In the late morning it stopped raining, and after a while they had to dismount, and lead Derry and Champion. Although there were still trees, these grew less thickly, and the ground was steep. After a while they came to a flattish place with grass and heather. "Rub down the horses," said Dorac, disappearing. Gormad peered into the valley below, and gratefully sat down on a stone. When Dorac returned, he was clearing another stick of bark. "I said rub down the horses. Do it now." When this was done, he tossed over the stick, and reached for the one behind his saddle. "Show me how you hold a sword. So. What did Captain Renatar and Marrach teach you?"

Dorac was one of the best swordsmen in the Thirty, Gormad remembered, so he was not surprised to be repeatedly disarmed and knocked to the ground. It was less humiliating than the same thing happening in the Castle yard, because there was no one to call mock advice or laugh. But it was more intense, and Dorac's silent grim figure was infinitely more daunting than the other squires, or even the Captain. *He wouldn't really kill me.*

"Get up. Right. Now -" The explanation was not very clear, but it was like what the Captain was always saying – "*keep feet apart for balance.*" "And before the fight starts, if you can, what should you always notice?"

"My opponent?"

"Plainly. What else?"

Gormad shook his head.

"Where you are. Notice where your ground ends -" he gestured to the rocky slope- "where there are roots to trip you – where there are buildings or stalls or hiding places for your enemy's allies. You need to use this knowledge. I will use it next time."

There was going to be a next time! The reason for the change flashed upon him. He was no longer just an incumbrance; he was not going to be sent home; he was being trained.

I am a real squire again.

They both sat down. "Tell me - North from Stonehill, a day's journey, where do you come to?"

"The city of Derbo."

"And after that?"

"The sea?"

"There's a long way between Derbo and the sea. Have you heard of Ebaya?"

"Yes, sir."

"What do you know?"

Gormad cudgelled his brain (*Geography!*); he could only think of snippets.

"Go on."

More snippets. He realised that, after the first few corrections, his new lord was no longer listening. He kept saying, "Go on," but even when Gormad dared to give deliberately wrong answers, he did not notice. He was staring back into the trees they had risen through, small eyes half-shut, face blank. Until at last, "Enough. Up." And they went

84

on, first climbing the hills, then descending, then rising again, sometimes picking a way through woodland, and sometimes over scrub. There seemed to be a path of sorts, but it was not easy to find, and they led the horses single file.

*

Gemara was annoyed with her king. The enquiry was hers; she should be in charge of it. Instead, Hassdan and Soumaki had ridden off to Ferrodach yesterday, and she had had the excruciating task of welcoming Saysh to the Six. Normally, this would have meant a cathartic and merry evening, with a few tears for the dead, and a hearty welcome for the newcomer. But Dorac was not dead, and there were only herself and Kremdar to be merry. She was not feeling merry.

Kremdar, although it was plainly an effort (*he made it plain*, she thought sourly), had done his best, and his best was good. There had been singing in the tavern, and he had invented a Southern Six "tradition", by which the newcomer had to tell five secrets in exchange for one from each of his new siblings. Gemara had found it hard to cooperate. Kremdar's "secret" was having lost his virginity to a fisherwoman in a boat during a storm. He made a fairly good ribald story out of it. Saysh seemed to have nothing much in return. He had dreamed of being in the Thirty all his life, he said. *Who hasn't?* Gemara almost replied, but bit her tongue.

She conceded that someone had to be there for Saysh, and that the citizens of Lenchen on the Hill could wait one day for their justice. And she could watch Kremdar as well there and in Stonehill as elsewhere. But she wanted to be at Ferrodach.

Instead they were riding east under heavy cloud: Gemara,

Kremdar, Kremdar's squire Tommid, a secretary, and a guard of three soldiers. No one was cheerful, even the soldiers, who had no particular ties to one Six over another. Gemara's silence, she knew, was infecting them all. General grief for what had come to them served as her excuse for a while, but it could not last.

She rode quietly, drawing strength from the bond with her chestnut Tara Maid, and then dissipating it again in fury. But how could she be civil and suave with this man? *You have a child; I have children; how could you? Dorac is your brother; he's saved your life; how could you?*

She had been twenty-one years in the Thirty, Dorac fifteen; they two longer than any of the others. The Six were rarely all in the same place, for one was almost always assigned to guarding the King, and the others were allocated duties at his discretion, except for the King's Gathering in late autumn, and the great feasts of Christmas and Easter. But each of them worked with all the rest; they were not brothers and sisters in name only. If Dorac were innocent, it was his brother who had destroyed him.

Hassdan would have done her task better. He was skilled at hiding his feelings. Gemara was not.

No hypocrisy so great had ever been required of her as this, when she smiled at Kremdar, and exchanged words about the weather, and the town that was their destination. It was a little place they both liked, the birthplace (as it happened) of Soumaki's husband Shoran. Kremdar speculated quietly whether news of events at Ferrodach would have reached Lenchen, and if this might make the King's judges of the Thirty less welcome than usual.

"Surely not," said young Jakali, naïve even for a lower

secretary.

"It might," said Kremdar. "It was a brutal thing."

Gemara gripped her knife, and longed to stab him then and there. She felt so much angrier these days, since Habbaroth's death.

(And that brought back *his* funeral, three years ago. Standing around the grave outside the city, her daughter's arms around her, Gemara had been grateful that all the Six had managed to be there. Hassdan had ridden through the night. Soumaki had found someone to care for her tiny baby, and was there with her husband. Kremdar had spoken generous words of praise. Kai had wept for her. Dorac had shown no sympathy. He never did. But he had come. They had all come, and as she said farewell to the husband of twenty-eight years, strength seemed to flow into her from her brothers and sister, enabling her to comfort the children, adults though they were, and to set Habbaroth free.)

They camped that night in a meadow near the road, all working together to put up the tents. Gemara kept an eye on young Tommid. One of the younger soldiers was practising swordplay with him. He didn't look as if he were hiding anything, or experiencing nightmares, but people lied, in body and word. Gemara preferred horses.

*

Gormad was wondering if one could eat bracken, when Dorac suddenly said, "Those fools who stopped us in the village. How many were there?"

"Four."

"Women or men?"

"Two women, two men."

"What did they look like?"

"One of them had an axe - He was quite young."

Dorac waited.

"One of the women was older and a bit fat. She had a blue hood." He struggled. "I - I think the other man was light-skinned, and had a beard."

"Moustache only, greyer than his hair. Tall or short?"

"I don't remember."

"Why not?"

"I don't know."

"Because they were not important enough to notice. Although they were threatening to kill me, and abduct you. If we come to a village, and one of those four is skulking in the crowd, waiting for a chance to steal your horse, or carry you off to their Lady Yenilda, you wouldn't notice, because you didn't mark them in your mind. The man with the sword was about thirty-five, reddish hair, reddish-grey moustache. He had a stall in the market, selling cheese and fruit. His jacket was green, with some embroidery on the right – I think right – shoulder. His boots looked new. If I'd killed him, I would have taken them. They looked my size."

"Oh," said Gormad.

"Shut your eyes. Stand still. What am I wearing?"

"A dark-grey cloak and hood. A brown jacket which laces criss-cross down the front, and the laces are black. And black hose - and boots. You have a belt with gold studs on, and a carving of - a curly thing - on the buckle, and a sword, and you have a pale-brown satchel with two buckles."

"Open."

Gormad looked embarrassedly at his companion, who seemed almost amused. "Bronze, not gold. I am not a great lord. The carving is a salmon. So you do notice something."

So it went on all day. A long silence would be abruptly followed by a command to recite the Ten Commandments, or to list the qualities of a good warhorse. Once he was asked to identify the direction of Stonehill, and was ashamed to be told he was pointing in completely the wrong direction. "You must know where you are." The absentmindedness had fallen away; he was corrected firmly when wrong, and learned to interpret a grunt as approval. But then there would be more silence.

They stopped in a dip between hills as the sky's colour began to turn. "I will look for water for the horses, and to cook these." "These" were four eggs, presumably from the market. "You gather wood, make a fire and clean your knife."

Gormad was left alone to revel in the moment. He was a squir*e. Wasn't he? No words had been spoken.* He was learning to fight; he was travelling with a real warrior, an innocent hero. Ballads could be written about this. Dorac seemed to be "learning to live again", as his father Ramahdis had had to do after the death of his beloved sister – Gormad had been a tiny baby at the time, but so the servants had said. One day he would be Gormad Kingsbrother of the Southern Six – or any Six – and King Arrion, or perhaps by then it would be King Jendon, would send him to battle the Jaryari -

He was standing over a fallen foe in triumph when Dorac

returned, half an hour later. "Where is the fire?"

"Oh - I forgot," he faltered, not liking the tone of voice at all.

He thought the blows that followed were quite unfair, as there had been no previous warning. But all children know idleness and disobedience will be punished, and if they do not know, they need to learn. That was what his mother would have said, and probably Dorac agreed with her.

They made the fire and poached the eggs, and they lay down to sleep. *Even the punishment proved he was a squire*, Gormad thought.

But they were still heading for the Old Stones. The Place to Die.

5 October 570

Quite early next morning, they came for the first time to a crossroads. There were four ways – their own and one sloping down to the south, both of which were mere paths, a road back north, and one continuing east. This one they took. It was wider, even in some places paved with stones, and they rode side by side.

Dorac abruptly stopped. "What do you see?"

"There's smoke ahead. Maybe a village."

"And those." On either side of the road, before it rounded a bend, stood a thinnish boulder, as tall as Champion's thigh, painted white. He had not seen such a thing before. "Go round the back, and stay out of sight. Meet me at the other end of the village. Do no damage, and stay out of trouble." Dorac rode on between the white boulders.

All grown-ups say these kind of things. Is trouble something you can decide to stay out of? Who chooses trouble? Gormad remembered yesterday's blows, sighed, dismounted and led Champion into the brushwood.

The village was small, and in fact there was no difficulty in skirting its edges and avoiding notice. A little after the last house, he saw two more stones guarding the path, but this time painted black. Dorac was sitting on the grass, his back to him, and asked without turning his head, "Did anyone see you?"

"No."

As they mounted again, "Why did I send you that way?"

Gormad felt cautiously proud of having worked this out. "In

case anyone tried to make me stay again, like the day before yesterday."
Dorac grunted, which meant "correct", and the boy ventured, "Please –
why did you go through the village? We could both have gone round."

"To confirm where we are. I asked the name of the place, and
it is called Wester Kleechit by some, and Dayspassing by others."

The first village is called Dayspassing; the second is called Daysend; the
third has no name. It hit him again: the Old Stones. *No! You can't!*

After a time they stopped for more practice with sticks. He
was clumsier and slower than yesterday. The sticks had no guards, and
mistakes meant sharp taps to the fingers, as well as thumps in the side,
and tumbles to the ground. But the sinister knowledge of where they
were still really going was worse, and as they were resting afterwards,
and he was licking blood off his knuckles, he dared to ask, "How far is
it?"

"We'll be there by nightfall." Surprisingly, Dorac added,
"There is an inn, they say. We can have a hot supper."

"Th-thank you."

Dorac had stopped asking questions. They rode on and on,
and saw nobody, and Gormad longed passionately for the sound of
human voices. Marrach had not been a talkative man, but there had
always been some conversation or other going on in his hall. That
seemed a long time ago. Going further back, he heard Kammer
nagging, and Beta shrieking, and he himself telling them both to be
sensible, and listen to him. And the squires in Stonehill were always
gossiping and putting each other up – or mostly down. And there had
been Jamis – he missed Jamis – with his endless flow of news. Talking
is what normal people do.

There were two more white stones ahead. Beyond them was a collection of three cottages, one incomplete. Two men were thatching its roof. They had arrived too suddenly round a bend to evade notice here, and they simply rode straight down the road, and through the second village.

A little further on, for the first time, they heard hooves coming towards them. They politely dismounted and stood to one side as two highborn-looking people passed by, followed by three servants or guards. One of the servants was leading a saddled but riderless horse, and another a pack mule. The whole company was silent and solemn. As they passed, Dorac pushed back his hood, bowed his head and crossed himself as if for a funeral party, and cuffed Gormad's head down also.

A riderless horse. *It really does happen. The third village has no name.*

The people passed, unspeaking but grand, like something in a dream. Gormad's eyes pricked for no reason. Now the silence was scary. Sometimes as they rode, he saw the man glancing at him. Wondering, perhaps, what his squire would do after he was dead.

*

So many memories -

Ilda, aged five, scowling as her nurse plaited her long brown hair. Gaskor, aged six, throwing a tantrum when his sister beat him in a race. Filana, aged three, whirling round and round in the middle of the kitchen while the servants around her laughed.

Hagouna sighed and laid down her accounts book. A tear had smudged the last entry. She sat in her steward's room, and the house of Ferrodach sat silent around her. It waited for its fate, and nothing much mattered. Since the deaths.

Only ten days ago. She had been trying to persuade her lord's senile cousin Derrian that the stable boy had not been deliberately insulting him, when she'd heard the noise. There was a confused calling out in the courtyard; steel clashed; people cried out. Making rapid excuses to Derrian, she hurried into the hall. People were pouring into it – their own guards and stable-hands were being marched in by grim strangers with drawn swords, and then she saw two men she thought she recognised.

"There are soldiers, madam!" Mabboran the gatekeeper cried. "They've killed Arator!"

"Where is the steward?" Kremdar Kingsbrother was demanding, and then he identified her. "This house is taken for King Arrion. Where is your lord?"

"What do you mean?" she asked, flabbergasted.

"They killed Arator!" Mabboran wailed. "They say Lord Gahran's a traitor!"

"Lord Gahran is accused of treason to the King. We have orders to take him to Stonehill for trial, but no one else need -" Dorac Kingsbrother was saying.

One of the soldiers interrupted him. "Where is he?"

The thought of treason in connection with her gentle lord was so ludicrous that Hagouna was filled with indignation. Somebody grabbed her arms from behind.

"We will find him anyway," said Dorac. "Save us all some trouble. Where is he?"

Perhaps her master would benefit from a little time, was her confused thought. "I will answer no questions from you."

He hit her in the face. "Where is he?"

"What is happening here?" Lord Gahran had entered the gallery above the hall, and was staring down at the chaotic crowd. Faces turned upwards, and quietened.

"My Lord," said Master Kremdar, "you are summoned to Stonehill to answer charges of treason. This house is under command of the King."

"Under command of a rabble, I think," said Lord Gahran. "Master Dorac, you are an honest man. What is going on?"

"Our orders, my Lord, are from the King. You are under arrest for treason."

The babble rose again.

"Treason! On what grounds?"

"The charges concern a letter written by you. You will hear more in Stonehill. We call on you to yield this house."

He had had to shout to be heard, but now again there was quiet. Everyone stared up at Lord Gahran, and it seemed to Hagouna that his face had changed.

"Where are my children?" he demanded.

"The children have not been harmed," Dorac promised. "Nor will they be."

"I yield this house. Do not hurt any of my people. They have committed no crime, and neither have I."

Dorac nodded to someone, and Hagouna felt her bruised arms released. Orders were given. Lord Gahran was escorted as a prisoner to his chamber; the servants were herded to the kitchen.

"Where are the children?" Kremdar asked her, and obediently she guided him and Dorac to the turret room where Sotras had been trying to teach arithmetic until the extraordinary noises from downstairs made it impossible. When they walked in, the elder girl was arguing vociferously with the tutor, the boy was leaning out of the window to try to see what was going on, and the youngest was sitting very primly and virtuously with her sister's book upside down in her hands.

"Children, these men are here from the King. No doubt everything will soon be explained, but for now we must do as they say."

"I don't obey anyone but my father," said Gaskor truculently.

"You obey the King's Thirty," said Hagouna.

It was the will of the King's Thirty, apparently, for the children to be taken downstairs, and shut in the little chamber opposite the steward's room, with a guard outside the door, and their bewildered tutor ushered away.

She had not seen them again.

Ilda, aged eight, proudly reciting the list of the kings of Israel and Judah. Gaskor, aged seven, rolling down the hill by the stables. The two of them allowed in to stare solemnly at baby Filana for the first time.

And so they had died, and their father had died, and the soldiers the Kingsbrothers had left behind allowed no one to leave, and Ferrodach would soon have a new lord, who might keep some and dismiss others to beg or starve, and would scorn them all as traitors. Traitors! It was still not possible.

The three standing in a little huddle at the funeral of their mother and infant sister. Gaskor saying to Ilda, 'When we're both in the King's Thirty, you'll be my double sister!' Ilda climbing trees. Filana crying because her brother had teased

96

her, but refusing to tell what terrible words he had used. Now they were both dead, and no one would ever know. That information was gone from the world.

But Hagouna still had things to do, and people to look after. Her steps were slow and heavy as she arrived at the bookroom, where that man had come to sit after promising to keep the children safe, and then slaughtering them. Here sat Sotras day after day, a tutor with no one to teach, the most pitiable person in the house. He lifted his red eyes to her as she entered. "I've brought you some wine, sir. How goes your work?"

He gestured vaguely at the desk. It had been Hagouna's idea to ask him to write a life of Lord Gahran, to honour and defend his memory – and largely to give Sotras something to do. The only thing accomplished so far was the complete disarrangement of all the books.

There was a call from downstairs. "Riders coming! Soldiers!"

What more could be done to them? she thought.

Ilda riding in the wind, hair flying loose, a wild grin on her face. Gaskor carefully jumping down the stairs two at a time.

There were six strangers entering the hall. No, four strangers, accompanying Hassdan and Soumaki of the King's Thirty. The King's Thirty again.

*

They rode in and out of woods as the path rose, and fell, and rose, and when the woods failed there was rough grassland splodged with sheep. As the afternoon began to wear away – he was so hungry – and a few drops of rain were falling, Dorac and Gormad came to the third village, with its white boulders. But first on the left was a small sheepless field. Instead of animals, there was an odd collection of items, some plainly old and weather-battered, others less so. There were several litters, once brightly painted and softly cushioned. There were tattered banners on poles, flickering in the wind. There were swords stuck in the earth, and there was a board with papers fastened to it, with a little roof to keep them dry.

They could easily have stopped to look more closely, but Dorac rode on.

On the other side was a graveyard. One of the humps was recent, and bare of grass. Gormad remembered the riderless horse.

Beyond were the white markers, and as he rode up to them his stomach tightened. He waited for the sense of doom as they stepped over the line. It did not come, but Dorac dismounted, and gestured for him to do so also.

This was a much larger place than the last – there were nearly a dozen small wooden houses on either side of the road, and even a lane running away to the left. In between the houses someone had planted shrubs, the kind with flowers. There was a small wooden church, and there were other buildings larger than the rest. Some even had upper storeys. Two women were sitting sewing on a bench in the large porch of one of these, and they looked up at passers-by.

A man stepped into the road ahead of them. "Welcome, friend," he said to Dorac. "Do you know where you've come?"

"I know."

"Are you wanting a meal, or – anything?"

"A meal, and a room, if there is one."

"The Crescent Moon at the end of the street. There is stabling there." The man bowed politely.

"Thank you."

All those days of sore, confused travelling, and it was about to be over. The last village. Then the Stones.

All those days when he should have been working out what to say, what arguments to use, and now there were twenty yards to the inn, and perhaps only an hour or so left. Twenty yards. Fifteen. But he did not dare argue, not just because of the threat and the stick, but because death (Gormad thought) is actually very frightening, and someone who wants to die is also very frightening, and - *Please, no.*

"Stables?" Dorac called, and a young girl appeared from the back to take the horses. "We will be here for the night." He ran a hand briefly over Derry's nose before turning away towards the main door.

Blood bubbling in his head, Gormad pulled at his sleeve. "Please." As Dorac glanced down – "I still don't want you to." No reply. Dorac pushed the door open.

The fuggy room was lit by candles on walls and tables, and by the fire in the huge hearth. It did have windows, but the shutters were fastened. The flat ceiling was high enough for a tall man not to bump his head against. There were benches round the walls, and several tables with more benches, and a half doorway at one end. Beyond in the back room Gormad could see a woman moving about, and there were barrels. In a corner sat a tall man playing gentle boring music on a lute, and being ignored. It was a proper tavern.

Two women sat at one table, a man and a woman at another. At a third was a man on his own, who looked up as they came in.

Dorac froze, so that Gormad bumped into him.

The man, who looked faintly familiar, stood up. "Brother," he said.

"Kai?"

There was a moment's pause. Then Dorac was across the floor in two strides.

*

The embrace, which was silent and still, lasted a long time. But at last they broke it, and looked at each other rather awkwardly, and both said almost together, "What are you doing here?" and the other man laughed. Gormad knew him now – Kai Kingsbrother, the good-looking one the girls squealed about.

"Plain enough what I'm doing here," said Dorac, not laughing. "Why are you here? Have you no orders?"

"I am here on business of the King. I'm here to talk to you. And first, to buy you a drink." He turned to the half-door. "Hostess! Another mug for me, if you will, and my friend will take one also." He sat down again.

Dorac stood staring at him. At last he said, gesturing towards Gormad, who had crept up to them, "The boy will have his watered."

"And a watered ale for the lad."

"At once, sir."

Master Kai looked at Gormad for the first time. "Gormad, son of Ramahdis, I think? You're a long way from home. Why are *you* here?"

"I -"

Dorac sat down. "He is a child I have not yet killed." Both the others jerked a little. "I'm saving him for breakfast."

It was only Kai's guffaw that told Gormad that this was –

almost unbelievably – an actual joke. The inn hostess pushed through her door with three mugs. Gormad sat at the table – and the truth hit him that, whatever else happened in his life, today he was sitting drinking in an inn with two of the King's Thirty. He wished that Jamis or Kammer or that oaf Hanos could see him now.

Everyone else in the room was watching them.

The hostess took another order and disappeared, and when the attention had passed on, Dorac said, "Talk to me?"

Kai's voice was low. "Gemara went to the King. He has asked her and Hassdan to investigate what happened at Ferrodach."

"Why?"

"In case Kremdar and Arvill are lying."

Dorac looked down at the table, and traced something on it with his finger. "They are lying. I did not kill Lord Gahran's children."

"No."

Gormad's heart leapt for joy. He waited for Dorac to say "You believe me!" as in the happiest bit of a story, and for all to be well. But Dorac was still staring at the table. Slowly he said, "It's too late to investigate. Investigation comes *before* the trial."

"They think there may be more evidence. They have forty days to take it to the King, and - he could change his decision."

"He couldn't." As Kai was about to speak, Dorac continued, "So. What are you doing?"

"I was sent to find you two days ago. Gemara said I was to ask you everything you remember about Ferrodach, and learn what you're going to do next."

"What I'm going to do?" Dorac sat back on his stool, and

looked at him. For no reason that he could understand, Gormad felt that an argument was coming. "I'm going to take a room for the night. A bath. A good supper. Tomorrow I'll tell you about Ferrodach if you like. A church to take the sacrament. I need to write my will."

"You've written your will."

"It needs changing. A few other things, if I have the money. And then I'm going to the Old Stones."

"No. You're not."

"I am."

"Weren't you listening? The King has ordered -"

"If I believe you and Gemara. It makes no difference."

"Dorac, you can't do this! Of course it does! You're an exile, you're not dead! You don't have to die!"

"Stop!" Dorac shouted, thumping the table so hard the mugs jumped. The inn fell abruptly silent. "Just stop talking."

The three sat still, and slowly the rest of the room started its business again.

"You are my brother, or you were, and you mean well. I will - let you try to talk me out of this. If you must. But not now - I can't do this now. I just want to drink - with my friend."

"With your brother."

"Thank you," Dorac whispered. "With my brother."

"If you've stopped shouting," said his brother, after a moment, "if this were my last night on earth, it's not a church I'd be looking for."

"Perhaps you're ready to face God. I'm not," said Dorac matter-of-factly.

A chill ran up Gormad's spine and settled at the back of his neck.

In a different tone, Dorac added, "I said 'other things'. We passed a whorehouse on the way in, I think. I can hope they don't only employ women - Before you get too drunk to remember, will you do something for me?"

"Of course. What?"

Dorac jerked his head at Gormad. "I was going to leave him with the priest, and ask that someone sent a message, but you'll do. Take him back to Stonehill."

"Oh - yes. Gemara told me to bring him along."

"He wants to be a squire. His lord is dead, and he's afraid his parents may call him home. I'd be grateful if you could ask the King's favour for him. I'll write him a letter to take."

"Who was he squiring for?"

"Marrach."

"Marrach who was dying?"

"He died."

"Ah." Gormad thought he saw sympathy as Kai glanced at him.

There was a pause, and then Dorac asked, "Has the King named anyone to replace me in the Six?"

"He hadn't when I left. I suppose he will have done by now. Most of the money is on Ralia, or maybe Captain Renatar."

Our Captain?

"What happened in the west?"

"What? Oh. The Haymonese came in through Kerrytown, and

burned a few houses." He leant back, and in a tone Gormad did not understand, he said, "Well met, then, brother. How did you get here? Which roads?"

They looked at each other, a strange grown-up look.

"I went out of the Wide Gate, and walked south on the main road about - nine miles, to near the charcoal-burner's place on Harro's lands. The boy caught me with Derry, and after the Wildfowl Lake we turned southeast. I suppose you did too. We slept that night in the wood about a mile from Little Barr. The next day we went to the market at Madderan, and there was some trouble with a few fools who wanted to rescue him from me -" (Gormad's ears pricked up, but Dorac continued), "so we cut through the woods to the little hill trail through Verkki's lands, and up to the crossroads just north of here, and through Wester Kleechit and the other village. There was no more trouble. We hardly saw anyone." He shrugged, and added, "And you?"

Gormad could not have believed that even a grown-up conversation could be so stupid. Kai's reply, happily, was shorter. "I came the main road, and no marketing. I've been waiting for you about an hour. Hoping I guessed right. What did you do to the fools in Madderan?"

"Scared them, perhaps. Where did you camp?"

Gormad's eyes were closing, but suddenly, "Can I get you anything more, sirs?" and he jerked awake.

"Yes, my friends will be joining me upstairs," said Kai briskly. "Is there space for them?"

"The bed is large enough, sirs, if you don't mind sharing. Or there is a better room with two large -"

"Just one. I have to account for the money I'm spending. And a straw pallet for the boy. And is there a place for a bath?"

It seemed there was a bathhouse at the back, and water could be heated in an hour. In the meantime, they ordered a supper which Kai paid for, and it was a far better meal than Gormad had enjoyed for a long time. He ate helping after helping. "Were you starving him?" Kai asked.

"Plainly I was."

Then they all went outside into the dusk and climbed the stair to the upper wooden gallery leading to the inn's three bedrooms. The room Kai had already spoken for was lit by candles ready for them, and had its own fire. To Gormad's surprise, a sweet fragrance met them as they entered – there were flowers in a bowl, and petals strewn on the bed, and fresh hay on the floor. The bed had a tall frame with hangings. There was even a tapestry on the wall, but it was too dark to see the design. It was nearly as grand as his parents' chamber at home, or Marrach's room on his estate, where as a squire he had slept outside the door.

"The bath is ready for you, sir."

"Dorac."

Dorac turned in the doorway.

"You promised to talk. You're coming back."

"I'm coming back. Cleaner." He paused. "Then we can talk." He walked out.

"Oh shit," Kai said, and sat down on the bed. Gormad wandered about, feeling very full, peering at the tapestry – it seemed to be a scene of martyrdom – and noticing the carved cross on the wall, and the bowl of water, actually scented, to wash one's face in.

"This is a fine place," he said.

"It disgusts me."

"Oh. Why, Master Kai?"

"I don't know. But it does." The man put his elbows on his knees and his palms over his eyes. "I thought the hard part would be finding him. I need someone clever. Hassdan or Brinnon or someone. He's such a stubborn bastard."

Gormad blinked. "What d'you think happens at the Place, the Stones?" he asked timidly.

"I don't know. Even Dorac surely can't think that God will reach down and strike him dead when he steps into the circle." Kai looked upwards a little nervously, and crossed himself. "But people do die. I should have gone up and looked around, but I couldn't risk missing him."

After three days with Dorac, Gormad was finding Kai's openness very refreshing. To keep the talk going, he asked, "Did you like the supper?"

"The stuffed wood-pigeon was very fine," said the other rather sarcastically, and then, "That's what disgusts me."

"The food?"

"It's like fattening a pig. People come here to die. Nobody should set out to die, and they make money out of it." He got up and started striding about the room, his voice rising. "'Welcome to the Village with No Name! We will give you everything you desire! Fine dinners, comfortable rooms, willing whores! We have churches for you to pray in, and baths for you to wallow in, and we'll charge you for everything. Because you don't need your gold any more, do you? We'll give you everything you want, except a reason not to die. Because if you don't want to die, we don't make any money. We're just a village on the edge of the mountains.'

"Shit, shit, shit." He sat down again. "Be a good lad, and don't talk to me. I need to think."

So Gormad lay on his mattress, and made shadow pictures on the wall. Kai would be able to sort things out. He was one of the King's Thirty. They could solve anything. After a while, Dorac's footsteps on the stairs returned, followed by himself, shaved and washed (presumably) and with his hair tied sleekly back.

"Very well," Kai growled. "But downstairs. There are too many flowers here, and I need a drink."

*

The new arrivals had been welcomed by the soldiers at Ferrodach with some enthusiasm. They had brought a guest-gift of a large live ox to contribute to food stocks, and their coming might possibly indicate that this dull and depressing assignment was nearing its end. By Lord Gahran's people, they were received with polite obedience barely masking hostility.

Meril dropped an armful of luggage while helping to unpack, and Hassdan swore at her, and told her to get out of his sight. So she had a good excuse and some free time to wander, noting the layout as she had been told. It was a fairly large house, and strongly built for defence, although less fine than she'd expected for a former queen's grandson. She visited the room she had heard about, where brown stains were visible on the walls and the floor matting, and felt her body clenching at the thought of what had happened there. Master Dorac had done that. Or had he? The room was being left unused, perhaps on purpose. Small and dark, it contained no trapdoors or secret passageways that she could discover (*but what do you know, Meril?*). There were no tapestries to hide behind. There were two benches, and a chest containing toys. As a toybox it was large, but an assassin could not have hidden inside. Meril gently touched the brightly coloured spinning top, and turned away. In the grounds, she found the household chapel, and its small graveyard. And two recent graves, one labelled on a temporary cross, *Arator, son of Otto. Died in defence of Ferrodach, aged 23 years,* and the other, *Ilda, Gaskor and Filana, Children of Lord Gahran and Lady Geril. Murdered 26 September 570.* She crossed herself, and said a dutiful prayer for the success of their mission. Although she was not sure what "success" would mean.

Supper in the hall (the one Master Dorac had crossed with a drawn sword on his way to kill the children. Or just to talk to them, he had said) was an awkward affair, but not as awkward as what followed. From her place at one of the lower tables, Meril watched Master Hassdan as he sat beside the grim-faced steward Hagouna. A minstrel had been strumming quietly for some time, but as the meal ended she stopped, to polite applause. Hagouna turned in traditional manner to the house's honoured guests.

"Would you care for some more entertainment, Master Hassdan? Mistress Soumaki?"

"Surely we would be delighted," Hassdan said.

"Who has something to offer?" asked the steward.

A tall elderly man stood up and strode clumping to the middle of the floor. "I have a tale to tell."

"Please tell it, Mabboran."

"Once there was a king," he began formally. "Once, and not so long ago. His name was Marod, and he ruled the fair land of Arbeth."

Meril saw Master Hassdan stiffen, and felt a sudden stir in the Hall, but she did not understand why. The man began telling of the War of Three Kingdoms, that had begun with the murder of Good King Marod two hundred years ago. The three lands of Arbeth, Qarath and Rachonda fought bitterly and viciously for twelve years, until Marod's nephew Tristar forgave the murders of his uncle and his wife, united the exhausted people in a single kingdom and called them after the last noble king.

Mabboran did not tell the long history of battle, siege and betrayal that always confused Meril totally, but dwelt instead on the gruesome stories that haunted dark nights still. The village children herded into a church and burnt alive. The nuns and monks raped and then flayed. The pregnant women ripped apart at Christmas "celebrations". And so on, until the Great Peace, when the new king gathered his lords and warriors, and appointed the King's Thirty to help make a better future. *Oh, I see*, thought Meril, ashamed of her slowness.

"And he stood on the steps of the Cathedral, and declared, 'From now on we will not be barbarians. Even in war, even in the worst of times, *we will not kill children*, we will not commit rape, we will not take pleasure in torment.' And all the people said -"

"AMEN!" finished the hall, and Meril felt the fury and hatred of Ferrodach walking up her spine.

Mabboran bowed to the high table, and walked back to his place, and there was a silence. Perhaps Master Hassdan, impassive and polite, would have said something, but it was Mistress Soumaki who stood up. "Thank you, sir," she said. "A tale well told, and a lesson to remember. May I offer something to the hall?"

Hagouna nodded, and Soumaki stepped into the centre to sing.

Her voice was sweet and true, but not loud, and the hall had to quieten to hear her. She sang the song of the Massacre at Bethlehem, the lament for the babies killed on the orders of King Herod, and she sang it simply and well. When she had finished, she bowed first to the steward of the house, whose guest she was, and then to the hall, and the song and the bows seemed to Meril to be a sort of apology for her brother's actions. The room felt slightly less angry.

Later that night, Meril reported to her master.

"The graveyard – where is it? Is it in sight of the house?"

"Of the highest windows, I think, but not the rest."

Hassdan said frowning, "The funeral was so hurried, so shabby. They wrapped the bodies in a sheet – one sheet – and interred them, barely three hours after they'd been killed. No wonder the steward feels insulted. I suppose Kremdar did have a lot on his mind." He made a steeple with his fingers, and frowned. "I had a strange thought about the violence and the mess, but it does not fit with the funeral. What do you think, Meril? If you were Lord Gahran, or Lord Gahran's steward, and the King sent soldiers to arrest you, and you knew you were lost, but you were desperate to protect the children at any cost -"

She looked confused.

"Dorac and Kremdar had never seen them before. How do we know it was indeed Gahran's children who were put in that room?"

"To be killed, sir?"

"To take the small risk of being killed - No one knew Dorac would hurt them. No one at Ferrodach heard Lady Sada's words at Council. The violence to the bodies, and even the speed of the burial, might fit with hiding their identity. But *our* people did that. Kremdar stitched up the sheet himself. Doubtless to spare anyone else such an unpleasant task.

"We need to talk to someone who knew them well. Not the tutor; he's half-witless already."

"The steward would know them."

He tweaked her ear. "If there was a plot to substitute Lord Gahran's children with others, to save them from the wrath of the King, who is the most certain to be involved in it?"

"I am sorry, Master."

"See if you can get someone to describe them to you tomorrow. I'll talk to the priests, the village man and the chaplain. St John help us. We're going to have to dig them up."

*

Kai had not thought it possible that The Crescent Moon could annoy him any more than it had already. But then he saw at least twenty people, more than the room could comfortably hold, crowding the benches, all pretending not to be expecting a show, but falling silent as they entered. One table had been left empty in the middle, ready for the performance. The glamorous strangers from the city were the entertainment for the night.

"We'll talk outside," he said.

It was almost dark behind the inn, where there was a little square with a few trees, between bathhouse, bakehouse and stables. A torch in a wall bracket provided just enough light to see each other's faces. The eager-faced but rather tired-looking boy sat down on a root. The two men stood with their mugs of ale at an angle in front of a tree that they could look at if the conversation became too embarrassing, and eyed each other warily.

"And so?" said Dorac.

Kai wished he had drunk less earlier. "I told you before. Gemara and Hassdan are looking for evidence that you didn't do it."

"The evidence was my word against theirs. Everyone believed theirs. The King decided, as he had to, and that will not change."

"If we prove you're innocent, it will change."

"No, it won't." Dorac stared at the ground, and his voice became strained. "The King can't forgive a murderer. What would happen would be people talking, gossiping, 'maybe Kremdar is a liar, maybe the King was wrong'. That would damage the Thirty more – and the Kingdom. I was found guilty. It is over."

"It can't be over. The King must be able to do something. I don't know the law of it -"

"There is no law to unmake sentences. You're a judge, Kai. I've hanged people, you've hanged people, who may have been innocent, who swore they were. Only God knows. I had a good life, and then it was my fate to be lied about, and to die."

"You're a Christian. You don't believe in fate," Kai growled.

"I believe that what has already happened won't change because you don't like it. Today the King believes Kremdar, the next day me, the next day Kremdar again? It's nonsense. Chaos."

"But you don't have to do this! Not here! What d'you expect to happen if you walk up that hill?"

"I expect to die."

"Struck by lightning, or devoured by a dragon, or swallowed up by the earth, like - like -"

"Some of Moses' enemies?" Evidently Dorac couldn't remember their names, either. "If it's God's will. But I expect it's something more earthly."

"You mean that someone hides in the trees and shoots anyone who comes? That's my guess, having seen this place. You don't think that's wrong?"

"Not as long as they shoot straight."

"That is not the right death for you!" Kai said.

"It's better than many."

"It's suicide. Isn't that a deadly sin?" His head was aching. He swallowed, and said, "Don't do it."

"Is it suicide? My life is over. This is a tidy way to finish it. After the battle, the hopelessly wounded are killed, and it's not murder. Because they're not going to survive."

Kai looked down at his hand gripping his mug, and said quietly, "I know you've been through hell. Kremdar saying that, and the King believing him. Losing your name."

Dorac absently stroked the tree bark in front of him. "Yes, it was hell. It is hell. Everyone who hears my name will think of murdered children. Forever."

"Not everyone. We know you didn't do it."

"Ah. Nearly everyone. Whatever King Arrion told Gemara, murdered children is what he saw, and murdered children is what people will see. It's what I see. I see them in my sleep, lying cut to pieces, the way Arvill said they were. After I promised they would be safe."

"It would be worse hell if you were guilty. We know you're not. There is hope." Dorac shrugged. "And even if there were not, this is exile, not death. It's hell now, but it won't always be. You will survive. You're too strong not to." He forced himself to say it. "You know what Gemara tells her grandchildren. 'The coward says the pain is unbearable.'"

He was relieved to see a flash of fury and hurt in Dorac's eyes. "You're calling me a coward?"

"I know you're not a coward. That's why you won't go to the Old Stones."

There was a long pause. Dorac slowly slid down to sit against the tree. "So, in that case - tell me what I do?"

Kai wasn't sure how much he had achieved. "You can go anywhere else outside the Kingdom. Anywhere."

"I can travel around Jaryar and Ricossa, and even down south, to the holy places in Defardu. I have no money, and I know no one. What do I do there? Starve?"

"Dorac. You're one of the best swordsmen in Marod. You wouldn't starve."

"I travel around Jaryar and Ricossa demanding food and

shelter, and killing anyone who doesn't give it to me?"

"You fool, you'd be valuable to anyone. Shit, they're fighting each other all over Ricossa! Or any king – any noble – would hire you. A bodyguard, a city watchman, a soldier. There is nothing dishonourable in it. Good people need bodyguards."

"I thought of that." Dorac fingered the hilt of his sword. "I did my little thing with the stones that you all like to laugh at. I thought I could kill myself. Or I could kill Kremdar." He swallowed. "Or I could go and find something to do, and the only thing I can do is kill people. Choose a side in Ricossa, or find some rich person who wants guarding."

Kai waited.

Even more slowly, as if the words were being dragged out of him, Dorac went on. "I know this will sound unreasonable. I'm forty-two years old. I've been fighting for my queen and my king and my country since I was fifteen. 'I will swear my sword to no one else.' I cannot do it."

Kai looked at him, and saw that, unreasonable though it was, he truly could not. He sighed.

"There must be something else you can do."

"I'm getting old. I can't see as well as I used to. Soon I won't even be able to kill as well." He shrugged. "Once I knew how to milk a cow. I looked at my stones three days ago, and prayed, and chose to come here instead of cutting my throat, to give God time to show me something else. Because I could see nothing."

So now he was speaking for God, Kai thought in despair.

"What do you see me doing? Shall I become a merchant, or a

poet, or a secretary?"

"No -" He searched for professions in his memory. "You're a holy man for a warrior. You could go into a monastery," was the best he could think of.

"'I had a strong vocation to worship God, but killing people for the King distracted me, until I murdered three children, and the King threw me out.' Any monastery would be delighted."

Suddenly Dorac glanced over at the boy, who was listening intently. "Gormad. I've changed my mind about thrashing you. If I don't go to the Old Stones, what could I do?"

He had plainly been longing to be asked. "You could become an outlaw."

Kai could not help laughing.

"An outlaw," said Dorac.

"Yes, fight evil lords, and live in the forest, and rescue people, and - hunt -"

"Like the Blue Lake Brothers, and Hardi of the Woods?"

"Yes!"

"What evil lords?" asked Dorac grimly. "Shall I murder that Lady Yenilda? Does King Arrion deserve to have me killing his tax collectors? Does even the King of Jaryar deserve that? Outlaws are criminals, and I've hanged them. I swore fifteen years ago to do justice. It would betray everything I believe in." He looked at Kai. "I can see nothing that is not a betrayal."

"If you die, you'll never know what you could have found to do." Kai pursued doggedly. "And if you're wrong – have you thought of judgment? The – the pit of fire and all that they say in church?"

"I've thought of it. I think of it before every battle. Perhaps you don't. I may go to hell. We all know that, all the time, and we trust in our Redeemer for salvation. God is merciful." Quietly he added, "God is good. If I believe anything, I believe that."

"Do you have any more to say?"

"You have friends who don't want you to die."

"Is their pain going to be unbearable?" asked Dorac dryly. "People die all the time. You'll miss me as much or as little whether I go to the Stones, or into exile. And I don't want your false hope. He can't change his verdict. I can't come back."

People laughed at Kai for weeping easily, and there were tears on his face now. "I can't argue like you can. You know that, you bastard. Just don't throw your life away. There is always something good, something to hope for. There *is*. I can't see why anyone would not want another day." He couldn't keep still, and he paced across the little space as he talked. "Don't miss the next sunrise."

"Tell me," said Dorac. "If you thought I had killed those children, would you still tell me life was good, and shouldn't be thrown away?"

After a heartbeat, "Yes."

"Ah - If you were sure I was innocent, you'd have taken longer to think about that."

"You *bastard!*" shouted Kai, because it was true.

"So you do see murdered children."

"I do not!" Kai said, and they both knew he was lying. He sat down against the same tree, staring anywhere except at his brother.

"Why did he have to be merciful?" Dorac asked after a

moment. "Why couldn't he just have hanged me?"

"You want to be hanged for something you haven't done?"

"It would be better than this," Dorac whispered. He put his face in his hands, and wept.

The other two waited. Kai's throat was raw, and he wanted to send the boy for more ale, but looking up he saw faces at the window, and round the edge of the building: clearly they were still the entertainment. Had he not been so tired, he would have got up and broken some heads.

So they just sat on, and at last Dorac wiped his face and stared up wordlessly at the sky where there ought to have been stars, but there was only black cloud. The silence went on and on, and slowly changed, as Kai had noticed silences do, from pity and embarrassment and pain, to a quiet that soothed a little, and did not want to be broken.

After a time, when the crowd had got bored, the three went up to bed. Dorac carried Gormad, who was already asleep.

6 October 570

The next day felt very strange to all three of them. Perhaps it was least strange to Dorac, who had a mental list of things to do, had made certain arrangements the night before, and went steadily through them.

Gormad was warm and well-fed and comfortable, and was not ready to be nudged awake.

"Up." The voice was firm.

His first proper thought was to wonder if Master Dorac would be embarrassed about having cried the night before. And it was true that he looked slightly less confident than usual, as he said, "When Master Kai wakes, tell him I have gone out. I will be back before noon."

"Where are you going?"

"That is not your concern. Practise your swordplay. You need to impress him."

In fact, Kai was waking up before the footsteps had faded down the stairs. He groaned and rubbed his face in a way Gormad remembered from Marrach's brother and from his own aunt Tisha, but once he had dipped his head in the bowl of sweet water, he was ready to hear the message.

"Hmm."

"Where d'you think he's going, please?"

"He mentioned a whorehouse and a church. The whorehouse comes first, I feel, and even he wouldn't have the gall to go straight from one to the other, so I suppose he'll come back in between."

They were breaking their fast in the empty room downstairs

when he added suddenly, "I should tell you he doesn't often go to such places. Not often at all."

Gormad blushed.

"But he must think if he's going to die today, God will understand and forgive."

"Will He? Forgive?"

"I don't know," said Kai. "That is why I prefer to stay alive."

"But the King's Thirty never fear death!" exclaimed Gormad. And then realised that he was implying that Kai was afraid, possibly a coward, and that might be unforgivable.

But Kai only said, "Who told you that?"

"People say."

"One of the Thirty is afraid of deep water. Another is afraid of loud noises in the dark. Death - Kremdar Kingsbrother is the bravest man I know, and he rides to battle without fear, but the rest of us - Surely your Captain Renatar has told you, 'Fear in your guts brings no shame, fear in your feet destroys your name.'"

"You mean you can be scared as long as you don't run away."

"Yes. Should you not be practising?"

As they left the room, Gormad said, "He seemed a bit happier. Do you think that's good?"

"No. It means that nothing I said – *we* said – made any difference to him. If we'd made any impression, he'd be angry as hell working it out."

Gormad dared to ask, "Do you believe him?"

Kai sighed, and tossed him a stick. "I believe him most of the time."

"Oh."

"What he wants, what I would want in his place, is for people to believe him because they know him, because they know he wouldn't do such a thing. That's what he wants. But what *I* want – the person doing the believing – is for a reason in the facts. I want there to be evidence, even just evidence that means something to me, and no one else, that he's innocent. The evidence is not good."

Gormad did not quite understand this.

"Very well. Find a place to stand. Attack."

Kai was a better teacher than Dorac, or at least a better explainer, and it was almost enjoyable. They were sitting resting against the inn wall, and Gormad was wondering how to ask the first of the hundred questions he had about life in the King's Thirty, when they saw that Dorac had returned and was looking down at them, very faintly embarrassed (Gormad thought), and munching an apple. "What d'you think?" he asked Kai.

"How old are you, lad? Ten? Not bad for ten. How's your archery?"

"Captain Renatar said I was just a little better than useless," Gormad admitted.

"You've plenty of time to improve. I have parchment," he said to his friend. "Ferrodach."

"Mmm." They both looked at Gormad, who tried not to look obviously hopeful. "Were you at my trial?"

"Yes."

"You can stay and listen if you like. Unless Master Kai objects."

"I can swear him to secrecy afterwards."

So they dragged a bench and table out of the inn, and sat in the space they had argued in last night, and Dorac talked and answered questions, and Kai wrote, and Gormad wondered for the first time who had killed the children, if Dorac had not.

*

In a pleasant room above a linen shop on one of the best streets in Stonehill, Lady Sada was visiting an old friend. The window was open, and the cries of street-sellers wafted up, along with the scent of their spices and cakes. Lady Karnall of Aspella peered out occasionally, between inspecting her embroidery and smiling at her guest. Long years ago, she and the Princesses Darisha and Sada had been the leaders of merriment and pleasant society in Stonehill. Long ago.

A hunting accident had killed her husband and crippled her, and she spent most of her time confined to this room, leaving her daughters and sons-in-law to manage the family estate in the west. She was always grateful for visitors, especially Lady Sada of the Council of Elders.

"So Gahran's treason was averted, thank God," she was saying, her grey head bent over her stitches. "I hope the King gave you your due for that?"

"Tcha. It was more thanks to your daughter and Lord Jovian, and no, he has not expressed much gratitude. It would have made another reason to call Ralia, but no."

"Ralia is a good girl. She knows no one has a right to a place in the Thirty. She can serve the King where she is now."

"Yes, but still - What my nephew was thinking of, I do not

122

know. He asked me for four names. I had *one* name, I found two more respectable ones, and I added Saysh to make up the list." Lady Sada wrinkled her nose disdainfully, and sipped her drink of newly-fashionable spiced morbah. "What does he want in the Thirty? Skill in battle, great skill, *intelligence*, honour, good family, a popular name with the people? Ralia has all these things. I do not flatter, though she is your granddaughter. To be passed over for Saysh, son of Adshan!"

"I know nothing bad about this Saysh."

"As strong as an ox, and half as clever. Heaven knows, Dorac was never the most sparkling of my nephew's brothers, but he could string two thoughts together. Saysh is built like a wrestler, and the women come to watch when he practises swordplay. I suppose he's loyal, and knows one end of a sword from the other. But so do all the rest, and the Southern already have one good-looking bonehead."

Lady Karnall chuckled. "Ah well. He sounds as if he has excellent qualities. Strong, loyal and handsome – perhaps that's what the King wants? Or the Queen -? I do hear titbits sometimes. Is it true that Saysh sits and gazes at her? And I suppose there's no harm done if she occasionally gazes back."

"Humph."

"Intelligent advice they can look for on the Council. From you, and others."

"Perhaps. As we have seen, Arrion is not always interested in advice. Though I admit he is less headstrong than his brother was. He has made a better king after all." Lady Sada turned her thoughts away from her dead elder nephew to her living younger one. She sighed, and fingered her heavy crimson skirt. "But I doubt if *my* advice will be welcomed much for a month or two. I am not popular. Mothers are pulling their children away from me in the street."

"You made a hard choice," said Lady Karnall gently.

"You think I was wrong? Perhaps I was."

"Does my opinion matter? You followed your conscience. You were right that the children were dangerous. Wolf cubs at play, I think I called them. Letting them live was a risk, and to believe otherwise is foolishness. Yet to kill them offends the Church, and the instinct of every parent. We both know that.

"I do not know if you were right or not. At least one of the Thirty evidently thought you were, however he tried to deny it afterwards."

A manservant knocked, and entered. "My lady, the man Attar is downstairs."

"Thank you. Do not fear, Sada. Your name will recover in time. It may even be praised. The King may not agree with what you said, but the courage was undeniable. Courage to say what to the conventional seemed wrong, but you thought necessary. Arrion must appreciate that. If war comes, which God forbid -" she shuddered " -we will need people with your sort of courage."

*

"I know I looked guilty," Dorac ended, tracing a pattern on the table. "I can't explain it. *They* lied so smoothly, and - I was asked to swear before God. I felt God was the only person who could believe me, and - the words went out of my head. So indeed God was the only person who did."

"I believed you!"

For a moment Kai thought Dorac was going to hit the boy. Then his face relaxed. "You must have done, or you would not have run off like that."

Kai looked down at all he had written, and back at his brother. "Is it possible," he said slowly, "that Kremdar is not lying? That there was someone else there?"

Dorac's face was very blank. "He said they went in a few minutes after I came out. There were no other doors. I saw no place for a killer to hide. And - he said I spoke of it beforehand. That I said it might be necessary, or some such thing."

"'Ugly but necessary', he said you said," put in Gormad shyly.

"I had no such conversation. He lied. I don't know why. Even if he thought it right to kill them, why lie about it, and about me?"

Kai looked away from the pain in that. He liked Kremdar, Dorac had liked Kremdar, and as far as he was aware, Kremdar liked Dorac. "There's something more, isn't there?"

Dorac opened his mouth and shut it again. At last, staring at the table, he said, "I think Arvill may just be saying what Kremdar tells her to say."

"Why might that be?"

"Because she is his lover."

"*What did you say?*"

"You didn't know. I don't think anyone knows."

"But he's married. It's adultery," said Kai slowly.

"Yes."

"How do you know?"

"About six weeks ago, I was walking along Oyster Alley one

evening, past The Shells and Bells Inn. There were two people kissing in the alley beside it. Then Arvill ran out, and almost crashed into me. She laughed and looked back, so I looked in, and saw Kremdar. She went one way, and I went the other, and then he caught up to me and said, 'Be a good fellow, and don't tell my wife. Or the King.'"

"And you didn't."

"I didn't tell anyone."

"But," Kai was struggling to make sense of this, "you could have said at the trial."

"I told Lady Kara when she visited me the day before. The King's Questioner is supposed to care for justice first. It took me some time to realise she was not going to mention it, so then I tried, but she wasn't letting me say much. And anyway," he said wearily, "they would have denied it, and I would be besmirching their characters again, and it still didn't prove they were lying about the children."

"No."

"That's everything." He hesitated, and then said, "You've done your duty. You don't need to wait till this evening. It's supposed to be by moonlight."

"I know. They say," Kai said brutally, "that the bodies are left on the field outside the village. They are found there in the morning."

"So I hear."

"We are staying till you leave."

Dorac turned to Gormad, and gave him a set of instructions that began with cleaning the horses' gear, and ended with having a bath. "I will see you later, then," he said, and walked away.

*

Gormad had not forgotten the mention of a letter to the King. It needed to say he obeyed orders, so he went to the stables, where Champion and Derry and Diana were pleased to see him. He worked through his tasks with the same sense of unreality that he had felt in Marrach's death chamber, and eventually found himself sitting in the bath with tears sliding down his face, but with no thoughts except a longing for someone his own age to talk to.

After the other two had gone out, Kai stared at the parchment in front of him for some time, considering his notes. *Hagouna - Braf - Laida - Arvill - Kremdar and Arvill -* At last he picked up his pen, and added a further three sentences to the report.

Dorac found the church. He confessed his sins, including those from earlier that day, and received the Holy Body and Blood. He could not bring himself to forgive his enemies, but he renounced vengeance on them, and hoped that was enough.

*

Gemara, Kremdar and their party reached Lenchen on the Hill mid-morning, and were greeted by the town elders in the marketplace. Gemara had asked Kremdar to handle the formalities, and he did it very well, as he always did. (Hassdan had once said that Kremdar reminded him of the statues of saints and kings in his native city of Makkera – always standing in a noble heroic pose. That was of course unjust, but Gemara was not feeling generous today.)

"We heard that Dorac Kingsbrother was exiled," murmured Bedala, who had managed Lenchen's affairs for seventeen years, and knew all the Southern Six well. "Is it true?"

"I am sorry to say it is." He paused to allow this to be

absorbed. "The King has appointed Saysh, son of Adshan, to the Thirty, and we are sure you will find him a faithful and fair judge when you see him. We are grateful for your hospitality, as always. The trials will begin at the hour of Terce tomorrow. Let all who have evidence to give be present."

It was the Southern's custom to wait until the next day to begin hearing the trials, to give the judges time to accustom themselves to each place, absorb the atmosphere and pick up any gossip. Hassdan had once overheard a woman boasting to her neighbour about the perjury she was about to commit, but even without such spectacular successes, Gemara felt the method was useful, and it helped bind the Six to the people they and the King served.

She watched Kremdar moving between stalls, smiling and talking, and making friends with his little purchases. More toys for his daughter Yaina, doubtless, whom he spoilt abominably. Yaina and her mother Praja spent half the year on their estate in the north, and Kremdar spent one month of that six with them; they came to Stonehill for the rest of the year, and saw him when his duties permitted. It was not the easiest way to be married, Gemara thought.

When they met to dine at the main inn, Dancing Fox, he had indeed bought a grinning puppet dressed as a minstrel. ("She has a queen and a warrior and a horse already. I know.") To Gemara's surprise, he had also bought a pretty necklace of beads.

"For Praja?"

"Er, yes. It's been too long since I bought her anything."

He was better at interpreting the towns than she was, so she was duty-bound to ask, "What did you learn?"

"I think people are a little quieter. It may be the talk of war. One woman wanted reassurance that we were not here to recruit soldiers. No one mentioned Lord Gahran."

"One did to me. He asked if it were true he was a traitor. I said yes. He asked if his lands were forfeited, and I said yes. He asked if I knew who was to receive them, and I said no."

Kremdar smiled sadly. "I would guess many people would like a share. I wonder if King Arrion will let the family keep any part, or if they are all tainted."

"Gahran's family are the King's family a few generations back. What were they, second cousins?"

"I believe so. Is that a close relationship? I barely know any of my cousins, first, second or third."

So they managed to talk until the music started up.

The second song the minstrel played and sang was the old tale of Renya and Korax and their tragic true love. Gemara, for whom "love" was the name men gave to their desire to seduce or even rape, hated such stuff, but Kremdar was always softer. She was still surprised to see the emotion on his face as he listened in silence. She remembered how obsessed he had been with Praja before they were married, but she had not realised he still felt so strongly. *True love. Noble heroism.* Perhaps she was wronging him. Perhaps it was all a mistake, her own arrogant belief that she knew Dorac better than the evidence.

*

By the time Gormad returned to the inn's main room, it was beginning to fill up again, and the sky was dark. There were pasties on the table, and it was Dorac's turn to be writing. He did this slowly and neatly; at last he pushed the parchment across to Kai and said, "Will you witness?"

Kai read it through. "Everything?"

"I owe him for a horse and saddle. Which he bought or stole."

"Bought. He left money in the stable, apparently." Kai wrote, *Witnessed this sixth day of October 570 Kai Kingsbrother of the Southern Six,* and folded it in three. Then they looked at each other.

"You can't stop me, Kai."

"I know I can't. You could knock me down with one hand. And if I stopped you today, there's tomorrow and next week." His whole body was tense, but Dorac seemed more at ease than Gormad had ever seen him.

"You can tell Gemara you did your best. I've no wife or children to leave, and I've had a good life. Well, since I left home, and until two weeks ago, a good life. That's over twenty-five years. More than most people have."

"I'm not coming with you," Kai said. "I think if you're determined to do something, to do something stubborn and pigheaded and stupid - it's easier to change your mind and come back if you haven't got people standing at your back watching. So I'm not coming, and neither is he. I'm going to sit here, hoping - and praying - that my brother comes back to drink with me tonight."

"You're a good man, Kai," Dorac said quietly. He lifted his satchel onto the table and began to search in it. From a pocket he took a very small scroll, which he tucked into his shirt. Then he pulled out a letter. "Gormad can give this to the King, if you think it will help him. Take my greetings to the others, if you would. And to Gamar and

Mayeel. Tell anyone interested that Lulet was a good steward for me at Valleroc. Tell her that - Don't trust Kremdar and Arvill."

"Anything else?"

"No." He unbuckled his sword belt, and laid it on the table, beside the satchel. "God go with you, Kai." He embraced Kai, and then looked down and awkwardly ruffled Gormad's hair. "And with you. Good luck. Be a great warrior." He turned and walked out.

"Wait -" Gormad began.

"Let him go."

"I only wanted to -" Gormad sat down again, and swung his legs violently.

Kai said nothing.

*

Beyond the black-painted boulders, the trees returned. Dorac marched along the path, neatly paved with small white stones, the better to be seen by twilight. It led uphill. One of the few roads in the south that he had never travelled before.

It was not yet quite dark, and there were clouds in the indigo sky, but not enough to obscure the moon. So that was all right. A *crescent* moon. The trees were fir, not close enough to the path to be menacing.

He longed to die, yet he was afraid. He had heard people wonder if you were faced at Judgment Day with the dead you had killed, and how they would look. *Lamb of God, that takes away the sin of the world -*

If God were very good, he might meet the other dead, the ones he wanted to see. He pictured the faces with just a little hope.

Ettuar, his first captain, who had taught him about honour, and God; Queen Darisha, who had given him his sword and won his loyalty forever; Taldim Kingsister, who had made him welcome in the Southern Six; Stimmon, its leader for so many years – and Tor. More than anyone, Tor.

I'll do anything. I can't bear to live without you. I love you, he remembered saying. But that was three years ago – no, four – and Tor had died, and of course one did go on living, and it possibly wouldn't have lasted anyway. But he wanted to see Tor very much, and he fingered the little scroll that was the only thing he had kept.

There was a light ahead. Someone had fastened a torch to a pole. A man was standing beside it, and he stepped out into the road. Dorac's hand went without thought to where his sword ought to have been. The man bowed his head, and Dorac bowed back.

"Do you know where you're going, friend?"

It was plainly a ritual. One he could have done without. "I know."

"From here on, you must go alone. Along this road is a circle of ancient stones in a place clear of trees. If you step into the circle and say 'I have come here to die', then Death will come for you."

"At once?"

"Death will come. Soon or late. Until you have said the words, you are free to turn back. Once you have entered the circle and said them, you will not leave alive." He bowed again, and stepped aside. "May God have mercy on your soul."

"Amen."

So he walked on, trying to pray, and not succeeding very well.

132

The trees surrounded the crown of the little hill, but the crown itself was bare. By daylight there would be a good view – back over Marod, forward to the higher peaks of the Jattamans. As he pushed slowly up the slope, the Stones rose before him.

They were not as large as he had expected. The tallest was perhaps twice his own height, and all were some six feet wide. One had slumped in the ground to an odd angle. On some he could dimly see carvings: knots and animals and lacy curves.

In the centre was a single stone, slightly smaller than the others. There was nothing else.

Dorac had not been impressed by the prevarication over timing, or the insistence on his going alone. He could not see anyone waiting in the shadows. But he had little doubt that Kai was right, and that the villagers who guarded this place took measures to ensure its promise did not fail. *As long as they shoot straight.* Mentally he rehearsed the words he must say.

He had only to step forward and say them, and the pain and the emptiness would go away. And the agonising false hope that Kai had brought. He wanted that very much.

What you want matters little in this world.

And there was nothing else he could do.

He stared up at the tall silent stones. Silver light touched his face. Slowly, he bent down and picked up a small pebble. And another.

*

When he pushed open the door, they were still sitting there as Kai had promised. The relief and pleasure on their faces when they looked up and saw him was more than he had expected. His voice sounded strange as he said, "If either of you weeps - or laughs - I'm going straight back."

He strode up to the table, picked up his will and the letter, which he would now have to rewrite, tore them across and threw them in the fire. Kai and Gormad had their arms around him by then, and he pushed them off with difficulty.

"Very well," he said, sitting down. "Tomorrow I will go to the border, and into Jaryar to find work. If I start early enough, I should have time."

"Can I come with you?" The boy, of course.

"No. You are going back to Stonehill. Kai will tie you up and strap you to your horse if he has to. You will go to the King, and he'll find you a better lord or lady than either me or Marrach of Drumcree, and you will have a good life. If you want reasons, I will give them you tomorrow, and if you say any more about it tonight, I will knock you down." He looked at Kai. "And now let's get drunk."

7 October 570 (St. Aidril's Day)

Meril woke early, but lay still and tense, shivering a little and dreading getting up. It was hard to believe that they were really going to do this thing.

Master Hassdan had spent most of the day before arranging it. He told her that nothing would make the inhabitants of the house accept a desecration of the children's graves; any explanation he could offer would be regarded as an insult. So Mistress Soumaki was to undertake further questioning of Lord Gahran's people that afternoon, all together in the hall, to keep them out of the way. Soumaki plainly thought this a waste of time, and a distraction from their task, and had said so forcefully. The possibility that the children might have been substituted was a very faint and unlikely one. Hassdan was in charge of the mission, so she had to give way, but she did not like it. Meril, excruciatingly embarrassed, had to witness their argument.

As they left the room, Master Hassdan had relieved his feelings by slapping the back of her head, and saying, "Take that smirk off your face. Go and make yourself useful in the kitchens." While she was doing this, he exerted the authority of the King's Thirty over the two reluctant priests, and talked to Captain Rabellit, whom Kremdar had left in charge. The captain was willing to help, he told Meril, but she had to select the least talkative of her soldiers to assist. "Not that there's much hope. Someone will surely let it out."

Meril, chopping vegetables and apologising for the ones she dropped on the floor, had been trying to learn what the dead children had looked like, but she had discovered little. They were all little angels.

135

Gaskor had a mole next to his eye. Ilda's hair was curly, and Filana's straight. This was all she could learn, apart from the colours of the clothes they had been wearing that day.

She had asked several people about the events of the funeral, and learned these by heart. Kremdar, Arvill and Braf had wrapped the children in a sheet and sewn it together "out of respect", before breaking the news and arresting Dorac. The actual bodies had been too terrible to be viewed, after what that monster had done to them. All anyone else had seen were the bloodstains on Dorac's cloak, and on the floor, and seeping through the sheet - and the fact of the children's absence. The remains had lain in the chapel with those of their father for an hour or so, for last rites to be spoken, and people to pray. Then they had been carried out to the graveyard by Captain Rabellit and one of her soldiers, with everyone else following behind. Lord Gahran's chaplain had spoken the words of the funeral service, and all had wept and crowded round while the bloodied sheet was placed in the earth, in a hole dug by the soldiers. The other body, that of the stablehand Arator, had been buried later.

"Very very odd," commented Master Hassdan. "Not even a coffin." It was clear, he said, and Meril earnestly agreed, that the people of Ferrodach could have had no part in anything suspicious after the murders, at any rate. Captain Rabellit seemed trustworthy, and she was sure the grave had not been disturbed since. When asked if Ferrodach had had enough warning of their arrival to organise a substitution, she had thought not. "Our scouts saw nothing, and when we rode up, everyone was very surprised. Or seemed to be."

So today they were to dig up corpses. Meril could not get her mind off this, wondering how horrible the sight and smell would be, and if she would disgrace herself utterly – throw up, or scream, or worse, in front of everyone. She thought of pictures of the opening tombs at the Last Judgment at home, which had given her and her sister nightmares. Her stomach was cold and heavy, and she could not make herself move from her pallet outside the Ferrodach guest chamber.

"Meril! You good-for-nothing brat! Are you intending to sleep till noon? St John preserve me from idle children." Hassdan kicked her up, and she stammered apologies. He was still complaining loudly about her laziness and clumsiness as they went down to the hall (the same stair that Master Dorac and Master Kremdar had used that day), and Soumaki gave her a compassionate look. It was almost funny.

*

The three rose early, and rode hard, despite the drink and the emotion of the night before. They could travel together as far as the crossroads. None of them was sorry to leave The Crescent Moon, and Dorac had a long way to go that day.

It was not until they stopped by a stream to rest and water the horses that Kai asked, "Why did you change your mind?"

Dorac fingered Derry's mane. "I realised I was committing the sin of pride."

"I dare say. How?"

"I said there was nothing for me to do in Jaryar. You let me say that. That's nonsense. I'm fit and strong. There are many things I can do."

"Ah."

"What things?" asked Gormad.

"Carrying packs. Sweeping streets. Cleaning stables. Many things."

"But that is work for poor people!" And then his face scalded, but he could never take the horrible words back.

"Yes. I have been poor before. And so I do not need a squire."

"I could help."

"You could not. You are not strong enough yet. I would have to earn enough to keep two, and you would be a burden."

"Children work!"

"They work for their parents mostly, and they are not paid." He eyed Gormad's rebellious face, and went on ruthlessly, "In a few years you might serve as a whore, which I certainly cannot. It's not a pleasant life, and your parents would die of shame. You are going back to Stonehill."

"In fact," said Kai, "you will give me your promise to come back with me, or I will truly tie you up and strap you on the horse. You can ride back that way. I will do it."

Both the men were staring at him. Gormad was trying so hard not to cry that he could barely speak. "I promise," he managed to mumble.

"Have you thought," Kai asked Dorac as they set off again, "that you don't look like a streetcleaner?"

"I know. I look like a dangerous foreign warrior on a horse. Who has been in a fight. I'll leave the horse with you, and the sword."

"You need your sword!"

"I need to look harmless. No one with a sword is harmless. I have a knife."

"Anyone who sees your arm will know who and what you are."

Gormad wondered, and then remembered. *Branded for the King.*

"Will they know that much about the Thirty?" asked Dorac uncertainly.

"Some of them will."

Dorac shrugged. "I'll have to keep my shirt on."

"You should change your name."

"You think they have nothing better to do in Jaryar -"

"Travellers gossip. It's possible your name is known."

"If it pleases you." He thought. "Ettuar. Ettuar, son of Araf."

"I'll tell Gemara and Hassdan."

A few miles later, Dorac said suddenly, "Will they take our money?"

"No. Look, give me the money, and you take the food. That's what you'll need."

"You'll need it too. This is Friday. You'll find no market closer than - Broch tomorrow, or Sendran on Tuesday. I don't plan to starve. I'll get work as soon as I can."

A little further on, "If your new sibling is Ralia - her fighting is good, but her manner is rather arrogant with ordinary people. Try and gentle her."

They came to the crossroads shortly after noon. The road behind them to the Old Stones; the mountain path that Dorac and Gormad had travelled; the road home that Kai must have ridden; and a little path into the trees to the south.

Dorac dismounted. He handed Kai his rewritten letter, and then passed Derry's reins to Gormad. "He's yours. Treat him kindly, or sell him to someone who will."

"You're giving me your horse?"

"You bought him. Did you think I'd forgotten?" He put his hands one each side of Derry's neck, and laid his face against the horse's nose. The other two looked politely away. Then he again unbuckled his sword belt. As he hesitated, Kai said firmly, "I'll take that. We'll store it at South Keep until you come home."

Dorac grimaced. Then he looked down the path into the trees. "Last time I went into Jaryar, it was to burn their fields," he said. "What do you know of their ways?"

"Try to look humble," said Kai. "The poor are called Lowly, and they bow if a great person passes, if they know what's good for them. That's probably anyone on a horse. And they boast about their city."

"Makkera, the Green City," Dorac murmured. "The green is the stone, isn't it?"

"Makka stone, yes."

The other two had dismounted also. "I gave you all my messages last night," said Dorac. "None of that's changed. God go with you both." He looked at Gormad and smiled. "Keep your knife clean and sharp. That's the only thing I've taught you."

He was really going. "Please -" said Gormad.

"What?"

"Will you give me your blessing?"

Dorac looked disconcerted. "I'm not your father. Or your

lord."

"Please."

"I don't know if I remember – if you wish."

So Gormad knelt before him, as he had knelt before Ramahdis the day he left home. Dorac placed his right hand on the boy's hair, and slowly spoke the ancient words. "The Lord bless you and keep you. The Lord make His face to shine upon you. The Lord lift up His countenance upon you, and give you peace. Amen."

He bent over, kissed the top of Gormad's head, pulled him to his feet, embraced Kai for the last time, and walked down the path without looking back.

"Come on," said Kai, and they mounted again and rode off north.

*

It wasn't long before people passed them in the opposite direction. Two riders, a man and a woman, looking sombre. The man nudged his companion, indicating Derry, and they both pulled down their hoods, and waited for Kai and Gormad to pass. A riderless horse, like the one he and Dorac had seen. Gormad wanted to explain, but the moment passed, and they went on.

Although this was a wider road, they still occasionally had to lead the horses. This was difficult with three. It gave them something to think about that wasn't sad, and after a little Gormad recovered enough to ask questions.

He was pleased to find that Kai knew Meril, and thought Hassdan was pleased with her. He was disappointed that Kai had not fought in the War from the Sea. "That was all happening in the north while I was at South Keep." It was after the war that the King and Queen had arrived unexpectedly at the Keep one day, talked to him about his duties, amazed everyone by camping overnight, and ridden away again. And a few weeks later, Kai had been called to the Thirty. "I suppose someone must've mentioned my name, but why or who I don't know. The King and Queen choose whom they like. Who can fight for them - and who they think will keep the oath." He sighed.

He had not known Marrach of Drumcree well.

"Master Dorac said they quarrelled many years ago. Can I ask what they quarrelled about?"

Kai looked him in the eye. "You can ask. And then I can tell you that I don't know. Nobody knows. It's one of the great secrets of Stonehill. In fact, if Dorac told you they quarrelled, that's probably more than he's told anyone else."

Gormad stared.

"I'll tell you what is known. Years ago – before you were born, I would think – when Dorac was fairly new in the Thirty, he was given command of a raiding party. Or maybe it was a counter-raid, or pursuing outlaws, or something like that. Marrach was a young man seeking adventure, and I suppose he went along. There was a group of ten, or twenty, or thirty - Anyway, they rode off on this expedition, whatever it was, and when they came back a week or so later, they'd done what they went to do, but Marrach had lost an ear. There'd been other people wounded or killed by the enemy, of course, but in Marrach's case everybody who'd ridden with them seemed to think Dorac was responsible, but no one knew, or would tell, any details. And Marrach and Dorac would not say. They would not say if Dorac had

142

cut it off, or if he had, why. Neither of them ever has. Mute as milk.

"Marrach made no complaints to any court – and his mother was all ready to make one – but he would not tell her. Dorac refused to tell Master Stimmon, who was the leader of the Six then. People say he refused to tell the King.

"And they never spoke to each other again. Not that they had been friends before. Everyone has a theory, and no one knows." Kai paused, and then asked, "Was Marrach a good master to you?"

"Yes, he was. He used to explain things, and he told me if I did well or badly. When he decided to spend the summer in Stonehill, he said I'd like the city, and he'd stay on for the King's Gathering at the end of October, and all the other squires would come, and it would be good for me. He was already coughing on the journey. Padac – that's his steward – wanted him to go home, but he said he wanted to be somewhere with a bit of - life."

"And then he got ill, and you had to watch," said Kai. "That must have been very hard."

This was the first consoling word anyone had said to Gormad about his master. He opened his mouth to say, "Thank you," and burst into tears.

Kai lifted him down, tethered the horses, and sat by the road with him. Gormad sobbed and sobbed onto his shoulder, and begged to be reassured that Marrach would go to heaven.

"If he died in the faith of his Redeemer, he will," said Kai firmly. "And you said he had a priest, so he must have."

They sat on for a few minutes after Gormad stopped crying. His head and his eyes ached.

Kai said, "Master Dorac said you should give his letter to the King if we thought it would help. So that means we should take a look at it, I think." He pulled the letter out of his satchel. "Can you read?"

"Of course I can!"

"Many great warriors cannot," said Kai with mock severity. He unfolded the letter, and they both read:

6th day of October, 570.

Dorac, son of Araf, to His Grace Arrion of the Marodi, greeting.

You will not hear from me again.

You will have been told that I was followed, and have been accompanied almost to the border, by the bearer of this letter, Gormad, son of Ramahdis. He was the squire of Marrach of Drumcree, until Marrach's recent death. I write to earnestly recommend him to Your Grace's favour, and to ask that you grant his request for a new lord or lady to serve.

I have known few of any age so brave. He is also honest, kindhearted and intelligent, and has some skill with horses, although he requires training in hard work and discretion.

I am fully aware that I have no right to make any request, but the child is not to blame for any faults of mine, and I am therefore made bold to plead for him.

It has been an honour to serve you and your family, one that I could never have deserved.

I remain Your Grace's obedient servant and subject.

Kai was silent. Then he said, "Well, you must have impressed him. I'm sure he'd never say anything as good as that about me. If I were King Arrion, I wouldn't hesitate."

"Really?"

"Really. But he does need to consult your parents. And we must go on. We should get back as soon as we can."

*

It was the festival day of St Aidril, one of Marod's few homeborn saints. So no work was done in Stonehill, and there was a commemorative service and pageant in the morning, and in the afternoon a feast to which all the King's servants, not merely the high people, were invited. This included even the secretaries, one of whom had to stand on the dais in the Great Hall and read the appointed portion of St Aidril's life. The honour this year had fallen to Makkam, daughter of Eve (sometimes called Makkam-Maid-of-Ice). No one envied her, for St Aidril's virtuous life had apparently been very dull, and her biographer totally devoid of literary talent.

And so after much prayer, she was sent out. And she was blessed for her journey by Bishop Mark Darro of Flet of blessed memory who was consecrated to the bishopric in the year 58 by Bishop Anna of Stonehill, and she was accompanied by fourteen companions, including Jabeth, the son of the Lord of Ritteri, and Bax, who was a child of only twelve years, but most zealous for the Lord -

Everyone dutifully refrained from conversation, and only the crackle and purr of the great fire and the wall torches competed with Makkam's voice, straining slightly so as to be heard at the back. She dared not hurry, let alone turn over two pages at once, although the food was getting cold, and the hungrier guests were glaring. She did not even create different voices for the different speakers, as she had half-planned, for that might be deemed irreverent. Now and again, she flicked a glance down the Hall – the long tables decked with steaming meat carcasses and pies and flagons; the guests in their colourful festival

145

gowns (floor-length and elaborately sleeved on women, knee-length to disclose flamboyantly coloured and embroidered hose on men); the torchlight dancing and crackling along the walls; the servants waiting with itching feet. And the wonderful taunting smells of roast mutton, goose and pork.

At last she was finished. No one applauded, of course, for this was an act of piety, not entertainment. Makkam bowed to the high table. The Bishop of Stonehill inclined her head graciously. The Queen raised an eyebrow in the smallest possible gesture of rueful sympathy. The King seemed not to be paying attention.

The Steward of the Feast thumped a staff on the floor, and Prince Jendon, the heir to the throne and nineteen years old, stood up. He was tall, well-made and elegantly dressed – a figure to draw admiration, until he moved or spoke. Everyone tensed. "Welcome all, in the name of the Holy T-t-trinity, and all the saints, most p-" (*oh no,* thought Makkam) "p-p-p-particularly the bl-blessed Aidril, to the feast." He sat down again, blushing after his ordeal, to be soothed by Ralia, daughter of Imali, who sat beside him, and Makkam was released.

She walked down the narrow passageway between tables and benches, ignored by everyone (eating at last), until she approached a little group of young men.

"I pity you indeed. Gemara's Six!" Torio Kingsbrother of the Western Six was saying teasingly to his companion.

Saysh, son of Adshan (now Saysh Kingsbrother, and therefore, it seemed, worthy of Torio's attention), drew his gaze away from the high table to ask, "Why pity?"

"You know they're all terrified of her. She scolds them like children, and sends them to bed without supper, and they piss themselves."

"You'd piss yourself if Gemara even looked at you," laughed Maros, of the Eastern, spearing a slice of beef. "The whole world is frightened of Gemara."

"She was civil on Monday night," protested Saysh. "Rather quiet, in truth. Perhaps worried."

"Worried how many more mistakes the Southern can make," Torio said, and looked up at Makkam, whose path was blocked by his outstretched legs. "Secretary?" he asked, his eyes roaming over her in a way that was probably intended to make her feel naked. It did not succeed.

"Yes, I am a secretary. May I pass?" she asked primly.

"What will you give me?" he said, managing to make even the suggestiveness bored and contemptuous. Makkam stared calmly back, and Maros nudged him, and he moved.

Of course it was unsurprising and correct that a member of the Thirty should think himself far superior to a mere secretary – a bastard-born secretary, at that. The lewdness was less excusable, and it would have been pleasant to say so. But she did not want to give him an opportunity to complain. The King was almost bound to believe a Kingsbrother's word over anyone else's. Even Torio's.

Do not be so quick to condemn, Makkam. That is arrogance.

She sank gratefully down among the other secretaries, a small group dressed in workaday black, not presuming to wear anything festive. The noise around the Hall was now considerable, almost louder and merrier than was natural. For there was a nervousness, she thought, after the last week. After Ferrodach.

*

Nor was Makkam wrong. At the second table, young Ralia demanded boldly, "But why should we distress ourselves about that 'Overlord of the West' legend? It's only something dramatic for old King Rajas to put on his coins." Formal long skirts and slashed sleeves looked wrong on Ralia. In the saddle, in training, striding tall and assured through the streets, she wore hose and jacket of good cloth and cut and bright colour, always healthy and active and vivid. Minstrels wrote songs about her gleaming hair, and sparkling eyes, and young squires admired her expert swordplay, and dreamed guilty dreams about displacing the Prince in her favour.

"Only an ancient legend," she finished now.

But those around her frowned. Lady Kara said sharply, "You do not have to believe the legend or the Dream. But if soldiers and peasants -"

"And priests -" said Lady Sada.

"– and priests believe it, then the lords of Jaryar can make use of it against us. The Dream was a prophecy, and they fulfil it by making war on our border. If Gahran believed it – I thought he cared for nothing but his studies and his children – others may too."

"Come, Kara, no one knows what led Gahran to do what he did," said Herion of Maint, a portly and imposing middle-aged figure. "I cannot believe that there are many disloyal lords."

"We know your family is loyal," Lady Sada said. Herion was the Stonehill representative of the mighty house of Aspella.

"Thank you for your confidence, which I trust we will always deserve. But I would hope, my prince -" – with a courteous nod to Prince Jendon, sitting silently beside Ralia – "that your parents can depend on all their lords."

"I am sure they c-can," said the Prince, and Ralia laughed and said, "No doubt of that."

In one corner of the Hall, bets were being taken on the loyalty of Lady Ferriol and Hassdan Kingsbrother, and even of Lord Vrenas.

But only one corner.

*

Despite her misgivings, Mistresss Soumaki had as agreed gathered the entire staff into the hall, and was politely going through Lord Gahran's actions in his last few days with the steward, the captain of the household guard, and the tutor. Meanwhile, Captain Rabellit accompanied Master Hassdan and Meril to the chapel in the grounds. There were also two priests, the household chaplain and Brother Joseph from the village, and two soldiers. No one spoke. They stood beside the children's graves while Brother Joseph made a long prayer, asking God's forgiveness for what they were about to do. "As Thou knowest, we are compelled by our oaths of temporal obedience to this sad action," he said. *Asking God to blame Master Hassdan and the King, and not him,* Meril thought indignantly.

"Amen." The soldiers stepped up to the grave, and began to dig. It did not really take very long, but the cold was seeping into Meril's bones by the time the sheet appeared, three feet or so down. Blood could still be seen on it, but there were other stains as well, green and brown decay. It was fully uncovered, and then carefully lifted out, and laid on the grass. Captain Rabellit knelt by the bundle, and drew her sword.

"Wait. Look at the stitching. Is that unchanged?" Hassdan asked. Sister Martha nodded curtly, her mouth a narrow line and her face taut. She had known these children all their lives. Meril wondered how she could tell, although the stitches did look small and neat, like Master Kremdar's work. "Cut beside them, not through the thread," Hassdan commanded. He was very pale.

It was like the chrysalis of some huge insect, Meril thought. Only dirtier. There were worms, and slime. And already a smell of something - not quite sweet.

Captain Rabellit rather clumsily inserted her blade, and carved the thing open. It made a sickeningly long ripping noise.

Sister Martha had her long sleeves over her mouth, and was sobbing. One of the soldiers turned aside and retched. It had occurred to Meril that almost no one had seen the bodies – could it possibly be that it was all a pretence of some kind, and no one had died at all? But she looked steadily down, *oh oh oh*, stomach twisting, and saw dead people. That had once been a face, skin now pulled in, something collapsed inside – but the hair was still there, holes for eyes - A faint voice was muttering prayers. The smell was terrible. There was a hand -

The captain pulled gently, and the cloth fell open, and the pieces - shifted. A red jacket, just as she had been told -

Meril gasped. Surely they would all have seen it in time, they would all have noticed what became suddenly so obvious, but still it was Meril who realised first, and whispered, "But Master -"

"Yes. Look," said Hassdan hoarsely. "Three children, we were told. Three children, cut to pieces. Here are only two."

Torio Kingsbrother was not foolish enough to gamble himself, but he took pleasure in watching a good game, studying the players' faces and analysing their errors. It was fairly late when he returned to his cell in the Court of the Thirty, a tiny room furnished as comfortably as he and his mother could afford, and found a folded and sealed parchment lying on the bed.

The seal was blank and anonymous. Torio opened the letter and read in Attar's precise bookkeeper's script:

My master agrees that the Southern want watching. He wishes to know about – and if possible, see – any mischievous reports they may convey to KA. Such reports will be written, copied, or at the least kept in the scriptorium, and to aid you in discovering them he encloses a key to that room. Use it warily, and not by night.

All at A will be grateful.

Torio smiled, stored the key safely, and burned the letter in the flame of his candle.

*

Dorac had walked into the night, rehearsing his story. He was Ettuar, son of Araf, from the small town of Queenshouse. He had worked as a general assistant and guard for a goldsmith in Marod's second city, Derbo. When his master unexpectedly died of some sickness, and he could not get on with his new mistress, he had lost his place. So he had decided to see the world.

It was not a very good story, but he had never understood why anyone would want to see the world.

In the late afternoon, he had remembered one more thing – the Lowly ranks in Jaryar cut their hair short. To keep it out of the way

151

for work, and to prevent anyone mistaking them for people of importance. Why had he and Kai forgotten that? His absurd attempts to cut his own hair with his knife made him look more like a vagabond than ever. A well-dressed vagabond. His clothes were dirty, but they were the better ones he had put on to be tried in a week ago. There was nothing he could do about this beyond smearing some earth on his over-fine belt. Perhaps people would only think he had stolen it. Which would not encourage them to hire him.

This path was not the main road into Jaryar. But after Kerrytown and Ferrodach it was possible that any border was manned, so he cut across land belonging to Lady Orria of Sparat. Under a chilly night sky, he found himself coming down the edge of a newly harvested field towards the River Lither, not yet as wide or deep as it would later become in the west, and beyond a similar-looking field. A Jaryari field.

Now was the time to regret his ignorance. In the south of his own country, he knew every village, almost every path. In Stonehill, he knew every street, and in the Castle every face.

He barely knew the name of the King of Jaryar. Other than Makkera, he could think of no cities. They spoke the same language and worshipped the same God – that was all he knew. And they died if you stuck a blade in them.

It was impossible that this was happening. He was walking into Jaryar, without a sword, without soldiers at his back. He was walking into Jaryar forever.

"God help me," he murmured grimly, and prepared to wade into the river.

From the Archives of Stonehill

The Trial of Dorac Kingsbrother

<u>The evidence of Kremdar Kingsbrother</u>

My name is Kremdar Kingsbrother of the Southern Six. I was called to the Thirty seven years ago, after the War from the Sea.

On 24th September just past, I was summoned to the Council of Elders, along with my brother Dorac. We were told that a letter had been found proving treason on the part of Lord Gahran of Ferrodach, and we were to go with some soldiers, and take the house and arrest him and bring him to Stonehill for trial.

Lady Sada made a comment. I cannot remember exactly, but she said something like, "Bring him back alive. If alive is not possible, no one will love me for saying this, but it might be better if he left no heirs." Someone protested, and she said, "The children of a dead traitor will grow up with a grudge, and three innocent deaths now are better than many in ten years' time." The King said, "I don't agree." That was all that was said.

While we were riding to Ferrodach, Dorac rode up to me, and asked me what I thought of Lady Sada's words. I said it sounded like an ugly thing. Dorac said, "Ugly things are sometimes needed."

[The prisoner interrupted, shouting that the witness was lying, and was silenced.]

There was no sign of trouble until we got right up to the house, but then some of Lord Gahran's servants tried to deny us access.

There was a short fight, and one of them was killed by the soldiers. Lord Gahran surrendered, and Dorac ordered him to be confined to his chamber and guarded. The three children were identified to us by the steward. Dorac had them put in a little room, the one marked on the plan. He sent their tutor away with the other servants. He did not say why.

Laida, daughter of Mab, from South Keep, called us to say that Lord Gahran had managed to take poison while her back was turned. Dorac and I went up to the room accompanied by Arvill, daughter of Eve. Dorac left Laida there with the body, and the three of us went down the stair. I noticed that he had drawn his sword, and I wondered why. Braf, son of Arro, was on guard in the passage outside the room where the children were. There was no one else. Dorac said, "They have to be killed." I think he said that, but at the time I was not sure, and I did not believe he could mean it. He went into the room, telling us to wait. He was in there for a little time. The three of us could not hear much, but somebody shouted, and I think the word was "Murder!" It was a child's voice. He came out. There was blood on his cloak, and his sword. There was not much light in the passage, but I could smell it, and see it glistening, fresh blood. He looked strange and unhappy, and he did not say anything. He just walked into the hall.

Arvill and Braf and I looked at each other for some minutes. I should have gone in sooner, but I did not want to believe it. I pushed open the door, and we went in, and the three children were lying dead on the ground, the boy in the middle of the floor, and the girls by the wall. Two of their heads had been cut off, and the other face was slashed. Some of the limbs were cut off too.

154

I confess I was not sure what to do. Dorac was in command of the mission, and he must have decided it was right, and Lady Sada said it should be done. But it was not right, and it was not ordered. I knew I had to arrest my brother.

We collected up the pieces of the bodies, and put them in a sheet together. It seemed respectful to do that. Then I took some guards and went and found Dorac. He was in Lord Gahran's bookroom. He had cleaned his sword, but the cloak was on a chair by the door, just as it is now, but wetter. I told him he was under arrest, and at first he pretended not to know what I was talking about, and then he attacked me.

The next morning, before we left, I went to talk to him. I thought if he could explain that he had meant it for the best, the King would be merciful. He attacked me again, and hit me in the face. He was shouting and threatening to kill me. His exact words were, "I will pull your fucking head off, and send you to hell in pieces."

I have served with Dorac Kingsbrother for seven years. I admired and respected him. I looked on him as a brother, and he has saved my life in the past.

[The witness identified the cloak, and took the oath.]

The evidence of Arvill, daughter of Eve

My name is Arvill, daughter of Eve, and I serve in the army of the Warden of the Kingslands. A troop of us were sent to Ferrodach, under command of Dorac and Kremdar of the Southern Six, and Captain Rabellit. I had not myself been present at the Council, but Lady Sada's words had been reported to me. They did not concern me, as I was confident none of the Thirty would order an attack on children. We all honour and trust their judgment.

I happened to be in the hall when one of the soldiers from South Keep shouted that there was trouble in Lord Gahran's room, and that is why I went there with Dorac and Kremdar Kingsbrother. As we came back downstairs, Dorac was in front, and I was at the back. Kremdar and I followed him across the hall, and I wondered why he had drawn his sword. He said, "They must be killed." I am sure he did. I remember feeling confused and worried. But I still did not think he was going to do it straight away. He went into the room. Braf was on guard. He is in my troop.

I heard a shout of "Murder!" When Dorac came out, I was afraid of the look on his face. His cloak was stained with blood: a lot of blood. It had been fastened, so there would not have been much blood on the clothes underneath. He walked across the hall. I waited for Master Kremdar to decide what to do, but I think we all knew, and did not want to admit it.

The three of us went in together. It was the worst thing I have ever seen. I have not fought in a great battle, but I have been in raids and skirmishes, and I have killed people and seen people killed. I have never seen anyone cut to pieces like that. The three bodies were all hacked apart. The boy and one of the girls had their heads cut off. There was a lot of blood. Our feet were slipping in the blood.

[The witness paused to compose herself.]

I was not with Kremdar when Dorac was arrested. I was sent to break the news to Lord Gahran's people. They were very distressed.

I do not know Dorac well, but of course I have seen him

around the Castle and the city. I have always heard him called a brave and loyal warrior, but also a hard man that people would not like to cross. I have never had reason to fear him myself.

[The witness identified the cloak, and took the oath.]

The evidence of Braf, son of Arro

My name is Braf, son of Arro. I serve in the Army of the Warden of the Kingslands.

Dorac Kingsbrother put the three children in a little room, and Kremdar Kingsbrother posted me to guard it. There were no windows in the room except a small slit for firing through. No one could have got in or out except through the door I was guarding. No one did go in or out except Dorac, until the three of us went in.

I have heard the evidence sworn by Kremdar Kingsbrother and Arvill, daughter of Eve, and I agree with it. When we went into the room, it was the most horrible thing I have ever seen. The smell was awful. It made me feel sick.

[The witness took the oath.]

The examination of the prisoner by the King's Questioner, Lady Kara of Meriot

Q: You are accused of murder. Are you guilty or not guilty?

A: Not guilty.

Q: At the end of your evidence, you will be required to swear to its truth before God. Do you understand?

A: Yes.

Q: What is your name?

A: Dorac Kingsbrother of the Southern Six.

Q: Before you were sworn to the Thirty, what was your name?

A: Dorac, son of Araf.

Q: How many years have you served in the Thirty?

A: Fifteen.

Q: Before that, you were a soldier?

A: Yes.

Q: For how long?

A: Twelve years.

Q: The day you left Stonehill for Ferrodach, were you present at the Council meeting mentioned in evidence?

A: Yes.

Q: Did Lady Sada say that Lord Gahran's children should be killed?

A: I don't remember exactly what she said. She said they would grow up, and were dangerous, and the King said –

Q: Did you agree with her?

A: It was no concern of mine to agree or disagree.

Q: What were the King's orders regarding Lord Gahran?

A: To take the house at Ferrodach and arrest him. Bring him back alive if possible. Find out what was going on.

Q: Who was placed in command of this mission?

A: I was, with Kremdar Kingsbrother, and Captain Rabellit.

Q: Who was in *command*?

A: I was.

Q: While you were journeying to Ferrodach, did you talk to

anyone about Lady Sada's remarks?

A: No.

Q: Kremdar Kingsbrother says you did.

A: He is lying.

Q: Did you bring Lord Gahran back alive?

A: No.

Q: Why not?

A: He killed himself while a prisoner.

Q: So you failed your king, did you not?

[No answer.]

Q: You failed your king, Master Dorac?

A: I was not able to –

Q: You *failed?*

A: He might have thought so. Yes.

Q: After taking the house, did you send Mari, daughter of Febana, to report to the King?

A: Yes.

Q: Evidence has been heard that you came down to the hall with Kremdar Kingsbrother and Arvill, daughter of Eve. Is that correct?

A: Yes.

Q: Who was in the hall?

A: No one. There was a guard in the passage outside the room. I don't remember his name.

Q: Was it Braf, son of Arro?

A: I don't know.

Q: Were you wearing that cloak over there?

[Pause.]

A: Yes.

Q: What did you do?

A: I went into the room.

Q: Which room?

A: There was a little room to the left behind the hall, where we had put the children.

Q: Lord Gahran's three children?

A: Yes. That is – the children had been identified to us by the steward, Hagouna, daughter of Lahni. I had never seen them before that day.

Q: You had ordered the children to be placed in a room without their tutor or any of the servants?

A: Yes. I suggested it, and Kremdar agreed.

Q: Why did you leave them alone?

A: We had been warned of treason in the house. Any of the servants might have been traitors. I wanted to keep the children away from them.

Q: I see. Before entering the room, what did you say?

A: I asked if there was any way out of the room, and I said I would tell the children –

Q: You said, "They have to be killed."

A: No, I did not.

Q: That is the evidence.

A: I said, "They have to be told."

Q: *Told?*

A: Yes.

Q: Told what?

A: That their father was dead.

Q: Anyone else could have told them that?

[Pause.]

A: Yes.

Q: The witnesses are lying about what you said?

A: Lying or mistaken.

Q: Did you go into the room alone?

A: Yes.

Q: Why?

A: I didn't need anyone else. I was only going to talk to them.

Q: Did you have any weapons with you?

A: My sword.

Q: Why?

A: I always carry my sword on the King's business.

Q: Were you wearing it on your belt, or holding it in your hand?

A: In my hand.

Q: You went into a room to talk to three children with a drawn sword in your hand?

A: Yes.

Q: Why?

[Pause.]

A: I don't know. [Pause.] We were in a hostile house.

Q: I see. You went in. Were the children there?

A: Yes.

Q: Three of them?

A: Yes.

Q: Was anyone else there?

A: I saw no one. I did not search the room.

Q: Were there any other doors?

A: No.

Q: Windows?

A: There was an arrow-slit.

Q: What were the children doing?

A: The youngest was sitting on a bench. The other two were standing together, playing some game. With string, on their hands.

Q: What did you do?

A: I told them their father was dead.

Q: What else?

A: Nothing else. I left.

Q: So you were in the room for how long? [Pause.] As long as that?

A: Longer than that.

Q: So you must have done something else?

A: The children were distressed. The – the boy was shouting, and he ran up and hit me.

Q: He hit you, and you hit him?

A: No. I grabbed his hand, and his sister called him back.

Q: What was he shouting?

A: He shouted, "Murderers!"

Q: He shouted, "Murder!"

A: No. "Murderer" or "Murderers". He meant that we had killed his father, and I explained that Lord Gahran killed himself.

162

Q: You agree that one of the children was shouting about murder?

A: Yes, but not because of anything I was doing.

Q: But there was shouting?

A: Yes.

Q: What did you do?

A: I said I – was sorry for their loss, and someone would bring them some food, and I left. I left them alive.

Q: You have heard the evidence given –

A: It's lies.

Q: Silence. You have heard the evidence read and sworn that you came out wearing that cloak – in the state it is in now – and –

A: He is lying! He is lying, he and his –

[The prisoner attempted to attack Kremdar Kingsbrother, and was subdued.]

Q: This mad violence will not assist you. The evidence says you came out of the room bloodstained, and no one else went in until your brother and the two soldiers became concerned at the silence, and they went in and found the children.

A: They are lying.

Q: They found the children dead. "Cut to pieces" were the words used.

A: I did not touch the children.

Q: You said just now you did. You grabbed the boy – Gaskor – grabbed his wrist -

A: Yes, when he ran at me. He was punching me in the stomach. I did not hurt him.

Q: Kremdar is your sworn brother. You have served together for seven years. Why would he lie?

[No answer.]

Q: Why would he lie? Had you quarrelled?

A: No. But he – he and Arvill –

Q: You killed those children because you had failed your King, and thought he would approve.

A: I did not. He is lying. Your Grace, they are lying!

Q: Do not address the King. You still claim the children were alive when you left the room?

A: They were alive.

Q: What did you do?

A: I told them to watch the door, and I went –

Q: Wait. Who was in the hall when you came out?

A: Kremdar and Arvill. And there may have been a guard.

Q: The same guard as when you went in?

A: I think so. I don't remember.

Q: Well, then. You were still wearing this cloak?

A: Yes. It was not –

Q: What did you do?

A: I went to Lord Gahran's bookroom.

Q: Why?

A: We were told to find out about his treason. I wanted to look for anything he had written or received.

Q: *Did* you send for food for the children?

A: Yes.

Q: Who did you send?

A: One of the servants. A man. I don't know his name.

Q: None of the servants at Ferrodach remember this. Are they also lying?

[Pause.]

A: I'm sure I sent someone.

Q: Someone who has disappeared. You sent no one. Because the children were already dead.

A: *I did not kill them.*

Q: Were you alone in the bookroom?

A: Yes.

Q: Wearing your cloak?

A: No, I put it on a chair.

Q: Where we have heard it was found. Covered in the children's blood.

A: Somebody must have taken it –

Q: Come, Master Dorac, you would have seen them. You remained in that room until Kremdar Kingsbrother came and arrested you?

A: Yes.

Q: Regretting what you had done.

A: I had not done anything.

Q: Did you find any treason in the books?

A: No.

Q: Later, after you had been arrested, did your brother Kremdar come to talk to you?

A: Yes, he came –

Q: To ask you for the truth?

A: He called me a murderer. He is an –

Q: Did you try to assault him?

A: Yes.

Q: Did you threaten to kill him?

A: I don't remember. I may have done. He was lying, and –

Q: So you say. You attacked him, just as you have done today. Just one more thing. Kremdar and Arvill have described the bodies of these innocent children – arms and heads hacked off, faces slashed –

A: I did not –

Q: Have you ever cut off anyone's arm or leg?

A: In battle, yes.

Q: Yes, in battle. Have you ever – think carefully – cut off part of anyone's body, not in battle? A hand, an ear, a nose -?

[Pause.]

A: Yes. Many years –

Q: You may take the oath, Master Dorac.

[With hesitation, the prisoner approached the book and was prompted through the words of the oath.

"In the presence of God -"

"Almighty God -"

"In the presence of Almighty God, Father, Son and Holy Spirit - er -"

"And as I shall answer -"

"And as I shall answer at the dread Day of Judgment, I declare that I have spoken the truth."]

Part Two – The Investigation

Gormad and Kai (8–11 October)

8 October 570

Kai had left him alone to guard the horses the night before, while he set some snares. ("If there's any trouble, yell." Gormad had sat cleaning his knife, jerking at noises, and reminding himself that Master Dorac said he was brave. There had been no trouble.) This morning, one of the snares was empty, and another Kai was unable to find again, but the third had caught a fat rabbit.

They had camped near the road, and they stuck to the road. "I came a different way with Master Dorac," he ventured.

"I'm sure you did. He will have taken you down all kinds of paths that he alone knows."

"Does he know many?"

"Everyone has their own skills. Dorac comes from the north. They say when he was named to the Thirty, before you were born, the only part of the south he knew was Stonehill. So he asked for a month without duties, and spent it tramping the land like a vagrant, and when he came back he knew every inch of it. And where the taverns are, and when the markets are held. You can imagine how useful – and annoying – that makes him." Kai grimaced. "I wonder how he'll get on in Jaryar, where he knows nothing. I'm not sure he knows the name of the king." He fixed Gormad with a stern eye. "Do you?"

"Umm -"

"Rajas the Second, of the House of Vend, I believe."

Gormad nodded respectfully. He longed to ask what Kai's skills were. "Will Master Dorac be all right?" he asked instead.

"I'm sure he will. He can take care of himself." Kai did not sound sure.

They made speedier time than he had made in the opposite direction, and they saw more people. Occasionally these people hailed them – "Godspeed, Kai Kingsbrother!" "Godspeed to you." Sometimes they looked as if they would like to stop and talk, but Kai rode on, looking unKai-ishly grim. Gormad realised after a while that the grimness was an excuse not to stop. "I haven't decided what to say," he explained. "Does the King want people to know I went after Dorac? Probably not. But everyone at Stonehill knows you did. So why are we riding together?"

"I don't know," said Gormad, once he had worked this out.

"I don't either."

They were riding through yet another hamlet, and a man called, "Did you find the murderer?"

"Did you kill him?" asked someone else.

"Dorac has gone into exile, as he was commanded. I went to fetch the boy."

"You're safe now, lad," said a kindly-looking woman. Gormad opened his mouth indignantly, and shut it again.

Kai asked him about his home, and he told him about his parents, and his brother and sisters, and a little about his problem with his father. In return, Kai said he had three sisters. He was the youngest of the family. He also had a stepmother and a young half-brother. Before becoming Kai Kingsbrother, he had been Kai, son of Vidrach. Catching the expression Gormad tried to hide, he said, "Indeed. I was once foolish enough to ask my father what made a parent name their son Vidrach."

"What did he say?"

"He did not *say* anything. I was answered as my insolence deserved." He grinned ruefully. He was the friendliest grown-up Gormad had ever met.

"Do your family live in Stonehill, Master Kai?"

"No, my father's lands are in Rayf, and Ebbi is living in Derbo. But I have other people in Stonehill." He seemed rather happy about this, but somehow Gormad didn't like to ask any more.

As the shadows began to grow, they found a place in the hedgerows to camp, make a fire and cook their rabbit. Kai showed him how to skin it, and spit it, and roast nuts in the embers. It was too dark to find mushrooms. ("Some of the ones round here are poisonous. Very poisonous.")

"Well," said Kai, as they were licking their fingers afterwards, "now how shall we make merry? What do you contribute to your lord's hall, young Gormad? Do you sing, or tumble, or play the lute?"

"Sometimes I sing," Gormad admitted shyly.

"And play?"

"No."

"Sing then." It was a strange and chilly place to perform, and at first he felt embarrassed, but yet it was fitting; music and stories were the proper things after food. Kai produced a small set of pipes from his satchel, and fitted a few notes to Gormad's tune. He sang the sad ballad of "Lovely Irria", which had been a favourite of Marrach's, so he knew it well, although he himself did not care for it. "Something else." So he sang the "Round Tower Ditty", and then dared to finish with his favourite, "The Angry Song of the Baked Lemon Pudding", and Kai actually laughed.

So then they were quiet, until Gormad asked timidly, "What do you do?"

"Ha," said Kai, as if seeing into his mind. "Sometimes I sing, less well. Or sometimes - I tell stories."

"Please! A story!"

"What about?"

"About the adventures of the Southern Six!"

"Oh, those adventures. Where we ride around the country, saving babies from burning buildings, and each of us fighting six foes at a time?"

"Err - yes."

"I fear that no one can truly fight six at a time – at least not if they're armed. Dorac and Kremdar are – were – our best swordsmen, and even they would have difficulty with more than two together." Kai leaned back against a tree, and put his hands behind his head before going on. It was too dark to see his face. "But I suppose we were at least *outnumbered* at that place near Ardo Vale. Very well -

"Once there was - a bad year. Once and not so long ago," he began formally. "You may not remember '66, when the storms were so bad, and so many crops were lost. Some people starved. And in Ardo Vale, in the southeast, it was even worse. The rains caused a landslide, and destroyed houses and the crops they had managed to harvest, and killed a few.

"We were sent out to do what we could. It was just after Soumaki had joined the Thirty. Mistress Gemara stayed in Stonehill on guard duty, and she put Hassdan in command, and we had some soldiers from the Kingslands, and we rode to Ardo Vale.

"We stayed there about a week, a little more, helping to rebuild, burying the dead. Amusing the villagers by our lack of building skill. It cheered them up to be instructing the King's Thirty. They were very welcoming." He paused for a moment, perhaps remembering something – or someone. "We'd brought some food, of course, from the King: two oxen and some chickens and vegetables. And the local lord and one of the neighbouring ones sent food too, which must have cost them and their people dear. There were two cart-loads of grain in sacks, which we guarded, and gave out as fairly as we could, not just to Ardo Vale, but to people coming in from the country round.

"Then one morning, we woke up to find our guard killed – his throat cut – and one of the carts gone. Hassdan asked the people, and they said there were two groups of scavenging outlaws nearby – one to the west and one to the east.

"So we argued over which way to go – west, east – or divide? Dorac said that the road to the east was barely a road at all, and could not have taken a cart. So Hassdan stayed behind in Ardo Vale with the soldiers, and sent four of us off along the west road to see what we could find. We took a man from the village, and extra horses to drive back if we were lucky, and we took turns to scout ahead.

"We passed through a small village – very small, I can't

remember its name. It had once been a larger place, and it had a biggish market square with houses all round. Soumaki said the folk there seemed scared. There's a feeling in the air when people are frightened, like before a thunderstorm.

"Kremdar came back to us to say that there was a large building half-hidden in the trees ahead, with a guard outside. So he and I crept up and jumped on the guard and knocked him out, and sure enough inside the barn was our cart, still loaded with most of the grain, and no one else in sight.

"We were very pleased with ourselves, great warriors that we were – so pleased that we were careless. The villager drove the cart, and Dorac and I walked alongside, and Kremdar and Soumaki were at the back, and it wasn't yet dark. We'd tied up our prisoner and slung him onto the cart too, and he woke up and struggled and cursed. Then he started to whistle. Kremdar gagged him, but by that time it was too late. The whistle was a message, I suppose.

"We were just coming into the little village square, when we saw a man at the far end of it. He had a young boy – about your age – held in front of him, with a knife at his throat. So we stopped, and all around men and women came out of the shadows, all in dark clothes, difficult to see. There were two of them on each side, and another beside the leader, about ten in all, and the leader said, 'You've stolen our bread, and my brother. Give them back, or the boy dies.'"

Gormad shuddered.

"I remember the man's face, very pale, very thin, and his voice like something dragging on the ground, and the boy trying not to cry. The grain was enough for a lot of people, who desperately needed it, but none of us liked the thought of testing his threat. We could see people peering out of their houses, wondering what we would do, and we guessed some of them were the boy's family."

"What did you do?"

"Dorac looked carefully all round, the way he does, making it seem as if he's defeated and weary, but he's really observing and planning. He said, 'How do we know you won't kill him anyway?' and then he said to me very quietly, 'When he falls, go left.' And at that moment," Kai said emphatically, "the leader fell with an arrow in his throat."

"Dead?"

"Not quite. Wounded and screaming like a rabbit in a snare. Dorac had seen that Soumaki'd slipped behind and climbed up on a cottage roof where she had an excellent view, and so she shot him down, and I went left, and Dorac went forward and Kremdar went back, and Soumaki shot one of the ones on the right.

"I was fighting two at once, I suppose – I had to knock one down while I was slashing at the other. She wasn't much good with a sword. So I was doing all right. I can't describe a fight," he added to Gormad's disappointment, "it's all too fast. I remember a cut just missing my ear, that's all. Then we heard a noise, slow like something tearing, but very loud."

"What was it?"

"One of the men had climbed up behind Soumaki to stop her. Of course, the thatch wasn't strong enough, and they both crashed through. Kremdar yelled, and went rushing into the house, leaving his man dying on the ground.

"He said that when he got in and stopped blinking, he saw the two of them rolling on the floor. Soumaki was jabbing the man with her knife, and trying to push him into the fire, but he was heavier than she was. Kremdar helped her with that, while Dorac and I finished off outside. So we ended up with five dead and four prisoners."

"Then what did you do?"

"Told the villagers to bury the dead, gave them some corn, took the others back to Ardo Vale, tried them and hanged them for murder and robbery – for stealing food we would likely have given them if they'd asked." He sighed. "And then Kremdar and Dorac said we should go back to the village."

"Why?"

"That's what I said. 'Why?' Kremdar said, 'To mend the roof Soumaki fell through.' He said, 'We've freed them from outlaws, and fed them – we'll be the most popular Six in history if we make all tidy afterwards.' So we did. He was right. The more popular the Six, the more beloved the king, and when hard times come, the king needs to be loved as well as feared."

"Were you rewarded?" asked Gormad.

"Rewarded?" Kai laughed. "Soumaki was praised. She'd done very well on her first mission, and got a broken rib to show for it. But the rest of us - when we got back to Stonehill, Gemara lined us up and said if we'd been children of hers, she'd have whipped us all for stupidity. She said that if they'd chosen a narrower place for their ambush with no houses for Soumaki to clamber on, or had come at night, or had used more than one hostage, it would have been very different. All because we were too confident to send out scouts on the way back, even though we knew there were more of them around." He grinned. "But on the other hand - I think we were the most popular Six in Ardo Vale's history.

"Are you sleepy yet?"

"Only a little." Gormad told himself *always send out scouts*, and then dared to ask, "What does Master Dorac do to entertain?"

"He doesn't sing, anyway. You sing well - If we are very bored, we play a game called Ask Dorac."

"What's that?"

"Someone says, 'How would you travel from - Lenchen on the Hill - to Easter Kleechit?' And Kremdar normally adds, 'You have a heavy cart and it's a muddy midwinter', or 'You don't want to be seen, but you do want to visit every monastery you can find on the way', or suchlike. And then Dorac tells you. We have never caught him out.

"If he's drunk enough, he'll arm-wrestle. Or argue theology, which is sometimes entertaining late at night. Mostly he applauds other people, which is also good."

Gormad could not imagine Dorac applauding. Kai said, "You've never seen him happy. It – it lights up the room." He fell silent then, and soon afterwards they went to sleep.

*

9 October 570

Towards the end of the next day, they saw the great gate of Stonehill looming up ahead of them. That meant proper beds and a warm fire, and not to be riding all the time. But on the other hand, Gormad was feeling very guilty about missing his master's funeral. It was a monstrously ungrateful thing to do, and he saw Marrach's reproachful face. Surely no proper squire - And -

"You'll be in a lot of trouble," Kai said quietly.

Gormad nodded, feeling himself shrinking. He knew he would, and even Kai could not help or reassure him, and did not try.

"Welcome back, Master Kai!" said one of the gatekeepers. "You found the lad, did you?"

"Thank you, yes. I fear I can't stop. I need to deliver him," Kai responded, and they were let pass. They approached the Castle by a side way to avoid some of the bustle, arrived at the stables and arranged things there with a little difficulty. No other squire owned two horses.

As they were crossing the courtyard, a voice called, "Brother Kai!" and Kai was embraced by a chunky young man with long hair and a flowing moustache. Gormad thought he was one of the Thirty but did not remember his name until Kai said, "Greetings, Torio. Are you well?"

"Oh, indeed, indeed. Congratulations, Kai! You must be very happy."

Kai blinked. "Yes, of course."

"And is it a little son of Adam or a little daughter of Eve?"

"A boy," said Kai firmly, after a moment.

"Oh? I thought the King said - and are mother and baby doing well?"

"Very well. That is, she is. The child is a little small, but no one is greatly concerned. He'll grow."

"God send he thrives. But, Kai, we all know the King will tolerate anything short of adultery, but the priests are spitting about your bad example. What is this – three? Be prepared for sermons on

176

sin."

"The baby is not the sin," Kai argued. "The sin is nine months earlier. Has the King named us a new sibling?"

"Saysh, son of Adshan."

"Oh. Was anyone expecting Saysh?"

"Everyone was a little surprised. Including him - He'll be able to give you all wrestling tips. And this is the truant boy?"

"Yes. I followed a rumour, and picked him up. And now I need to report in, and find someone to take charge of him."

Torio let them go.

"Shit," Kai murmured.

"What was that –?"

"Not just now."

They reported to the Lord Marshal himself, Lord Vrenas. He was not tall, but very broad, and his hair and beard were bushy and white. Gormad stared meekly at the floor, as the Marshal said, "I believe the King will want to see you both very shortly, Master Kai. My apologies, but could you wait in your cell?"

Gormad had never been into the Court of the Thirty, a square of roofed stone passages, which he had heard called a quadrangle, open on the inside to a courtyard with benches and grass. Opening from the passages were the cells: a tiny room for each Kingsbrother and Kingsister. Some of them had no other home in Stonehill, and some, he had heard, had no other at all.

So it seemed to be for Kai. "It's not very tidy," he said as he pushed open his door.

The cell was about ten feet square, with a shuttered window

high in the wall. It contained, as perhaps all of them did, a bed, a chest, and a rack to hang clothes on, and these items filled most of the space. Kai's cell also contained extra garments piled on top of the chest, several cushions on the floor, a shelf with a real book and some parchments held down by a carving in the shape of a cat, and what looked like a set of painted stones for the children's game Dabbydown. A huge old-fashioned sword hung on the wall, and a clumsily-woven straw hat was perched on a peg, looking like the work of a child.

It was the most fascinating room Gormad had ever been in. He decided that when he grew up he would have one just like it.

Kai fastened a candle to a bracket on the wall, and cleared a portable writing-desk and a lute off the bed so that they could sit down. He then impressed Gormad further by remembering the earlier question.

"It looks as if the King excused my absence on Monday by saying I'd become a father again. And with a one in two chance of guessing the right sex, I chose wrong. Karila will not be pleased." He put his elbows on his knees, and splayed his fingers over his cheeks, staring over them at the door.

"Please, why did you say the child was small?" asked Gormad, after digesting this.

"Because since he does not exist, he had better die soon. I don't want to be answering questions about him in six years' time." Kai sighed, rubbing his bearded chin. "If we're going to see the King, we'd better smarten up."

They went to the lavatories at the end of the passage, and washed and brushed themselves. Tiny creatures were jumping crazily about Gormad's insides, and they became more frantic still when a servant arrived to say, "Master Kai, the King requests his brother's presence in the Small Chamber. And the squire."

*

King Arrion was alone except for a dark-faced woman in a long black gown. Gormad had never seen the King except in a crowd. There was a strange fascination about him, because he only had one arm, and it was very rude to look, but almost impossible not to. He had been terribly wounded fighting Ricossan intruders in the east two years ago, and people had whispered that he might die (the gossip had even reached Dendarry), "but he killed his man, and won the battle", Marrach had said. Now there was just a scar down his neck, and gowns made with only one sleeve. Gormad stared instead at the kingly face. *What did he mean by "kingly"? Did he just mean not cross or silly?*

"Welcome back, brother." The King embraced Kai. "I see you found the boy. Did you see Dorac?"

"Yes, Your Grace. I met him at the last village before the Old Stones, but he changed his mind, and he headed towards Jaryar the day before yesterday."

"Well done," said the King quietly.

"I doubt if I had much to do with it."

"Has anyone told you that I have provided you with a new daughter?"

"Actually a son, Your Grace. I met Torio outside, and - I guessed wrong."

"My mistake, then. So this is Gormad?"

Gormad bowed.

"Yes, Your Grace," said Kai. "He has a letter to present to you."

"Later. Young man, Makkam here will take you to a place to wait. Master Kai is going to report to me. Do you have it written?"

"Yes, Your Grace." Perhaps responding to Gormad's pleading look, Kai said, "He heard all that we said at the Old Stones."

"He may have heard all your secrets, Kai, and all Dorac's, but he is not going to hear all mine. Go, boy."

So the woman took him through two doors to a small room, and left him. Gormad scowled. There was nothing interesting there, except a large map hanging on the wall. It showed the whole continent of Ragaris, from the northern islands off Baronda to the hot countries and the Long Bay in the south, from the Jaryari coast and Haymon in the west to Ricossa in the east. He traced the borders of Marod in the middle of the northern section. He'd just found Stonehill, and was looking for Makkera, where Dorac might be going, when someone came up behind him and he spun round.

It was a tall, big lady in white and blue, her black hair piled up on top of her head. The Queen! He bowed low.

"Gormad, is it not? Do you like the map?" she said. "It was painted long ago for my husband's brother, Prince Rafad."

Gormad scurried through his memory. "The one who died," he remembered proudly.

"Yes, he died just before his mother, so that then Arrion became king. What are you looking for?"

She showed him Makkera, and Ricossa's capital City Qayn. His home, Dendarry, was not marked, of course, but she pointed to where it probably was, and enquired politely after his family. Gormad put on his best manners and tried not to look bored, but all the time his ears were on alert for the secretary's return. It seemed a long time before she did come back; she smiled and bowed to the Queen, and said, "The boy is wanted."

*

As the door closed behind the slightly downcast boy and the black-pillar secretary, King Arrion said, "You talked to Dorac. Is he guilty or innocent?"

"Innocent," said Kai. "I would stake my life on it." He supposed he would.

"I would not, though. Your report?"

They both sat down at a table, and the King read it, and when Secretary Makkam returned, she was permitted to read it too, while Kai rubbed his hair and fretted. The King's face, scarred down the neck to the right, was the dignified kind loved by sculptors; he had thick silver hair and beard, narrow features and high cheekbones. His gown was a deep red, from neck to floor. Makkam, standing at his shoulder, was slim and still, all dark except for a white collar. Together they seemed to embody wisdom and judgment, qualities that Kai admired greatly from a distance.

Dorac's further evidence, given to me at the Old Stones.

I talked to Dorac at length. Dorac insists he is innocent. He stands by all his evidence at his trial, except that on thinking it over he is not sure that Braf was the guard at the door. He is not even sure that there was a guard when he came out.

He also says that he was surprised by the people at F. The house was not strongly guarded or fortified and everyone seemed distressed and angry at the suggestions of treason. However he does think Lord G reacted to the mention of a letter.

He thinks when he entered Lord G's room after he was found dead there was a piece of parchment or something similar on the table but it was not there when he left. Perhaps Laida would remember. Laida is scatter-brained. He left her with the body when he and K and A left because she is nervous of corpses which she needs to learn to endure.

He says he thinks that someone could have taken his cloak from the bookroom while he was reading, as he was tired and finds it difficult to read complicated records.

He says K and A are lovers. He saw them together in an alley in Stonehill a few weeks ago and K asked him not to tell his wife. He mentioned this to Lady Kara. He thinks A may have been influenced in her evidence by K.

This is what Dorac says. However, Arvill and I were lovers for a time last summer. I do not believe she is a person who would say anything she did not want to say.

Kai Kingsbrother

"Hmm." King Arrion raised his eyebrows at the last paragraph. "Yes. Arvill - And Lady Kara did seem very forceful against the prisoner, and interrupted him a few times. She is like that. Makkam, who chose her to be King's Questioner in this case?"

"I think it was Lady Sada."

"Yes. Ferrodach, also - But the main point is Arvill. Arvill, daughter of Eve. A bastard. Who is Eve in this case? Can you tell us,

Kai?"

"I don't think she ever mentioned her mother's name to me, and certainly not her father's, if she knew it. I believe she said her mother was dead, but I am not sure."

"Where does she come from? Any brothers or sisters?"

"She never mentioned any. I can't remember – I think she may have come from the country -"

"Like most people," said the King dryly. "Were you together for one night, or more than one? You plainly did not do much talking."

Kai shifted uncomfortably. "It was about four months, Your Grace."

"So you were strangely incurious, or strangely *forgetful*," he shot a sharp glance at Kai, who felt instantly guilty of something, "*or* she was strangely secretive. It is not for me to tell Mistress Gemara how to manage her investigation, but Mistress Gemara is not here, and time is short. Copy this report and send it to Gemara and Hassdan. Then find Arvill, and speak to her, and to Braf."

"You want me to -" Kai could not hide his dismay. "But -"

"You have suspicions of criminal activity. Adultery is a crime, I think. Unless you become convinced that Dorac is lying or mistaken about them, you will arrest her. And you will get the truth from her, and from Braf. I don't care what you did with her, or how you feel about her now, but that is an order, Kai."

"Yes, Your Grace."

"Makkam, find out where she's been sent. And now I suppose we need the boy back." As Makkam left, he asked more warmly, "What did you think of him?"

"He seems a well-disposed lad, loyal and affectionate and honest. Dorac recommends him very strongly in his letter."

"Mmm. I'd always take Dorac's views seriously - He recommended you, you know."

"Me?"

"Everyone was giving us names after the war. There were so many spaces to fill. Mostly they were names of their kin or their friends, of course. Dorac said, 'You should consider the Captain of South Keep', so we did. And so he never told you. How like him."

*

When Gormad returned, Kai and the King were sitting at a small table, and Kai was folding up a piece of parchment, not looking happy. He made a tiny gesture to Gormad, who went down on one knee, heart thudding. Patches of cold seemed to freeze and melt on his head and shoulders.

"You have a letter for me."

The King read Dorac's letter carefully, and then read it again. His face was very still.

Then he said, "So. After Marrach died, and you ran off, I wrote to your parents, and now I will write again to tell them you are safe. When the time comes, I will take this letter, and your wishes, into consideration, but I can make no promise. For the time being, you will go back with the other squires. Kai, find someone to keep an eye on him. Perhaps Sheru Kingsister."

Somehow Gormad sensed Kai's surprise at the name. "Yes, Your Grace."

"That is the first thing I have to say to you, Gormad. The

184

second is this. People will ask you where you have been. You can tell them where you went, and what you did. If they ask you *why* you went, you can say what you like. But Dorac killed the children at Ferrodach, and no one here doubts that except perhaps you, and no one is listening to you.

"The only people you can say anything different to are myself, the Queen, Makkam here, and Kai, Gemara and Hassdan of the Southern Six. Do you understand?"

"I understand, Your Grace." Gormad tried desperately to learn the list of names, counting behind his back on his fingers.

"Very well. And the third thing. Your actions have been a serious nuisance to me, and to other people. Do not do anything like that again."

"No, Your Grace."

"No. Take him out and thrash him, Kai, and then put him back where he belongs."

*

"You're going to hate me," Kai murmured as they entered the courtyard a little later. Gormad's arse was sore, and he thought he hated him already. But he hated him a lot more when Kai dragged him by the arm up to the other squires being herded together by Captain Renatar to go in to supper, and said loudly, "Here is your truant. The King has had quite enough of him for now. Chasing after murderers, fighting with villagers, horse trading, running off to the Old Stones, and causing enough trouble for twenty boys in a year. However I think -" with a hard look, "he has now learned his lesson."

Then he turned around, and marched away to his glorious free life in the King's Thirty, and left Gormad standing there.

"Learned your lesson, eh?" said the Captain, staring at him. "We will say no more about it, then. Clean yourself up, and see if there's any food left."

There were a few sniggers, then and later, but as he unpacked his things before bed – he had a new shirt, anyway, and somehow that made him want to cry – he found people gathering around him, and even girls creeping in from the other room, and suddenly the questions burst out.

"Did you really go to the Old Stones?"

"Did Dorac hurt you? Weren't you scared?"

"What did the King say to you?"

"What did he mean, 'fighting villagers'?"

And from one of the girls, "You were camping with Kai! Boys have all the luck."

Even the bully Hanos said enviously, "Must have been exciting."

Gormad could not resist. "Master Dorac says 'exciting' is just children at a fair."

Of course Hanos clouted him, but it was worth it.

In bed at last, he suddenly thought, *but Kai knew that's what would happen.* He started to giggle, so hard he had to stuff his mouth full of pillow.

But he wanted to talk to Meril. Surely the King would allow that? She would know what Hassdan knew. He hoped she would come back soon.

*

After leaving Gormad with the squires, and talking to Sheru Kingsister, Kai did his duty, and sought out his new brother. His main memory of Saysh was of having been beaten by him in the wrestling contest the Christmas before last. Saysh, like Hassdan, was tall and pale-skinned, but across the shoulders he would have made two of Hassdan; his hair was a strange shade, almost the colour of firelight, and his big-chinned face was scattered with freckles.

He seemed very happy to go to The Merry Miller for a drink and a slice or two of mutton - and happy, too, to pay his share, which was fortunate for Kai's light purse. But the conversation did not flow well. From Saysh's point of view, Kai recognised, he had been called to the Thirty in circumstances that forbade rejoicing, and almost forbade congratulation, to a Six in turmoil who were dashing around the country - and perhaps he had realised that no one was being entirely frank about why. At any rate, they exchanged stilted words about Stonehill news, and Saysh toasted his latest bastard (*Shit. What would Karila say?*) and then the talk turned to Saysh's romantic life, and he became enthusiastic. It seemed he was highly in favour with a delightful gentlewoman called Videnna. After praising her beauty, ancestry and talents, he began to hint at the more personal ways in which she was willing and eager to be delightful. Such details as these Kai thought should really remain private between the people concerned. Gemara would have boxed his ears, but that would not have been brotherly, and also Saysh was much bigger than he was.

They parted reasonably amicably, and Kai headed with some misgivings for the prosperous wood-carving business Karila ran with her brother and sister-in-law, and above which they lived.

She grimly allowed him to enter the dimly lit shop. He began awkwardly and truthfully, "I've missed you," and she slapped him stingingly in the face.

"You bastard. You *bastard*. How many more gullible women have you got strewn around the South?"

He had shared her bed when in Stonehill for the last three months, and all this time some other woman had been growing fat with his child, and he had not mentioned it. So obviously he shared this other woman's bed when he was not with her. It was all too probable, and Kai had no defence except impromptu and implausible lies, which she did not for one moment believe. She allowed him to stay only long enough for her to list all his flaws, more of them than he had remembered, and then turned him out, telling him emphatically that if they met in heaven, or indeed hell, it would be too soon.

By now, Kai felt like a jug full of secrets, which might spill disastrously if one drop of alcohol were added. So he dared not go to a tavern, but returned to his cell in the Castle, where he spent a night that was quite as miserable and lonely as Karila could have wished.

*

10 October 570

The next day he went to the scriptorium and spent a weary time copying up his report and writing to his siblings, under the watchful eye of Secretary Makkam. She brought him a cup of ale unasked, and mercifully made no sarcastic comments about Arvill, but she did not seem inclined to be friendly. She did however tell him that Arvill and Braf's troop had been sent off to the northwest to replace the soldiers sent to Kerrytown on the Haymon border. So it was there he was to go.

He left the scriptorium, avoided Torio who was hanging around the corridors for some reason, and sought out Gamar the saddle-maker and Mayeel Kingsister to give them Dorac's farewell. Then, more happily, he went to the church on Tailors' Street. On Sundays people worshipped God there, but during the week it was one of the city's childpens, where children too young to be useful fought and played and learned to obey adults, thus freeing their parents for trade or profession or service. He had obtained permission from the boy's mother, and so was permitted to walk off with three-year-old Edric, son of Adam – in this case, son of Kai – who was touchingly pleased, bouncing along next to him like a sparrow.

He took Edric to the child's favourite place, the big house on the hill where Kai lived, and generously allowed the King and Queen and some of their friends to live also. They watched some people pretending to fight, and Edric explored the smells and textures of the herb garden, and on the way back Kai tried to answer his questions – "Why do horses have tails and people don't? Why are brown leaves hard and crackly, and green leaves soft?" – and bought him a sticky bun. They arrived at the close down which Edric lived, and his mother Mritta said dryly, "So you have another now? Why aren't you there with her?"

"I was there. I was in the way." He told Edric a story, and sang to him. Perhaps some day Gormad would teach him the "Lemon Pudding" song. Edric would like that. As he sang, he wondered fleetingly what his life would have been like if Mritta had agreed to marry him when she became pregnant. But she had said, "When I have a husband, I want to wake up next to him every morning", and one of

189

the King's Thirty could never give her that, and soon afterwards they had parted.

As evening came on, and he grew hungry, he went to make some enquiries in Oyster Alley.

*

11 October 570

Two days after their return, Kai rode away. Before he left, he took Gormad aside and said, "Sheru Kingsister will take as much notice of you as I do of the bishop's sermons. Practise swordplay, and keep your eyes open."

That same day, as the squires were gathering for lessons, Jamis came running up to cry, "Gormad! Your father's come!"

Gormad felt at once dismayed, and then guilty.

"He went to see the King," Jamis added, confirming his fears. A boy ought to love his father and mother, and his home. He did love them. But he wanted to stay here – and if they sent him back, he would never know what happened next.

He was particularly stupid at his history, and Sister Susanna rapped his head with hard knuckles.

Book lessons finished, and the squires dispersed to various errands. Gormad, masterless, kicked his feet around in the courtyard, dreading the summons, and still there was no sign of Ramahdis. But after hours and hours a servant approached him, and said, "You are to come to the White Hall." The creatures in his stomach were back, but this time their dancing circled a lead weight. He cleaned himself up as best he could, and made his way to the hall where Dorac had been tried, and where the King and Queen issued commands. Today the dais was empty, and tall grandly dressed shapes were standing around making stupid conversation. Their faces seemed to be showing off how happy they were, and their eyes kept creeping to the King, who was talking about hawks with some old people. Eventually Gormad found his father standing alone by the wall. He edged up, his scalp pricking, not sure whether to kneel in his presence, as he would have done at home. He bowed instead.

"Well, lad. Here you are." There was something unusual about his father's voice.

"Ramahdis of Dendarry." The King had strolled up to them. To Gormad's horror, everybody around fell silent.

"Your Grace." Father and son bowed. Gormad stared at the floor again.

The King asked pleasantly about the journey, and the health of Ramahdis's wife and younger children, and then went on, "You have come seeking this rascal, sir? I'm sorry we took such ill care of him, but you see he returned from his escapade in one piece."

"As you say, Your Grace. I am relieved."

"We are all saddened by the death of Marrach of Drumcree. I don't think he had any complaints about the boy. Captain Renatar and his tutors think there's something in him, and he has requested a new service. How say you?"

Gormad tensed.

"Your Grace, we miss him at home, but we will not stand in his way. If his sins can be overlooked, and someone is willing to train him, we would be most grateful."

"I will find someone shortly, or the Captain will. And now I'm sure you and he would like to go and talk." The King nodded and turned away, and it was over.

He had got what he wanted: so easy, so quick! *Why?*

Ramahdis walked out into the garden with his son. He said nothing until they were well away from the buildings, and then laid a hand on Gormad's shoulder, and said heartily, "My boy. Are you well?"

"Yes, father."

"No one has – hurt you?"

He had been beaten by adults, knocked about by bullies, and bruised in swordpractice, but he knew the right answer. "No one, father." He looked up shyly, wondering what the question really meant. Ramahdis was a big man, taller than Dorac, broader than the King, fairer-skinned than either, with the curly hair ("Dendarry hair", people said) that he shared with all his children. He always knew everything and commanded everybody at Dendarry. But here at Stonehill he looked odd – worried, or ill, or older, or something. Gormad looked round, but there was no one about, except one soldier standing not far off.

"Listen to me," Ramahdis said abruptly. "Listen carefully. Are you loyal to the King?"

"Of course, father," said Gormad in amazement.

"This Dorac hasn't taught you anything different, anything treacherous?"

"There's no one loyaller than Master Dorac!"

"Hmm. Good. Whatever happens, Gormad, whatever anyone says to you, or offers you, or threatens you with, do not betray the King. Do not disobey the King. If you do, you risk your life, and others' lives as well. Is that clear?"

"Y-yes, father." *But why would he? Why would anyone?* He tried to sound cheery. "'I will swear my sword to no one else.'"

"What?"

"It's part of the oath of the Thirty."

"I know it is. You are not one of the Thirty," said his father, sounding crosser than Gormad ever remembered. "Well, aren't you going to ask after the family? Your mother is well, Kammer is taller than ever, the harvest is good. We do miss you, lad – the house is too quiet."

They went in, and Ramahdis listened to reports from Captain Renatar on Gormad's swordsmanship *("Fair")*, and archery (*"Poor but improving"*) and from Sister Susanna on his general education (*"You gave him such a good start, sir, he's ahead of most of the others. Sometimes a little inattentive"*), and then he blessed Gormad, and went away. Gormad offered to come to the stables with him, but he said no. He smiled as he went, but he did not look happy.

*

Kai was not wrong about Sheru Kingsister. Every morning Gormad went to her cell, and asked if she had any tasks for him. Sometimes she sent him on an errand; sometimes she did not. He stood and knelt beside her at Mass, and at the Monday audience. Occasionally she stopped to watch him at practice on her way across the yard, and gave him a few useful hints. Once she took him to wait on her at a supper in the town. He did this very badly, for he had never done it for Marrach, and she told him how stupid he was in different ways all the walk home. The rest of the time she left him alone.

He did lessons and practised swordplay, and pictured Dorac fighting the Jaryari. He rode in the woods and attended chapel, and pictured Kai arresting the real murderer. He squirmed happily at the other squires' questions, and pictured Meril's face when he told her everything. Remembering Kai's words about paths and villages, he tried to learn every inch of the Castle and gardens, and as much of the town as he could.

The glory of his escapade faded. Only Jamis still seemed impressed, and his hero-worship was very pleasant.

(Jamis's own master was Aros, Ralia's brother. Everyone knew Ralia, whose swordplay was dazzling and whom Prince Jendon was madly in love with, Hanos said. Aros, on the other hand, had never done anything distinctive in any way that his squire could boast or look happily modest about. No wonder Jamis was so interested in everyone else's news. "I wish I could have an adventure like you," he said wistfully. "It was quite frightening some of the time," Gormad said as a consolation, but Jamis was not consoled.)

Life was not bad; and the King had almost promised him a proper lord. *When*, though? But for a few days he had been part of something big and real and deadly serious; the life of a squire, especially Sheru's squire, felt like sitting in a box after that. He could do nothing for Dorac but pray, and he did this, but doubted that God had time to listen to him.

The worst was being unable to talk to anyone. He had no access to any of the people the King had mentioned. Sometimes the thought that Kai had said they had forty days to investigate, and two weeks of it were over, and not being able to tell anyone who would understand almost drove him mad. Then he would snap at, and even fight with, poor Jamis, and feel guilty, and stalk off to find something to kick. He lay in bed at night imagining talking to Kai or Meril or Dorac, or even his tutor from home, or his mother. The conversations repeated themselves unsatisfyingly, and did not help him to sleep.

Hassdan and Meril 1 (8–20 October)

8 October 570

Having issued certain commands, Hassdan knocked on the door of the steward's room.

"How may I help you, Master Hassdan?" Hagouna asked with punctilious courtesy.

He seated himself opposite her. "You may have remarked that several of your visitors absented ourselves for much of yesterday. We were making investigations. May it please you to read this? I fear it may distress you."

She eyed him suspiciously as she took the parchment. Her lips moved as she read.

On the seventh day of the month of October in the five hundred and seventieth year of deliverance, under the orders of Hassdan Kingsbrother of the Southern Six, and in the presence of Captain Rabellit, Sister Martha of Ferrodach and Brother Joseph of Ferrodach Village, the grave of Ilda, Gaskor and Filana, children of Gahran and Geril of Ferrodach, was opened. We proceeded with prayer and all possible reverence.

"You -" She was looking at him as if he were the devil himself. "Continue, please."

In the view of the Captain and Sister Martha, the grave looked not to have been disturbed since the burial on the twenty-sixth day of September, when both were present. The sheet in which the bodies had been wrapped also appeared unchanged. Within the sheet were found and identified by Sister Martha and Brother Joseph the heads and bodies and limbs (although separated) of Ilda aged twelve and Gaskor aged nine. Ilda's head was completely severed from her body, and one of her legs also. An attempt had been made to decapitate Gaskor, but incompletely. There was no sign of the body of Filana, aged five.

In order to ascertain if her body could have been removed and reburied with that of Arator, son of Otto, this grave was opened. It also did not appear to have been disturbed before. The coffin contained the body of Arator, again identified by Sister Martha, and no one else.

We have taken oath to confirm the truth of the above.

Martha

Joseph

Rabellit, daughter of Bella.

Hagouna laid down the paper with a shaking hand. Sobs croaked from her as she rocked back and forth. Hassdan watched her and waited.

"What have you done with her?" she wailed at last.

"I have done nothing with her. Surely you must comprehend that. This is a mystery that I want you to help me solve." She said nothing but appeared to be listening, so he pursued the subject. "Madam, I am not your enemy in this. We all expected to find three bodies, and there are only two. Why would anyone be at removing a dead child? She may be alive. Do you know where she is?"

"How should I know? Your brother killed them. Your brother put them in the ground."

"But Filana is not in the ground. It appears that somebody took her away. One of your people, or one of ours. If she's not with an adult, then she's a small child alone, and therefore she's in danger. If she is with someone, then -"

"Then she's safe. Safer than she would be with you."

Hassdan sighed. "You must be a little curious, surely. Have you any thoughts of where she could have gone or been taken?"

"What I know is this. Your Dorac and Kremdar took the children and shut them in that room over there, and I never saw them again. I was told they were all dead. Now you say Filana is alive. How can I know?"

"The murders of Ilda and Gaskor were an abominable crime. No one is wanting to repeat that. No one here has any reason to hurt her."

"Do they not?" Hagouna glared into his eyes, ceasing to rock and ignoring the tears pouring down her cheeks. "Her family are all dead. She is the direct descendant of Queen Arrabetta. Some people might think she is the true Queen."

"No one is thinking that," countered Hassdan impatiently. "You don't think that. But if you say it again, I shall wonder what else you're thinking or you know."

"I have not hidden her. But whoever has has my blessing. I will not help you track her down like an animal."

So that was that. He called in the soldiers who had been waiting outside. "The steward will give you her keys. When her chamber has been examined, you will escort her there, and search her, respectfully. She will not leave it without my order, or Captain Rabellit's."

"But you're not my enemy, are you?" taunted Hagouna as he

left.

His mood was not ameliorated as he crossed the hall to see Soumaki approaching him, carrying what appeared to be a record book. He recognised her expression – it was the countenance of one compelled by conscience to speak harsh but necessary truth.

"I need to talk to you, Hassdan."

"And I need to talk to you." He smiled pleasantly, turned back and ushered her into the opposite room to the steward's, the one no one was using any more, with the brown stains.

"Where is Meril?" Soumaki demanded as soon as the door was shut.

"I sent Meril off this morning with an urgent letter for the King."

"Is Meril a squire or an errand-girl?"

"She is a squire, and like all squires, performs occasional errands. What have you got there?"

Soumaki's glare informed him she had not finished about Meril, but she answered the question. "This is a record of the servants. I learned from it that Ben, son of Andor, died last February."

"Yes?"

"Last February."

"I am sorry," said Hassdan, "but you will have to explain."

Soumaki's wrath burst forth. "Hassdan, what is wrong with you? We are here to work, we have a task from the King, and you haven't even read the case against Lord Gahran! I know it was terrible about Dorac, I know you are distressed, but we have a duty and we need to do it. You've done nothing since we arrived but desecrate graves and mistreat Meril. Meril is a good girl, she hasn't complained, but she doesn't deserve -"

Hassdan roared with laughter.

"Soumaki, sister, I am sorry. You are right. We have a duty. Now read this. This is what we found when we were desecrating graves."

She took the report from him with a look as suspicious as Hagouna's, and read it with increasing astonishment. "*Two* bodies - this is extraordinary."

"Is it not?"

"Extraordinary. What possible reason could there be? To kill two children, and not the third?"

"Or to kill three, and remove only one body. I can think of none. I thought the King should be advised immediately, so I sent Meril this morning with an escort. She should arrive the day after tomorrow. I sent Meril because I trust her absolutely. I've been a little unkind to her in public, I admit, in the hopes that she might be able to discover more from people here if she seemed deserving of compassion. I should have told you."

"Extraordinary," said Soumaki again. Then, "Did you suspect this? Is this why you wanted to dig them up?"

"No. I had no idea. I only knew something about that funeral was wrong." He lowered his voice. "It makes no sense for anyone to do it, but it is explaining so much about what was done. A funeral so rushed, no one permitted to view the bodies, put together in one sheet instead of proper coffins. It may even explain the brutality, which was extraordinary also, whoever did it." He could not conceal his distaste. "I think they were cut up to justify hiding them, to help conceal the fact that there were only two. We didn't realise at once yesterday, and they were lying right in front of us." There was a pause.

"Kremdar buried them," Soumaki said slowly.

"Yes."

"And he swore there were three - He lied. This is about the children, not Gahran. You came here to find out about the children. Hasscan, what have you not told me?"

He explained about Gemara's visit to the King. Soumaki turned away. "You didn't tell me -"

"We considered - perhaps you were the only sensible one. The evidence was so strong, yet Gemara had a wild idea, and Kai did, and I - I was a little less convinced perhaps, but maybe we were all being led astray into madness. Someone had to be looking at things straightforwardly. As you have. You read the report on Lord Gahran."

He was not sure how much of this she accepted or had listened to. "So Kremdar must be lying - If Dorac is innocent, I can never look him in the face again."

"Yes, you can."

She turned back with tears in her eyes. "I believed Kremdar as a matter of course. I like him, we're friends. We enjoy the same things, I like his wife, the children play together. Dorac is different. And – I suppose – because it was children - the rest of us know what that means. We have children."

"I have none."

"But you will have," said Soumaki, tactlessly. "But someone like Dorac -"

Hassdan decided to take a little revenge. "I understand. Dorac lies with men rather than women. So you believed he could not care about children, because he can never have any of his own."

Soumaki looked so distressed by this that he relented. "And also because no squire has managed to endure him for more than a month. Come, Soumaki. We all think things we should not about people. And as you said, we have work to do. I confess that I did not read the report about Lord Gahran. Tell me about this man who died – Ben, was it?"

Taking a few deep breaths, Soumaki returned to her duty. "Ben, son of Andor. He was a trusted servant of Gahran, and took messages for him. And in the report that Lady Sada brought to the Council, it says that he stopped off at an alehouse while carrying a letter with Lord Gahran's seal, a letter to King Rajas, but he left it behind by mistake. So the alehouse keeper showed it to a soldier, who showed it to her commanding officer, who opened it and read it, and showed it to the local lady, who showed it to Lady Sada, and all agreed it was treasonable. And this happened at the end of August. But the man died in February."

"It is being certain that he died?"

"It's in the records of the house; there's a note of an allowance for his widow; and I've just been to the graveyard to look at his grave. Undisturbed. And he's certainly not here now."

"So the messenger in the alehouse gave a false name – but why would he? – *or* - there's something very wrong with the accusation." Hassdan shook his head slowly. "And now Gahran and two of his children are dead. Was this a conspiracy against him, and not against the King at all?"

"And Gahran is dead."

"I'm beginning to be suspicious about that death. Suicide - We need to know what poisons they have here. Was it his own, or did someone give it to him?"

"Laida was in the room. I don't think she's a poisoner."

"If she killed him, it's surely the first efficient thing she's ever done."

"The letter was sealed with Gahran's seal," said Soumaki thoughtfully. "Could anyone else have used it?"

"According to Hagouna, no one had access to the seal except herself and him."

"Do we trust Hagouna?"

"She is stubborn and angry and grieving, and I have just ordered her imprisonment. I think I do believe her." Hassdan sighed, and went on. "We need to investigate all this, but we are also needing to find the child. I have soldiers searching the house and the estate, but if - Filana - is with someone, they've had nearly two weeks' start. They could be anywhere."

"She could have wandered out alone, and been taken in by someone. Everyone round about would know her, and most would want to help her."

"But how could she wander out? The doors were guarded. The room was guarded."

They looked at each other.

"So we do have work to do," he said. "Kremdar we must leave to the King."

*

When Meril was first put on a horse, at the age of three, and her fingers encountered the rough softness of the mane, a horrible shudder surged through her, making her cry and want to be sick. Over the years, she learned to control herself a little, but no slaps or scoldings could cure her revulsion from the feel of mane or tail. Riding remained a trial for her, and the horses sensed her distaste. This seriously hindered her usefulness to the family. It was plain nonsense, she knew – a proof of weakness of character, and her parents could not conceal their contempt.

It had taken only a few hours' journeying with Hassdan and Alida before they noticed, and Alida questioned her gently, and learned the shameful secret. And when they arrived at Stonehill, Hassdan had a pair of riding gloves made for her, and the problem that had soured the past nine years went away.

It was then that Meril fully realised that Alida and Hassdan were the most wonderful people in the world, and to be Hassdan's squire the greatest honour a girl could possess.

Life with them, and centred on Stonehill, was good.

Not all the Thirty had squires, and most of the other great people who did spent the majority of their time on their estates. So the number of squires in the Castle was frequently quite small, increasing gradually over the summer as people began to arrive after harvest to gossip and prepare for the King's Gathering in late October ("They make laws there!" Meril exclaimed excitedly, amusing Hassdan and disgusting the other children by finding this interesting.) She found it hard to make friends among these few, for she was a serious dull girl who did not understand mischief, but she learned to make up for this by being kind to anyone new or miserable, like the boy Gormad, and in any case her need to love was absorbed by Hassdan and Alida. Her adoration only increased when Alida confided, as between women, that they were a little worried - two years married, and no sign of pregnancy -

So she was happy, very happy, to be trusted with the crucial letter that might help to prove Master Dorac's innocence, and to be riding back towards Stonehill in the company of two of Captain Rabellit's soldiers, Anni and Josper. The soldiers themselves were the only problem. They were fully armoured, with mail shirts and helmets and greaves, such as the Thirty only wore into actual battle (or sometimes to train) and this made them even more daunting than ordinary grown-ups, but they did not leave her alone, and seemed to expect her to converse. Josper was eighteen, handsome, and knew it. Every time he looked at her, she was conscious of her bushy hair and the spots that Alida kept assuring her would eventually fade. He pestered her about the contents of her secret letter until Anni ordered him to stop. "Meril is the messenger. We are merely the armed escort, who should treat her with respect," she said, grinning at Meril. And it became clear that she and Josper did not like each other at all. Sometimes, it was true, they would get on to the subject of hawking, and argue happily for ages, and Meril was free to daydream about finding the missing child and saving the Southern Six, or more simply just of growing up to be competent and beautiful. But when they were not doing this, they needled each other, and Josper annoyed Anni by teasing Meril about whether she had a sweetheart.

"She's young yet. Leave her alone."

"I know the rules, Anni. No one touches squires. But you're looking forward to growing up, aren't you? Finding out what a man is for, and where the herbs grow?"

Anni told him angrily to be quiet, and she was his superior, so he obeyed for a time. Meril was not as grateful as she should have been. She had heard the saying *knowing where the herbs grow* among the older squires, she knew it had something to do with fornication, and she was sinfully curious to find out what.

They camped the first night on a farmstead with permission of the farmer, and shared the family supper and singsong round the hall fire. The next day was hot, and Josper was bored. He took off his helmet, and mocked Anni's home town, and teased Meril with obscene riddles. "Where's this place?" he asked as they entered a little copse in the late afternoon. There was a narrow path off the road to the right, and then this path divided again.

"I believe there's a village down there, left fork," said Anni. "But we're going straight on."

"Come now, we need to eat. Let's find the village, and see if it has a decent tavern."

"There is no need -"

"I'll take the right way, and you take the left, and whoever is last to find the drinks pays for them." He laughed, and turned off the road with a merry idiotic shout.

Anni exclaimed in annoyance. And then, just before he was out of sight, something sang in the air, and they watched him topple off

206

his horse. A person was striding towards him, a huge person. He was struggling to get up, but the person was raising her sword.

"You are the messenger – go!" And she slapped Meril's horse, and Damson leapt forward on the road. Anni was already riding back. Meril was carried away.

It was all so quick, so beyond belief; she struggled to understand what had happened. Was Josper dead? Was Anni? What enemies were these?

You know how important it is that this reaches the King as soon as possible. Hassdan had told her that, her and not Anni, but still Anni had protected the messenger. Meril hung on in terror (*"Our Father who art in heaven, hallowed be Thy name -"*), and rode – but what could she do? If they killed Anni and came after her they would take Hassdan's letter, and the King would never know, and it was there in her satchel, ready for any thief - (*"hallowed be Thy"* -) -there were hoofbeats behind her. But she could not stop to hide it. She slipped her hand down and fiddled with the satchel tie. For a wonder it pulled open. She seized the letter, fastened with the seal of the Southern Six, and struggled through the jolting to slide it into her glove.

Her distraction had conveyed itself to Damson, and he had slowed. The hooves were louder. It could be Anni, but Anni would have called out.

"Go on!" she cried, and Damson bounded forward, but abruptly stumbled, and Meril felt herself sliding sideways, clutching desperately, and then hitting the ground with an agonising jar on the shoulder, and a scrape down her face, and Damson was falling too, and she jerked almost clear, but the horse landed on her ankle, and she screamed.

Damson scrambled up again, but Meril could not. Her shoulder and her foot were coming apart with pain, and her head was ringing. And there was another rider, dismounting from Anni's horse. Huge and dark and angry, carrying a sword with blood on it. Anni -

"Please," Meril squeaked.

"Childkillers," said the woman deep in her throat, and spat on the ground. She bent down and seized Meril's satchel, and tossed it aside. Then she raised the sword.

"Stop, Raki, what are you doing? Stop!" Or something like that – and the woman turned and ran off with the satchel, and there were other people, and Meril tried again to get up, and the pain was everywhere. But there were other faces, none of them familiar, looming around her and looking concerned.

"Are you much hurt are you much hurt are you -?"

The ringing was getting worse, and her leg was on fire, but if she was dying only one thing mattered. "A letter for the King," she said, pulling it out, "for the King, for the King," and she kept on saying it until the world slid away from her.

*

The house and grounds were thoroughly searched for any sign of a living or dead person who should not be there. The fish pond was dragged and the well explored. Nothing suspicious was discovered, except someone's secret store of coins under a loose board in the wash house, and a plate with crumbs in one of the stables. Soumaki checked and questioned all the household children, but none was remotely the right age or description to be Filana.

208

"If she left the house with someone, that person was here and now is not," said Soumaki on Sunday evening. "So that person is also missing."

"Perhaps. They could have taken her to a friend and then returned. But I understand what you mean. I asked Rabellit. All the soldiers who arrived with her are still here, except the eight who left with Kremdar the day after the murders to ride back to Stonehill, and also Laida. Kremdar dispatched her to the garrison at South Keep, it seems."

"Laida? She could hardly take a child to South Keep."

"If she went there. I will write to the Keep to see if she did arrive. I'd already asked Hagouna if any of the household managed to slip away when Kremdar and Dorac arrived, or just after. It might be tempting to do so, if one saw soldiers storming in, and had any guilty knowledge. I had intended to investigate those who seem not to be here – Inda, daughter of Jaki, and Dav, son of Andor."

Their eyes met.

"Any kin to Ben, son of Andor?" asked Soumaki.

"His brother. Tomorrow we must make enquiries, and check against your records, in case Hagouna was lying to me. And start searching further out. If you had a child to save from the murderers of the King's Thirty, where would you go?"

"I would not stay in the lands of Ferrodach, unless I had a very good hiding place."

"No. And if Lord Gahran was secretly talking to the Jaryari, and I knew about it, I might be going to Jaryar. With the little heiress."

"Poor child," sighed Soumaki, rather irritating him. She added,

"But now we think he may not have been. Talking to the Jaryari, I mean."

"In conclusion, tomorrow we send out the soldiers to search. I don't know what explanation to give them, though."

"The truth."

"Soumaki, I do not want the entire countryside to know that Queen Arrabetta's great-granddaughter is alive, and possibly on her way to Jaryar!"

"They will guess. And the soldiers certainly will. Some of their comrades dug up a grave, and you need them to search for a child. Tell them the truth, and appeal to their honour and loyalty." She added sternly, "It isn't only the Thirty who can be loyal to the King."

Sometimes Soumaki's truths were indeed necessary. Hassdan sighed, acknowledging again the parts of himself he did not like. "You are in the right. As I said yesterday, we all think things we should not."

"I didn't understand what you meant."

It was late at night. He was missing his evening talks with Alida, and perhaps he owed Soumaki something for the earlier concealment. "Trusting common soldiers - Shall I tell you a story? A confession?"

"If you wish," she said, sounding surprised.

"As you may have heard," said Hassdan, leaning back in his chair and fingering his cup thoughtfully, "I was fifteen when my parents quarrelled with King Rajas, and we had to leave Makkera. Twelve years later, I was called to the Thirty. I considered that to be sufficient time to establish my loyalty, but Dorac did not agree. We were supposed to be brothers, but every time I was put on watch at night, he would sit up too. Surely to prevent me from slitting everyone's throat, or making off with the horses. Every time I passed him a message he checked it with someone else. This went on for months. It was - wearying."

"What did you do?"

"Complaining to Master Stimmon seemed rather childish. Probably I should have knocked him down. Kai or Kremdar would've done, but he'd have got up again and broken most of my bones, so it would merely have been a more painful way of complaining, or so I thought. I did consider poisoning his ale, but that would rather have proved his point. Once, in the beginning, I said to him, 'You don't trust me', and he said, 'No. Should I?' and I said, 'King Arrion does', and he shrugged. I don't know how he was reconciling it all with his oath. Or with his Christian charity.

"Eventually Stimmon and Gemara made him stop the worst of it, but he would still glare at me across the room. And then slowly he got a little better - And then, about eighteen months after I was branded, I was in the stable brushing down Vixen, and he appeared in the door. He said, 'Brother, I treated you badly. I was wrong.' I said, 'Yes, you were.' He said, 'I am sorry', and - bowed - and walked off, and as they say, the matter was never discussed again. And he stopped glaring.

"But the comical aspect, and the reason for telling you this, is that I had similar thoughts about him. Do you know where Dorac comes from?"

"Somewhere in the north."

"He was born in a one-roomed cottage in some nameless northern village. I believe his parents owned a field and one cow, or something like that. In Jaryar, such a person could never come to be anything – or almost never. They are the Lowly. They are there to be servants, and to work the land and, when we need them, to fight and die in battle. Very, very rarely, one might rise to be a minstrel, or a wrestler. But my family was one of the highest in Jaryar.

"So when Dorac looked at me, he was seeing an enemy who would stab him in the back, and when I looked at him I was seeing an upstart ploughboy. He wanted to send me home, and I wanted to order him to clean my boots. I merely concealed it better."

"You behaved better."

"Yes, I did. We have better manners in Jaryar."

"And then you became brothers."

"Yes. As long as he's innocent. If he's guilty, I still don't like him very much - We'll send out tomorrow."

*

10 October 570

Hassdan and Soumaki gathered the majority of the soldiers, and sent them out in twos, to search every path and track, and enquire at every cottage, offering money judiciously for information. "At the end of two days, if you have found no clue, return," said Hassdan. "If you find any indication, one of you follow it, and the other come back to report. The child may be alone, but more probably with someone: the man Dav, or indeed with someone else." (Inda had been tracked down the night before, living semi-secretly with her parents in the village.)

"If you find her alive - keep her safe, at all costs. Bring her back here, yes, but keep her *safe*, and do not hurt her – or Dav, if you can help it. If they refuse to come back, still do not hurt them. One stay

212

with them, the other return and report. If your search takes you to the border" (this was the nightmare) "talk sensibly to the Jaryari border guards. You're searching for a missing child who's wandered off. Don't name her. No fighting if you can avoid it.

"And -" – they had thought hard about this – "she is only five years old. Do not question her about what happened. If she says anything interesting, or if Dav does, remember it, write it down if you can, but ask the child nothing, and do not question Dav in her presence. What she remembers may be very important, and we must not muddle it or interfere. Don't upset her, don't confuse her."

"Play with her," Soumaki suggested.

"Yes - keep her happy, if you can, without lying. Bring her back here. But of course, she may not be alive. You are also looking for rumours, or signs, of a body."

They knew little about the man Dav – his brother had been trusted with secret errands, and his sister had been one of the Ferrodach soldiers. He had worked in the kitchens. There was nothing to suggest he would make an understanding children's nurse.

So five pairs of soldiers set out in different directions, leaving a worryingly small garrison – small enough for Hassdan and Soumaki to know how important it was to look confident as they searched through records and gave household commands. And waited for news.

*

13 October 570

They were gazing together at Lord Gahran's letter, which had been translated by Lady Sada's assistant from its fairly simple code, and then copied.

2nd day of August, 570

Gahran Lord of Ferrodach son of Prince Karac, son of Queen Arrabetta, to Rajas of House Vend, Lord of Jaryar, greetings.

I return humble thanks for Your Grace's good wishes. Your Grace's words are wise and generous. I have never sought high office. But if ill should come to our Lord Arrion (whom God protect) and if the people call me and Your Grace assists, I would accept the heavy burden of the crown. I have come to this conclusion after much internal debate and prayer.

I remain Your Grace's humble servant and friend.

"Well," said Hassdan.

"It would be good to read what King Rajas originally wrote to him," said Soumaki obviously. "But still it must be treasonable. If he wrote it. And it was his seal. People are careful with their seals."

"Could it have been mistranslated? A - mistake - with the code?"

"I did not translate it myself, but I saw the original document. It was a code with numbers for letters, you know? There were a few smudges on the page. Some letters might have been wrong. But there would have to be a lot of errors to change the meaning. *I won't actually say I want harm to come to the king, but I am Queen Arrabetta's grandson, and if it does, I want his throne –*"

"Most reluctantly," agreed Hassdan.

"*– and I'll take it if you give it to me.*"

"Indeed. Where were the smudges?"

Soumaki stared up at the ceiling, as was her way. "One near the top, and one towards the middle, on the left."

"Hmm."

Soumaki's husband was an apothecary, and she knew something about medicines and poison. Lord Gahran had died from a dose of empodene, kept in most great houses to kill vermin, or, in very small quantities, to take away pain. The little bottle he had used was not like any of the other bottles, including one of empodene, in Hagouna's box of physics, but that did not prove it had not been his. Hagouna had denied knowledge of it. "And he would not have had time to go to the steward's room after the house was attacked," said Soumaki thoughtfully. "Either someone gave it to him, or he kept it with him, on his person or in his chamber."

There was a commotion in the hall outside. A messenger had arrived from the King.

*

It was not, however, the messenger they were hoping for. Drac was unaware of any message having reached Stonehill from Ferrodach, so presumably Meril had still been journeying when he left. Assuring himself of this, Hassdan stifled a misgiving that in that case they should have encountered each other on the road. But the King had ruled on Ferrodach's future.

They gathered the people in the hall, to be told that the lands were to be divided – part to Lady Rakall and Lord Jovian of Aspella, adjoining Ferrodach to the west, who had exposed the treason; part to Lady Orria whom everyone knew the King and Queen had wanted to honour for some time; and the central, smallest portion, including the house itself, to be retained by the few family members left alive, like poor old Derrian. Since both the King and the Queen were cousins of Gahran's, this was possibly a concession to ties of blood.

Soumaki gave orders for this decision to be proclaimed at all the appropriate places, and enquired how soon the new lords or their representatives would take possession and establish new boundary markers. The messenger did not know. However, he did have a personal letter for Master Hassdan.

They waited until they were alone to break the seal, and read Kai's letter and report. Soumaki shuddered at the mention of the Old Stones, but both were more interested in the suggestion about Kremdar and Arvill.

"I never really trusted her."

"You never like any of Kai's women," said Hassdan.

"Why can't he find someone suitable and settle down? But Arvill seemed a little too eager to please everyone. Poor Praja! Kremdar seemed so devoted to her."

"Oh, he was. You won't remember the wedding. People called it a vision out of a fairy tale – such a handsome couple, and so much in love." Hassdan smiled cynically. "In the weeks beforehand he made us sick talking about her. Kai and Dorac would see how drunk they became, wetting their throats every time he said her name. He was in ecstasy. He was giving gifts to everyone."

"What, to his brothers, at his own wedding?"

"Yes, he gave me a painting of St John. I have it at home. It must have been very expensive. And he didn't give Kai anything, but he paid off one of his debts. Which was very thoughtful."

"What did he give Dorac?" asked Soumaki.

"I don't know. Dorac looked a little embarrassed when I asked," Hassdan said mischievously. "It was before he met Tor, so I always assumed it was a visit to a whorehouse, since Dorac doesn't care for *things*. Gemara doesn't either, so he found out which of her daughters had least money, and bought a gown for her. He was overflowing with kindness to the world. And at the wedding feast he sang to her – to Praja – that song about her being the dew on the daisy, the frost on the leaf - Some of us were sniggering, I fear, but it was a sweet thing. Well. That was five or six years ago."

"Marrying for love. It rarely lasts," said Soumaki – tactlessly again, as Hassdan and Alida had done so. He went back to Kai's letter.

"Well, we knew they must be lying, anyway. It's interesting, what Dorac felt about Ferrodach. But not as entertaining as wondering how he'll get on in Jaryar."

They decided not to write to Kai or Gemara about the bodies – Gemara because of the risk that Kremdar would see the letter, and Kai because they did not know where he was. He had said he was being sent to question Arvill and Braf, but not where.

*

Slowly the soldiers filtered back. Six had found nothing. Then one arrived to say that a man and child had possibly been seen on the south road, and another reported that they might have been heading east. So these two possibilities were followed up, and they tried not to wonder how the Jaryari would react to their searchers.

Apart from missing his wife, Hassdan appreciated life at Ferrodach. He had been born into the Jaryari aristocracy, after all, and this was a larger, more comfortable house, with better-trained servants, than any he had stayed in in nineteen years. (Stonehill Castle was an exception, of course, but even the Castle had been built in ill-assorted

217

stages, and had inadequate drains. And a Kingsbrother's cell was far from luxurious.)

The long-dead builders of Ferrodach had plainly had some idea of proportion and grace in stone, and the more recent improvers, who had added chimneys, gargoyles and occasional glass, had not spoiled the earlier work. All of this was rare in unbeautiful Marodi architecture.

He especially liked the chapel. Sunset light poured through coloured panes onto the altar. Above it were skilfully carved cherubs, and on the left and right the wall-paintings of Christ's life, if simply done, were vivid and evocative. The smell of incense hung about the place. He found it easier to pray in a setting like this, and as he became concerned about the lack of news, he went there at least once a day.

By the time Meril had been gone ten days, he was seriously worried. Two years ago, he had chosen her over the other children because she was the only one who knew how to keep a secret. He had not realised until now how deeply she had settled in his heart.

*

"She may be dead," he said soberly to Soumaki one night. "Filana."

"There are many dangers for a child alone."

"Indeed, but I meant, she might have been removed dead. We said we could think of no reason to do so, but - suppose in ten years' time King Rajas or his son produced a young woman, and said 'This is Filana, Arrabetta's great-granddaughter. She escaped the murderers' – the story would be more convincing if the body were not in the grave."

"Yes," said Soumaki slowly, "but -"

"But in that case would someone not have been wanting to

218

draw attention to her being missing early on? No one did, until you and I."

"If they drew attention to her being missing, there would have been a search. As there is now. Whoever removed the body would not want that, perhaps."

"Indeed. Perhaps. It still makes little sense."

*

20 October 570

Soumaki was out inspecting the roof of one of the outhouses, and Hassdan was listing the whereabouts, ages and possible disloyalties of Lord Gahran's more distant relatives, when he heard a dismayed noise outside the steward's room.

Captain Rabellit entered, looking grim. "Barad is back, Master Hassdan. He and Lakker have not found the child, but they found two of our soldiers killed. Anni and Josper."

Hassdan ran into the hall, where a tall, weary-looking soldier awaited him. "Barad? What did you see?"

"They were killed with a sword, it looked like. I left Lakker searching the area. The bodies had been dragged off the road, and covered with bracken. On the road to Stonehill, just within the border of Ferrodach lands."

"Meril? My squire?"

"We only found the two bodies, but I came straight back to tell you. There may have been more."

He saw Meril's proud eager face as she had ridden off. He pictured it turning to terror. *Dear God, not Meril. Mother Mary, St John, have mercy.* But two soldiers murdered – that was bad enough.

Pray later. Think now. "Fetch Mistress Soumaki," he ordered. "Barad, you need to rest and eat. And tell me everything."

An hour later, he walked into the steward's private chamber, and this time he was accompanied by Captain Rabellit, and he did not knock.

Hagouna had been sitting in the window, stitching at some embroidery. She scrambled to her feet, her face anxious, but he felt no sympathy.

"Have you found her?"

"I am not here to talk about Filana." He placed his hand on the hilt of his sword, but did not draw it. Not yet. "Eleven days ago, I sent a message to the King, with two soldiers and my squire, a girl of fourteen. You may remember her. Two of these three have been murdered, the third is missing, and so is the message." He stared at her as remorselessly as he could. As Dorac would have done. "I have every reason to suspect that someone in this house knows something about this crime, and I will act on that suspicion."

She swallowed. "No one here -"

"If you want me to believe that, you need to be more helpful. I have no time to waste. Tell me everything you know about the village of Saint's Rest."

Torio (10–17 October)

10 October 570

Torio had watched the last of the pen-pushers leave the room – fortunately they all seemed to want to attend Mass or run their little errands this morning – and then he stepped cautiously up to the door, knocked, waited and inserted his key. And the scriptorium, where dull secretaries scribbled and studied, and Kingsbrothers wrote reports, opened for him.

It was a long thin room with shelves up to the ceiling, and ladders to reach the higher ones, and candles everywhere to make up for the lack of daylight, but firmly fixed in sconces to avoid fire. And books. Laws of the Kingdom, commentaries on the Bible, lives of the saints, poetry about love – tedious. Tales of battles, histories of struggles for influence and authority, descriptions of far-off places and times – less so. Some day he would have time to read these.

A room which most Kingsbrothers, unlike him, did not appreciate. But today the books interested him less than the report that one of his more annoying siblings had almost certainly been writing that morning. If he was unlucky, it would already have been filed away, even locked in a drawer. But so far he had been lucky -

There were several tall desks, and each had its pile of parchments, some tidier than others. He started with the neatest pile and flicked through; then the second neatest. It was covered with a blank sheet, as if for temporary concealment. And sure enough -

Dorac's further evidence, given to me at the Old Stones, read Kai's easy untidy script on the page underneath.

Dorac's further evidence.

And still no one came in. Torio deftly snatched up a spare parchment and pen, sat down and started to write. He watched his hand copying fast and smoothly, intrigued by his own detached excitement. Rising, he knocked the little pile to the floor, picked it up and replaced it with a curse, and left the room. The scribbler Makkam was hurrying back towards it. He had seen her dressed up for Sundays and festivals, and she was not ugly, might be quite bearable naked if the insolence could be wiped off her. He did not think she had seen him leave, and so would not understand the triumph in his smile.

Arrogant bitch.

Alone in his cell, he carefully read the document.

-This is what Dorac says. However Arvill and I were lovers for a time last summer. I do not believe she is a person who would say anything she did not want to say.

Kai Kingsbrother

Torio chuckled at the thought of Kai having to present that last paragraph to the King. It was very pleasant to have outwitted Kai, who was so irritatingly, effortlessly liked, and had never had to pay a woman in his life.

And the others would think he had done well. He knew he had done well. He had no duties today, so he took the copy and his news promptly to his mother at her home on Little Church Street. Marbi praised him, as indeed she always did, but with even more than the usual fervour. And the next day he was invited to sup at Herion's house.

*

Gardai, leader of the Western Six, might suspect that Torio was going to a whorehouse rather than to his mother's as he claimed, but there was nothing he could do about that, and as stars were beginning to show, Torio dressed himself smartly, and passed through the Castle gates and into the town. He strolled down familiar streets, lit by occasional torches, enjoying being a Kingsbrother to whom people bowed respectfully, and checking now and again that he was not being followed. And so to Herion's.

There were two Torios. There was the one who fought and fucked and killed. His preferred places to be were a comfortable bed with a pretty and enthusiastic and docile woman - or a battlefield with a wet sword, and a dead enemy at his feet. Four so far. But there was the other Torio, the one who liked books, and Cathedral rituals, and understanding the ways of power. And for that Torio, Herion's house was his favourite place in the world.

Herion, son of Vestor, was the nephew and representative of Lady Karnall, legal head of the house of Aspella, and the first cousin of the managing head, her daughter Lady Rakall. (Torio had carefully learned the Latin terms *de jure* and *de facto*.) And in his own right Herion had considerable lands in the southeast, at Maint. But most of his time he lived in Stonehill, on King Tristar Street, near the city walls.

These were good houses, built of stone, four stories high. There were gardens at the back and glass windows upstairs. Glass downstairs would be too great a temptation for riff-raff. On the stone above the lintel was painted the first lord of Aspella, Feodor, who had lived two hundred and fifty years ago. He looked stern but calm, not unlike Herion in feature, but Herion's expression was normally more benevolent.

Torio was greeted at the door by the softly-spoken steward Attar, whose bland expression he never quite liked, dressed in Aspella green. As he was led to the stair, tossing his cloak to a servant, he caught a glimpse of a non-descript woman he recognised coming out of the kitchen. Her name was Sil, and he had gathered over the years that she went up and down the country on errands for Herion. Marbi had once said that she did not want to know what these errands were. Torio, on the other hand, was very curious.

He was ushered into the upper room with those windows, faintly perfumed candles, patterned blue and green carpet imported from the south decorating one wall, and painted woodland on the others. Here Herion greeted him warmly, in his usual unhurried manner, a well-built, well-fed man, with thick hair and beard of a mid-brown colour that was distinctive in Marod, and a ready smile. Some people who smiled a lot were taken advantage of, Torio had noticed, but Herion never was. People, the highest people, listened when he talked.

They ate relaxing on cushioned benches by the low table, in what was apparently the ancient Roman way, waited on with impeccable silent efficiency. The food – commencing with truffled larks – was not as good as feast-day fare at the Castle, but up to the regular standard, which meant that Herion ate as well as the King. And the service was quieter and more formal, and there was something about having all this courtesy, and a lute playing in the background, just for the two of them, that thrilled and expanded Torio, as indeed did Herion's presence, and this whole civilised and clean house. "Your swordplay is good, very good," Herion had said to him in this room. "Keep practising, and we may be able to get you into the Thirty." And so they had. Four years later, he was still not entirely sure who "we" were, but he knew that he was one of them, and that was enough.

So they ate, and made conversation about the inanities of the priest's homily at the Cathedral last Sunday, and the drunken antics of apprentices – "I chose this street for its quietness," said Herion ruefully – until supper was over, and his host dismissed the musician and other servants with a nod, and brought out a bottle of red wine from Tell in the south of Jaryar. "One of the better vineyards, so I am told by those who know," he said modestly. "But we are celebrating. Tell me."

"It was obvious, as we suspected, that the baby story was nonsense. If Kai's woman were with child, we would all know about it. And he'd brought the boy back, so he must've known where to find him." Torio tried to sound matter-of-fact, but could not keep the pride out of his voice.

"Yes. Our King's lies are usually more convincing than that." Herion smiled, and lifted his silver cup in a toast. "To your good work. Well done, indeed. You were quick, you were observant, you took all your opportunities, and now we know more than other people, which is always what we want." He glanced through Torio's copied writing again, and they shared a comfortable smile. "Poor Kai. He seems to think confession is good for the soul. It really isn't - but it's useful for other people. You have done very well, and I must find some way to express my gratitude."

"Thank you. Is it important, then?" Torio sipped his wine as his mother had taught him to, rather than gulping it as Maros or Saysh would have done.

"Saysh said Gemara was worried, and now we know why. We already knew that the Southern are a troublesome Six, always liable to meddle and waste everybody's time on nonsense. But now she has persuaded the King to assist them in their meddling. As if he had nothing more important to think about, but our King has his oddities, if one can say so without treason." He smiled again. "Almost certainly he's asked Hassdan and Soumaki to ask questions at Ferrodach that it would be better they didn't ask, and almost certainly he's going to make trouble for poor Kremdar. Which is undesirable for everybody. Did you say that Kai was off again?"

"Yes, he left this morning. The guards said he went southwest."

"Hmm. I would have expected him to be sent after Kremdar or Arvill. Now, as to your reward. My friend, the reward for doing a task well is to be given another one." He smiled at Torio again, and refilled his cup. The smoothness and richness of the wine was like drinking honey – but honey that tasted exotic and even sinister, as honey does not. "A few of the gatekeepers are susceptible to money. I will give you names. Offer them silver to bring you instant news of the comings and goings of the Southern Six. If Hassdan or Gemara or Soumaki or Kai ride home, I want you to know it at once, and to leave a message at a place I choose. If they send a letter, I want to know also. Letters from Hassdan and Soumaki in particular. Gemara is only judging, and I think we can manage Kai."

"If I had one of their seals, the guards could pass me a letter, and I could read it and re-seal it, and no one would know."

"Yes, but we must not expect miracles. Use your key with discretion. Not at night, for that would look very odd if you were seen. It is a pity it's usually occupied by day - Perhaps you can encourage one or two of the secretaries to cooperate - but do not be rash. It is important that no one knows you are interested in Ferrodach."

Torio had a question, but Herion went on. "I presume you have noticed the difficulty in this plan?"

"Whom do the guards report to when the King sends me away to judge or make war?"

"That's one way of putting it. Or, how do you avoid being sent away? I think you may have to have an accident, Torio, so that Gardai and the King allow you to stay in Stonehill."

"What kind of accident, sir?"

"Something that looks worse than it is. Attar will manage it. There will be a little pain, I fear, but I can rely on a Kingsbrother's courage. And nothing that need prevent you visiting Madam Leta's. How much does a night there cost these days? Or two nights?" He casually lifted a bag of coins onto the table. Madam Leta's was the best and most expensive place in Stonehill. Torio could rarely afford her prices, and tried to conceal his pleasure. *Pretty, enthusiastic, docile and skilled*. But he was also curious.

"And all I have to do is look out for the activities and letters of the Southern?"

"Look out thoroughly. I want to know as much as possible of

227

what they're doing, and reporting, and thinking. All at Aspella will be grateful. Talk to Saysh. It's not very likely that anyone has trusted him with anything, but it is possible. And he may have disreputable secrets of his own." Again they shared a smile. There were things that everyone knew about Saysh. "And meanwhile I shall send news of all this to our friends, praising you, you may be sure. Lady Karnall was most impressed by your quickness. And I'll have a little errand for Sil and her partner. You don't need to know about such things, but in due time, I may be able to tell you more. One day you may be giving such orders. Now, you look as if you had a question."

Very pleased, but still a little nervously, Torio asked, "What is it that they mustn't find out? What was wrong about Ferrodach? Who - who did kill the children?"

"Dorac killed the children. Brutal and loyal and stupid, but with just enough wit to understand that they were a danger. Of course he did."

"He swore to Kai that he did not."

"Naturally. He was saying farewell to his brother, whom he'll never see again. He's probably in love with him, like half of Stonehill. There are tales, you know, of what goes on in South Keep. Of course he swore. He's still as guilty as sin."

"And Lord Gahran?"

"Lord Gahran was slightly less guilty. Guilty enough, though: he deserved death, do not fear." He looked thoughtfully at Torio, who glowed in the calculation and respect in that look. "Gahran, son of Karac, son of Arrabetta: the grandson of a Queen. He thought that should matter, and perhaps it did, and he grew ambitious. Ambitious," he laid one finger on the table, "then treacherous," another finger, "then cowardly, and then - inconvenient." He smiled. "And then unlucky, because Lady Karnall and I do not permit people to be both treacherous and inconvenient. So, like his grandmother, he lost everything.

"He was guilty, Ferrodach is destroyed, we gain. We grow strong, with your help. It is sad about the children, but do not worry about Gahran. One part guilt, one part foolish cowardice, one part bad luck." He smiled again. One part compassion, one part triumph, Torio thought.

"More wine?"

*

There was pain, but Attar did his task well, and the foot was not actually broken. Torio had to endure a certain amount of impertinent teasing as to his carelessness, but being officially unable to ride or walk without crutches confined him safely to the city. He was surprised at how much he missed swordplay with his friend Prince Jendon. (The Prince had been born clumsy, and practised hard with Torio, Ralia and others to make up for it.)

But the nights at Madam Leta's were everything he had hoped for.

The guards Herion had mentioned were eager to help, but nothing much happened for some days. The fool Saysh had nothing to tell. No messages came from Ferrodach.

Then, six days after the supper, he learned that a letter had arrived from Gemara Kingsister in Lenchen.

Makkam and Gormad 1 (17–18 October)

17 October 570

When Makkam had been promoted to the rank of higher secretary, her friend Queen Malouri had said, "Remember, any dalliance with my husband, and I'll cut your toes off." Makkam had laughed, as she was meant to. Perhaps it was the first time she had laughed since the man she loved had been found beheaded with three others on a northern beach. The wedding had been five weeks away, Joseph was not a soldier, and they had thought the war could not touch them. Queen Malouri, on one of her regular retreats, had plucked her from the monastery where she had been drearily realising that a broken heart did not make a religious vocation, and brought her to Stonehill, and found her employment. It was kind of the Queen, who knew her mother, and so Makkam strove to adjust to city bustle, to do her duty and care about her work, and not to hate all men (or, more precisely, all young men) for being alive when Joseph was not. And two years on, she was made one of the inner circle of royal secretaries, and told not to flirt with her friend's husband.

But in fact her toes were quite safe. Makkam had no desire to dally with the King (or with anyone) and the King had shown no interest in her.

She had served him conscientiously (except for her tendency to doodle on parchment). She had prayed hard for his recovery when he was wounded and lost his arm. She respected him and obeyed him, and even admired him, but she was not sure how much she liked him. His sarcasm was too hurtful; his jokes could be too cruel. The meeting with Ramahdis, for instance. Ramahdis, who was now sitting in a dungeon -

And once she had been passing the royal bedchamber, and heard him calling his wife a "bloody obstinate bitch". As someone who had spent years, both as a child and since, in a monastery, Makkam was aware that her standards might be unreasonably prim. As a virgin, she had no right to judge other people's marriages. But still she loved Malouri, and she had been shocked.

Each of the higher secretaries had their own areas of secret responsibility. Dendarry had been Makkam's, until Mistress Gemara had paid her visit to the King, and she almost accidentally acquired another one. She was the only person outside the Thirty who knew of the forty days' enquiry - and sometimes she wondered why Mistress Gemara and Master Kai, and even King Arrion, seemed to think that Dorac might be innocent, against all the evidence, just because he said he was.

Early on Monday morning, a messenger arrived with a letter from Gemara Kingsister, and once the King and Queen had read it, they sent for Makkam.

15th day of October, 570

Gemara Kingsister to His Grace Arrion of the Marodi, greeting.

In haste. Kremdar has told me he must leave Lenchen at once, and visit his home. He has received news of murders there. He was agitated, and unlike himself. I will follow and try to understand. I have received Kai's letter. He should speak to Arvill, daughter of Eve.

I remain Your Grace's obedient servant and sister.

"Murders in – where is Kremdar's land? Gisren?" said the

King. "More murders?"

"Or more lies." The Queen tapped the letter thoughtfully, and handed it to Makkam.

She just had time to lock it away before attending Mass.

But the priest today introduced prayers in remembrance of the dead in the War from the Sea. She had thought she was at last healed, but it seemed she was not, and she slipped out early, and so came back down empty corridors to find Torio Kingsbrother turning a key in the lock.

"Sir? Master Torio?"

He jumped.

"May I help?"

"What are you doing here?" he demanded angrily. And then there was a gap in time when they stared at each other, seeming to share a confusion with the situation. "Beautiful Makkam," he said, bowing with an aggressive flourish, and hobbled away on his crutch.

Makkam's worst sins were an overly harsh assessment of people, and a tendency to bear grudges. She knew this well, and confessed it often, but alas improved little. Just as Kai was an unchaste young man, with a suspiciously pleasant smile (crinkling round the eyes), and Gemara was a dictatorial old woman, who rarely smiled at all, Torio was a bully, whose sneer somehow reminded her she was a bastard every time he looked at her. But all of them, she remembered firmly when she caught herself thinking these things, were brave loyal warriors whom she had no place criticising.

Still, as she re-lit candles and returned to her desk, she wondered a little about his behaviour. *What am I doing here? This is where I work. What are you doing here? Had he been turning a key? Why would he have a key to the scriptorium?* Torio did not often come down here (happily). She had not seen him in these corridors since - since Kai had been writing -

Kai Kingsbrother's report. Gemara Kingsister's letter. He had a key.

It was as if someone had hit her in the stomach. And the brain, at the same time. She felt for a bench and sat down slowly. She could not be thinking such a thing about one of the King's Thirty.

But she was.

She read and re-read it in her mind, and wondered if it were nonsense, and perhaps (probably?) it was. It was only her prejudice, making her think such things. Torio was an arrogant gutter-minded man whom she disliked, and so she was inventing crimes for him. How like her.

But if she was not inventing it, she must tell the King.

She must go to him at once, and tell him what would be very bad news. Which he might not believe. Which was (*perhaps, partly*) her fault.

Torio Kingsbrother is spying on the Ferrodach investigation.

And - very reluctantly - even if it were nonsense, that was for the King to decide.

She could speak to the Queen? But today it was the Queen presiding at the Monday audience, and after that she was riding out with Lord Vrenas and his lady. It had to be the King.

Makkam slowly stood up. Her legs were shaking. Then she sat down again. She could not go now, because that would leave the room empty with all its secrets, and he had a key. And also she must see the King alone. She was a secretary; she was entrusted with royal business, and called to secret meetings at the King's pleasure. She did not initiate secret meetings. Only the Thirty (or Lady Sada or the Marshal) did that. The Thirty had their watchword, which the higher secretaries and the most trusted servants knew, but did not themselves use.

The watchword was "fifteen".

I can't.

Makkam had watched men and women ride out to war, knowing they might never come back. Some had not come back. That was courage. And she did not dare to go to her master, and tell him of a problem. He had never been unkind to her, but she realised now that she was very afraid of him. As one should be, of a king.

*

She'd been summoned six days before, in the early afternoon. "Ramahdis of Dendarry has come. You are to go to the King in the Small Chamber, and bring the Dendarry papers." *Ramahdis of Dendarry!* She couldn't help feeling a flicker of excitement, which she tried to conceal the only way she knew how – with a rigidly severe countenance. She had gathered the documents (hoping she had not absent-mindedly drawn animals on any of them), and obeyed the summons.

"Your Grace, I can hardly express my gratitude," Ramahdis had said with pompous humility. He was a big bluff man with receding curly hair, and a face that was trying to be calmly confident. *It was such an extraordinary feeling,* Makkam thought, *and not a very charitable one, to be aware of what he was not aware of, of what was probably about to happen.* "To think that our son should have behaved so ungratefully – it has shocked me and his mother. I shall lose no time in removing him, and beg pardon for the trouble he has caused."

"There is no need for that. Your concern is most commendable, but Gormad has been punished for his escapade. In other respects, he is well spoken of. He has asked for a new lord, and with your permission, I shall look around for one."

"Your Grace is too good. But if I may be frank," (*Indeed!* thought Makkam scornfully) – "he was anxious to leave Dendarry, and clearly he only wanted to be free of the discipline of home. When he did not like the discipline required of a squire, he ran away. The trial has failed, and he will be better restrained back with his family."

"We all like him here," said the King mildly. "With your permission, I shall find him a new lord."

Ramahdis now seemed to understand. "But, Your Grace, I have not given my permission."

"But you will."

"Your Grace? Forgive me, but it does not seem wise to me. And he is *my* son."

"We both know that is not true."

Ah.

Ramahdis jerked. "Your – Your Grace is surely jesting. I have absolute confidence in my wife's honour," he said uncertainly.

"I'm sure you have, but he isn't your son. He is your sister's bastard, and you are a traitor."

Ramahdis goggled in horror – *like a frog*, Makkam thought, *except his mouth was too small. Concentrate!*

The King went on pitilessly. "For one thing, he is so much braver than you are. That must come from my side of the family.

"My brother told me about the delightful young lady –

Thahdi, wasn't it? He didn't mention the baby - but perhaps he never knew. And nobody at Dendarry considered it necessary to tell my parents about their latest grandchild. He was being brought up in your house, as your son.

"A royal bastard in the family is often very valuable, so I was puzzled that you wanted to keep his existence so secret. And then I spoke to a man called Desor, son of Shar, and I understood."

Ramahdis sank to his knees, his hands over his face. Makkam (pitying him after all) thought he might have been wise to have done this sooner.

There was a silence.

"This is what is going to happen now. You will go aside with Makkam here, and write and swear a full confession of all that has happened, or been *planned*, at Dendarry since Prince Rafad tumbled your sister. Make sure to include a list of everyone who knows about the matter – those you told, or those who found out in any other way. I will then compare it with the names I already have, so it had better be complete." (As far as Makkam was aware, he had no such information.) "You will write to your wife, and explain that you are unavoidably detained in Stonehill. Then you can see Gormad, and tell him you are happy for him to stay here – where I can keep an eye on him – without telling him why. Do you understand?"

Ramahdis understood, and this indeed was what happened. No one, except perhaps young Gormad, seemed to notice anything amiss in his manner.

Makkam's duties and privileges did not include visiting the Castle dungeons, where she supposed Ramahdis was sitting, waiting for the King to decide what fate he deserved. And ever since then, whenever she saw Gormad in the corridors, she went a little cold inside, because he thought his father had ridden off home, and this was not the case.

*

One should be afraid of a king. And she was.

I can't do this. Dear Saviour.

The other secretaries returned from the chapel, so it was safe to leave. Makkam walked slowly to the door, and slowly along the passage. She remembered where he was; she came to the room, lifted her hand to knock - and walked away. *Coward.* She needed something (or someone) to make her.

A tall pile of linen was marching towards her, with a mass of curly hair on top. "Gormad?"

*

Gormad was a squire with an inattentive mistress, and thus, much of the time, he was "an idle boy hanging about". Anyone – almost anyone – could demand assistance or work from him. Some of the better-born squires resented this rule, and were careless or sullen in their obedience, but Gormad had noticed that Marrach and Dorac and Kai had always been reasonably courteous to common folk, and it was them he wanted to copy.

In any case, he would not have dared to be rude to Secretary Makkam. He was carrying a pile of precariously balanced laundry along a passage when she suddenly called his name, and he almost dropped it.

Makkam put out a steadying hand. "What are you doing?"

"I've to take this to the wardrobes upstairs, madam."

"Can you come back here afterwards?"

"Of course, madam."

When he returned, she was pacing up and down. "Will you do something for me? Just walk with me to – to the Willow Chamber, and wait for me outside. I will not be long."

"Yes, madam. Should I carry that for you?" Surely the only reason for her to need company was to carry things, but her bundle was not large, and Makkam said no. Or could she be afraid of being attacked? That was even more absurd. But she did look nervous as she walked along clutching her documents. On one parchment, to Gormad's amusement, was a little pig, drawn in a corner away from the official writing. He could not believe it had any proper business on her document, or anywhere in the Castle.

Outside the Willow Chamber, they stopped. "Wait. Try to look as if you ought to be here," said Makkam, her voice almost hoarse. She cleared her throat and went in. He waited, out of place, rather like the pig. There were voices.

"My friend Karnall tells me you have been calling on her with Ralia, Jendon." Were they Lady Sada's gruff tones? "That is very kind. Confined as she is, she appreciates -"

Makkam's voice squeaked. "My apologies for interrupting, Your Grace, but perhaps you could look at these. Page fifteen, in particular."

"Hmm?" The King. "I don't have time this morning. Put them somewhere, Li."

And Makkam was out again, without her papers, and looking more frightened than ever. "Thank you. You can go," she said, and walked away while he was still bowing.

Grown-up people were very odd.

*

Makkam sat at her desk, shaking and dizzy, until the servant Li came to tell her to go to the Small Chamber. Chief Secretary Andros raised a curious eyebrow, but said nothing.

The King was sitting at a table alone, and he did not look happy. A stern face, with a touch of disgust. "Makkam. When did I appoint you to the Thirty?"

She wondered if she should be on her knees. *Like Ramahdis, who might even be dead.* "I ask your pardon, Your Grace. I wanted to speak to you."

"And so?" He tilted his head impatiently. She took a deep breath.

"Your Grace. The day that Kai Kingsbrother returned from the Old Stones, he mentioned seeing his brother Torio. The next day he wrote his report, and letters to the others in the Six, and left them with me in the scriptorium. I went to find a messenger for the letters, and I locked the door, but I left the report on my desk.

"When I came back, Torio was in the passage. I went into the room, which was empty, and I think – I am sure – that my papers had been disturbed, or rearranged. I did not say anything at the time.

"Then, this morning, you received Mistress Gemara's letter. I left chapel early, and I found Master Torio trying to open the door. I am sure he was. He seemed to have a key. I spoke to him, and he looked angry at being disturbed, and went away. He gave no reason for his presence. He does not normally come near the scriptorium."

That was all.

The King said slowly, "You left a paper on a desk. And you object to where my brother chooses to walk in the Castle."

"I think he is looking for information about Ferrodach, Your Grace."

"Ferrodach has nothing to do with the Western Six."

"No, Your Grace. "

A pause. "So you think his interest is suspicious."

"I – I don't know."

"That is what you are suggesting. Do you like Torio, Makkam?"

"I know no evil of him."

"That was not my question."

"I do not like him very much."

"So you invent lies about him."

"No," she whispered.

"Three years ago, Torio, son of Izzan, took a solemn oath to be loyal to me and the Queen, though it cost him his life. He is my brother. You have taken no such oath. Why would he break it?"

"I don't know."

There was no trace of kindness in his face. He stood up, and turned his back to her. "You may consider the very serious things you have accused him of. Then, if you wish, you may decide that these are without foundation, and leave. We will forget this conversation, and you will lock secret papers away more carefully in future."

Dear Saviour. Help me.

When he turned back, she was still there.

"I may be mistaken in my conclusions," Makkam managed to say. "But what I said was true, and I thought it not right."

"Do you still think so?"

Dear Saviour. "Yes."

"You come to me with these wild allegations, or perhaps spiteful lies, and you expect me to trust you, rather than my brother's oath and love?"

"Your Grace, I have never given you reason to call me a liar!" She tried to meet his gaze steadily, and could not.

"Until today. Get out, Makkam. Come back when the bell rings at noon."

*

When she came back – and how she longed not to have to – the King was not alone. Queen Malouri was sitting on the other side of the room. Neither of them was smiling.

"Makkam," said the King, "put your hand on the reliquary." Her heart thumped. It was a wooden box, decorated with gold and pearls. She knew what was inside it.

"Can you swear on the holy things that Kai's report had been moved or interfered with?"

She hesitated, her hand clammy on the box. "I cannot swear that it had been. Only that I think so."

"Can you swear that you told me the truth this morning?"

"Yes. I swear."

"Very well. Tell the Queen what you told me."

He had plainly told the Queen already, as she showed no surprise. When she had finished, King Arrion said to his wife, "So

Makkam is lying, or she is mistaken, or Torio has a key that he should not have, and is meddling where he has no business." His voice was grim.

"Yes. And although she might be mistaken about the report, and even about the key, if he had a good reason for wanting access to the scriptorium, he should have said so and sought her help. Why would he not?" She stood up, frowning, and turned away.

"You understand," said the King, turning back to Makkam. "Gahran writes treasonable letters to the King of Jaryar, and that is only him and his people, and King Rajas. As far as we know. Which is ill news enough. Dorac kills the children, and that is only Dorac. Or perhaps Kremdar and Arvill killed them, but that is only Kremdar and Arvill. But this - if Torio is spying on this investigation, he cannot be alone. This is a conspiracy. An unknown group of people, doing unknown things for an unknown purpose. And some or even all of these people are our brothers and sisters.

"I hope you can understand why this thought made me a little harsh this morning."

"Your Grace." She always forgot to give him credit for this: he apologised.

"Torio. Why Torio? Is he reporting to the Jaryari? He has no connections to Jaryar. He comes from the east.

"He has read Kai's report. He was interested in Gemara's letter. That means he – or his masters – have some concern in Ferrodach that we do not know. He read Kai's report, but not Gemara's."

"He may have read Gemara's," said the Queen. "Makkam saw

him at the door, but he might have just come out."

Makkam gasped.

"True. He knows we – I – am not satisfied with the story. He seems to want to know of anything the Southern Six do."

"And somehow he has a key to the scriptorium."

"Yes. So," said the King, "one of the secretaries carelessly mislaid her key, so the lock needs to be changed. And if anyone enquires, Makkam, the careless secretary is you."

She nodded, feeling this was just.

"But how did he know there was a letter today? The gatekeepers know. They look out for messengers with the seals of the Thirty. So someone should talk to them. Someone we can trust." Something about his voice made Makkam shiver.

"His injury," she said suddenly. "Your Grace, his injury means he stays in Stonehill, and has not been sent to the west."

"Yes. Yes. The injury that happened when? Just after Kai came back. I can ask Master Gardai about that. If I trust Gardai."

"Can you not question Master Torio?" Makkam asked tentatively.

"Can I ask my brother if he is spying on me, because one of my secretaries saw him in a passage? No, I cannot. I cannot arrest him or question him or treat him as suspect in any way, without much firmer evidence. I hope you are wrong, Makkam. I will ask one of the guards to keep an eye on him from a distance, perhaps, but not to follow him about. Besides, we don't want these people to realise we know anything about them. And we know practically nothing. Who are they, and what do they want?"

Queen Malouri had withdrawn from the conversation, and stood staring out of the window. Now she said suddenly, "What do they want? What have they *achieved?*"

"Go on," said the King.

"There was a letter accusing Gahran, and he and the children are dead. Some or all of that may have been planned. What it achieved was, first, the destruction of the Ferrodach estate. We have split it up into three."

"Makkam, do you have parchment?"

"Yes, Your Grace." *A secretary without parchment is as useless as a well without a bucket*, as the saying went.

"Make a list of people, and look for connections between them. Dorac, Kremdar, Arvill, Braf, Gahran, his late wife, Torio; then those who benefited, Lady Rakall and Lord Jovian of Aspella, Lady Orria of Sparat - and whoever is Gahran's next heir."

"That would be me," pointed out Queen Malouri, as Makkam scrawled furiously.

"Yes, but when we said the family could keep a third we weren't intending you to take it. Any surviving members of Arrabetta's line, then. Your sister, who doesn't like me."

"But also," the Queen went on, "there were the murders. The result of those was that Dorac was exiled. And Saysh was appointed to his place."

"We suspect Saysh? Wait, though. He was not the obvious choice. Makkam, add Saysh, but also the other names we considered. Lady Sada suggested Ralia of course, and – who were the other names? Helena, daughter of Sibel, and -"

"Captain Renatar."

"Yes, him. Is there anyone else who may be connected? Makkam?"

"I was wondering" – she had already dared so much – "Master Dorac said he told Lady Kara about Kremdar and Arvill, and she ignored it."

"Yes, add Kara."

"Your Grace, what am I looking for?"

"Any connection between any of these people. Are they related, do they owe each other money, are their lands close together – Dorac had an estate at Valleroc which I took from him, and haven't yet given to anyone else – do they enjoy the same pastimes, have they quarrelled, do they go to the same whorehouses -?"

"Torio goes to whorehouses, I understand," said the Queen. "Perhaps we could find out something there. I hear no one gossips more than whores and squires."

"*I* hear that the best whores know that their customers value discretion," responded the King. "Squires, on the other hand -" He suddenly grinned. "Do you think young Gormad would like to help?"

Makkam was leaving with her head dizzier still, and her list tightly gripped in her fingers, when the King said, "Makkam. Do not pretend to be a member of the King's Thirty again. My aunt was most uncomplimentary about your presumption, and you do not want to annoy Lady Sada. Why could you not have spoken to my wife?"

"I thought she was riding out with Lord Vrenas and Lady Yolu."

"I am. They are waiting for me. Well, if Makkam is not in the

Thirty, and she needs to speak to us, what should she say?"

"A new watchword, for secretaries with secrets. You could say
_."

"You could say, 'The Queen is wondering how much longer
you are going to be?'" suggested his wife with a smile. The King looked
at her reproachfully. (Makkam realised abruptly how wrong she had
been about them. She would be thirty in a few weeks' time, and a sick
jealousy stabbed her for what she would never have.) "Mention
'Monday', in memory of today," he said. "Now go."

*

18 October 570

The day after Secretary Makkam had asked Gormad to walk to the
Willow Chamber, a servant stopped him on his way out of the Great
Hall, and sent him to her again. She looked serious, but less upset than
before, and smiled at him. "Come with me, please." They climbed one
of the back stairs to a room Gormad had never been in. There was a
guard outside, but inside there was only Queen Malouri, sitting with a
large book in front of her. She closed it as they entered, and he bowed
nervously.

"This is the boy."

"Yes, I know. Gormad, son of Ramahdis. Gormad, are you a
loyal servant of the King?"

*Why did everyone ask him that? Did he have a sign on his forehead
saying POSSIBLE TRAITOR?* But she was smiling.

"Yes, Your Grace."

"And would you like to do something that might help Master
Dorac and Master Kai?"

"*Yes*, Your Grace."

And so he was given his mission. He and Jamis were to learn anything they could about Master Torio, and notice his actions. Not follow him around, or annoy him, just find things out quietly. Bring news to Makkam.

"Is that clear?"

He supposed his instructions were clear. The reasons for them he would probably never know. He felt very honoured, but also a little cross.

*

Jamis was entirely thrilled. They crept out to Gormad's place under the bushes, and debated what Torio's crime could be. He must be a criminal, gleefully shocking though that was. Gormad wriggled with frustration at not being able to mention Lord Gahran's children – *how could Torio have killed them? He had not been there. Perhaps he had paid a poor scoundrel, one of the "scum without loyalty or honour" that his mother talked about, to do it for him.* Jamis thought he might be planning to kill the King, or kidnap Princess Daretti and force her to marry him, "like that ballad, you know, the 'blood and sorrow, tum te tum' one." "Or he could be a spy for Jaryar or Haymon. But how can a Kingsbrother be a spy? He doesn't have a foreign accent."

They felt no regret at thinking evil of Torio, who was well known for being "high-stomached", as the squires called it. He would push, swear at or insult anyone he thought beneath himself. Like servants, swordless commoners, or children.

But that night Gormad thought about the oath of the King's Thirty, inscribed on the wall of the Castle chapel, and he shuddered. If

Torio was a murderer or a spy, he had terribly broken that oath. And that did shake the world. A little bit.

*

Makkam knew what it was like to have no one to talk to, and the Queen had agreed to her suggestion that Gormad be allowed to involve his friend in his enquiries. But it was not clear how much information the squires could provide.

Makkam had her list, and she began searching the scriptorium library. Records of charters, land sales, genealogies. Uneasily she felt that this was not going to be enough. She needed to talk to people and hear gossip, and so she began to spend less time in the chapel and the scriptorium and her small rented room near the Wide Gate, and more in the Great Hall and the courtyard, trying to remember how to be sociable and friendly, something she had never been skilled at. (She had not been looking forward to that part of being a priest's wife, seven years ago.)

In fact, people were quite endurable, but they were not talking much about Torio, or indeed any of the names on her list. They were talking about the latest arrivals for the King's Gathering at the end of the month, and their thankfulness for a good harvest, and their individual quarrels. But some of them were talking, a little worriedly, about the Dream.

Fifty or so years ago, King Asatan of Jaryar had had a dream. The same dream (so it was said) three nights in succession. So he had consulted priests and judges, and then had had the dream written down and proclaimed throughout his realm. Copies had also been sent, with a polite letter, to all the other kings and queens on Ragaris, and the higher bishops.

He had seen a bright shining light in the shape of a man. Plainly an angel (the interpretation said). "Watch and remember. This is for your children," he was told. He had been lifted up and carried on the wind over the lands and mountains, from Derbo to Tell, all the west of the continent of Ragaris, and the message was clear.

And that was why the kings of Jaryar had the words *Overlord of the West* on their coins. In the expectation that God would give it to them.

Or perhaps they could just take it.

("Would it be bad to be part of Jaryar?" Makkam, aged ten, had asked – and was whipped for treason and impertinence.)

In the east, the rulers of Ricossa, larger and richer than Jaryar (and not included in the angel's bounty), could afford to smile. The people of Marod, Haymon, Baronda and Falli could not. The Queen of Falli had indeed commented, "When I eat too much cheese, I dream of naked men and giant lobsters, which is far more entertaining." King Lukor of Marod reacted more practically by marrying his daughter and heir Darisha to a Fallian prince to build up northern solidarity, and even tried unsuccessfully to extend the alliance to the fiercely independent people of Baronda. The King of Haymon acknowledged Jaryar as his overlord, and the others did not, and there were border skirmishes, and the more serious War of the River, and more recently bitter suspicions (almost certainty) that the Jaryari had encouraged Baronda in the War from the Sea. But mostly there was an uneasy peace.

Until King Rajas promised the throne of Marod to Gahran of Ferrodach.

How many of the people on her list could be reporting to Rajas?
Makkam wondered. Others had similar thoughts. "Hassdan
Kingsbrother was born Jaryari", she heard someone speculate quietly at
supper in the Castle, "and so were Evda and Jos the goldsmiths. Who's
to say what side they're on? And that's where Dorac's gone to, you can
be sure."

Gardai Kingsbrother of the Western Six rose in majestic
wrath, and forced the speaker at knife point to retract the slander on
Hassdan, but what you force people not to say they can still think.

Sometimes, terrifyingly in the night, Makkam felt that the
King had entrusted her, without meaning to, with the fate of the realm.
This was absurd presumption indeed, and she tried to laugh at herself.
She distracted herself with thoughts of the other task he had given her,
and had perhaps forgotten about.

Kai 1 (11–15 October)

At the last minute, Kai had added Dorac's sword to his luggage, although South Keep was a little – more than a little – out of his way. He had promised to deliver the sword - and more importantly it occurred to him that someone should speak to Laida.

Or possibly he was just postponing his meeting with Arvill.

Each Six had a Keep, and each Keep had a small garrison of soldiers.

Of course every lord or lady had armed retainers to guard them and keep order in their lands, and every lord owed service to the king in the form of armed men or (less commonly) women. Nominally, and in times of emergency – in other words, war – the crown could call on them all. But most of the time the king and his Thirty relied on these tiny garrisons, and on the troops supported by the Kingslands, the estates around the city managed by the Warden. The post of Warden was not hereditary, but it was always someone closely akin to the monarch, and was currently King Arrion's ancient and redoubtable aunt, the dragon Lady Sada. Arvill and Braf were Kingslands soldiers, as Dorac and many others of the Thirty had been once, and so could be sent anywhere.

Otherwise, there were the Keeps. Here twice a year were the People's Meetings – not held inside the Keep, where there would have been no space, but on the hill or plain or square outside. There, under the leadership of the regional lords, anyone could gather and debate and question local issues – or bigger ones. The lords and ladies governed

251

the meetings and made the decisions, but they did so knowing that four or five of the Six were watching and listening, and ready to report to the king. Sometimes the king or queen themselves attended, but even when they did not, the Kingsbrothers and Kingsisters were trusted to bring them word of what their people thought. 'The king trusts the Thirty, and the Thirty trust the king. The people trust the Thirty, and the Thirty listen to the people.' Or so it was said.

None of the Keeps were beautiful or comfortable buildings – they were built strictly for utility. Kai's life there had been as austere and dull as a Sunday in Lent for four-and-a half years. He rode up to the simple square stone tower, three storeys high, with stables to one side, and was pleased that he was noticed and challenged as he dismounted. "Stop. What is your name and – oh, Master Kai!"

"Kai Kingsbrother, on the King's service."

"Welcome, most welcome." Captain Dakos, who had been Kai's second-in-command, looked a little nervous. "I hope you are here to sleep? Arran, take Master Kai's horse."

"Thank you. One night only, if you would be so good as to feed and house me and Diana, and tell me the news. I'm on my way to the Haymon border."

So he shared an awkward and gloomy supper with Dakos and the others, sitting round the fire outside under the dark cloudy sky – awkward and gloomy because of the disgrace Dorac had brought on the Southern Six, which was naturally felt at their Keep. As soon as was decently possible, Kai stood up, thanked his host and said, "Laida, I have something to deliver upstairs. Can your captain spare you for a short time?"

Inside the tower was a square room, with a ladder to a trapdoor. Above that were the sleeping quarters partitioned between the sexes, and another ladder to the storeroom. Nothing had changed in seven years. They climbed in silence. At this time of year there was not a great deal stored there; that would change soon with preparations for winter. But there was a chest of items, mostly memorabilia belonging to the Six, past and present. When Laida had lit a candle for him, Kai wrote out a docket on a piece of parchment, wrapped it in a cloth with the sword, and placed it in the chest, and Laida brought him a book to enter it.

"Laida," he said. "You heard about the trial."

"Yes." She sounded a little annoyed to have missed it.

"Why were you sent here from Ferrodach?"

"I don't know. Master Kremdar sent me. He said the Keep needed to be at full strength in case the Jaryari attack. It felt like a punishment. Not quite fair."

"A punishment for what?"

She did not look him in the eye. "I couldn't have known Lord Gahran would take poison! I couldn't have guessed."

"No, I suppose not. Tell me what happened."

She snuffled defensively. "He came into his chamber, and went and prayed in the corner, and then sat down and wrote something at his desk, and then I think he prayed again and – he walked over to the window, and suddenly he -" She leaned forward, hugging herself as they knelt beside the chest.

"He did what?"

"He gasped, and I looked over, and he was falling, and

reaching for the bed. He just fell to the ground, and choked, and his face went all purple. He looked frightened." Her voice was small. "I called out, and Anni came in, and we tried to lift him up, but he – jerked and died. So we put him on the floor, and Anni ran for help."

"Kremdar and Dorac and Arvill?"

"Yes."

"And the bottle?"

"He dropped it when he turned round, and I picked it up. The stopper had fallen on the floor. The bottle smelt foul – like garlic but stronger."

Kai knew little about poisons, and longed for Soumaki. He thought back. "You looked over when he fell. What had you been looking at before?"

"I didn't know he would do that! I didn't keep my eyes on him every moment. I was standing by the door looking round the room – such a grand room, with pictures on the *ceiling*."

That sounded like Laida. "You said he was writing. What was he writing?"

"I don't know. Something on a piece of parchment."

"But did you read it afterwards? What happened to it?"

"I don't remember seeing it. I don't know."

"This writing disappeared? No one mentioned it at the trial."

"Well, I didn't see it or steal it. I don't see that I was to blame."

"Did he say anything to you? Anything at all?"

"Not one word. He looked sad."

"Did Dorac say anything about the children? Did anyone?"

"No. He just went out."

Kai supposed he had finished, but the missing parchment chafed at his brain. "When Dorac left you in the room, after he and the others went out, did you look around at all?" *Find anything hidden on the body,* was what he really wanted.

"No, when I came back I stood as far away -"

"You came *back?*"

Suddenly Laida looked so guilty that he remembered an earlier question that had not quite been answered. "What did you do?" he demanded sternly.

"He was dead, Master Kai! He was only just dead, and his ghost might have – I couldn't bear it, and I went out after the others, and stood on the gallery -"

"What gallery?"

"The gallery above the hall."

Kai struggled to remember the plan of the house at Ferrodach. "There was a gallery above the hall at one end," he said slowly, "above the room where the children were put."

"Yes, I stood there, and watched Master Dorac and the others cross the hall, and he had his sword drawn, and he must have been planning to do it -"

"You saw Dorac and Kremdar and Arvill cross the hall and go into the space between two rooms, under the gallery?"

She nodded.

"And then what did you see?"

"The guard came out and walked away, and a little later Master Dorac came out and walked away, and I was thinking I should go back in case he came up and caught me, and - I wandered up and down a bit - and then Master Kremdar came out, and looked round, and he saw me. He was very distressed, of course; he'd just found them. But I didn't know that. I went back to the body. He was angered with me afterwards -"

"He was angered with you, and sent you to South Keep."

Laida nodded.

Kai looked at his hands, and saw they were trembling. No one had asked Laida any of this before. "You saw Dorac walk away after he had killed the children? Do you remember how he looked?"

*

12–14 October 570

So he rode on the next day, with Laida's sworn statement in his satchel. "Evidence, even just evidence that means something to me," he had said to Gormad, and now he had it.

He rode and rode, and the first night he camped alone, but the second and third nights the weather was so wet and blowy that he exercised the privilege of the Thirty to shelter at farmhouses. He offered to pay, but the offer was declined, as usual – although a little less readily than before his brother had murdered children. People sounded polite rather than pleased at the name Kingsbrother these days.

He rode through wind and rain for three days, enduring ice-cold trickles down his back, gusts of water in his face, and angry snorts from Diana, and he had plenty of time to think: never his favourite occupation. Time to ponder Laida's statement, and to wonder if he'd found out all he could. How nearly he had missed the vital piece! He had time to miss and mourn Karila – independent, brisk, beautiful Karila. He had time also to feel for Dorac, and to wonder how long his friend could possibly stay out of trouble in a strange land.

And to think about Kremdar. Kai loved and respected all his siblings in the Six, and would have trusted any one of them with his life. But when it came to companionship, there was no denying that Gemara was sharp-tongued and impatient, and Dorac was taciturn and unsympathetic, and Soumaki's conversation was largely domestic, and you never knew what Hassdan was thinking. But Kremdar was good company. Kremdar would drink with you and laugh at your jokes and lend you money if you needed it, as Kai all too frequently did. His courage was legendary and infectious, an inspiration to lesser brethren. To think of Kremdar the way he was now thinking of him was hard.

But most of all he thought about Arvill.

*

"I'd annoyed him somehow – I don't remember exactly how, but I was an impertinent boy – and he took me down to the stream – said he was going to teach me how to fish. And he said, 'You're an insolent brat, Kai, aren't you?' and pushed my head under the water." He paused to breathe. Arvill was silent. "I was certain I was going to die. And then he pulled me out, and said, 'Very insolent', and did it again." *And again, and again. One of the Thirty is afraid of deep water.*

They had been sitting, he and Arvill, under the trees on the banks of a slow-moving river, on a bakingly hot June Sunday, eating fresh bread and strawberries, and drinking cheap wine. Discovering that neither of them had any desire to attend Mass at the Cathedral had drawn them together, and inspired the outing. He was wondering whether she liked him as much as he liked her, and hoping she did, and they were talking, and somehow he found himself telling her about the most terrifying experience of his childhood.

"How old were you?" she asked gently.

"Nine. One of the servants heard the noise we were making, and called my father. And my sister cried for a week, and never spoke to Harv again. And found a better sweetheart a few years later."

She was stroking his palm, tickling.

"So that's why I still don't truly like rivers. This one is pretty, I will concede."

And they went on talking, and tickling, but a little later – surely his memory was right, and it *was* the same day – she wandered a few steps away, and balanced on an overhanging root over the water, looking back at him mischievously, and he was trying not to say, "Be careful", when she slipped, or jumped, and screamed, and went straight in.

The water was slow, and not deep, and neither of them were in any danger, but Arvill was soaked from head to foot, and Kai nearly so by the time both were back on the bank. "What the hell were you doing? What the *hell?*"

"I knew you'd save me," she said, her eyes big and bright. "I'll have to take this shirt and hose off, I think." And suddenly she was kissing him, and sliding her hand between his legs, and equally suddenly Kai was fumbling with her laces, and his only coherent thought was to hope that no one would choose to wander by for half an hour or so.

No one did come by, and it was some time before their clothes were dry enough to put back on.

It occurred to him later, of course, that she really hadn't needed to ruin two sets of garments in order to seduce him that day. A simple "Shall we -?" would have been enough. But that, he learned, was Arvill. Unpredictable, infuriating, irresistible Arvill.

He had to get the truth out of her. Whatever the truth was.

He thought about Arvill until it became a torment. Arvill pulling faces to make him laugh in church, so that Gemara and Hassdan glared at him. Arvill rolling about on the floor to entertain young Edric, who adored her, although Mritta did not. Arvill undressing with a mock shyness that drove him wild. Arvill listening raptly to every detail of his life, knowing exactly when to sympathise and when to distract. (Kai was always easy to distract.)

Arvill, exactly the same height as him, which meant tall for a woman. Sleek black hair, which she cropped short, and often wore daringly bareheaded, in defiance of convention. Arvill with her kind heart and mischievous eyes and fascinating dimples. If Arvill instead of Kremdar had told the story of Ferrodach, would he have been less likely to believe Dorac?

Arvill, daughter of Eve, wearing her bastardy with a defiant openness that had touched his heart from the first, and made it impossible, for him anyway, to probe for inevitably hurtful details.

Now he realised, perhaps rather belatedly, that her attention might not have been as sincere and flattering as he had thought. What secrets had he told her? What kind of a fool had he been?

He thought of Arvill in bed with Kremdar, and did not like the thought, and did not like himself for not liking it. It occurred to him that when he had seen her lately, her head, when not helmeted, had been covered by a decorous kerchief. Perhaps that was Kremdar's influence: an unpleasant idea.

Kai was thirty-two, and not the youngest of the Six – Kremdar and Soumaki and now Saysh were all younger – but he had somehow always felt the junior, the boy among adults. Now he had to grow up, as they kept telling him to do. He had to do the task he was entrusted with.

Was the King expecting him to torture her?

He knew two things for certain about Arvill – that he still found her intensely desirable; and that she was cleverer than him.

It rained and it rained.

*

15 October 570

The Kingslands troops were billeted in various villages along the borders with Haymon and Falli, and it took Kai a little while to identify the right one. At noon, however, he presented himself to a Captain Garnoch, and after the normal greetings and pleasantries said, "I have to talk urgently with two of your soldiers – Arvill and Braf."

"You won't be able to talk to Braf. He's dead."

Kai stared. "How did that happen?"

"Two nights ago. He was out drinking, and it seems he stumbled into the river on his way home." Seems.

"Do you think he did not 'stumble'?" asked Kai cautiously.

"Braf did drink; he was careless. To be truthful, it may indeed have been an accident. There was no sign of violence or robbery. But some of the soldiers are saying – begging your pardon, Master Kai – that your former brother might have followed us here."

"You think Dorac killed him?"

"They say he was swearing revenge at his trial."

Kai had excellent reasons for believing that Dorac was several days' journey to the southeast. But if you didn't know that, the theory was plausible. "Braf had little evidence to give. It was Kremdar he'd want vengeance on, if anyone. Maybe Arvill."

"Yes, indeed. Arvill puts a brave face on, she always does, but I think she's nervous."

"I need to talk to her," Kai said, setting aside this mystery for the moment. "In private."

This was difficult in a village of tiny homes, but at last he was offered the church. He had a table and two stools brought, stationed soldiers outside, and asked Captain Garnoch to send for her. While he waited, he took off his still dripping cloak and lit extra candles, the better to see her face and reactions. The rain pounded down outside, and the nave was dreary in shadow.

She came in, and he was slammed with a longing for her so intense that he almost gasped. He wondered if she knew exactly how much he wanted to pull off her clothes right now. In church. Probably. Arvill always knew.

But she came towards him with hands outstretched, sympathy radiating from her like sunlight, saying, "Kai. It's good to see you. I'm so sorry – it must have been terrible for you about Dorac."

"Yes," said Kai briefly, and indicated that she should sit down opposite him. Then he took a deep breath and said, "I need to talk to you about Ferrodach."

"Is there anything more to say about it?"

261

"About whether your adultery with Kremdar influenced your evidence."

"My what?"

"I'm here to talk to you about that."

Arvill's eyes glittered with anger. "You're here to ask me if I've been lying with your brother? Is that the kind of mission the King sends you on, or was it your own idea?"

That hurt, a lot. He said, "I know you are lovers."

"We are not."

"You are. There are witnesses."

"Ooh, witnesses!" exclaimed Arvill. "Peeping in my window to watch me in bed – is that what you do?"

"I've spoken to people."

"You've spoken to Dorac, perhaps? He hates me, he always did. You remember that."

No, it was Arvill who had never liked Dorac, he remembered. *And that it had always puzzled him.*

"I've spoken to people in Oyster Alley where you used to meet. You're lying about that, and you're lying about Ferrodach. I've also spoken to Laida."

"Who's Laida?"

"Laida is the soldier who found Lord Gahran dead. She was watching from above as Dorac crossed the hall, after you said he killed the children. He was not distraught, and he was not bloodstained. He took off his cloak as he walked away, and there was no blood on it. You and Kremdar were lying, and you have to tell me *now.*"

"You believe this Laida? You've put together a horrible story

262

– adultery and murder, is that it? And you want it to be about me? Do I have to tell you that's not true, Kai?"

"It is true. Stop playing games. The landlord of The Shells and Bells – do you want to be on trial, with him telling a court what you and Kremdar -"

"You enjoyed questioning him, did you?"

He actually had to shut his eyes for a moment so as not to see the contempt in hers. "We can sit here until tomorrow morning," he said at last, "but you are going to tell me."

Arvill was very still. Then she took a deep breath, and put her hands palms down on the table, spreading the fingers and staring at them. Her lovely hands, slender-fingered, the colour of brown egg-shells. *Good enough to eat,* he used to say. He held his breath. At last she said quietly, "Yes."

"Yes, what?"

"Yes, we have committed adultery. Yes, we've met many times, in Oyster Alley and other places. *Yes*, I love him." She looked up defiantly, but there were tears in her eyes.

"And 'yes, you lied about Ferrodach'?"

A pause. "Yes. But only a little. It didn't make any difference."

"How can you say that?" Kai exclaimed.

"Dorac killed the children. We just - we only changed things a little."

"What things?"

Arvill shook her head.

"Arvill, I'm here to arrest you for adultery and bearing false witness. It'll be worse for you if you don't tell me the whole truth *now*."

263

"Will it be worse for Kremdar?"

"I don't know. That depends what the truth is. But you have to tell me."

Tears were trickling down Arvill's cheeks. "We meant to act for the best, Kai. We did. Very well. I'll tell you everything.

"I met Kremdar – well, of course, I'd met him before when I was with you, but I met him properly about a week after Easter. We were both in a tavern one night when some fools got rowdy, and we helped the host throw them out, and Kremdar bought me a drink, and we talked. And - we just went on talking. We talked for hours. Then we met again two nights later, and we - didn't just talk.

"You must understand he was very lonely. He sees so little of Yaina and Praja; he loves Yaina so much. I suppose I was lonely too." She slid a look at him. "I know it was sin, but it didn't feel like sin. It felt as if everything was suddenly right.

"We were happy to be sent to Ferrodach together, although of course it was awkward – we couldn't do anything on the journey. We had to be discreet. And he told me – Kai, you weren't at the trial, were you? Have you read the evidence?"

Kai nodded.

"He did tell me that Dorac said it might be necessary to kill the children. He was very distressed. 'He wouldn't do that, he couldn't', he kept saying, and I was trying to reassure him.

"We came to Ferrodach, and you know all about that – Lord Gahran and so on -"

"Wait. When you went into Lord Gahran's room, was there anything on the desk?"

"I don't remember. What kind of thing?"

"A piece of parchment, maybe a letter, a prayer -"

"I don't remember. There may have been. I didn't touch anything, if that's what you're asking. Except the bottle. I took it from that soldier – Laida? – and put it on the table. We went downstairs – it's all true what we said. Dorac went in with his sword drawn, and he did say something that sounded like 'they have to be killed'. There were three of us outside, waiting. But the guard wasn't Braf. The guard was Berden."

"So that was a lie."

"Yes. Kremdar sent him away. I'm not sure why. I think it just seemed absurd for three of us to be standing there in this tiny space. And of course Kremdar and I wanted to be together, and it wouldn't make any difference to Dorac which soldier was on guard. And all the time we were waiting and listening.

"We did hear shouts, and then silence. He came out, and no, his cloak was not stained. I don't know how he managed that. He went off. Then Kremdar went in -"

"Kremdar went in alone?"

"He's braver than me," said Arvill simply. "We were both frightened of what we might find. He went in, and I waited."

"For how long?"

"I don't know. Not long. What do they say – long enough for one of the really long psalms. A little while, less than a quarter of an hour. I can't remember. He called my name, and I went in.

"They were lying dead on the floor. They weren't as we described them – cut up – they were just dead. The boy's throat had been cut, and one of the girls – maybe it was both of them – had been stabbed in the chest. I'm not sure. Kremdar was standing there, shaking. He looked at me, and he said, 'He did it. He really did it. My brother.' I said, 'What do we do?' He said, 'I have to arrest him.' But then he said, 'And he will explain it away. Lady Sada recommended it, and he's done it for good reasons, he'll say, and the King will allow it. Everything Dorac says is right. He lets Dorac do anything.'

"You know that's true, Kai. He said, 'And that's what we'll be – childkillers. The King's Thirty.'"

Arvill looked him in the face. "That was the worst for him – the thought that the King could be persuaded to approve and allow it – perhaps had even ordered it secretly. Kremdar honours King Arrion so much – to think that he could be corrupted - I can't remember exactly, but I think I said, 'But they won't allow it. When they see how horrible it is – *children*' – and that gave us the idea. To make it worse – more brutal even than it was – to show up the evil - after all, it couldn't hurt them any more."

"Whose idea was it?"

"Kremdar's. But I helped, I did just as much. I slipped out and went to the bookroom – we guessed that was where Dorac would go. I got his cloak – we used that to keep the blood off us as we cut them up. It was horrible, but they hadn't been dead long. We managed to spread the blood around." She was no longer looking at him. "It's difficult to believe we did that. And Kremdar found Braf – we thought he'd be the easiest to bribe – and persuaded him to support our story."

"But you knew Dorac would deny it."

"We didn't know he would deny killing them. We were rather

266

surprised by that. People do go berserk, and that's what everyone would think. We weren't making him any more guilty than he was. We would've admitted our part, and explained, if he'd admitted his, and accepted that it was wrong." Arvill shrugged. "So now you know."

"Do you expect me to believe that, Arvill?" Kai asked quietly. But he couldn't stay quiet. He banged his fist on the table and jumped up. "D'you expect me to believe that you believe it? It is nonsense. You walk into a room, and your lover's standing over murdered children – he tells you to lie about it – to create false evidence – and you tell me you think he's innocent?"

"He is innocent!" cried Arvill through her tears. "He would never have killed them."

"You trust him," said Kai with sarcasm.

"I trust him because I know him. I love him and I know him. Just like – if it had been you, Kai. I know you're a good man, you would never do such a thing, no matter what, and neither would he."

Kai had no answer to that. There was silence, and Arvill wiped her tears away with the backs of her fingers.

"I have to arrest you," he said, and she nodded sadly.

"Write out what you've told me – two copies – and swear it. We'll leave tomorrow for Stonehill." He would have to write to Gemara, so that Kremdar could be arrested too. Suddenly he said, "One more thing. You said you bribed Braf – where did you get the money?"

"I had a little, Kremdar had a little. We put it together, and it was enough for someone who'd never had much. Poor Braf – he didn't have much time to spend it."

He was turning away when she added shakily, "Kai. What I've - we've - done - is it bad enough - to mean death?"

"I don't know," said Kai honestly. He felt that every part of his soul was hurting. At the door he let in the soldiers waiting outside, one man, one woman. "Arvill, daughter of Eve, is under arrest. Search her – decently – and keep her here. She will need parchment and ink." He went out and wept a little.

Later that evening, Arvill's confession was brought to him. He read it through, and it matched what she had said. He wrote a letter to the King to enclose her statement and Laida's, and then he sat and looked at what he had written, as he had done nine days before at The Crescent Moon inn. He slowly added the words *Either Arvill is telling the truth, or she is a very good liar.*

Still more slowly, *I think she may be a very good liar.*

He sat on, wondering whether he wanted to believe Arvill because he loved her, or whether he wanted to disbelieve her because he no longer loved her, and how it could possibly be that he didn't know which.

Dorac 1 (10–20 October)

10 October 570

He learned the country as he went. Woodlands, quiet. It was irritating, like an itch, not to know the path, but the trees, clean sombre dark green pine changing as he descended to ash and elm slowly turning brown, were the same. And the squirrels, and the honking of migrating geese overhead, and the rich smell of autumn rot. Rabbits, wood-pigeons, rooks. Sometimes pigs, rooting freely, branded on their hindquarters with queer marks to show who they belonged to. Or, if it were very quiet, a glimpse of a deer. He could almost smell the roast venison or the tangy bacon at feasts at the Great Hall of Stonehill. *No.*

He ate the pasty they had bought – *they* – in the Village, and gathered wild garlic and chanterelles, and filled his water-skin at a stream. As he walked, he chanted psalms to himself, and prayed for the welfare of his homeland, and for the few people he loved.

Mostly woodland, but as time passed, more and more farms. Much like Marodi farms, but the buildings here were more often stone. And on the wall by each of the doors, someone had painted or scratched a picture of a man or woman or a crowd. Sometimes more than one.

Hassdan was the only Jaryari he knew, and he had expected the people to be pale-skinned like him, but the few he saw were the same mixed-mostly-brown assortment as in Marod. The short hair was different, but the clothes were similar.

The wall paintings were guardian saints, he realised. They liked saints in Jaryar. Hassdan had said that everyone had their own saint, and at his christening he had been assigned to the protection of St John. Dorac tried to find this interesting.

On that first day, he spoke to no one. *A day's walk at least, before asking anyone to trust a foreigner*, he thought.

It was almost pleasant.

Perhaps he could make a new life. As he had done before. Walking alone twenty-three years ago from Bello in the north all the way to Stonehill, with Captain Ettuar's letter of recommendation in his pouch, and very little else. He remembered his first sight of the city – a town surrounded by walls, higher than he had thought walls could be. Carvings of saints on the gates that kept out the enemy. The Castle itself on the hill. *Stone Hill, a hill covered with stone buildings*, he had understood with sudden awe. The huge King's Square in front of it, a square that would have taken the whole of Dorac's village.

Hassdan and others said that Stonehill was nothing to Makkera, but to him it was a city as great as Jerusalem or Rome. And there the Captain's letter, whatever it said – he could not read in those days – had indeed found him a place among the Kingslands soldiers. A year later he had been lucky enough to help Princess Emmia, now of the Northern Six, when robbers attacked her. And at the next Christmas feast the Queen had rewarded him with the gift of a sword. In Stonehill he had found his place, and also, for the first time, love. Perhaps he could do that again. But he had no letter this time.

He found the main south road on the second day, and started to ask for work. He quickly learned many things.

He learned that he was in the province of Marithon, but he was pronouncing it wrong. He learned to beware of dogs. He learned that even the simplest work was jealous of its skills. "I could help you do that," he said to two men who were building a wall. "Do you know how?" "I can lift stones into place." "You don't, then." Generally, he learned that he was a thieving Marodi savage who should go back where he came from.

None of this surprised him. What did was what he learned about himself. He had been stared at as a Kingsbrother for years, but still he was shy of strangers. Who were not enemies, because Marod was no longer his home. The loneliness was also worse than he had expected. He missed his friends; he missed Gormad; he missed his city; he missed Derry; he missed his sword most of all.

On the third day he walked up to another farmhouse. A saint in a boat. Two rooms inside, probably. A man and two women were sitting on a bench beside the door. The older woman stood up.

"What do you want?"

"God guard this house, madam," he said politely, pulling back his hood. "I am looking for work. Do you need anyone?"

"You're not from round here."

"No."

"We don't. Go away." As he turned, "You can have a piece of bread, if you like."

His face burned. "Thank you, no."

Walking back to the road, he heard footsteps behind him. He put his hand uselessly where his sword was not, and turned.

It was the younger woman, and she did not seem threatening. She looked at him, and he looked at her. Not much over twenty, small and slim, with the short hair that looked strange to him, and a dull green kirtle.

"Madam?"

"What is your name?"

"Ettuar." In Jaryar the poor had only one name.

"I - I think I know you from somewhere," she said uncertainly, to his surprise.

"I don't think that's likely. I don't come from near here. What's your name?"

"Melina."

There was a Melina in a ballad Dorac had once heard. He knew no other. She didn't look familiar. "You are thinking of someone else, madam."

"We *have* met before."

He shrugged. "Do you know anywhere I could find work?"

"What kind of work?"

"Anything honest."

She thought. "D'you know Vinkler village?"

"No."

"It's about five miles further on. On the left as you come to it is an inn called The Hanged Man. I think they may need someone to do stable work, and that sort of thing."

"Thank you." He bowed, and left her, and felt her puzzled eyes on his back as he walked away.

What person in their senses called a drinking-place The Hanged Man? Who would come to drink there?

But The Hanged Man existed, and looked as if it did well. A solid stone building, with smoke drifting from a chimney, not a smokehole. On a stake outside there was a painting of a gallows. Empty, despite the name. St Peter and his keys were painted by the door. So perhaps The Hanged Man had hopes of heaven, after all. When he walked in, he saw an inside staircase, something he'd not often seen in the countryside. (*Like Ferrodach. Down the stair, across the hall, into the little room* -)

"God be with you. My name is Ettuar. I'm a hard worker, and I heard you needed someone."

"With hair like that, you'd make a good scarecrow, but it's the wrong time of year." The man looked him up and down. "Who told you?"

"A woman called Melina."

"D'you know her?"

"No. I met her earlier today, and she was kind enough -"

A grimace. "Come on, then." They went to the stables, which held three horses, but had space for several more, and looked not to have been cleaned for several days. "Get that muck shifted, and then we'll see."

At least, if they were good Christians, they would give him supper.

Two hours later, he was hired. The man Artos and his wife Sali ran the inn with the help of one servant girl. "You don't serve customers – don't talk to them if you can help it, you sound foreign – and you don't cook. You'll do anything else. And look after the horses, mainly. Keep them groomed and fed and tidy, and walk them round if they need exercise and if the guests please. And if you steal one, let me tell you, Lord Ramos will hunt you down, and by the time he hangs you, believe me it'll be a happy release." Sali shut her mouth tight. Then opened it again. "A penny a week, and food and lodging. And keep yourself clean, if you please – the bath's at the back. You can sleep in the outhouse."

"And meaning no offence, but you'll be barred in at night," her husband added. "We don't know you, you see."

After he had accepted these terms, Sali sat him down and neatened his hair. She cut it almost as short as a priest's. Then Artos pointed him to a logpile to chop wood. He hadn't used an axe for many years, and made a poor job of it, but it was a start. A new life.

*

So at last, two weeks after the murders at Ferrodach, he had a place. He had work and reliable food. The Jaryari did not trust him, but they had no reason to, and they were not monsters. Things might get better.

They did not. He had finished his journey – journey to his trial, towards death, towards work. It was over. He was at rest, and there was nothing between him and that day in Stonehill when Kremdar and King Arrion had taken from him everything he had.

He woke next morning to find an invisible weight pressing down on him. It was so heavy that he could hardly drag himself upright. There was a fog so thick that he could barely see his employers, or hear them speak. He could not get rid of either.

He couldn't understand what was happening to him. It must be his weakness and sin that made him unable to think of anything good, or care about anything at all. He prayed and prayed, and it made no difference. Alcohol might have helped, but he had no money, and he wasn't welcome among the guests. He went to church on Sunday with his master and mistress, and for perhaps half an hour the fog lifted a little; and then it came down again. Nothing else broke through. Except when he remembered *The King has asked Gemara and Hassdan to investigate what happened at Ferrodach.* Then the agony of hope was worse than any physical pain he had ever known.

The days were not as bad as the nights. In the daytime he had something to do. He cleaned and chopped, carried and groomed, and was forced to pay some attention to those around him. The work itself was hard and dirty, but it was decent work with an end result. As far as he could like anything, he liked the horses. Sali and Artos provided water for him to wash himself thoroughly, although they saw no reason to heat it. No one interfered with him, and he had not expected kindness.

It was at night that his soul fell apart.

He lay in his shed, and rested his tired body, but he could not rest his mind. It showed him everything he did not want to think of, over and over again. He wept and wept, and despised himself for weeping, and could not stop. He was so alone and sorry for himself, and he relived obsessively every moment of the hour he had spent in the village whorehouse, disgusting himself more every time, and again could not stop. At last he would fall asleep, and then there were the dreams.

He dreamed of murdered children, as he had told Kai, but now he was killing them. He dreamed of his trial. It wasn't always King Arrion who judged him. It might be Queen Darisha, or Captain Ettuar, or his father; and once it was God. But always there were the eyes, and always the judgment, and the certainty that he must be guilty, his cries of innocence a lie. Surely these people would know.

But the worst dream was quiet and gentle. He dreamed of one of the nights camping in the woods with Gormad. In the dream Gormad was smaller and younger than in real life, and he had a nightmare. Dorac put his arms round him to comfort him, as he'd seen parents do to children. That was all; and then he woke up. The feeling of soft humanness next to him was so strong and good that he smiled. But lovers hold each other as well, and it had been so long – *had he really wanted to do that, to a child?*

That was what he was. Thank God Gormad was safe from him now. His body and soul felt filthy to him. In that hour he would have confessed to any crime, rape, murder, even treason, if it would have bought him a quick death.

He lay as dawn came, thinking of his knife, and too cowardly to use it.

So it went on, day after day, and night after night. And he might have as much as ten years to live, or even longer.

*

20 October 570

But, as Kai had said, travellers gossip.

He was plugging holes in the stable walls with moss one afternoon, when Sali interrupted to send him to the village with a message. This had never happened before. When he returned half an hour later, there were horses in the stable that he had not put there. He would have gone to check them, but Sali met him in the yard. "Wash yourself, you're a sight. And then come inside. Hurry up."

He was working harder, and sleeping less, than had been the

case for many years. As he came into the hall with its benches and bright fire, and noise, the only desire he knew was for rest. Sali shut the door fussily behind him, and said, "There are two people to speak to you."

But there shouldn't be. *Kai*, he thought for a bewildered moment, and the world seemed to stop.

A man and a woman, strangers, were sitting at a table. The man was older than Dorac, thick-set and tall, drumming his fingers, thick brown hair plaited down his back. The woman was young, perhaps only twenty, thin and curly-haired. Both wore fine jackets (blue and green), and both looked out of place in The Hanged Man.

"You are Ettuar? Come and sit down, friend," said the woman, standing up courteously.

There was a screaming inside Dorac's head. "That is not my place, my lady."

"An honest man in an honest inn – why should it not be your place? What will you take to drink? I am Igalla of Arabay, and this is Ramos of Marithon. We wish to offer you work."

Slowly Dorac crossed the floor. As he walked, the dreadful fog lifted a little. *This was not right.* His body tensed warily. He could almost feel himself turning back into himself. But still he was very tired.

He sat down, lifted the cup he was given, and said, "My thanks to you, my lady."

"So," said Lady Igalla – as she must be – "you are Ettuar?"

"Yes, my lady."

She smiled. A friendly smile, almost shy. "We could play games, but we will not. You are Dorac Kingsbrother of Marod." She said the quaint foreign name carefully.

"No."

"Yes. You were branded fifteen years past. King Arrion exiled you twenty days ago. You travelled to a village near the border, and had a secret meeting with one of your brothers, perhaps to receive instructions. Then you came here. As a spy, or as an assassin, or what?"

"I am neither of these things."

"Then what are you doing here?"

His head was throbbing. "I am an exile, working for my living. I mean no harm to anyone in Jaryar."

"Has that always been the case?" demanded the man.

Lady Igalla frowned at him.

"I've fought for my king against his enemies," Dorac answered quietly. "Sometimes they were Jaryari. I intend no harm now, and I'm doing no harm."

"And we mean you none," said Lady Igalla. "But consider our king's thoughts. You are known to be a faithful warrior of the Thirty, loyal for many years. King Arrion decides to excite himself about ancient history, and sends you to Ferrodach. You do whatever you did, out of loyalty to him – and after all those years, and all that service, you're exiled. And now you're here. If you're not a spy - this work is not fit for you. You have a better future. We have come to invite you to Makkera, Master Dorac."

Dorac cast an eye around the room, and saw that people were leaving quietly.

"I am content here."

"In this shithole?" exclaimed Lord Ramos.

"You cannot be content here. A man of your skills is needed – and valued – anywhere. King Rajas himself has sent us to call you." He stared. She said, "I am not lying. You'll have a place of respect, and work for a noble king. We have been enemies before, but we all serve the same God, with the same honour. Makkera is a great city, and you can make a home there. I cannot promise boundless wealth, but enough to be comfortable. King Rajas, unlike some men, does not forget his friends."

Dorac thought. Then he said, "You're right. I served King Arrion faithfully, yet he chose to believe lies about me and banished me. So now I will serve another lord and take his money, and this will be my revenge. Isn't that what I would say, if I were indeed a spy?"

Lady Igalla was taken aback, but she said, "I don't think you are a spy. There's nothing in Vinkler to spy on."

"That makes me a stupid spy. One that your king wouldn't want to hire."

The room was now empty except for the three of them, and Sali peeping through from the back. The conversation was not going to end well.

"This is nonsense," broke in Lord Ramos. "King Rajas wants you, and will reward you, and you hate living here."

"He is most kind," said Dorac, "but I swore an oath. In Marod such things matter. I will serve no king but my own. If King Rajas is as noble as you say, he will understand."

They both had swords, but so far undrawn. He was between them and the door, but he only had a knife.

"So you refuse to come to Makkera? That is a pity," said Lady

Igalla.

"I refuse."

"It is not for you to refuse," said Lord Ramos. "You'll be coming with us whether you wish to or not."

"I will not. After all," he added recklessly, "as you said, I already know what a shithole looks like."

He jumped up, and Lord Ramos shouted, at the same instant. Dorac upturned the table against them, and made for the door. But it was already opening. The four soldiers who ran in hadn't drawn their swords either, but they were all armed in mailcloth and helmets, which hindered his knife. He got in one slash before they were on him. They were six and he was one, and very tired, and he was on his back on the floor almost instantly. Two of them held him down, and he stared up at the eyes.

"A real Kingsbrother of Marod," said one of them, grinning.

"Indeed, Milna," said Lord Ramos. "This is one of the noble King's Thirty. The ones who excite themselves by carving five-year-old girls to pieces." He kicked Dorac in the side, but the words hurt worse. That was what the nobles of Makkera were saying about the King's Thirty. "To think Lady Igalla wasted courtesy on you."

"What d'you want with me?" he asked, but he knew.

"As the lady said, we were sent to bring you to Makkera. If you're sure you don't want to fight for King Rajas, you can be useful in other ways. You can supply information, for instance. I'll tell you more later. We have all night."

"We need to confirm who he is," said Lady Igalla.

They took off enough of his clothes to confirm the brand on

his shoulder - and then they took off some more, because they could. *Their hands.* They stole his knife, and bound his hands and feet, and left him on the stone floor with one of the soldiers pointing a sword at his throat. Then they discussed plans, while Dorac lay and cursed his cowardice at the Old Stones.

There were Lady Igalla and Lord Ramos and four soldiers. One of the soldiers was to ride back at once with the news. There were no other guests staying at the inn, so it could close for the evening, and in the morning the five remaining would leave with their prisoner. In the meantime, Sali and Artos were to send their girl home to her parents, and to prepare food. These orders were given, and the messenger rode away.

While supper was being cooked, Ramos came over to relieve the soldier standing guard. He brought with him a bottle of the best wine The Hanged Man could provide, and he sat down at a table, and drank greedily, and kept his promise to tell Dorac more about what awaited him in the Green City.

All the King's Thirty had permission where necessary to use violence to obtain evidence. None of the Southern Six liked this (*"We do not take pleasure in torment"*), and it rarely went further than breaking or dislocating a few minor bones, joints or teeth. But it seemed that in Makkera things were different.

"The entrance to the dungeons is down a little street which some people call the Alley of Screams," he said genially, "though that's not its formal name. The first thing they do is strip the prisoners – in case they're concealing any weapons -" – he flicked at the braies which were all they had left Dorac – "and then bath them in fresh cold water.

281

Very cold. So then they warm them up.

"I see someone's been flogging you for some reason. But perhaps only with a stick? Imagine an iron bar that's been heating in a brazier for an hour, laid gently on your back, and then lifted off again - The skin pulls away. That's entertaining. Smells quite horrible. There are so many things they can do with hot iron." He went on to describe them. *Oh God.* "They say the biggest men scream loudest. I'm not sure if that's true."

Now and again, he kicked his prisoner. Once Dorac kicked back, but his bound feet only collided with the table. The bottle fell off and broke, and Ramos gathered up the glass, and carved a small additional scar on his naked back. "One more makes no difference, does it?" Dorac managed not to gasp.

Then they heard Lady Igalla cough loudly, and say that the food was ready. A different, silent soldier took Ramos's place. Dorac was left with his terror.

He was not brave enough for this. He had never been brave enough, and God certainly knew he wasn't brave enough now. To die under torture without betraying a single secret. He could not do it. Unless he was granted a miracle of courage, he would end his life a traitor. This time, he would be guilty.

It seemed that it would take three days to reach Makkera. So in those seventy-two hours he must either escape, which seemed highly unlikely, or find a way to die. As he had failed to do before, when it would have been so easy. To die he needed free hands, a knife or a noose, and a few moments alone. None of this seemed likely either. But it was a smaller miracle to ask for.

282

Oh God help me to die. Oh God help me to die.

They ate and drank and told stories, but always one of them had a sword pointed at him. They might be reluctant to use it. They plainly wanted him alive. That might be a tiny advantage.

"Ancient history." *Ancient history?*

Sali and Artos cleared away, eyes on him all the time, and went upstairs. The front door and the back kitchen door were barred. One soldier (Milna) was stationed outside the front, and one inside; the third in the kitchen. Lady Igalla was to take the best upstairs room. She promised to come down later to relieve one of the guards, and said as she went up, "Give him a drink. And a blanket."

He was indeed cold and thirsty. Lord Ramos's chunky cruel face loomed over him, pouring water into his mouth and over his face, so that he spluttered. That was amusing. Then the lord pulled up a chair and sat down, with his sword on his lap. He left a few candles burning, and began to talk again.

"But of course you're thinking you have little to tell us. We know all about your foolish little barbarian kingdom already. We know where its soldiers sit and shit themselves, we know who you're trying to ally with. We knew where you were, *Ettuar*. That's all true. But there are a few questions you could answer.

"The King's very curious to know one thing – who is really Prince Jendon's father? Everyone knows it's not Arrion. He's only interested in raping priests. Who was that one – Lumia, I think, was her name? – who he got a child on, and she was so shamed she killed herself? Very sad. There are songs about her in Marithon."

It was not Arrion, it was his brother Rafad. She wasn't raped. She died in childbirth. Dorac said nothing. Ramos moved on to the real purpose of the King's Thirty being to provide a lusty set of lovers for the King and Queen. "I can picture you there, you fine fellow, licking your lips as you wait your turn to tumble the Queen. Or does even that bitch Malouri have some standards?"

He must not react. He must not react.

A reaction would be interesting, and he needed Ramos bored. Bored and sleepy.

The man at the door wasn't likely to fall asleep. He was standing up, and his only concession to night had been to remove his helmet. But Ramos had drunk and boasted, and was looking comfortable. His talk died away after half an hour. And at last Dorac dared to shift about under his blanket, searching with very little hope for a piece of glass.

He didn't know much about glass. But he knew that it breaks when dropped on a hard surface. And broken glass is sharp. Sharp objects cut. He had hoped and prayed desperately that Ramos might have missed a piece or two. One that was big enough to use.

Cautiously he moved his body and his stiff hands around the flagstones, and at last was rewarded with a jab of pain in his side. He got his fingers to it and clumsily started to work on the rope. The candles burned lower. Ramos nodded, drowsing now and then, but reviving to grunt or kick.

It took a weary age, but at last his hands were free, and he forced himself to be patient, to massage them into fresh life. Now he could cut his wrists surely – would that be enough? But slow. If he could free his feet too, he might be able to grab a knife?

Ancient history.

He was bleeding already, in any case. He cast a look around before drawing up his stiff knees. The table partly blocked the door guard's view, but at any moment he might grow suspicious. Slowly, slowly, Dorac worked, until at last the ropes were cut. He could choose his time to jump up to attack two people - who had three other people within call, and who were all armed. He needed a knife and a very short space of time. And courage. *Oh God help me to die.*

Lord Ramos was definitely asleep. Dorac was still hesitating when there was a noise – voices? – outside the front door. The man turned to unbar it and investigate, and Dorac leapt up.

He sprang onto Lord Ramos, pushed him over backwards, chair and all, and thumped his head hard back on the stone. He just had time to grip his sword when the man from the door came running over, shouting, still not drawing himself, and Dorac reared up from his knees and slashed him across the throat, and blood rained down. He looked surprised, and Dorac pushed his dying body backwards, and pulled away the sword.

None of this had happened silently. There were footsteps running through the kitchen, and the front door was opening. Two at once, and he ought to have just died as he had intended to, but instinct was too strong. He ran forward to meet the soldier coming from the kitchen. Huge joy welled up in him as their swords clashed. But at the same time he knew this one was good, and he himself out of practice, and now he parried desperately, in a blur -

And the man looked over his shoulder and gasped. Dorac had time, lots of time, to knee him backwards and drive his sword through his chest, and kill him more easily than he had expected. And then turn to see what had surprised him.

The outside guard Milna had run in, but was grappling with someone – a woman – who had seized her from behind, and was trying to pull her down. She did not succeed, but she held on long enough for Dorac to run over and thump Milna's head with a candlestick from a table, and she also went down. Dorac turned away to see Lady Igalla on the stairs, running towards him with a sword.

She was so young and shocked; it was too easy. He sidestepped as she charged forward, and flicked the sword from her hand, and kicked her to the floor.

And then he stood bewildered in a shadowy room with two dead enemies, and two unconscious or dead, and one on the ground with his sword (Ramos's sword) at her neck, and a strange woman staring at him - and Sali peering in horror from the top of the stairs.

Now – *now!* – he must think, think quickly, and think right. He grabbed a bench and pulled it onto Lady Igalla's legs, to keep her down. He looked up at Sali and said roughly, "Get your husband and sit on the stairs." Then he glanced over at the woman. It was the one he had met at the farmhouse – Melina. "Is there anyone outside?" he asked her, and she shook her head.

"Bar the door. Then see if any of them are breathing. You," he said to Lady Igalla, "lift your hands slowly and put them under your head." Cautiously he bent down and took her knife. Kicked away her sword. "Sit on the stairs where I can see you, with your hands on your heads," he ordered Sali and Artos.

"She's alive, and so is Lord Ramos," whispered Melina.

She seemed willing to take orders from him, so he nodded brusquely, and said, "Tell me if they start waking up." He took time to make himself as intimidating and vicious as possible, and looked down at his prisoner. He was almost naked, spattered and stinking with her companions' blood. She'd left him humiliated and helpless. He knew he was terrifying.

"Now," he said, "we will talk, and if you're helpful, I will not kill you."

"You'll have to kill me. I won't tell you anything," she said breathily. *As he might have said, in the dungeons.*

"I didn't say I would kill you straight away." He looked her up and down. "You have ten fingers, I suppose ten toes, two ears, two *eyes*. You'll still be alive when I have removed them all. Lord Ramos was very clear about the kindness I could expect in your king's prison, so I am not feeling merciful. We have all night."

He gave her time to think about it, and himself to consider what to ask. "So." He moved the tip of the wet sword to beneath her ear. A drop of someone's blood trickled down Lady Igalla's neck. Tears were oozing from her eyes.

He wondered if Melina would try to stop him.

He slapped her face with the flat of the sword, lightly but to sting. "Who sent you to look for me?"

"The – the King. And Lady Ayella."

"Who is Lady Ayella?"

"The King's Chancellor." *A stupid question.*

"What do these people want with me?"

"What we said – to see if you would serve King Rajas. Lady

Ayella thought – if King Arrion had wronged you – you might be an angry man."

"I am. Very angry. To serve the King willingly - or unwillingly?"

"Lady Ayella said preferably willingly."

"But she's not here. Where are the rest of your soldiers?"

"There are no more."

"The truth," he said with contempt, flicking her again.

"There are no more! I swear it! We didn't want to attract attention. Please."

"What did you mean by 'ancient history'?"

She stared.

"You said Ferrodach was ancient history. Why did you say that?"

"It - it was all over two years ago."

"What was two years ago?"

"The - the letters."

"Tell me about the letters."

She gulped. "In summer two years ago – it may have been June – King Rajas wrote to Gahran of Ferrodach, but there –"

"What did he write to him?"

"I don't know, I don't know exactly, but something about his being the rightful heir, and a league of friendship between Jaryar and Marod if he became king –"

"If your king deposed King Arrion for him?"

She bit her lip.

"Go on."

"There was no reply for a long time, but eventually one was delivered that didn't make sense, asking the King to ignore his previous letter, which was written in a fit of madness. But there was no previous letter. So that was all."

"What other letters were there?"

"None! None! I swear by St Bridget. Nothing after August or September of '68. So the Council were surprised when King Arrion sent soldiers to Ferrodach last month."

Dorac considered. "I see no reason to believe any of this. You are young. Why would you know these secret matters?"

"My – my father told me."

"Why would your father know?"

She licked her lips nervously. "My father is the Commander of the King's Army."

"What's his name?"

"Rodas of Garo."

Dorac had no idea if this were true. Hassdan or Gemara would have known. Kremdar probably. Soumaki and Kai, perhaps not. He stood still a moment too long, and became aware of how exhausted he was going to be as soon as he stopped being desperate and fierce.

Four pairs of eyes were looking at him in terror. Lady Igalla said with tremulous courage, "I have answered your questions, sir. Kill me if you're going to."

"Why should I kill you?" He almost added, *You are not five years old. It wouldn't be exciting.* Instead he said, "If I kill you now, and then find out you've lied to me, I can't come back and kill you again. Slowly."

It seemed an absurd threat to him, but she gasped with fright. Good. He jerked his head at Melina. "There's a crucifix on the wall. Bring it.

"Lift one hand – slowly – and take the cross. Swear you've told the truth about Ferrodach."

"I swear."

"About Lord Gahran and about the soldiers."

"I swear."

"Kiss the cross." She obeyed. He took it back, and turned again to Melina. "There's rope in the stable. Bring it." The candles were almost burnt out. He struggled to push away the unclean feeling that such conversations always left behind. *Get this right.* He wondered how long it was till dawn.

Melina returned, and he took the risk of handing her the sword to keep the prisoner still while he bound and gagged her. Then he turned to Sali and Artos, still sitting on the stairs. "Come here."

He tied them up, too, back to back on a stool. They stared at him. Then he told Melina, "There are horses in the stables. Saddle two of them, and put harness on them all." She went out.

Methodically he removed all knives and swords from every living or dead person. He even went through the kitchen for more knives, in case one of them managed to get in there. He turned Lord Ramos and the other unconscious soldier onto their sides and bound them also. For a moment he looked down at Ramos, and felt the others' eyes on him. The temptation was strong, but it would have been pure revenge. Captain Ettuar would not have approved.

Then he went back to the kitchen to steal a bag, and some

food and drink to put in it. He wiped the sword on Ramos' cloak. Finally, he put on the hose, shirt, jacket, cloak and boots that his enemies had stripped from him, and pocketed his piece of glass.

Nearly finished. "Remember I did not kill you," he said to Lady Igalla. "And one more thing. The people here did not know my name. They did not help me in any way. I shall be - very angry - if they suffer more because of tonight. Do you understand?" She nodded.

The two men he had killed lay on the floor, staring upwards. It was not for him to close their eyes, but he commended their souls to God. Then he went out, pinching all the candles on the way, to leave the living in the dark also. There was no reason to make it easy. There were perhaps four hours before the servant girl returned, and the alarm was raised. Less time if one of them freed themselves sooner.

He threw down the swords and knives, except the ones he had chosen to keep, and almost forgot to collect his own satchel from the shed where he had spent such unbearable nights.

*

Melina had made no progress in the stable. She was plainly scared of the horses, and made them skittish. He was too tired to curse her. He moved gently to stroke noses and soothe them with stableman's words. "Stay back," he said to her, and then, "You probably saved my life. Thank you. Why? What are you doing here?"

"I came to help you," she whispered. "I was going to give the guards money to let you escape." He almost smiled at the absurdity of that.

"Why?"

She paused. "I - know of Lord Ramos. He is very cruel. When

291

he comes here, people die. I heard them talking in the village about arresting a foreigner, and I knew it must be you."

"That is not a good enough reason." He was buckling on a saddle, trying not to let the horse feel any tension, but ready in case she attacked him from behind. Why should she not?

"We have met before."

"We have not. My name is not Ettuar."

"I know. You're Dorac Kingsbrother of Marod."

That did surprise him. "Why would you want to help Dorac Kingsbrother? When did we meet?"

Instead of answering, she took a deep breath and said, "When you were in there just now - did you kill Sali and Artos?"

That took some courage, perhaps. "No."

"Are you going back to Marod?"

If you ever return, I will have your life, King Arrion said inside his head. "Yes. When did we meet?"

She shook her head. "It's a long story."

Dorac gave up. The woman's behaviour was only one of his problems. The most pressing was how long he could stay awake.

"Lord Ramos will kill me if I stay here, won't he?" she asked timidly.

"Yes."

Plainly she was hoping to come with him. Another Gormad, but less use.

He had to hoist her into the saddle, but at least she seemed able to hold on. They rode slowly away from The Hanged Man, Dorac leading the remaining four horses. Lady Igalla had brought one for the prisoner. About half a mile down the road, he released them, hoping they wouldn't simply amble back to the inn.

So many problems and puzzles. *Two years ago. We have met before. I will have your life.*

But he had a sword, and he had a horse, and he was going home.

Kremdar and Gemara (14–20 October)

14 October 570

Kremdar and Tommid had been practising just outside Lenchen town, and were walking back as the afternoon waned. Tommid brandished his sword happily at any shadow, even challenging some of them aloud. Sometimes he fumbled and dropped the sword. His master hadn't yet had the heart to mention how much his enthusiasm outmatched his skill. Instead, "Is it dull for you here, lad?" he asked. "All that standing around listening to witnesses contradicting each other?"

"Sometimes," Tommid admitted. He was a solid boy of thirteen, already wearing his hair long and tied back, in imitation of Kremdar and other warriors. "But sometimes I like it very much. Yesterday, when Mistress Gemara proved that man was lying – that was wonderful. She was so clever."

"Yes, she's good at that. Occasionally a little over-suspicious, perhaps. I once had to point out to her that if someone looks shifty and frightened of her (and who isn't?), it's not always a sign of guilt."

They grinned at each other.

"She talked to me afterwards," said Tommid.

"Oh? On what matter?"

"She asked me about Ferrodach – whether I'd been distressed by Dorac and the murders. I suppose it was horrible – worse for you, sir – but such things happen, don't they?"

"Yes. Not often as horrible as that."

"It's the Ferrodach people who would have been most distressed, I think - Sir, there was one thing. Before it all happened, when we came in and the Lord – who was it? - Lord Gahran - surrendered, I thought I saw one of the soldiers talking to him, just for a moment. I didn't know why they would've needed to." His shy expression begged Kremdar to tell him this was nothing. "Should I tell Mistress Gemara?"

Kremdar frowned and considered. "Who was talking to him – one of our soldiers? And was he talking back?"

"I only saw a moment – the soldier was saying something, and then turned away. It was on the stairs. I didn't see who it was – a woman, I think."

"We don't want any of the Kingslands soldiers mixing in treason. It is odd, and I'll mention it to the Marshal when we get back. Remind me to do that. There's no reason to concern Gemara – it is not really a matter for her." He smiled reassuringly. "You did well to speak to me, but do not worry."

"No, sir." As they approached the square, "Tell me a story tonight, please."

"Which one?"

"You and Kai and the brigands – when you saved his life."

"Hmm, perhaps not that one again." To be honest, Kremdar didn't really want to think about Kai. Not now that he had learned what his brother was really like, when doors were shut. Not after what Arvill had told him. "I'll tell you about my first mission abroad with the Six – when Master Stimmon and I were sent to talk sense to the Consuls of

Haymon, and I fought a duel with their gigantic champion."

"Did you win?"

"Wait and find out," said Kremdar with a modest shrug that meant "yes".

It was growing dark as they approached the inn, and Kremdar kept a hand on his sword. No harm in being ready, just in case a violent and vengeful man leapt out of the shadows.

But he wasn't afraid of Dorac. Everyone knew that Kremdar wasn't afraid of anything.

*

Kremdar was twelve when his older brother was killed in front of him by the leader of a band of robber outlaws attacking his home. At that furious moment, the terror and confusion in the boy's mind was suddenly pushed aside, and he launched himself at the murderer, waving his small sword, and caught him off guard, and killed him.

The killing was a lucky stroke, everyone agreed, but the courage was undoubted. In the midst of the family's grief, there was pride, and the story briefly became well known in the north. Kremdar himself wept for his brother, and made up his mind to live a life worthy of Karac. He realised that it was possible, most of the time, to push away fear to do what had to be done. He seemed to be better at this than many people. And he also realised that the praise earned by a noble and brave act was the greatest thing in the world. Sometimes such acts were not acknowledged immediately, but in the long run they were recognised. From his brother's death onwards, he wanted to be a hero.

He was his family's hero, of course, and a hero to the people of Gisren, and for a magnificent time Praja's hero, as well as being one of the Thirty, who were heroes to all of Marod.

And then he was Arvill's hero.

Now, at Lenchen, he wasn't doing anything particularly heroic, but he was at least carrying out his duty. He heard cases as fairly as he could, trained and encouraged Tommid, and tried not to think about the events – horrible, indeed – at Ferrodach.

Then the messenger came.

*

15 October 570

Gemara's certainty that Dorac was innocent and Kremdar guilty had been shaken by the week in Lenchen. Kremdar wasn't his usual self; he was less cheerful and confidential. That was surely to be expected, and in some ways it was a relief. But he did not look haunted by conscience, and when she watched him at swordplay with Tommid, and chatting genially with the local people, she knew doubt.

He had never done anything to warrant a belief that he could kill children. Look at the foolishly fond way he behaved with his own.

Neither had Dorac. But where Dorac thought his duty was involved, he could be very hard. His behaviour to Hassdan was an example of that. And there were the painful conversations he and she had had about Master Stimmon, four years ago. Stimmon was a leader Gemara loved and reverenced, but he did not seem to realise that his body was shakier, and his mind less clear, than they had been. He was no longer fit to serve in the Thirty, far less lead the Six, Dorac had said.

"He can't stand upright for even an hour at a time any more! He cannot guard the King!"

"He may improve. Wait a month," Gemara ordered, although she had no right, other than seniority, to order Dorac to do anything. He'd waited however, grimly, and during the month things only got worse.

"If you don't tell him, Gemara, I must." He'd been right, and they had spoken to Stimmon and to the King, and Stimmon had been retired with honour. But it had not been pleasant for him, and he had died fifteen months later, a warrior with nothing to do.

If King Arrion had ordered the killings, or Dorac had thought he had -? She could not believe it, but she was not sure why. Some people claimed that women had an instinctive understanding of certain truths denied to men. Gemara had no time for such ideas. It was only a short step from believing that to the views of the heretics who thought that men and women had been made by God so differently that they had entirely separate roles in life. *Women cannot be rulers, or priests, or warriors. Men cannot be cooks, or care for children.*

But if her belief was not female wisdom, was it only wishful thinking, born of the fact that she had known him so long?

She set this aside, and tried to deal with the work in hand.

She had been sitting with two jurors for a long afternoon, in one of the tents erected in the town square for the trials. They were trying to decide if Garos the carpenter had stolen seventeen lengths of cloth from his neighbour's shop, or if this was a calumny thought up by the neighbour because Garos was too friendly with his wife. At last they rejected the evidence of one of the two witnesses, and one witness was not enough, so Garos was allowed to go, smirking in a suspicious manner.

Kremdar had finished earlier. Through the tent flap, she could see him talking to someone who'd apparently just arrived in the town, and was still holding his sweaty horse. *Look after that animal, or you don't deserve her,* was Gemara's instinctive reaction. But then Kremdar broke abruptly away, walked across and entered the tent.

He looks ill, she thought suddenly.

"Mistress Gemara, may I speak to you?" He hadn't addressed her so formally in years. Gemara rose, said a few polite words to her jurors and walked out with him. They headed towards the church, and she eyed him curiously, but he was staring straight ahead and not looking at her.

"I have received ill news from home," he said. "I am sorry, but I must leave at once."

"What news?" *His daughter,* she guessed with pity. Children's lives were so frail.

"There have been murders committed on my land. It seems ruffians broke into one of the outbuildings, and slaughtered children – I'm not sure of all the details. Praja and Yaina are very distressed. I must go."

"We're nearly finished here," said Gemara after a moment. "Two more days, and then you can request the King -"

"I need to go now. I must investigate – I can't leave them alone."

"But surely Praja can do what needs to be done. Or your lord – who is it?"

"Lady Ferriol – but I can't leave it to them! This is children – and just outside our house! I need to go and help Praja – I – I am sorry,

Gemara," – he seemed to be trying to pull himself together – "after – after what happened at Ferrodach, I can't endure it. I must go. You must understand." *Now* he was looking at her, his face full of pain. *Beseeching* was the word for that look. Gemara had often seen it, although not often on him, and had rarely given in.

But she was here to watch him, to see if he did anything odd. This was odd. "Very well. I will speak to the elders."

"I don't want to hinder your work. And – may I leave Tommid with you?"

"Am I a nursemaid?" snapped Gemara, who always found Tommid's clumsiness irritating. "I will not be responsible for your squire. Keep him away from the blood if you like – send him to play with Yaina – but take him with you. I suppose you want to leave today?"

"Yes, I must. I'll go and tell him." He walked away, and Gemara hurried over to Secretary Jakali.

"That man over there – he brought bad news for Master Kremdar. Find out what it was."

She had a decision to make, and she missed her siblings. Not Soumaki or Dorac – Soumaki would have sympathised and Dorac would have understood the problem, but both would have left the choice to her. But Hassdan would have given thoughtful advice. As for Kai, he would have dithered about what was best until she acted decisively out of sheer irritation. But none of them was here.

She couldn't see the urgency that Kremdar claimed was obvious, even assuming his story were true. Murder unfortunately was not unknown; there were people in Gisren to deal with it. But Kremdar would be disappearing in an hour or two, and he might not be going to Gisren at all. So she needed to find out, and there was only one way to do that.

Jakali reported that Kremdar's steward had sent word that a man and a young girl had been killed while sheltering (with his permission) on their estate. Gemara made polite excuses to the leading townsfolk, asking them to keep the remaining accused in prison a little longer. She wished Kremdar and Tommid Godspeed when they rode away, and decided she had just enough time to write to the King before setting off after them. Jakali she sent back to Stonehill with her letter and two of their soldiers, but she selected Morvan to accompany her. He didn't look pleased at the prospect, she noticed grimly. She had never been particularly popular.

*

16–18 October 570

There followed a tedious few days of riding, and camping, and saying very little. They skirted Stonehill to the east, but at each town and village Gemara made enquiries, and it seemed that Kremdar and Tommid were indeed heading north for Gisren, just a few hours ahead of her. She didn't want to catch them up, for what would she say? She wanted to arrive at the same time, or even a little later, and find out what was going on.

Stimmon had insisted that the Southern Six should have contacts and friends throughout Marod, not only in the south, and Gemara had continued this policy. So now she forced herself to be sociable and drink wine with Lord Dekker of Krayl in his draughty hall, in order to hear his stories and his gossip.

"I don't know of any particular trouble at Gisren. Praja and their steward – can't remember his name – run the place well. Maybe a little too tolerant of vagrants and idlers – Lady Ferriol complains about that. Kremdar and Praja are very well liked."

"So all is well, so far as you know?"

"At Gisren, yes. There was a report that came in to me of a disreputable character travelling these roads. You don't remember Sil, daughter of Jarri?"

Gemara thought. "She was suspected of something -"

"Suspected of killing people for money in the northwest, but got off at her trial. There were rumours of friends in high places, and bribed or threatened witnesses. That was about eighteen months ago. She's not been heard of since, but if she were sensible she'd go to another part of the country and change her name. Anyway, someone said they thought they'd seen her travelling north with a man – oh, about ten days ago. And then someone else round here said they thought they'd seen her the other day. Also travelling north, also accompanied. So either one of them was mistaken – which is quite possible, one violent peasant is much the same as another – or she's going along this road to and fro, to and fro" – he gestured – "like a wave on the shore. But no one has any lawful reason to stop her. If it was her."

So a paid assassin was in the area, interested in the north. Maybe. "What does Sil look like?"

"One of those faces that people recognise but can't describe. Normal height and medium colouring and all that, broken teeth. A scar on her hand, don't ask which one."

"Hmmm."

As Gemara got up to leave, he added, "Don't sleep in the woods; everywhere is sodden with all this rain. They say the bridge over the Poto is down."

Gemara and Morven slept one night on the road, one night with Lord Dekker, and two in inns, sharing a room or a blanket with little embarrassment, and no lust. Morvan was thirty years younger, after all, and had no conversation worth listening to, and to him she was doubtless the type of an unfavourite aunt. And no men but Habbaroth meant anything to Gemara.

Forty years ago and more, riding on an errand for her parents at the age of fourteen, she'd been dragged into the bushes by two men, robbed of horse and money, and raped, and left in the undergrowth to live or die. When the physical injuries had healed, she had left home for the city, and come to Stonehill to find work, swearing to let no man touch her, ever. Habbaroth's endless patience and good humour, as friend and business partner, and finally as more, had eventually won her round, but only for him.

They rode on through a soggy landscape of woods and fields, and at last reached the borders of Kremdar and Praja's prosperous estate.

*

19 October 570

The house was long, two-storied, and wooden, set conventionally on one side of a courtyard with stables and bakehouses and such on the other sides, and the well in the centre. Gemara and Morven were challenged at the yard's arched entrance, but then she was recognised and they were escorted to the main hall.

Praja had set up a loom, and was flicking the shuttle to and fro with enviable skill, while her child sat on the floor carefully wrapping pieces of wood in a spare length of cloth, presumably as some sort of game, and a servant in the corner scoured pots. It was a peaceful domestic scene, attractively alien to Gemara, with the loom's clicking almost musical.

"God's greetings to you, Praja."

"Gemara Kingsister!" Praja rose and curtsied, not too low. "This is an honour."

"Is Father coming?" asked little Yaina, looking up hopefully.

"I believe he is. I seem to have overtaken him on the road. He wanted to be here, after he heard of trouble on your land."

"What trouble – oh, poor Gan and his daughter? It's rather unpleasant to think of that happening so close to the house, but we have guards and locks. He really needn't worry. Did you say he was coming here? Lukor," to a portly man who entered at this moment, "it seems the master is coming."

"Yes, madam. He's already here; he spoke to me, and said he would come to the house later," said the steward.

This was plainly news to Praja. "Where is he now?"

"He asked me about the – er, the murders -" (he whispered the word, presumably to spare Yaina), "which had grieved him greatly, and he wanted to see the place where it happened. He seemed to think it was someone else who had been killed, but I explained. I thought I'd put it in my letter –"

"Someone else?" Gemara hoped things would become clear

soon; they were very far from clear at the moment.

"Oh, Mistress Gemara!" He bowed. "Yes, he wrote a short while ago to ask me to give shelter to a poor family we know from a neighbouring estate, and so we let them stay in one of the sheds, and someone broke in, probably looking for something to steal – but the master seemed to think that he had meant us to help someone else entirely -"

"But had he named these people – Gan, was it? – that he wanted you to look after? Did you keep his letter? Can I see it?"

She had sounded too eager. The steward looked fussily at his mistress.

"One moment, Mistress Gemara," said Praja, in the sweet voice that always means trouble. "Surely you are not questioning my servant, about my husband, in my house?"

Gemara met her gaze. "I am enquiring about a murder."

"The murder was committed on our land, and it is for us to investigate, or for Lady Ferriol. Unless the King has given you particular instructions, it has nothing to do with the Southern Six.

"But I am forgetting. Would you care for a drink, Mistress Gemara, and you, sir? I am sure Kremdar will be here soon."

"Thank you. I'll be happy to talk to him when he comes," said Gemara, because Praja was right in her legalistic way, and one should choose one's battles.

"When is Father coming?" whined the child, pulling at her mother's kirtle.

The steward disappeared. She couldn't prevent this, but it was annoying. He could be warning Kremdar, or destroying evidence –

destroying evidence! What was she thinking? They sat down with cups of ale for the adults and goat's milk for the child. Praja expressed polite horror at the Ferrodach business – "I must say, I was surprised to think it of him. Though I never knew him well" – and Morvan at last earned his place in the party by commenting intelligently on the local livestock.

Kremdar walked in a quarter of an hour later. He stopped abruptly on the threshold, with Tommid just behind him, and Yaina squealed with joy and ran to him before the others had registered his presence. He scooped her up in his usual informal way, and stroked her hair, but his eyes were on Gemara, as if she were something out of a nightmare.

"Welcome, husband," said Praja, walking calmly into the embrace of his free arm. "It was kind of you to come to us, and kind of the King to spare you."

"He asked my leave to come, and I was pleased to give it," said Gemara. "And I was also concerned. Have you managed to find out more about this crime, Kremdar? Are the murderers still at hand?"

"It - seems not," said Kremdar slowly. "Lukor says there were strangers seen in the neighbourhood the night before – a man and a woman – who haven't been seen since."

"On my way north, I heard tell of a woman called Sil with a dubious history seen travelling this way with a man. But who were the people killed, and why would anyone want to kill them?"

"Gan is – was – a decent man, but shiftless, especially since his wife and two of his children died last year," Praja explained, since Kremdar seemed unwilling to speak. "He and his daughter lived a few miles away, but their landlord was always threatening to turn them off for delays in their rent, and he did, and so they came here. And Lukor followed his instructions, and helped them."

"How very Christian. You knew beforehand that they would be evicted, and wrote about it?"

"I - guessed it was likely. Gemara, I'm sorry to have brought you so far. Did you say a woman called Sil?"

"Yes. Praja can make enquiries. You and I have finished in Lenchen for the time being, and can return to Stonehill."

"But I need to investigate – to follow this woman -"

"Other people can do that."

"You must all be tired," said Praja. "I will have beds prepared, and supper."

"Supper would be most welcome," said Gemara. "But we must be on our way tonight." Everyone stared at her. "We are required in Stonehill, and it's a long way. Better to get moving."

"Don't go, Father," murmured Yaina. Her father, who until now hadn't taken his eyes off Gemara, put her down and said gently, "I have to go after supper, Duckling." (*Duckling?*) "I'll sing you a song first. And I brought you a present from the south." Yaina put her fingers in her mouth, and smiled up at him tentatively. Kremdar's eyes kept flicking from her to Gemara. Hardly at all to his wife.

"Shall we see to the horses?" Gemara included Kremdar, Morvan and Tommid in her gaze. She would never neglect Tara Maid, but she mustn't allow Kremdar any further opportunity to be alone with his people, who might be part of it, whatever "it" was. This was why they had to be out tonight. Supported by Morvan, she talked horse and journey steadily through their time in the stables, passing on the little information she had about the mysterious Sil. Tommid volunteered that they had seen a wedding celebration in one of the villages on the road, and took several minutes trying to remember the names of the bride and groom. He waggled his fingers in frustration, a frustration Gemara fully shared.

It was a large party that gathered for an early supper, with all the household and farm staff sitting around tables set up before the meal, and dismantled afterwards. All was informal, and everyone chatted to his or her neighbour, or exchanged general news. As well as the murder of Gan and his daughter, there was much talk of the bad weather, and confirmation that the bridge was down. "I hear one of your siblings was delayed, Master," said one man. "Master Kai, is it? He was going to Stonehill with a prisoner, and had to turn south."

"A prisoner? What prisoner?" asked Kremdar abruptly.

"I don't know, Master. A woman, I believe."

Arvill, hoped Gemara. So perhaps they were making progress after all. Her forty days were wearing away. She wondered how far Kai had had to travel in their direction before finding a ford or bridge. And how many mistakes had he made?

She itched to be on her way, and the tension and mystery conveyed itself to the rest of the household. Yaina clung tiresomely to her father, and Gemara was forced to take her eyes off him long enough for him to carry her upstairs and sing to her. (The songs came drifting down: "Ten Little Ducks", and "Lullaby Sweetling".) Praja stood in the hall, watching Gemara darkly. Gemara looked back, trying for the unruffled expression that Hassdan or King Arrion would have produced.

Kremdar came down and kissed his wife, and the four travellers left. It was already dark, and threatening to rain again. Tommid looked downcast.

They rode for about half an hour – not fast, in the dark. Then Kremdar drew up beside her, and said quietly, "Gemara. I cannot go back to Stonehill with you."

"Why not?"

"I can't explain – it's not for me to do so – but I have a task to do. I must find these killers, this woman Sil."

"Other people can do that. Why does it have to be you?"

"I – there are reasons -"

"This is a murder of one man and one girl. You can ask the King to let you pursue it, if you like. I suppose you'll give him your reasons."

"Why won't you trust me? I tell you, I have to go. You would trust any of the others," he said incomprehensibly.

"I would certainly not trust any of the others to dash around the country outside the south on their own idea of what was important, without consulting me or the King, and without explaining why," said Gemara angrily. "I am ordering you to Stonehill. Give your reasons to King Arrion."

"Very well." He bowed his head meekly.

Was he jealous of the other members of the Six? Had he lied about Dorac because he was jealous of him? Jealous of Dorac, who had so little, when Kremdar had so much?

They went on a little further before she ordered camp, in an abandoned homestead near the road that still had most of its roof –

fortunately, since it was beginning to rain again. Kremdar and Tommid made a fire and cooked bacon and nuts, while Gemara and Morvan saw to the horses.

"One of us must keep watch all night," Gemara murmured. "I don't trust him to stay here. I don't want to arrest him, but his behaviour is so erratic – I think he may be mad." Morvan looked alarmed, as well he might. She remembered what had happened to Dorac, and added, "He may try to persuade you that I am a traitor or a criminal, and it's your duty to help him. He is a good talker."

They ate without conversation, and lay down. When the others were quiet, Gemara sat up again, wrapped in her blanket. A long, slow, cold watch, staring at the embers and the horses, and the three humps of people. She wondered what Kai was doing with his prisoner; how Dorac – prejudiced fool that he was – was managing in Jaryar; and why there had been no news at all from Hassdan. Most of all she wondered whom Kremdar had expected to find dead in his outbuilding. It was plainly not this Gan. He had been her brother for seven years, and she understood nothing.

Halfway through the night, she roused Morvan with a word of apology, and wrapped herself up to sleep.

*

20 October 570

Gemara was very cold and stiff – *getting on for sixty* – when she woke, and it was broad day. There was silence, except for the birds.

Kremdar was gone. Tommid was gone. Their horses were gone. Morvan -

He was lying on the ground, with a gash on the side of his

310

head. But he was still breathing.

Gemara cursed, but she had no time or energy to waste in cursing. She pulled herself together, and found the tracks, leading back to the road. With an enormous effort, she heaved the soldier onto the back of his horse, and led him there, where she examined tracks again. It was all very muddy, but she thought she could discern that they had headed south. *Did this have anything to do with the news of Kai?*

She came to the next substantial farmhouse, and assumed her most authoritative air.

"I am Gemara Kingsister, and I am in urgent need of your help. Please look after this man as well as you can. When he wakes, give him a letter I'll write for you. If he doesn't wake within the next hour or so, send the letter to the King by someone you can trust. In the meantime, gather three or four trusty people and come after me. You may have to help arrest a dangerous criminal. And give me a drink."

She wrote:

20 Oct. K and his squire attacked soldier and escaped west of Arjan. Am pursuing. Find out what Praja and Lukor know. Woman called Sil may be involved. G.

And she set off again.

She couldn't ride as fast as she wanted, because of the mud after the rainy days, but the same would apply to them. How much of a start did they have, or think they had?

For the first time, it occurred to her to wonder if she ought to be afraid. Forty years ago, after it happened, she had set herself to become the best fighter she possibly could, so that it could never happen again. It was not only or even mainly sword fighting, for she was a horse trader and not a soldier. But there were techniques for combat suited to women and those of lighter build, and it was her expertise in these that had first drawn her to the notice of Queen Darisha, and led in time to her being called to the Thirty. It was not so much that Kremdar was stronger and heavier and better with a sword than she was that concerned her now, but that he was half her age.

In early afternoon, she crested a hill, and looked down, and saw them. The woods had largely been replaced by fields, and they were standing under a lone tree in the drizzle, examining one of the horses. Riding too hard on slippery ground had evidently led to an accident.

She could trust Tara Maid to stand. She led her off the road and left her among the bare harvested rigs. "Wait for me. Wait," she said, caressing her horse's nose, and set off on foot along the edge of the field where she could keep low.

Gemara was very quiet. They were so absorbed they did not hear her coming until she stepped up, sword in hand, and said, "In the name of the King, stand still."

Tommid gasped, and Kremdar stared at her, his face sad and unreadable.

"I am arresting you, Kremdar, on charges of assaulting a soldier in the King's service, disobeying my direct orders, and abandoning your duty. There are soldiers on the way. Give me your sword."

"You cannot do this, Gemara," he whispered. "Please."

"Give me your sword. Tommid, stand back."

Tommid stepped away obediently, several paces, until he was standing against the tree. Kremdar slowly drew his sword, turned it hilt outwards, stepped to the side, and knelt to lay it at her feet.

"I had orders," he said. "I did have orders. From King Arrion."

That was impossible – he was fiddling with something –

"Help me!" Tommid screamed.

Gemara could not but turn her head to look at him, and in that moment Kremdar had his knife out, and was up and slashing at her throat. She had no time to do anything but stare before it was over, and he pushed her away to die at his feet.

*

Kremdar cleaned his knife on Gemara's cloak, and picked up his sword. He stood and met Tommid's horror-stricken eyes. "I am sorry," he said uselessly, and the words seemed to come from a long way away.

Part of his mind knew that his actions were insane, and that he had destroyed himself as surely as he had destroyed Gemara. But the other part, the tired and dreamy but determined part, said that at least she could not stop him now. He must go on. He must protect the child. He must find Arvill.

Arvill my soul -.

He had to find her, and look in her eyes, and ask her if she had betrayed him.

There was a rustle, and Tommid was gone. Poor Tommid.

She had said soldiers were coming, but that might be a bluff.

Knowing it would not buy him much time, he dragged Gemara's body off the road and into the ditch. He couldn't dig a grave, and he couldn't bear to throw leaves or soil onto her, so he closed her eyes, and covered her face and body with her dark-coloured cloak.

It was not possible. He had killed his sister.

He set this aside. Over the last few weeks he had learned that he was good at not thinking about things.

Kai had a woman prisoner somewhere between here and the Poto bridge.

He slapped Tommid's lame horse until it ambled off, mounted his own, and rode on.

Makkam and Gormad 2 (20–23 October)

20 October 570

Gormad and Jamis sat in the chapel with Secretary Makkam, and told her the things they – mainly Jamis – had picked up.

"Torio comes and goes as he pleases with his broken foot. Brinnon Kingsbrother's squire says he's very mysterious about how he injured it, and swore at someone who asked."

Makkam made a note.

"He laughed a lot because Kai Kingsbrother's lover in the town quarrelled with him and threw him out because he had a child with another woman. I don't know her name, but she keeps a wood-carving shop on Battle Lane."

"But -" Gormad stopped himself.

"That is sad," said Makkam, frowning, and made another note. She asked if they knew anything about several other names. "Ralia is your lord's sister, isn't she?" she asked Jamis.

"Yes, but they don't talk to each other much. Aros says Ralia has grander friends than him. She talks a lot to Prince Jendon. And so does Torio – I think he practises swordplay with him."

"Torio is a distant cousin of theirs, I think?"

"Is he? I didn't know that. Aros and Ralia did have a cousin in the King's Thirty, I know, but that was a woman, and she died."

"What was her name?"

"I don't know. She died in the War from the Sea. My lord told

Ralia once, 'Don't be so sure the King's going to name you just because I-can't-remember-her-name was named ten years ago.' He was cross. I think it began with G."

He listed the friends of Ralia's that he had heard Aros mention, and they both detailed everything they knew – or suspected - about the severe Captain Renatar and his family, and just before they left Jamis volunteered that he thought the dead Kingsister's name might have been Gara or Galla. Makkam was drawing a rabbit, which she hastily crossed out, and wrote this down. She met Gormad's eyes, and grinned guiltily.

That seemed to be all.

Gormad thought that the conversation had wandered rather far from Torio. But if Jamis didn't feel he was being disloyal to Aros, that wasn't for Gormad to worry about, and anyway it was all for the King. It must be. Surely it couldn't be what his father had forbidden. He told himself that King Arrion himself had said he could talk to the Queen and Makkam, so he must trust them. The Queen, after all -

He wished something would happen.

*

21 October 570

And then abruptly something did.

The squires had finished their Friday lessons, and were looking for amusement. A few grabbed sticks, and began hitting a stone about the courtyard. The game would be stopped by an interfering adult very soon, and in any case Gormad preferred to watch and dodge. The smaller boys sometimes got hurt.

Suddenly he noticed that a strange girl had crept up, and was staring from the edge as well.

She wasn't a squire – in fact she was barefoot, ragged and a bit tear-stained. Perhaps she wanted some help begging food from the kitchens. Gormad sidled up to her, and said, "Who are you?" in a friendly tone, though it made her jump. "I'm Gormad. I live here. Are you from the town?"

She shook her head. "I need to find the King," she whispered in a poor person's accent, hard to follow.

"You can't just 'find the King'. You need to be summoned. Why d'you want to find him?"

"I have a message. A letter. For the King, and no one else." She drew out from her shirt a rather battered and dirty parchment. But it was sealed, and Gormad recognised the seal. Kai had used it. The seal of the Southern Six.

"Who's it from?" he asked excitedly, and more loudly than he had meant. A few heads turned.

"A girl, a rich girl gave it to my aunt."

"Was her name Meril?"

"I don't know. It's for the King."

"I'll take you to him," said Gormad. He had the right to see Makkam, and surely Makkam could find the King.

"You're going to see the King, Gormad?" said his enemy Hanos, and people laughed.

Gormad had to choose whether to shrivel or stand firm. "This is a messenger with an important letter. I think she needs to see the King." The girl shrank close to him, and he felt strong and protective. But he was still one of the smallest people in the group.

And then there was someone much taller looming above the children. "A message for the King? I'll take it for her."

Torio.

"She is to deliver it herself, Master Torio," Gormad dared to say.

The girl nodded vigorously.

"Insolent boy. Give me that." When neither of them moved, Torio reached out, snatched it, and turned away. Hanos laughed.

Gormad was humiliated and angry, and desperate to do something useful. Again he chose, and threw himself at the man's hateful back.

Torio was leaning on his crutch, and they both went down onto the muddy ground. Gormad, on top, seized the letter from his hand, but the man was shouting, and rolling over onto him, knocking away all his breath.

Someone else tore the letter from him, and ran.

*

Makkam did not need to use her new watchword. The King asked her openly one day to attend on him in the Willow Chamber, a room he liked to use for private conversations. There was a window alcove where they could not be overheard.

She told him that Torio and Ralia were distantly related (third cousins), that Lady Kara and Helena, daughter of Sibel, shared a passion for chess, that Lady Kara and Braf had been born in the same town, and that Lady Orria and Lady Geril had both travelled to Makkera (many years apart). And that no one seemed to know anything about Arvill, daughter of Eve, before she had joined the Kingslands army at the age (she said) of nineteen.

"Not much so far," said the King, as if reading her own thoughts. "Do you have anything else?"

"There is something I want to explore. Something the boys said. And, also, Your Grace," she said very nervously, "when Mistress Gemara first suggested that there might have been a - mistake - about Ferrodach, you asked me to look into the law. The law about changing a conviction and sentence."

"Yes, I did. What have you found?"

"Not much, Your Grace. We only have accounts of trials for about fifty years back, and only those of the highest people. I found one man who was hanged for a murder, and two years later another man confessed to it, among many others. So everyone realised that Lord Derrian had been innocent, and there was a church service to honour him, but of course he was already dead. And there was a woman who was exiled for treason, and then recalled by King Lukor, and it seems certain that she had been wrongly sentenced by his sister before she was removed. Queen Arrabetta condemned many people unjustly, but there were not often trials."

"Very interesting," said the King, not sounding interested, "and your conclusions?"

"Your Grace, you are the king. If you believe Dorac is innocent, or that he's been punished enough, you can call him back. No one could prevent you."

"I can fill my castle with murderers if I choose, you mean?"

"Yes. That's the first solution. Or you can pardon him for his crime, and again bring him back."

"If he's guilty, I don't want to pardon him. If he's innocent, a pardon suggests he's guilty, and that's not good enough."

"If you find evidence against someone else, you could try that person and find them guilty. But then you'd have two people condemned for the same crime, which is illogical. It seems wrong."

"The second trial would overrule the first."

"But why would it? Unless there was a rule, an arrangement -"

"You are about to be presumptuous again."

Makkam looked down at the floor, her ears and shoulders strangely cold, and explained her presumptuous idea.

"I still think," said the King eventually, "that I should be able to say, 'He is innocent. Here are the proofs', and deal with it that way. If he is."

"Yes, you could, Your Grace. But that would just be for Master Dorac. Judges make mistakes. Justice should be for everyone, not only the king's brothers."

"What makes you so interested in justice, Makkam?"

Makkam made her face rigid. "I knew a man, a priest, who visited people in prisons. Because Jesus commanded it."

"Ah, a saint. What happened to this man?"

"He died, Your Grace. In the War from the Sea." And at last she could talk of it without her throat swelling, and tears.

"Leaving his high thoughts with you. First you want to join the Thirty, and now you want to change the law. Is there no limit to your ambition, Makkam? I make no promises. Devise me a plan, then, that satisfies your thirst for justice."

They left the Willow Chamber and walked away, followed by

320

Olda Kingsister and a guard. They were almost at the door to the Great Hall, when there was a sound of running footsteps, and shocked shouts, and two children ran up to the King.

One was a ragged and unfamiliar girl; the other was Gormad's friend Jamis. "A letter, Your Grace," he gasped. "A letter from Meril."

*

Torio thumped him in the face – *ow!* - and struggled to his feet. "Where did those children go?" Gormad looked up at the legs and then the faces of the circle of squires, and saw with pleasure that none of them seemed willing to help Torio.

Who dragged him up from the ground.

"I'll teach you respect for the Thirty!" was all he said between blows. Gormad squirmed and wriggled, and tried not to squeal.

"What is going on?" demanded Captain Renatar, appearing in the midst of the confusion.

"This boy attacked me and knocked me down – whose squire is he? I –"

But suddenly silence fell in the excited courtyard, and everyone turned. King Arrion was striding calmly towards them, accompanied by Secretary Makkam, several guards, the ragged girl, and Jamis.

Gormad, Torio and the Captain bowed.

"Brother, what is wrong? The noise we heard suggested a riot."

"That urchin claimed to have a letter for Your Grace. I was proposing to bring it to you when I was knocked down by this brat, and his friend stole it."

"You," the King said to Gormad, and at the cold fury in his face, Gormad felt himself shrink. "You *again*.

"Brother, for your comfort, the letter has been safely delivered. The little messenger deserves food and drink – see to it, Li." He smiled at the girl. "Captain Renatar, I'm most displeased by the licence these boys seem to think they have. An unprovoked assault on an injured man – this is not just a childish prank. I am sure, brother, that we can rely on the Captain to see that they are severely punished. Lock them up somewhere to start with to think about what they've done. You are not hurt, Torio?"

*

Gormad and Jamis were put in a small windowless storeroom, and left in the dark.

"They won't hang us, will they?" asked Jamis, trying to sound brave, and failing.

"Of course not," said Gormad crossly. His face was bruised, and his shoulders were sore. He had never seen the King so angry. He wondered if watching Torio had all been a mistake, but the *Queen* -

The door opened, and Makkam came in carrying a candle and a bowl of water. "Show me your face," she said, and she knelt down and began to sponge it gently. "The King has a message for you, Gormad."

"Ow! – What message?"

"He says," Makkam said smiling, "that he now realises that Master Dorac was not exaggerating in his letter. He is most grateful to you both, and hopes you will understand that he had to pretend not to be."

"He was pretending? He pretended very well," said Jamis.

"Yes. I sometimes think he would have made an excellent mummer in the mystery plays. He would not have wanted Torio to see that letter, but he doesn't want Torio to know that. Even less would he have wanted to lose it."

"Was it from Meril?"

"Who is Meril?"

"Master Hassdan's squire."

"Ah. The letter was from Master Hassdan. He gave it to his squire to deliver, and she was attacked by someone on the way. It's not clear who attacked her. She was injured, and passed the letter on to the villagers, and they sent the little girl to deliver it. That was eleven days ago."

"Is Meril – is she all right now?"

"I don't know," said Makkam seriously. "People are being sent to find her. At least it explains why no one has heard from Ferrodach." She looked thoughtful.

"What did the letter say?"

"I don't think I can tell you that. I'm sorry." Then she relented. "It does confirm that what happened is more mysterious than it first seemed."

"Perhaps Meril was attacked to stop the King reading the letter! By friends of Torio?"

"Perhaps. Perhaps. The King can't be sure. But he is going to keep a much more careful eye on his brother. You two, however, should stay out of his way.

"In the meantime, you're to be punished. Captain Renatar has ordered that you eat nothing, and drink only water, until Sunday morning, for the good of your souls."

Jamis looked horrified.

"This means that when we're all eating, you two will stand at the back of the Hall looking repentant and hungry. Make sure you look repentant and hungry. Afterwards, you may come to me in the scriptorium, and I will get you something to eat."

*

22 October 570

She was better than her word. When Jamis and Gormad called for food the next evening, she did not merely take them aside to a private chamber and feed them cold pie, cold chicken, apples and watered ale, she also gave them more news.

"The King and Council think they need to know more about the earlier trial. They're sending soldiers to try to find Master Dorac.

"Don't look so hopeful," she added. "According to you and Master Kai, he went into Jaryar. The soldiers will have to be tactful at the border. He may be difficult to find."

"But there were only forty days given to prove he didn't do it!"

"Yes. Well. We'll have to pray."

"Suppose he doesn't want to come back?" asked Jamis.

"He'll come back if the King asks him to," said Gormad confidently. He knew that, at least.

Makkam laughed. "How strange – that was exactly what one of the soldiers said. 'He might refuse to return with us. Do we force him?' and Pr – someone said, 'I think he will come back at the King's request.' And the King went -'' Makkam put on a very superior expression. Neither of the boys knew if this was an accurate imitation of King Arrion, but they both laughed. "The King said, 'I am not 'requesting'. I am ordering him to come home. Make sure you tell him so.' They're leaving tomorrow."

*

"Galla, daughter of Palla, was named to the Queen's Thirty in 558 at the age of 20. She was noted for her skills in hunting and with the bow. She served with honour, and died in battle at Rayf in the early days of the War from the Sea. She was replaced in the Southern Six by Hassdan, son of Yrass. She was unmarried and left no children."

Makkam stared at her notes. Galla of the Southern Six. A first cousin once removed of Ralia, daughter of Imali. Then she looked at her second, larger parchment. As neat and clear as she could make it. Once again, news – no, not news, merely a theory that the King would not want to hear.

She had managed to speak to the Queen at the end of chapel. "Your Grace, you asked me to look for connections between people."

"You've found some? I will send for you later."

Torio was in the corridors. He had not looked at her, but his presence made her nervous. Warriors have weapons. But so, in their way, do secretaries. Makkam's weapon was a genealogical chart.

So she waited, running over phrases in her mind, and absently drawing a timid-looking spaniel on the edge of her notes.

A knock, and Secretary Andros went to the door. Li said, "Secretary Makkam is wanted in the Willow Chamber."

Now to be presumptuous again. She swallowed a vile taste, and found her mouth dry.

*

Gormad was struggling to look as sorry and suffering as he was supposed to. Jamis, very excited, made ridiculous grimaces that surely would make anyone suspicious. But fortunately no one seemed to be looking at them. Everyone was talking about Master Hassdan's letter, even though no one knew what it said. Dorac had been sent for; that much was known. Perhaps he had committed more crimes – or perhaps Lord Gahran or his steward had. There was an excited air about the Castle, and Gormad did not know whether to feel nervous or smug.

Sheru Kingsister chose that Sunday to send him with a gift to a friend in the town. This friend kept him waiting for a long age, and it was nearly supper-time when he returned, kicking a pebble along the road, and pretending it was the King of Jaryar. He slipped through the courtyard, arranged his face to look sad, placed his hands on his supposedly empty stomach, and hurried into the Great Hall.

The huge room was almost silent. There was a whispering at the tables, and a few people looked up at him as he entered, almost as if he might have brought news. Something about the way they were sitting and looking at each other was wrong. Gormad glanced up at the King and Queen at the high table, and gasped at their faces. As he edged along to stand next to Jamis, he caught a few words from someone. "The Southern Six is cursed."

"What's happened?" he muttered to Jamis.

Jamis seemed unable to answer. But the person in front turned round to say, "Have you not heard? Gemara Kingsister is dead."

Bassdan and Meril 2 (10–23 October)

10 October 570

When Meril woke up, it was almost completely dark. She was indoors, lying on something, probably bracken. There was a strong smell of smoke, and cow – or goat? Her head hurt, and her shoulder hurt worse, and her ankle was agony. As she shifted, the bracken crackled, and all the pains churned sickeningly.

"Pl-please?" she asked in a wobbly voice. Even that sound was frightening, in an unknown dark place. There was no answer.

Someone had attacked Josper. Someone had attacked *her*. She had given away her letter. She was hungry and thirsty - probably not many hours had passed. That was all she knew, and all she knew for a long waiting time. *Please please please.*

Then the hut door opened, and people were finishing a conversation in the doorway. Most of it was too faint to hear –

"But if she doesn't die, then –?"

"Shh!"

One person went away. The other approached, carrying a foul-smelling rushlight. It was a poorly dressed woman, who peered down and seemed startled at Meril's open eyes.

"My dear," she said awkwardly, "are you – how are you?"

"Please – where am I?"

"You're in my house. I am Finya. Have some water - er - my

327

lady."

My lady?

"My name is Meril. I'm the squire of Hassdan Kingsbrother. He will pay you for helping me. Please send a message – he's at Ferrodach."

Finya looked frightened, and her hand shook on the cup she was holding to Meril's mouth. "I don't know -"

"There were people with me -"

"I don't know about anyone else," said Finya firmly. "We found you in the wood, on the ground. You had fallen from your horse. You were injured. Does your leg hurt?"

"Yes, but – there were two soldiers -"

"No, we have not seen them. No." She was lying, Meril was sure, and she felt sick at the thought of Anni and Josper.

Finya leaned very close, and Meril shuddered at the scent of her. "We saw no one else. There was no one else." More quietly still, "I sent your message with my niece. Don't tell anyone."

Who shouldn't she tell? Meril drank, and then was given some porridge, and Finya said nothing more. Instead, she rolled herself up in a blanket, and told Meril to go to sleep.

All lights went out. In the hut corner, some largish animal snorted and pawed the ground. Meril tried to make sense of what had happened. If Anni and Josper were alive and well, they would surely have come for her. They would have come. So they were injured at best, dead at worst. Finya was frightened, perhaps because she or people she knew had killed them. She had said the message had been sent, but that might have been a lie.

"If she doesn't die -'" they would kill her? *If she doesn't die of her injuries. If she doesn't die.*

Slowly the pain became more bearable, and she slept a little. Morning came, dim light crawling in through cracks in the stick-and-mud walls. Finya rose and rubbed her eyes, wakened the fire and heated more porridge. She did not ask how Meril was, or seem to want to talk at all, but her manner was gentle as she propped her up to eat and drink. It was then that Meril discovered that she could not move her right arm, from the shoulder down. Any attempt hurt.

The animal was a goat, which was let out.

She was in a home half the size of Hassdan and Alida's kitchen. There were no windows, so when the door was shut it was little brighter than at night. But its upper half was usually open, letting in chill air. The hut contained a fireplace, a pile of cooking utensils, a box, a few blankets, and some tools hanging up, all neatly arranged, and nothing else.

"Where is this place?" she asked timidly.

Finya bit her lip and hesitated over even this information. "The village is called Saint's Rest. Our lord is Beriot, and his lord is Gahran of Ferrodach." Her face showed a sudden realisation that Gahran was no one's lord any more, and again she looked frightened. She gulped and said, "How did – how did you fall off your horse?"

Meril had had time to think about this. "I'm not sure. I was riding with my friends, but it's confused in my mind. I think I hit my head." She noticed the woman's obvious relief. *So I haven't denounced your friend. If she is your friend. Please don't kill me.*

Again she tried to persuade Finya that Hassdan would reward

her for news, but the woman walked out of the house. Meril wept with frustration, and then she went on weeping for other reasons.

The next uncountable days were frightening, pain-filled and tedious. She lay or sat in Finya's house, staring at chinks in the walls. She was fed, and had access to a necessary bucket, but apart from her grazed face she was not washed, and no one looked at her injuries, which began to worry her more and more. The final awfulness was when the cramps and the trickling told her that her moon-time had come round, and she had to beg for some rags for the blood. She did not get rags, only moss. Finya was sympathetic but embarrassed.

Meril grew steadily more disgusting.

She wondered what had happened to her letter.

And if she would ever get away from here. And, if she did, if she would ever walk again. The foot, like the shoulder, hurt unbearably if she tried to move it.

A squire who could not walk, or ride, or fight. A cripple. It might be better to be dead.

Her family were decent and God-fearing. They would not turn her out to beg by the roadside, like the people one sometimes saw, whom Alida might give a penny to. She would have a home, where she would be useless and resented, and would spend her life sewing. If she could even sew.

If she got out of here.

Finya was afraid. Someone in this village must know who had attacked Josper and Anni. That person might want to kill her.

And she could do nothing to help herself, or her master, or anyone else.

Her thoughts went round endlessly.

There was only one thing she could do. She could listen. She could try to talk to Finya, listen if anyone else was nearby, listen and remember.

One day someone might ask her questions. *Please please please.*

*

22 October 570

Captain Rabellit remained behind at Ferrodach when Hassdan and Soumaki rode out with Barad and three other soldiers, which was the most they could possibly spare. It was not enough. From what Hagouna had said, if she could be trusted, it did not seem likely that the village of Saint's Rest was a focus of active rebellion against the crown. But to murder two of the King's soldiers was a terrible crime.

The soldiers rode in armour, but Hassdan and Soumaki did not. They instructed everyone to look calm, unafraid and unaggressive. This was a simple criminal investigation, and a search for a lost child. Two of the soldiers were sent scouting forward, back and around.

One of them came riding back with Barad's comrade Lakker. "I have found nothing, sir," Lakker reported. "There is no sign of the squire in the woods. The villagers have seen nothing."

But somebody had hidden the bodies, Barad had said, moving them from where they fell. Lakker had not managed to deduce where the attack had happened. Admittedly, it must have been well over a week ago, but still he seemed useless.

They rode down the little path into the village, pretending that no one would think of troubling them. There were about six houses clustered together round a well, and a string of other dwellings further down the path as far as the eye could see through a few trees. Hassdan ordered a trumpet sounded immediately. Four long blasts. Then he waited. To the first person who stepped out of a house, he ordered, "Call the people together," and in a quarter of an hour or so there were about twenty men, women and children congregating in what passed for a village square.

Hassdan had not dismounted. He smiled serenely, and nodded to Yalli to sound the trumpet again.

"Greetings in God's name. I am Hassdan Kingsbrother and this is Soumaki Kingsister." He paused. "Four weeks ago, a terrible murder was committed at Ferrodach." Another pause. "The King utterly condemned this murder, and sent the criminal, who was a member of the Thirty, into exile. Since then the two of us have been making investigations at the house. I sent three messengers to Stonehill. As you've been told, two of them were attacked and murdered not far from here. I know you will be frightened at the thought of killers nearby.

"We are here for justice for those soldiers. We're also here to find any news of the third messenger, a girl called Meril, and to find any trace of a five-year-old child who may be travelling with a dark-skinned man. If you can help us, there will be rewards.

"If you do not help, if you have knowledge and hinder the King's work, you will face his wrath. He is not forgiving. But I can be, if you have reason to be afraid. Talk privately to me, or to Mistress Soumaki.

"Who are your village elders?" When two men crept slowly forward, he said, "Go with Barad here, and give him a list of everyone living in the village and five miles around. Now, if you please."

He swung himself down, and watched the little crowd murmur and disperse. "What did you see?" he asked Soumaki.

"They are all scared. Scared, I think, rather than angry. They know something. There were a few glances towards the cottage at the end, where we came in, and a few down the other way."

Hassdan nodded. Soumaki turned one way, and he the other, wandering casually up and down, trying to intuit whose attention was most intense. Yes, that woman was looking at him steadily, and fingering the folds of her kirtle. He allowed his steps to drift in her direction, with Lakker a few paces behind. The woman edged along the side of a house. Hassdan followed, and she threw herself at his feet.

"I meant no harm, sir, Master, I swear, I have her safe. She said you would reward, please, I did her no harm -"

The hovel was one of the furthest from the village entrance. Its roof would be too low for him to stand upright. The woman opened the door and stepped back. The smell revolted him. It might be a trap, of course, although the hut was not big enough for many assassins, and Hassdan said, "Wait for me" to Lakker, and ducked into semi-darkness, with his sword drawn.

"Who is here?"

He heard a gasping "Oh!" which he recognised.

"Meril! Thank God."

The place stank of many things, including blood. She was lying on the ground, and seemed unable to get up. "Give me your arm."

"I can't, Master – not that side." So he got to the other, and half-dragged, half-carried her out. Meril flinched and raised her good hand to ward off the brightness, and his heart contracted as he saw her so filthy and thin, and the sickeningly wrong shape of her shoulder and ankle. At least there seemed to be no open wound and no gangrene.

"Get Yalli," he ordered. Yalli had the greatest knowledge of wounds and their treatment. He sat on the ground, propping her up against him. "Where are you hurt? Who did this?"

"I – I don't think anyone did, Master. I fell off my horse, and hit my head." But she twisted round, grimacing, to look into his face, and he clearly understood the message. She went on, "This woman has been kind to me, fed me and sent on my letter."

"Ahh."

"Anni and Josper – are they -?"

"They are dead. I'm sorry. When did you come here?"

"You sent us out on the Saturday, and I was injured the next afternoon. What day is it now?"

"Today is Sunday the twenty-third. So you've been lying here for two weeks."

Yalli came hurrying up, clucking at the sight of Meril, accompanied by Soumaki. "I need cloths and clean water."

"You. Fetch water." That got rid of the Lowly woman. "You were attacked?"

"Yes," gasped Meril, bravely trying to ignore Yalli's probing fingers. "Josper rode off the road, and someone threw something at him, and there was a tall woman -" She described the attack. "Finya knows something, I think, but the people from the village scared the woman off. Graki, or Raki, they called her, or some name like that, a 'rak' in it, I'm not sure. I tried to listen when people talked, but hardly

334

anyone came to the hut. Only one man, and he whispered."

"Did you hear anything of interest?"

"Nothing about children – or Ferrodach – or Anni and Josper. I heard whispers, a few names -" She screwed up her face. "He said 'in the chapel', and 'that fool Duff or Daff', and once 'Thank St Aidril she's gone'. I think it was 'she', not 'he'."

"St Aidril. I see."

The woman was back with water. Yalli had opened Meril's shirt, and probed gently. "Only dislocated, I think. This will hurt, but -" She looked at Hassdan. "Can you hold her still?"

He stared. After a moment it was Soumaki who said, "I will," shifted Meril across, gripped her firmly and nodded to Yalli. Meril squeezed her eyes tight shut, tearing Hassdan's heart again, and Yalli twisted something in her shoulder, and she screamed.

"Is that better?"

Tears were streaming down her face, but she nodded, and her shoulder and arm no longer appeared misshapen.

"Now I'll look at that foot."

Barad was approaching them with a parchment. The list Hassdan had asked for. He called himself to his duty. "I'm no use here, I think. I will be back, Meril. Well done." He squeezed her good shoulder, and he and Soumaki left her with Yalli and the woman, who continued to stand trembling and twisting her hands together, until Yalli started giving her orders.

The list told him where to go: to a rather larger cottage at the other end of the village. One of his soldiers was standing outside it. He had a brief discussion with Soumaki, who went off with Lakker, and he entered with Barad.

This one, happily, smelt only of smoke. There was one person there, a frail-looking elderly woman, at least fifty, sitting by the fire. "God's blessing on this house," said Hassdan, his voice much less friendly than the words. "You are Vetara, daughter of Janika? And, I believe, widow of Andor."

He looked round in the murky light from the door and single window. "Look over there." Barad pulled out a satchel from beneath the bed. "That belongs to my squire, I am thinking."

She was silent. Hassdan squatted down in front of her. "I want to talk to you about your children."

*

Dorac would have known at once. When St Aidril decided to spend her remaining days in prayer and solitude, a local lord built her a tiny stone chapel in the woods. The village of Saint's Rest did not exist then; it grew up later. Anyone riding or walking from Ferrodach to Stonehill could deflect down a meandering path, which then divided again. The village to the left; the chapel to the right. Josper had gone right.

Dorac would have known, but he was not there. Hassdan had had to rely on Hagouna and Meril, and now Vetara. His soldiers were spread terrifyingly thin, but he left Barad and Yalli in the village, and everyone else surrounded the little glade where the chapel was. "Yes, he's in there."

"Good."

St John, pray for us. Hassdan walked into the glade, alone, tensing for arrows and spears. He stopped about ten feet from the door.

"I am Hassdan Kingsbrother. I am here to talk to Dav. I am unarmed, and I swear by St Aidril that I mean no harm to the child."

There was silence. But he had heard something before, when they had seen him coming. He took out his water-skin and drank, then sat down and brought out apples and bread from his satchel.

"I can wait to talk to you. Although I would rather not be waiting too long. This place is surrounded. You cannot escape." *Unless you have many friends. If God is good to us, you have not.*

"There is no child here," said a man's voice from inside. A good beginning.

"This is a sacred place. Don't lie. I have spoken to your mother – who is well – and I know there is." He took a mouthful of bread and cheese, nonchalant. He knew Dav was not a soldier, but the other -

The chapel door opened. A dark bald man of about thirty emerged, a small child clinging behind his legs. Hassdan knew little of children's ages, but she looked right.

"God's greetings. Do you want something to eat? I will call my friend. Soumaki?"

Soumaki emerged from the trees, smiling and unthreatening. Hassdan addressed the girl. "Little lady, I need you to sit over there with Mistress Soumaki, and have some bread and cheese, or a pear, or something nice, while I talk to Dav."

"Don't hurt Dav," she whispered.

"You can sit and watch, and see that I don't."

She looked up at the man, and he nodded. She released him reluctantly, and sat down next to Soumaki. They had brought one of

337

the few toys the village possessed, a little wooden horse and cart, but she batted it pettishly aside, and stared at the men.

Dav walked over to Hassdan and stood over him.

"Sit down."

Hassdan had rarely seen anyone look so defeated. Yet Dav said, "I don't care who you are. If you hurt her, you will be cursed and damned."

"I have no desire to hurt her. I have sworn it, and I will swear it again, by any saint you please. Sit down and eat."

Dav obeyed. He was not starving, but once he had taken the bread he ate it fast.

"Speak quietly, please. Tell me what happened at Ferrodach. After the Kingsbrothers came."

Dav finished the bread. He hunched his shoulders, and glanced over at the child. Then he sighed, and said, "They said our lord was a traitor. It's not true. They shut us up." He was sitting cross-legged, staring at his hands. "I had to go to – to take a shit – and I met one of them in the passage. He –"

"Which one?"

"I didn't know their names. One of them was older and broader across, and one was thin, with a scar on his face. It was the older one. He told me to fetch food for the children from the pantry, and go to the little room under the gallery. I got the food, and the other one, with the scar, met me. He told me his brother was mad. He'd killed Ilda and Gaskor, and Lord Gahran. He opened the room, and showed me the children's bodies -" Dav looked away. Hassdan remembered the corpses he had seen. "He said I could save the youngest. Even Hagouna the steward and one Kingsbrother couldn't defend her against this Dorac and all his soldiers, so I had to get her away. He got rid of the guard at the door, so we could get out. He said, 'Take her to the stables, and hide and wait.' I did that.

"Later on, he came and gave me money for the journey. I still have it, I've only spent a little, I'm not a thief. He said she'd be safe at a place called Kisren –"

"Kisren?"

"Kisren, or Gisren, somewhere in the north. He said it was his estate, and he would order people there to help us. He'd make arrangements, persuade the King to let her live. He made me swear to protect her."

"Go on."

"I - He ordered me to go north, but I didn't." He met Hassdan's eyes with a despairing defiance. Lowly though he was, Hassdan was starting to like him very much.

"Why not?" He could guess.

"She - I - I don't know how far 'the north' is, but it would've taken - it took us nearly a week to get here. She doesn't walk fast, I had to carry her sometimes, and we were hiding all the time. I couldn't have done it. I don't know how to look after children."

"So you brought her here, and talked to your mother."

"My mother isn't to blame. I didn't know what to do. We were trying to think. I stayed here with Filana, and then you came."

Now the hard part. "I sent two soldiers along this road, and they are dead."

"I didn't kill them! I swear I did not." The resemblance in his face to his mother was clear. Hassdan wondered if Meril would also have seen a resemblance to her attacker.

He took a drink, and passed over the water-skin. "My squire is injured. I am needing to send word to Ferrodach, and to the King. For the time, you'll both come with me to Saint's Rest, and we will make camp."

He stood up, and Dav stood also.

"If you or the King hurt her, my ghost will haunt you. I'll make you pay."

"If you wish. Why leave the task to your ghost? You seem very sure you're going to die." Dav looked at him. "You took a child from her home, but you acted for good reason, and under the instructions of one of the King's Thirty. You later disobeyed those instructions, but that is not itself a crime." *Now for it. May the dead forgive me.* "You know more than you've said about a murder. You may be lying. If you had part in that murder, ordered or encouraged it, you will die. But the eyewitness account is of a single attacker, a woman.

"Your sister Raki fought in the War from the Sea. It's not known what she did after that. I am told she wanders around, but frequently visits her mother."

"Raki has nothing to do with this."

"This is a sacred place. Don't lie."

After a long pause, Dav said, "She saw terrible things. Ever since then - She's not right in the head."

"And she wanted to protect a child. Has she gone away?"

"Yes."

"I can't say what the King, or the new lord of these lands, will see fit to do about Raki. But you and I will go back to the village. With the child. Filana!" he called, and she looked up at once. "You and Dav are coming with me to see Dav's mother. And then I'm going to send for your friend Hagouna."

Kai 2 (19–23 October)

As he rode up to the impressive towers at Dendarry, Kai's primary hope was that there would be a good fire. He seemed to have been cold and wet for weeks.

It had taken a day in the village of Pendafor to arrange for the blacksmith to make manacles for Arvill. He wasn't going to let her ride free, but binding wrists firmly for days at a time was cruel. Then they set out – himself, Arvill on a led horse, and three soldiers – through drizzle and sodden fields. He warned the soldiers not to speak to the prisoner more than they had to, and tried not to do so himself. Arvill rode meekly, occasionally dropping a tear, but mostly just silent, looking about her with interest. With the interest of someone possibly on her last journey, Kai thought miserably, or perhaps not, for sometimes she hummed a little, but none of it was like the vivacious teasing Arvill he remembered. At night he set a guard to watch her, and took his own turn, and once or twice saw her lying awake staring at him, with a gut-wrenching lack of reproach. It was almost unbearable.

And then the next morning their way was blocked by the high water of the River Poto. Apparently everyone had been predicting that the bridge would collapse one day, and now it had. "We might be able to ford it further south," said Venner, the most local of the soldiers, so they turned that way. It wasn't truly raining any more, but it wasn't truly dry either. They came to what was normally a ford, but the water was high, and it looked very dubious. Venner volunteered to test the crossing, and lost his balance, and there was nearly a disaster.

Arvill started shrieking as he waded in, which was not helpful.

Venner almost drowned, one of the horses was swept away – *Gemara would flay him* – and before Kai and Jax could pull Venner out, Jax had torn his leg badly on a submerged branch. Kai dragged the two, one at a time, up the bank to where Kalla was guarding Arvill, and realised that warm shelter as soon as possible was a priority. Kalla bandaged Jax as well as she could, and after Kai had relieved his feelings by swearing at everybody and then apologising, he gave up his horse to the wounded man, and they accosted the next person they met to enquire about the local lord.

It had taken him several minutes to remember that Dendarry sounded familiar because it was Gormad's home. Well, possibly they owed him a favour.

"I am Kai Kingsbrother. I am escorting a prisoner to Stonehill. One of my men is injured, and we seek shelter for the night." The porter looked scared at the request, but ushered them into a small gatehouse, and sent word to his lady. It had been a climb to get there at all. Dendarry House was built on a hill, and built high, like a set of towers from a children's story. On the far, northern, side, the slope was even steeper, almost a cliff.

The man who'd been sent returned to escort them across the courtyard to the hall. There they were greeted by two women. "Farili, lady of Dendarry." Farili was tall and thin, leaning on a gold-topped cane. She was grandly dressed in a full green overgown showing silver beneath – a gown that even Lady Sada might have coveted. There was silver embroidery in the cap that covered most of her neatly coiled hair, and a gold chain about her neck. These were confident clothes, and she held her chin high. Yet despite this, her manner was awkward, and she did not step forward at once at his words.

Her companion, to his astonishment, was Mayeel Kingsister of the Northern Six, a stocky woman in her forties, wearing businesslike dark-blue jacket and hose. She seemed equally surprised to see him. There were other soldiers about, he realised.

"Er, greetings, Master Kai," said Farili after a moment, looking at him as if he had brought news of a dead relative, and seeming uncertain whether it were for her to speak, although this was her hall. "Be welcome, in the name of my husband Ramahdis, who is in Stonehill at present, and myself. We are sorry you've met with misfortune. How can we assist?"

"I'm travelling to Stonehill, but the river is too high to cross, and this man is injured. I would be grateful if we could trespass on your hospitality for the night, and borrow a horse and a soldier in the morning – and some local knowledge of where best to cross the Poto." He might be over-cautious, but he wanted three soldiers. Arvill might possibly have friends.

Farili glanced sideways, and it was Mayeel who answered. "I am sorry to say there are no soldiers to spare. I was ordered here by the King. There has been some local trouble, and we cannot send any away. As for crossing the river, you may have to wait until it goes down."

This was more and more strange. Kai had seen no local trouble, and he felt crossly sure that Mayeel, with her cream-curdling face, was just being difficult. But it would have been undignified to argue with her, and indeed who was Kai to argue with the King's command? And on the other hand, it might indeed be quicker to wait until the river went down than to trudge an unknown distance to the east, and Farili diffidently offered to send to a neighbour lord for a spare escort.

And there was a fire, and Farili seemed, despite the soldiers billeted on her for no apparent reason, to have space for three extra men (one injured), and two women. Arvill could be accommodated in a tower storeroom.

Arvill, until then appropriately silent, suddenly said, "That will be most comfortable, I'm sure, madam. I shall feel that I'm treated as one of your own kin." A most peculiar sarcasm, Kai thought – was it directed at Farili, or at himself?

It was very plain that something wasn't right at Dendarry, for when at supper Kai mentioned Gormad – "I travelled a little with your eldest two weeks ago. I trust you heard that he's back at Stonehill safe and sound?" the surely innocuous remark seemed to agitate rather than please his hostess.

"Yes," she answered, after a moment. "My husband wrote that he'd seen him. Ramahdis is staying on at Stonehill with Gormad for the King's Gathering." Her voice crackled a little. "We are most grateful to you for bringing him back. And to His Grace. My husband said he spoke very kindly, and forgave the boy's reckless behaviour."

"A little reckless, but brave also," said Kai smiling. "He seems to have many good qualities. I'm sure he'll be an excellent squire." No one answered.

He exerted himself to be as pleasant as he could, but an invisible something in the room defeated him. Before he went to sleep that night, dry at last, on a pallet on the hall floor, he reflected that the soldiers seemed to have nothing to do, that there was definite tension between Mayeel and her hostess, possibly some suspicion towards himself, and that Farili and her steward were as jittery as two cats in a roomful of dogs. However, none of this was his business, and what he needed was to sleep while he could, before getting up to relieve Kalla guarding Arvill.

*

20 October 570

The next day there was no better news of the river, and no sign of a free soldier, and Jax was feverish. Farili dutifully urged him to remain as long as necessary, as it was an honour to serve the King and assist His Grace's brother. She showed no curiosity about the prisoner, although others did. "She is suspected of various crimes," was all Kai said.

That day and the next, he made and remade his decision – to stay, or to leave? The King had given them forty days, and these were wearing away alarmingly, but the waters were going down, and the ford, they told him, would soon be passable.

He wondered if he had ever worried as much about a prisoner. He borrowed books and a lute from the family to give her something to do, while she sat in her small room, with a window too narrow to get out of, and a sheer drop, and a guard just outside, for there were no lockable doors within the castle. Kai and his soldiers took turns. He would sit outside the room, knowing that she knew he was there, unable to stop remembering last summer, her teasing, the scent of her, her breasts. Neither of them spoke. The door next to her room led to the roof, and Kai went up one night, after Venner had taken over, and gazed at the stars, that he and Dorac and Arvill all loved - Or Arvill had said she loved.

When he wasn't guarding, he tried to be helpful as a Kingsbrother should, and rode out with the steward to inspect the lands and repair storm-damaged fences. Farili thanked him, but made no unnecessary conversation.

The soldiers were busy after all in the daytime, riding out and back on mysterious errands which they reported to Mayeel, and occasionally sorting through chests and desks. Sorting, or searching?

Mayeel told him nothing. They were siblings, and in the evenings they played a few games of abysmally unskilled chess, or sat exchanging stilted words about Stonehill. She was a friend of Dorac's, but Kai had never warmed to her. As humourless as unspiced pottage, with a thin-lipped disapproval of obscene language, excessive drinking and loud song, a poor memory for gossip, but an excellent one for small sums of money loaned out and not yet repaid. Her company was no more entertaining, although less uncomfortable, than Arvill's.

More cheerfully, having enlisted the boy Kammer's advice as to books, he continued to make friends with the children. Kammer was eight, thin and gangly, and his mother and sister said he was far too fond of reading. Beta was six, and bonny, and lively outside her mother's presence, and the little one, Kiri, toddled round after them. They were all curly-haired, but otherwise did not resemble Gormad particularly. Nor, surprisingly, did they talk about him much.

But on the second day, when the sun had come out, and Kai was sitting on the courtyard steps polishing his sword, Kammer and Beta sidled up to him, and Beta presented him shyly with a daisy chain.

After amusing them by wearing it in every possible way, he draped it on his sword hilt.

"Master Kai," said Kammer hesitantly, "why are Mistress Mayeel and the soldiers here?"

"Mayeel Kingsister has nothing to do with me. She said there's been trouble. Perhaps your mother didn't want to worry you."

"There's been no trouble," said Beta scornfully. "Father went to court to bring Gormad back, and he hasn't. But all these horrid soldiers came instead. And now you've come."

"We do fill up your home," Kai admitted. "But I'm truly only here until the floods go down."

"If you knew the King's secret orders to Mistress Mayeel, you wouldn't tell us," said Kammer wisely. "You would lie and keep the King's secret."

"If I had to, yes, I would lie and keep the King's secret. But I truly know nothing. I swear," he said with mock solemnity. They giggled.

"Master Kai," said Beta, "what do squires do?"

"They serve their lords or ladies, and they learn things. Mostly how to fight, but other things as well. And they play as much as anyone lets them – at least I did."

"I want to be a squire when I'm older."

"Maybe you will be."

"Can I be your squire?"

"Beta, you mustn't ask!" said her scandalised brother.

Kai laughed, and said, "I have no squire. No parent would ever trust their child to me." The children laughed too, although it was perfectly true. Those looking for someone to guide their son's or daughter's development generally wanted a person of good conduct and sound moral fibre, and Kai did not meet these standards.

The children begged, as their brother had once done, for stories of the Southern Six, and he told them the adventure he'd told Gormad, and then, wanting to give good measure, about the time he and Soumaki thought they'd discovered an assassin waiting to kill the King, but it was only some lord's younger son who'd lost his way in the passages.

So that was all very friendly. But later that evening, anyone passing the steps to the east tower could hear the plaintive notes of the "Soldier Marching Away" ballad drifting down. Arvill was not expert on the lute, but she could play a few popular tunes well. Annoyed to find Kammer and Beta and the cook's son sitting on the stairs listening, Kai reflected uneasily that a sad lady imprisoned in a tower would always attract romantic interest, and not just from children.

*

22 October 570

There was a commotion in the hall. Kai had just been relieved by Venner, and was coming down the stairs when Farili's maid scurried panting up to him. "Please, Master Kai, the mistress says can you come?"

He entered the hall to see Mayeel and Farili staring at four slightly bedraggled-looking people. Three were unknown to him, but the fourth was Kremdar, and his hands were bound.

"Master Kai," said Farili in a confused voice, "this man is Fen, one of my neighbour's liegemen." The eldest man bowed. "He says he

349

has arrested your brother."

She clearly found this unbelievable.

Kremdar stared at Kai, his face blank as unwritten parchment. "Brother."

"Why have you arrested him?"

"Mistress Gemara's orders, sir. She came to my farm with a wounded soldier the day before yesterday, and left these instructions, and commanded me to gather strong people, and follow her." He handed Kai a piece of parchment. "The priest read it to us."

K and his squire attacked soldier and escaped west of Arjan. Am pursuing - Kai read aloud, omitting the rest. His head hurt. "Where is Tommid? And where is Gemara?"

"I don't know. I did not attack the man she mentions – I suppose it is the soldier with her, a man called Morvan. I was with Gemara, but we separated. Tommid was with me, but he ran off. I was looking for him when these people attacked me." The man Fen began to speak, but Kremdar overrode him. "I asked them for news of you, as I'd heard you were in this area, delayed by the flood waters. I thought Tommid might've come to you. They seemed to find my question suspicious."

"But why did you leave Gemara?"

Kremdar hesitated. "Kai. I need to speak to you alone."

Kai saw Fen bristle indignantly, like a guard dog, almost showing teeth. Mayeel, on the other hand, looked puzzled but indifferent.

"Very well. But first let me make this clear. This letter clearly justifies these people in arresting you."

"If Gemara wrote it —"

"And," Kai went on, "if they had not done so, and you had arrived here alone, I would have arrested you myself."

"On what charge?"

"Committing perjury at our brother's trial." Kremdar's face became blanker than before. "Now. You wanted to talk."

They went into the steward's room, and Kalla waited outside the door. This was hardly necessary, Kai reflected, as no one else was going anywhere while such exciting things were happening.

"Is Arvill here?" demanded Kremdar as soon as the door was shut.

"Why would you think that?"

"I heard that you were travelling with a prisoner, and you mentioned Dorac's trial just now. And one of the soldiers said so." He smiled faintly.

"She is."

"I need to talk to her."

"You said you wanted to talk to me."

"And Arvill. Kai, I — can't fully explain. Gemara and I came north because I'd received news of a murder on my estate. I couldn't be wholly frank with her about why I needed to look into it further. She — she spoke harshly, as Gemara does, and we quarrelled. But I had no choice. I have orders from the King."

How many secret orders has King Arrion given? Kai wondered.

"Gemara said you attacked this man."

"I did not."

"What are you investigating?"

"I can't tell you."

"Arvill told me you are lovers. Is this true?"

Kremdar hesitated a moment. "Yes."

"You lied about the deaths at Ferrodach. Tell me the truth."

"I don't know what you mean."

"You do know what I mean. Arvill has admitted that you lied about the bodies."

Kremdar said, "Let me speak to Arvill. Then I may be able to answer your questions."

"Very well. You can talk to her."

"Alone."

"No."

"I must. Kai. We are brothers."

Kai hit him in the face.

"We were brothers." He thought of Dorac weeping at The Crescent Moon because to be exiled was worse than to be hanged, and hit him again. "Dorac was your brother, too; had you forgotten?"

"Dorac killed the children."

"And you and Arvill cut up the bodies to make sure he was blamed."

"Yes," said Kremdar after a pause.

Kai had a moment, one of the longest in his life, to realise that he was just as stupid as Gemara (and his sisters) had always told him he was. But a sneeze cannot be unsneezed, as Soumaki might have said.

"I will have her brought down."

They waited in the hall, surrounded by the curious inhabitants of Dendarry, while the maid took the message, and Venner re-shackled

Arvill and brought her downstairs.

"Arvill," said Kremdar.

"God be with you, Kremdar," she replied in a low voice. She smiled a little, but did not look happy to see him, as was perhaps natural, considering. "I – told him. I'm sorry. I told him about us, and that we – what we did to the bodies, and our reasons."

"I know."

"I'm not ashamed. We had to make it clear -"

"Yes. Arvill, some people killed a man and a child on my estate."

Her eyes opened wide.

"A man and a child."

"How terrible," said Arvill. She blinked a few times, staring at Kremdar. "Do you think Dorac killed them? Out of revenge, looking for you? Braf is dead, and they say Dorac killed him."

"Dorac is in Jaryar. He hasn't been killing anyone in the north," Kai interrupted – giving them more information, again.

"Who could have done this? Who would even know where they were?" Kremdar asked hoarsely, his eyes fixed on Arvill. He was visibly trembling.

Arvill shook her head. Then she said slowly, "But we were talking about your plans on the way back from Ferrodach – don't you remember I said someone was listening? Someone – I don't understand why they would want to, but - but this is terrible." Tears welled up in her eyes. Kremdar continued to stare at her.

Kai was beginning to feel very suspicious of Arvill's tears. "You were returning from Ferrodach with a troop of soldiers, and you think one of them decided to desert to the north to commit a murder at Gisren? Madam," to Farili, "I am sorry to have to ask you for another place to secure a prisoner until we leave for Stonehill."

Mayeel said, "The news is good of the river. You might be able to leave tomorrow. And I think – things are a little calmer here -" – *Are they?* wondered Kai – "and I can spare a soldier to accompany you."

"I would be happy to travel to Stonehill with you if needed," said the man Fen, clearly relishing his role.

So it was arranged. Arvill was taken back upstairs. As she turned to leave the room, Kai caught a glimpse of her expression: one not aimed at him, or at anyone. He had never seen her look so frightened. But even as he watched, her face changed, freezing to a bleak hardness that again he wouldn't have believed, and which haunted him long after.

He took Kremdar back into the steward's room, and said, "You've seen Arvill. Now what more can you say?"

"Nothing. I am sorry. She was not able – Kai, I know it is strange, but trust me. I cannot tell you more, but there is a reason. I have done nothing wrong. You cannot arrest me because other people are making a foolish mistake. The King would want you to trust me."

"And Gemara would not."

An answer that admits unapologetically to being mysterious and incomplete has a strange power. Kai was indeed tempted to trust him. But he had to hold to his orders from his King and his leader. Kremdar was imprisoned in a hastily emptied storeroom – Kai's conscience smote him, and he insisted on one with some natural light, for he wouldn't trust a prisoner with a candle – and guarded, and more manacles were ordered.

He copied out a map of the route they would need. Then he visited Jax, who wasn't well enough to travel and was remaining behind, though seeming to be out of immediate danger. And he was entering the hall again when he saw his soldier Venner come up shyly and approach Mayeel. No one else was in the room.

"Your pardon, madam -"

"What is it?" asked Mayeel.

"I've been watching the prisoner Arvill. She asked me to ask you -" Venner swallowed. Mayeel was not looking encouraging. "She asked if she could speak with you. She said I was to tell you that she would be *very grateful.*"

There was a pause.

"Arvill, daughter of Eve, is Master Kai's prisoner. If she has anything to say, she should say it to him. I have no interest in the matter." She turned abruptly away towards Kai, whose presence she had probably already noticed. Venner bowed confusedly to a space between the two of them, and hurried away.

Kai ought to have followed, but he said, "Why are you here, Mayeel?"

"I don't have leave to share my orders with you, or anyone else. It has nothing to do with Arvill or Kremdar. As you heard, I am not interfering with you."

And she made this plain by ostentatiously remaining within his view all evening, very plainly not visiting Arvill's tower.

Kai half-wondered if Venner would bring him a similar message, but nothing came. He placed a second guard, choosing Fen,

355

who was eager to be helpful, at the foot of Arvill's staircase, and longed to be away.

That night, Arvill wept. She didn't do so loudly or hysterically, yet somehow everyone knew that she was crying, a pathetic and ceaseless sound, even when they were out of earshot. Perhaps, Kai thought, she loved Kremdar so much that his capture meant more to her than her own. Somehow this seemed unlikely.

He had another horrible idea before he went to sleep – that the child Kremdar said had been murdered might have been Tommid. This did not fit all the information given, but by now he was so confused that it barely mattered.

*

23 October 570

But at last they were leaving, and the sun had come out. Kai and his assorted soldiers gathered with their horses. Most of the inhabitants of Dendarry were also standing around the courtyard, as they waited for Venner and Fen to bring out the prisoners from their separate cells. Mayeel watched impassively. The children were hovering on the edge of the crowd, willing to smile shyly at Kai, but seeming more interested in the door to Arvill's tower.

Kremdar was brought up, blinking in the light, looking as if he had not slept much. Then Arvill, glancing meekly at Kai, as if asking where she should stand. He gestured to a horse, and to the groom waiting to help her mount. She walked briskly a few paces in that direction, and then turned and spoke.

"Farili, daughter of Nara, I thank you for your hospitality here, although it was not of either of our choosing. You have treated me kindly. Fare well. And you," she said, smiling and holding out her manacled hands to the children.

Everyone was watching, secretly admiring her calm and poise – and beauty. Kammer stepped towards her, and suddenly Kai sensed the wrongness. "No, Kammer!"

He was too late. Quick as lightning, Arvill threw aside the chains (*how?*), seized the boy, and pulled him off his feet. "Stand back!" she said harshly, and everyone froze.

Kammer was struggling and kicking, but Arvill was strong. She had twisted him around, and had one arm across his stomach; the other was dragging his head backwards by the hair.

"If anyone moves," she said clearly, "I will break his neck."

One of the horses skittered and clattered its hooves, infected by the terror in the courtyard, and Farili screamed.

"You bitch, you bitch, you *bitch!* I did what you wanted! "

"Make her be quiet," said Arvill, and Farili gulped to silence.

"Now, Kai, we will talk. I am not going with you."

People fell back to leave a clear space between Arvill and Kai. He felt the weight of their dread, and his own, pressing on him. "Arvill, put him down. This cannot help you."

"Nonsense. It's got your attention. Do you remember -" – her voice became mockingly dreamy – "when we did it the first time, and I asked you to tell me a story? 'In exchange for my virginity,' I said. And you told me about your adventure in Ardo Vale, where you were all so careless about the scouts. That was when I realised how very soft-hearted the Southern Six are about children. Except Dorac, of course - I *will* kill him unless you do exactly what I say."

"Arvill, please." It was Kremdar, staring with as much apparent horror as the rest.

"I'm sorry, sweetheart, I'm not as gentle and kind as you thought me," she said briskly, and turned her attention back to Kai. "Listen to me. I'm not going back to Stonehill."

"You can't escape. There's nowhere for you to go."

"I'm not trying to escape. I want you to kill me, Kai. Kill me now, quick and clean, before the King gets his hands on me."

"I don't understand."

"You're so stupid sometimes. I've told you everything, Kai - or almost everything - but the King won't believe that." Her voice was harsh. "He'll have me tortured, you know he will, and I can't bear that, so you have to kill me now."

"He would not - I don't know what you think happens to people -"

"I know bad things happen to people, and so do you! You've done them yourself, Kai! Don't you remember what you and Dorac did to that man in Broffam? How you cried afterwards, and I comforted you? Bad things happen, so kill me now. Or I'll kill the boy."

"Not my son! You can't, *please!*" wailed Farili.

"He's not the heir," said Arvill cruelly. "Get more children, Farili. Don't you like fucking?" She turned back to Kai.

"Swear by your children's lives, or your honour as a Kingsbrother, or your immortal soul, or whatever you hold sacred, that you'll cut my throat. Then I'll let him go. Come on. It's only doing what the King will do anyway."

She knew things about Ferrodach, and so the King needed her

evidence. Dorac needed her evidence. But he could not let Kammer die. Somehow he felt she would really do it. He was dizzy with horror and doubt. *Kai, who always dithers.*

"I will count to ten, and then I will kill him," said Arvill. "One -"

"Oh God oh God oh God oh God -" someone was gabbling behind Kai.

"Two."

"Arvill, you're not a monster! Don't do this!"

"Three. I am whatever I have to be," she said, bafflingly. "Four. Five."

He could not do it. But he couldn't let her -

"Six."

There was a movement at the edge of his sight, to the left. Kai stepped to the right, to draw Arvill's attention, and said desperately, "If – *if* – I promise – you will put him down unhurt?"

"That's what I said. Seven. Hurry up and swear."

"But how do I know -"

Something struck Arvill on the side of the head. She jerked; Kammer wriggled; Kai leapt forward and grabbed him. He pushed the boy behind, and turned back, but Arvill was already running.

She did not run towards the horse or the gatehouse, but back to the entrance she had just come out of. In the doorway, she pulled down a chair to block the path for a few moments, and raced up the stairs.

Kai pounded after her – "Watch Kremdar!" he yelled back – hoping she would meet some servant to delay her, but everyone had been in the courtyard. People were coming behind – he hoped someone had heard his shout, that Kammer was all right –

Up again. Now he knew where she was going. She passed the door to the room she had sat in, and wept in, and played her bloody lute in, and darted through the other, up the last flight, to the tower roof where he had looked up at the stars, and down, far down, at the valley. Twelve feet square, with a low parapet.

He was in the doorway, but he had no breath to call out. Arvill did not pause, or look back, or speak. She ran across the roof space, put one hand and then one foot on the parapet, and jumped.

*

When Kai returned to the courtyard with Venner, who had followed him, they found Kammer being comforted, and Beta being praised by Mayeel. Beta had thrown the stone. "Like Mistress Soumaki in your story," she said with tearful pride. "But I didn't have a crossbow." Farili was sitting weeping on the ground with her son in her arms, her hand covering her face. Others had thankfully kept close to Kremdar, whose head was bowed and who was very still. Kai wanted to hit him again.

Instead, he went away for a little to work out what he had to do next. Gemara or Hassdan or Dorac would have known at once. He sat, seeing Arvill's beautiful laughing face from last year, and hearing her cruel words from today. She was dead. Having thought, he ordered her body to be brought in, and the courtyard cleared first. He must prepare a report, and question everyone who'd spoken to Arvill since her arrest in Pendafor for any clues to give to the King. He also needed as full a written description of her as possible, since her origins were still a mystery.

His own reputation was a tiny thing in the midst of it all, but he did wonder fleetingly if the people at Dendarry now pictured him as a man who rode about the country seducing naïve virgins ("It was a jest. A jest, Kai!" she'd said. "But I still want a story.") Rather more painfully, he wondered if they were all speculating on what he and Dorac had done to the man in Broffam, and whether it could be described as torture. He was wondering the last himself.

*

"Your man Venner said she wanted to speak to me – that it would be better for me if I went," Farili said. She was sitting in a small room, facing Kai and Mayeel. Her body shook continuously, and she kept glancing at the door, as if she feared spending even these moments away from her children. "She said she wanted to try to escape. That she was less guilty than you believed – or pretended to believe – and she asked me to find her a key to undo her shackles. She told me such locks are usually similar, and we would probably have a key that fitted. Of course I refused." She swallowed, and lifted her chin so that she was gazing over Kai's head. "She then threatened to denounce me to you as a traitor to the crown."

"*She* threatened to denounce *you?*"

"My husband is a prisoner in Stonehill. We are - accused of treasonable activities. The Kingsister is here to look into the allegations."

"More than allegations. Ramahdis made a confession," Mayeel said sternly. Before Kai could put the same thought into words, she went on, "But the treason is already known, so what could Arvill threaten you with?"

"She said the King didn't know everything. She was going to lie, and make it worse. She said she was at Ferrodach, and if she swore Gahran had named us as conspiring with him, it would be believed. She would implicate the children." Tears began to bubble from her eyes. "She said I would never see Gormad again. That the King would hang him, maybe Kammer and Beta -"

"You believed that of King Arrion?" Kai exclaimed.

"The Ferrodach children were cut to pieces. He might have ordered it. She – she promised she only wanted to escape. She would do no harm to anyone who didn't stand in her way - So I fetched all our keys, and one of them fitted, and I left it with her."

"The guard let you do this?" Kai thought to ask.

"He let me talk to her alone. I ordered him, and he obeyed. He was too stupid to realise. Arvill said she wanted to pray with me, and to seek my advice as to the law. He believed her."

No, thought Kai, *he wanted to believe her, because Arvill was beautiful and sad, and looked at him beseechingly.* Venner deserved whipping, but he had not the heart to order it. He himself had been distracted by worrying about Kremdar, but he should have thought to investigate why she was sending messages to Mayeel, and whether she was doing so to anyone else.

He would have to include this in his report. For now, he wrote the basic facts only, needing to get them to Stonehill as soon as possible. Any more evidence from Arvill was lost forever, and any chance, he felt, of understanding what she'd done, and why.

*

The day passed. Arvill's body was hastily coffined, and buried in the local churchyard: the furthest corner, as befitted a suicide and a criminal. Kremdar quietly asked to be allowed to attend. Kai permitted this, ordering heavy guards, but he didn't go himself, and was almost alone in the house, when a maid came to say that a boy was begging to see him.

It was Tommid, looking half-starved and miserable. "Welcome, lad!" Kai said heartily, relieved that something was right. He held out his arms to him, and Tommid burst into tears.

Kai heard his hysterical confession, ordered him fed, and then sat alone, absorbing the nightmare he was living in. When Kremdar was back in his storeroom, he went there with Fen. "Do not leave me alone with him," he said, at which Fen stared.

"I've been speaking to Tommid."

Kremdar flinched.

"If I were a merciful man, I would kill you now," Kai said. "But I am not. The King will want that pleasure himself."

Torio and Gormad (24–25 October)

24 October 570

"I am sorry, Master Torio. We cannot help you."

Torio hobbled crossly away from the Wide Gate. Everything had been going wrong of late.

It had seemed good fortune when he entered the courtyard three days ago, and overheard a conversation about a message for the King. If it wasn't sealed, he could read it, and if it was sealed, even news of it would be useful to Herion, and its delivery might win him favour. But the upshot had been humiliating, and even his royal brother's sympathy, and the knowledge that the intolerable children were being duly punished, could not make it otherwise.

He'd reported the matter to Herion's steward Attar (the ugly fellow with the insolent eyes) at the appointed alley. Attar shrugged, and said he would pass on the news. Torio longed to knock him down.

And now! "Hassdan's little girl's been found, did you know?" Hayn Kingsbrother greeted him. "What's-her-name whose letter was brought in by a beggar the other day. It seems she was attacked, and broke all the bones in her legs, and her comrades were killed. Poor brat. She's been all this time in some villager's hut."

"How d'you know this?"

"Soumaki rode in this morning. Hadn't you heard? She said no more than that."

Torio knew better than to trust Hayn for accurate reporting, but it seemed definitely to be true that Soumaki Kingsister had arrived, and had gone straight to the King. And his two informants at the Wide

Gate hadn't told him.

Most indignantly he headed for the guard-post, intending to remind them icily that they were taking his money to ensure that he was the first person to know of the movements of the Southern Six. And now he was told that neither of them had arrived for their duties that morning. Perhaps they were ill.

Or perhaps the world was conspiring against Torio Kingsbrother.

He supposed he should tell his friends the small amount he knew, and then try to wheedle more out of Soumaki, excruciatingly dull and respectable as she was. There would be no one waiting in the alley at this time, and he never went to Herion's uninvited, so he made for his mother's.

"I am sorry, Master Torio, my mistress went out. I'm not certain when she'll be back, but I think not for some time."

As he was departing, his mood worse than ever, he caught sight of Attar, haggling at a stall. "God's blessing on you!" he exclaimed, exchanging snarl for smile. "What brings you out today?"

"And on you, sir. A few minor purchases. No, I think I will not take it. May I accompany you as far as the Church of Obedience, if you're going that way?"

It seemed, oddly but fortunately, that Attar had been waiting for him. In a low voice, and once they were away from prying ears, he said, "You went to the guard-post, sir?" His tone was less than respectful.

"Hest and Arbodan are failing us there. Soumaki Kingsister has returned, and they hadn't told me."

"Hest and Arbodan are under arrest."

"Under *arrest?*"

"Yes. At this moment, they're probably telling the Castle soldiers that you were bribing them for information."

Torio felt cold. But there must be a solution. "I can deny it – or simply say I was interested in Ferrodach. Whether Dorac was innocent. Why should I not be? What does Herion say?" he asked, noting a quality in the other's silence.

"My master sends you these." A letter, and a bag of money. "Your horse has been brought from the stables, and is waiting for you outside the East Gate. The guards there will let you pass if you go quickly."

"What -" Torio unfolded the letter.

The King is not as stupid as you thought. Go now. Make for Ricossa. The landlord of The Huntsman Inn over the border will help you. We will bring you back when we can.

"Make for *Ricossa?* What -"

"And destroy that letter, or give it to me to destroy," said Attar. Torio, staring at him, realised that the man was actually frightened.

"Herion's telling me to flee Stonehill?" Saying the words aloud proved their absurdity.

"Yes. Unless you want to explain to King Arrion why it was more important for you to read his letters than for him."

"The King is my brother," said Torio angrily.

"He has had you watched for some time. Go now. That is Herion's order. He is not your brother. He expects to be obeyed."

366

*

It was the best thing that had ever happened. Gormad was shaken awake by grumpy Sister Susanna in the early dark. "Get up quietly, and pack for a journey. Come to the stables as soon as you can. Hurry."

His head whirling, Gormad tried to act as Dorac or Kai would have done. He washed his face to wake himself, said the Our Father prayer, and remembered to pack a change of clothes. *What journey? Was he going home after all?*

A sleepy groom had Champion already saddled, as well as four other horses. Three of their riders were already gathered, all members of the Thirty – Soumaki of the Southern Six, Gardai the leader of the Western, and Sheru, who gestured him over and fussily straightened his jacket. Saysh of the Southern hurried in, looking as confused as Gormad and surely more untidy. And then came the King.

They all bowed. "Gardai, Soumaki, you have your orders. Tell the others as you go. Ride swiftly, and God speed. And I want to speak to the squire."

So while the others were mounting, Gormad stepped aside with the King. He knelt, remembering their earlier meeting.

"I am sending Sheru Kingsister on an urgent mission, and you are going with her. You can trust her and the others. I give you leave to tell them any of the secrets you know. But try to keep out of trouble. Do you understand?"

"Y-yes, Your Grace."

"Go, then. And Gormad?"

"Your Grace?"

367

"Ride safely. Come back."

Someone lifted Gormad into the saddle, and then they rode out of the Castle, and away from Stonehill. Four of the King's Thirty, and Gormad, riding east into the dawn.

In the dark they could not go fast, but they did not talk, for they had to watch the road and their horses' footing. When the sun rose, however, they increased their speed. Gormad felt the cold adventurous air sweep gloriously by him, and knew that he was again part of something. The fact that he had no idea what it was hardly mattered.

But at last they had to stop, to rest and water the horses. Everyone else looked at Master Gardai and Mistress Soumaki, and Soumaki gestured to the senior Kingsbrother. He looked unhappy, Gormad thought.

"The King gave us our orders. I can hardly believe them. We are riding in pursuit of Torio, who has fled the city. We are to find him and bring him back, preferably alive."

Only "preferably" alive! A Kingsbrother! Surely such an order had never been given before. Sheru and Master Saysh looked as astonished as Gormad felt.

"But what has he done?"

"I don't know. The King told me some days ago that he had reason to distrust Torio. He didn't say why."

"But it has something to do with Ferrodach," said Mistress Soumaki.

And then Gormad realised what the King had meant. *"You may tell them the secrets you know."*

"Torio tried to steal – to take – a letter from Mer– from Master Hassdan," he said with a scared gulp. "My friend Jamis and I stopped him."

Everyone stared.

"You were in trouble for that, I recall," said Sheru slowly.

"The King pretended we were. Secretary Makkam said he was grateful, that he would not have wanted Torio to see the letter."

"When did this happen?" asked Gardai.

"Last Friday."

"Four days ago." Gardai nodded. "It was on Friday the King spoke to me, and told me Torio was being watched. He was followed tonight when he met someone – a servant – and apparently decided to run away."

"You are a mysterious boy. You ran off after Dorac, didn't you?" Sheru said.

"I suppose everyone's guessed by now," said Soumaki, "that the murders at Ferrodach are more complicated than it seemed when Dorac was tried. I can't see any connection with Torio, but - we have our orders."

They mounted and rode on, and Gormad noticed all the grown-ups giving him odd looks. He had not enjoyed his moment in the centre of attention very much.

They travelled through the day, and at every village they sought news. Torio, well known in the centre of Marod, was riding east the fastest way, and making no attempt to hide his passing. He wasn't making for the familiar enemy, Jaryar, but the larger land currently confused in fighting, Ricossa.

"Be wary. He's a skilled swordsman – not as skilled as he thinks he is, but good. He is dangerous. And we must find him before he reaches the border. If anyone falls behind, we leave them to catch up," ordered Gardai. "And we may get fresh horses at Mebb."

But the next time they stopped, Saysh said, in a rather shy voice for a Kingsbrother, that he had a suggestion.

*

No one can ride forever. So towards dawn Torio stopped at an inn, demanded food and a room, and told them to wake him in three hours. And now the sun was up, and he was riding again. Confused, and very angry. He longed for someone to kill. He should have killed Attar.

How was this possible? Fleeing to Ricossa – him, a Kingsbrother? But again and again he came back to Attar's face – insolent but frightened – and his words, "Do you want to explain to King Arrion why it was more important for you to read his letters than for him?"

I did nothing but ask a few questions, and pass on a few pieces of parchment! "I renounce all allegiance save to God, the kingdom, the King and Queen and the Thirty" – no one takes that seriously, do they? Do they?

He'd been given money, and told to ride, and he was riding. Was it really possible that he would never come back? What was Ricossa like, anyway? Which side was he meant to be on in their idiotic turmoil – the Banners of Joy, or the Banners of the True Daughters? He was going into exile, like his brother Dorac, and it was not amusing.

He rode, and stopped for food, and rode on again. The east part of Marod wasn't very familiar to him – he was in the Western Six, and his family's lands were in the north. Still, the main road east was straightforward.

He was approaching a crossroads with a few trees when two riders suddenly emerged from the north path and stilled their horses, facing him together, blocking his way. As he rode nearer, he recognised them, and went cold. Master Gardai, his own leader, and that idiot Saysh.

Perhaps he should have charged straight on, but the habit of outward deference to Gardai was strong. He drew up six feet from them.

"What are you doing, Torio?" asked the older man. He was thick-set and grey-haired, and Torio had often speculated among his friends how long he could last.

Old fool. Brazen it out. "I have an errand in the east."

"What errand?"

"I'm going to reinforce the border guards at Makaim."

"No, you're not. You are under arrest by order of the King."

He gasped. "For what crime?"

"That is the King's business. But first, for deserting your post. I did not authorise you to leave the city."

The look on Gardai's face made him feel like a naughty boy about to be beaten. But he was not a boy. Saysh was bigger and stronger than he was, but no one had ever said much about his skills with a sword. Torio knew he was better and quicker than Gardai.

"Do I need your leave for every step I take?" He felt himself growing more and more frightened, and therefore more and more angry.

"I'm not arguing with you. Surrender your sword, and return

371

with us to Stonehill."

He hesitated for a moment, and then said, "I will not surrender to an old man, who should be praying in a corner. And not to you," turning to Saysh, "you're only in the Thirty because the Queen finds your dumb adoration amusing."

"You are insulting your brother, and the Queen." Gardai drew his sword. "Surrender now."

Torio kicked Longtail into action: wonderful animal, faithful and quick as always. He made for Saysh, his sword out, and slashed him across the body before the fool could even react. Wheeling, he clashed swords with Gardai. The old man was stronger than he'd realised, and was stretching for Longtail's rein with his other hand. Torio punched him, while pulling his sword back, and readying it for the killer thrust.

That was when something struck him in the back. At first he was only aware of a blow, and a strange coldness – between the shoulder blades, but lower. Then there was a vagueness in the world, and Gardai had pushed him away, and he was falling backwards.

He landed hard, and the pain was much worse, tearing, and his mouth was full of blood, and he saw the bolthead sticking out from his chest, where his own weight had pushed it through. There were more people around him, and a strange rasping noise, and part of him wanted to curse, and part wanted to call for his mother, but he died before he could do either of these things.

*

It seemed that Saysh knew the east better than any of the others, and he'd thought of a quicker path, recently improved by a local lord, that avoided the town of Mebb and joined the main road thereafter. So he,

Soumaki and Gardai had ridden that way, and Gormad and Sheru had followed the better-known and signposted route, not talking, Gormad in agony in case he was missing the fighting. Then they rode up a little slope, and looked down to see three men facing each other. Mistress Soumaki was nowhere to be seen. *Had Torio killed her?* And then the fight did begin. Torio, unbelievably, was attacking his own leader. And it seemed that Soumaki had been waiting in the trees by the roadside, readying her crossbow. Gormad saw the bolt fly, and for the first time appreciated the beauty of its flight as Captain Renatar would have wanted him to - and then they were pounding forwards towards the three injured men, and their distressed and rearing horses.

Kai had said, he remembered afterwards, that each member of the Thirty had particular skills. While Soumaki gathered and soothed the animals, Sheru was pulling out cloths, staunching bleeding, and calling with curses for Gormad to bring water.

They could do nothing for Torio, who gave Gormad an angry look, and died with a little burst of red on his lips. But Saysh had blood pouring from a slash across chest and neck, and Gardai's face was cut, and he'd hurt something where he'd hit the ground after being thrown. "Only my pride, lad," he grunted, but it was not. He stood breathing hard and leaning on the boy – and looking down at the dead man. Something in Gardai's face hurt Gormad, and he blinked, feeling sick.

He had seen death before – his grandfather, and a child who fell off a roof at Dendarry estate; and he'd attended a hanging. But this was Master Torio. Someone he knew had killed someone else he knew.

That was what the King's Thirty did.

"I killed my brother. I killed my *brother*," Soumaki said, and

373

suddenly she vomited into the grass at the side of the road.

Sheru decided that Gardai had broken his collarbone. She bound him up, and stopped Saysh's bleeding, and they tied the body onto the back of his horse, and started slowly home.

The King and his Enemies (26–29 October)

26 October 570

"What is the town saying? *Was* young Torio a traitor? Do you have the truth of it, Sada?" Lady Karnall of Aspella had actually set down her embroidery to gaze at her guest.

"He was certainly riding without permission in the direction of Ricossa, and he seems to have defied instructions to surrender. If that's treason - And now he's dead, and cannot explain or defend himself. I can't say I ever warmed to Torio, but he had good qualities."

"I know his mother. I can't believe he would have assisted the Jaryari – and if he were doing so, why ride east? A longer journey." Lady Karnall shook her head sadly. "Torio wasn't popular. Could someone malicious have dropped poison in the King's ear?"

"Arrion has been talking a lot to one of the secretaries," said Lady Sada thoughtfully.

"Ah. A pretty female one, perhaps?"

Lady Sada looked up sharply. There was a pause. Then, with a shrug, "Perhaps his innocence will be established in coming weeks, too late. And speaking of establishing innocence, it seems that it will soon be possible for the criminal to disregard the judge and jury, and demand a second trial before he's punished. Arrion has some new preposterous idea to present to the Council. 'An Appeal', it is to be called. This is not what he should be thinking about at times like these."

"No, indeed. What an extraordinary notion, Sada. Who put that thought in his head? An idea of the Queen's, or -?"

"It's about Dorac, of course. Hassdan believes there may be

new evidence. Arrion is very loyal, and he knew Dorac a long time. He was shocked by his crime, and would love to think that it was all some kind of *mistake*. Tcha!" Lady Sada snorted.

"Yes. I see. So if someone had a reason to want this, they might have found him easy to persuade. It speaks well for the King's kindness."

"Less so for his good sense. We do not need kings to be kind." Lady Sada seemed to realise that she was, after all, speaking of her liege lord, and went on, "At any rate, this proposal is to be put to Council, and if they approve it, to the Gathering."

"I would love to attend that Council meeting. But alas, I'll have to rely on you, and on Herion, to tell me what happens. When Herion finds the time to visit his old aunt. If you see him, my friend, you might say that I would be grateful for some attention. You are almost my only companion."

Lady Sada smiled, and promised to call again soon.

*

"You wanted to talk to me, Aunt?" King Arrion asked. He had been frowning over a map of the Haymon border, but he had other documents close at hand.

"Yes, I do. I have been reading this proposed new law of yours."

"'On the Making of Appeals', yes. I hope I can rely on your support when it comes to Council?"

"You can *not*. What nonsense is this?"

"Judges aren't infallible, and it seemed -"

"There are strange rumours about Ferrodach, I understand. I

assume you were planning to talk to me about this at some time. And now this horrible business of Gemara. If you think Dorac was innocent, recall him. But what's this rigmarole you're foisting on us? Every pickpocket is to be allowed to challenge the judge before he's hanged?"

"He could hardly do so afterwards."

"Arrion," she said, and her voice was gentler, although still irritated, "what are you doing? We have no time for this playing."

"I'm hoping that it will not take much time. I am not playing."

"Why did you not come to me with this idea? It is that jumped-up secretary Makkam, is it not? You've been spending a lot of time with her. What does Malouri think of this?"

"You will withdraw that insinuation," said the King, looking up at her and speaking very quietly.

Lady Sada met his eyes and then nodded.

He glanced again at his map, and went on more lightly, "I am thinking of having you arrested, Aunt."

"On what charge? Is it a crime to disagree with the king?"

"No. It is a crime to present false evidence to Council, with the result that innocent people die."

Lady Sada's eyes narrowed. "Are you saying that I have done this?"

"You presented the letter from Lord Gahran that apparently proved his treason. I have now learned that that letter was not written nor sent this summer by Gahran or anyone else.

"Then there is the matter of Torio."

"Torio?"

"I was thinking back to when we called him three years ago. We were also considering Achad, son of Garas, were we not? And we rejected him because you told us about Achad's ill-treatment of some tenant on his estate. Quite an unpleasant story. Which later turned out to be mistaken."

"I don't understand."

"A few other matters also," he interrupted, and handed her a parchment. He watched as she glanced down the neat chronological list, and saw her face grow pale. When her eyes reached the bottom, he took it back.

"What are you saying?"

"For the time being, I am saying that I want your support in Council for our new law. And in the meantime, I would prefer that you didn't leave the Castle."

"You cannot believe -"

"And I want you to think about that list. That is all."

She stared into her nephew's cold eyes, curtsied, and left the room.

*

It was the man and child in Gisren that worried Herion most. Surely everything else, or almost everything, could be explained as excessive loyalty, or attributed to Kremdar's madness. But to send killers after little Filana without telling anyone – this could not be justified. If the King's people sniffed out Sil and her man. If Torio were caught. If Attar talked - *When* Attar talked -

There were soldiers outside his house day and night, front and back. Servants were allowed to leave, to go to the market, but they were followed there and home again. Herion had no doubt that he would be followed, and any letter he tried to send intercepted.

He had looked out upstairs and seen the red cloth hanging as if to dry from Lady Karnall's window. He knew the meaning of the message. *"Take the decisive step."* She was only a few streets away, and he could not discuss matters with her. He was alone.

His small bookroom was a pleasant place to sit in, cosy and wood-panelled, the shelves and cabinets containing many other things than books. A place of pride and pleasure for years, but now the walls were closing in. Herion shut his eyes to look at another place, far from Stonehill.

He saw the greatest castle in the west, scene of battle from the War of Three Kingdoms long ago, when its lords had ruled a kingdom of their own. Now, in times of peace, there were rolling slopes of flowers behind the towers. There was a hall grander than Stonehill's Great Hall, with tapestries and carvings to match any in Makkera. He had never owned the place, or lived there, but it was his heritage, and that of all his kin.

I will not let our dreams go. And so it is time.

If that girl has done her work well - If the boy has listened to her - I think she has. Then we can win. We can win absolutely. Despite everything.

He gripped the arms of his chair, back in the enclosed shadowy room, breathing hard, choosing. The Council was meeting tomorrow.

*

27 October 570

Makkam waited nervously by the wall as the Council of Elders filed into the chamber and took their seats. Bishop Abigail of Stonehill was sharing a jest with the Marshal. Abbot Simeon of Lintoll came in frowning. Lady Sada (terrifying Lady Sada; Makkam looked down at her feet as she passed) was talking to Herion of Maint in the doorway, and swept in last.

Eleven of the twelve were present, and seated. They rose for the King and Queen.

She had never attended a Council meeting before. The room wavered before her eyes, as she frantically ran over and over what she must say.

"You will be called last," the Queen had told her, and it was true. First there was a report about the flood of Ricossans in the east seeking refuge from their country's troubles, and debate as to how far Christian charity required that these beggars be welcomed and assisted (and who was to pay for it). And then the Council grew animated, as they discussed the provocations from Haymon (ordered from Jaryar), and the need to punish the recent raid on Kerrytown. Queen Malouri herself was to lead out soldiers for this purpose in two days' time. Extra troops had been quietly gathered, it seemed. "Good, good," murmured Lord Tarron, in whose lands Kerrytown belonged, and impulsively offered twenty of his own to join the expedition.

"And, finally, as you've been told, there is a proposal for a new law to be placed before the Gathering on Monday. I've often thought," said the King, "that we send criminals – probable criminals – to death rather too quickly. Some of these executions may be mistaken. Lately, I have been made aware of several cases of doubt over guilt. Several cases," he emphasised. "Makkam?"

Makkam, clammy all over, but steady now the moment had come, read out the proposed new law, and then went through it paragraph by paragraph, explaining how it was intended to work. There was only one question on the detail, and then she stepped back thankfully. King Arrion gestured with his one hand, to open any debate.

There had been several uneasy looks, and now Lady Ferriol said, "Your Grace, is this really necessary? Are our judges so flawed?"

The King repeated in different words what he had said earlier, adding complimentary words about the standard of judging by the Thirty in general.

"Forgive me," said Lady Ferriol, clearly unconvinced, "but if people are wrongly convicted, it is because witnesses lie. People will always lie." There was a murmur of agreement. "This law gives more time for criminals to arrange and pay for more lies."

"If they're rich enough. I agree that this is a danger. I intend to counter it by increasing the penalties for proven perjury, and making them penalties affecting rich and poor alike." Death or mutilation, was what that meant.

"At a time like this," said Lord Tarron, "do we wish to distract ourselves, and the Thirty, by tinkerings with legal trivialities?"

"By that rule," said someone else, "we'd never make any change except at a time of absolute peace. But that never exists. We're not at war yet."

"At any moment we could be. This will throw the country into chaos! There'll be no justice done, no order -"

"I hope there will be better justice," said the King. "There is precedent. St Paul, if you remember, appealed to Caesar."

"Are you suggesting, Your Grace," asked Lord Tarron, daring sarcasm, "that Marod should be managed in the same way as the mighty empire of Rome? We are a small kingdom."

"But our standards of justice should be no less high. It's not for the minor criminal, only for those for whom the penalty is very great. Innocent people have been hanged before now. God requires us to do justice. We cannot prevent mistakes entirely, but we can attempt to make them less likely."

There were a few nods, but the Abbot of Lintoll cleared his throat.

"A more fundamental matter, Your Grace. Before every trial, the judge prays to Almighty God for guidance and truth." He raised a hand towards heaven. "Do we not trust that this is given? To say – to encode in law – that a trial verdict may be wrong – is this not doubting God, the first step towards atheism?"

He looked, everyone looked, at Bishop Abigail, who perhaps knew more of God's opinion than most, but she said nothing.

"It is not doubting God, I think, to acknowledge that prayers sometimes go unanswered," said the King. "As my prayers for my daughter's life did five years ago." Makkam had never before heard him mention Princess Nadya, dead of fever at the age of ten. The reference brought a still sad moment to the room. "I think anyone who prays remembers such prayers."

"We are not saying that judges shouldn't seek God's help, or that He doesn't give it," the Queen insisted smoothly. "But all human justice is flawed. We've just heard that witnesses lie, and may be bribed. Judges may be wrong. We know these things. This is a fallen world."

382

("It is indeed," sighed Bishop Abigail, sycophantically.) "A broken world. It is my belief that God gives us the responsibility to deal with that brokenness."

Makkam was realising that she was not the only person who had prepared carefully for the meeting, and this distracted her from a momentary theological panic that the Abbot might be right.

"It is a fallen world," said Lady Sada, who had been silent so far. Everyone looked at her, expecting something definitive, Makkam thought. "I think the King is right. You said, my lord, that we shouldn't be distracted at a time of danger to the realm. There is danger. We know King Rajas means us ill. And if war comes, what are we defending? Our people, our King, our land – but also our ways. Our way of being, in this little kingdom, is to value justice. This is part of what we are."

There were nodding heads around the room. "I agree."

"And I agree. The rules seem straightforward. Our judges can learn them easily enough," said the Marshal.

And only Lord Tarron and the Abbot stood out for "Nay" (although Lady Ferriol still looked doubtful), and the law On the Making of Appeals was agreed to be put to the King's Gathering in a few days' time. The King smiled and the Queen winked at Makkam as they left.

*

Attar the steward had been arrested two days ago, shortly after his conversation with Torio in the alley. When he asked why, he was told "on suspicions of conspiracy", which could mean anything.

At first he had been confident that his master would get him out. But the hours passed. Then he began to be frightened.

He was taken from his cell and shown Torio's dead body. An arrogant youth whom he hadn't known well. The soldier escorting him asked, "Do you have anything to say?"

"About what?"

"About Torio Kingsbrother. About Ferrodach."

"No." If he admitted nothing, they could know nothing.

He was fed, and his cell was not unbearably cold or dark, and he had nothing to complain of but solitude and boredom. And fear.

"Our king is far too soft-hearted for torture," Herion had told him once, detecting a troubled moment. "And our friends are too powerful for him to move against. That protects me, and so you. If you want to leave my service, I will be very sorry - but of course you may." And Herion's service was well-paid, and there were promises of great things in the future. And he was not absolutely sure that if he left, the woman Sil might not be sent after him. As she'd been sent after that captain, who'd threatened to go to the King three years ago, and whose death had been blamed on footpads. Though, looking at Herion's benign face, he found that difficult to believe. So he stayed.

And staying had led to this cell. No one came to him.

Until now. Two men walked in: Lord Vrenas, the Marshal of the kingdom, and a guard. "Good day to you, sir. Please come with me." So they ushered him out, and along a corridor, and he wondered how much pain he could bear, or was willing to bear, to keep his master's favour. *God help me*. But the room they entered was a pleasant enough ordinary room, with natural light, and a table and chairs, and wine. The Marshal poured for them both, and sipped his wine first, as if to reassure.

"Attar, son of Garodoth. You have been here longer than you might wish. You do not have to stay. I'm here to give you a choice. You can talk to me fully, and tell me everything - or you can go."

Or? He stared, wondering if he had heard right.

"To be frank, the King and Queen suspect your master of involvement in a number of serious crimes. You've been his steward for years, and it seems likely that you know of them. There is evidence that points that way. So, as I say, I'd like you to tell me all about it."

His voice croaked. "And if I don't, because there is nothing to tell, what will you do?"

"I will open the door. You can leave. But before you go, think about where you would go, and whom you might meet."

"I would go home," he said cautiously. Surely this could not be a suspicious answer.

"The King will not permit you to approach your former master, or any of his people or family. I have authority to give you ten silver pieces, if you need them, to find accommodation elsewhere."

Where could he go, without Herion's protection? He could find work surely? He had relatives and friends. Lady Rakall would welcome him at Aspella. Or would she? Torio had been sent to Ricossa -

What did he mean by "whom you might meet"?

"There are likely to be announcements soon," said the Marshal, examining his cup. "About the King's suspicions."

He could walk out, that meant, but he would walk out as a named suspect. A suspect in the murder of Gemara Kingsister (*but he had known nothing about that, nothing! How could he, or even Herion, have guessed?*) and of the children at Ferrodach, and that other man and girl at Gisren. A lot of people might be very angry about all those things. They were enough for bloodfeud, and vengeance. Gemara had a son and two daughters, and none of them were likely to forgive a mother's murder. Nor were any of the Thirty. And Herion, it seemed, could not protect him.

"You can walk out, or you can talk to me," said the Marshal. Attar saw him struggling to conceal his contempt. "And if you tell me everything, and none of it is proved to be a lie, then the King will undertake to spare your life, no matter what it is. I cannot promise more."

*

29 October 570

"Wait outside, please," said the Queen, as she walked into the room. The guards bowed and obeyed, leaving her with her husband. He was sitting at a small table, absently stroking Sidon's nose, and rereading a report that had recently been brought in. Kai was expecting to arrive a few days after his message, with Kremdar and his squire as prisoners.

"Are you ready to wish the troops well?" the Queen asked. "Not too stirring, as this is merely a routine mission, but we agreed they deserve a word from the King, did we not?"

"Yes." He stood up and came towards her, smiling determinedly. "I hope the sight of you in armour doesn't have the same effect on the soldiers that it has on me." His eyes travelled down from helmet and mail shirt to greaves and boots. "Malouri -"

"There is no time now."

"That isn't what I meant."

"No, but we have had this conversation. No one will believe in the routine raid story if you come. But one of us needs to go. So it is me. Aren't you feeling well?" she added, frowning.

"It's nothing."

"Have you warned the garrison at Kerrytown? And the Consuls of Haymon?"

"The messengers have left. We've had the conversation, but I do not like it. I don't like sending you into danger."

"We send soldiers out all the time," said the Queen sternly. "Many of them have husbands and wives. These people take the risk, and you have to take it." She laid a finger on his nose, hesitated and said, "You remember before we were married, when you said 'absolute honesty', and told me all your disreputable secrets?"

King Arrion looked at her, opened his mouth, and shut it again.

"And I said my secret was not knowing how to love. I said I didn't think I could die for anyone. That was twenty years ago."

"Don't."

"I would die for my children. I would have died for Nadya. And -" She drew her blade, and used the traditional soldier's oath. "My sword for the King."

He put his arm around her, and buried his head on her shoulder. "Don't die," he whispered. "Come back."

"I shall do my duty, and then I shall come back."

He straightened up, and nodded. Then they both went out to the front courtyard, to meet the soldiers that Queen Malouri was leading out west towards the border, because those Rajas-loving murdering bastards in Haymon needed to be given a bloody nose. The city was full of people, for the King's Gathering was starting in two days' time. Sending out soldiers was a more cheerful activity than listening to strange rumours, and the Queen and her army were given a raucous send-off. The troops marched away, and the King went back inside. He felt very tired, and a little sick.

But less sick an hour or so later, when a young man marched up to him, saluted and knelt.

"Jendon, be welcome, son." The Prince rose, and his father embraced him. "Is there news of him?"

"We have found Master Dorac. B-but I think – it seems he may be guilty after all."

Dorac 2 (21–29 October)

He had a sword, and he had a horse, and he was going home.

But in fact he did not keep the horse long. When they came to a place he thought he remembered, and his eyes were almost shutting of themselves, he dismounted, and turned to Melina.

"I am going to walk. You can ride on if you wish."

She shook her head. He lifted her down, and slapped the horses away. Then he led her off the road into the trees, wading a little way up the stream he remembered in case they brought dogs, and washing the blood off his face. On, on, to a gap in trees where there was at last space to lie down.

He should have questioned or killed her, but he had no energy. All he could do was grip his knife, and hope to have time to use it if he needed to. He slept dreamlessly. Some hours later he woke, cold and damp and stiff, but alive. How strange that he was alive.

He rubbed his face, and prayed the Gloria, as he hadn't done for days. He was realising that he had been mad for a time. Perhaps even demon-haunted. It seemed that was over, thank God.

He drew Ramos's sword from his belt, and studied it with eyes and fingers. It was heavier and larger and grander than his own, with a green jewel set in the hilt, and carvings of fanciful dogs near the top of the blade.

Probably it was an ancient sword, with a name. Like Kai's, he hung on the wall of his cell. It had belonged to his grandfather, and even Kremdar could barely lift it.

Dorac's sword had no name. Or perhaps it did, he thought suddenly. In his mind it was always the Queen's Gift.

But this one would serve for now.

He had to decide what to do. *Ancient history.* So he gathered some little stones. Kremdar would have laughed. He scowled at that.

He could plainly not stay in Jaryar, so there were only two choices. It took him longer to choose than it should, and he was ashamed of his cowardice. "Amen." He tossed away the last stone, and considered the next problem, which was Melina.

She lay curled up asleep a few feet away. She looked as innocent as all sleeping people do – quite pretty, he supposed. He still couldn't remember ever meeting her before.

He knew of ballads where a warrior was helped against their enemies by a mysterious stranger of the opposite sex. Kremdar and Soumaki liked such stories. Kai and Tor found them funny. Most of them ended with the couple's marriage. He smiled grimly. Apart from all other reasons, she was young enough to be his daughter. If he'd had a daughter.

She could still be an enemy, or a spy. She had asked if he were going to Marod, and her actions did not make sense.

It was already full light, so he nudged her awake with his foot. She opened her eyes to see him standing over her with a sword. Reasonably enough, she whimpered, and shrank away.

"So," he said, crouching down. "Why did you help me last night?"

Melina wet her lips. Her voice croaked. "I hate Lord Ramos, and you had done no harm, and we have met before."

"Where did we meet?"

She turned her face away.

"So," he said slowly, "you've betrayed your own people to help me. I don't like traitors. And you won't tell me why. I do not trust you, and if I see the need, I will kill you."

Another whimper.

"They'll be coming after us. If they find us, they will kill you, and take me off to kill me in Makkera. Do you understand?"

She nodded.

"If I think that is likely to happen, I will kill myself, and they will kill you."

She nodded again, as he gestured she should.

"So we are unlikely to live long, but if we do, I am going to Marod. That will take more than a day. If I get there, you should know that I'm an exile. Anyone there may try to kill me, and would be right to do so. They will not hurt you, but they won't trust you."

"But why –?" she asked, gaping.

"It's a long story," said Dorac dryly. "So you can come with me, if you do what I say. Or I'll tie you up and leave you somewhere for your friends or enemies to find."

She didn't ask what he would tie her up with. "I'm coming."

"Very well." He handed her a piece of smoked meat, bread and a handful of raisins, and a water skin. They ate and drank, and then set off.

Neither then nor afterwards did she ask why he had abandoned the horses, so he did not have to explain his reasons, which were roughly:

We need secrecy more than speed. Horses are faster than people, but we cannot ride to the border without stopping. Horses are faster than people, but not much faster in the dark on an uncertain road. You have no skill in riding; you're already in pain, and it will get worse. If they think we're mounted, they may look for horses, and they may look mainly on the road, but there are woods here to hide in. People move better and hide better in woods. And horses need to be fed.

*

It was a largely cheerless day, drizzling with autumn rain. Dorac struggled more than he liked to find his way in the unsettlingly unfamiliar landscape, brown and grey. They were not following a track, and their journey took them through brambles and ditches, so they both became colder, wetter, and muddy. Now and again the woods failed. Then they had to creep around buildings and along hedgerows, hoping not to be seen by farmers or labourers.

All the time he was on edge for the sound of pursuing soldiers, and the fear of what the Jaryari would do to him – to them – if they were caught. Lord Ramos's taunting echoed dizzyingly in his head when he let it. Melina seemed equally or even more nervous, and started constantly at natural noises.

She was no help. This was her home, yet she could not tell where they were, or even in which direction they were headed. She could not walk quietly. Surely any Marodi countrywoman would have been able to, even hampered, as Melina was, by several layers of skirt. Other than at festivals, the men and women he knew wore jackets and hose for riding and fighting and ploughing. He was not familiar with the fashions for indoor-living people.

And she complained. Not loudly or continually, as he'd heard children do. He had vivid memories of Princess Daretti, aged seven. But several times that day she said, "I'm so wet" or "it's cold" – and she was an adult.

Neither of them said much else. They walked, and walked, and rested and ate a little, and scrambled on. Dorac saw again the faces of the man and woman he had killed the night before. He heard their voices, making ordinary conversation over supper, and walked on.

When it was too dark to see, they stopped. "Are we going to make a fire?" asked Melina, rubbing her hands together to warm them.

"No."

"Why not?"

"Damp wood smokes." She seemed to understand the meaning of that.

There was soggy bread, smoked fish and raw turnip. They sat and ate, not too close together. By now he knew that she did not want to marry him. If he had to help her across a ditch, or even handed her something to eat, she shrank away, with what seemed revulsion or fear. She wanted to accompany him, but she didn't want him anywhere near her. He wasn't surprised, after what she had seen and heard him do.

But now it was awkward. Between them they had one blanket, and their cloaks, and the evening was chilly. Dorac spread out a cloak on the muddy ground, as he had done for Gormad. "I'm not going to hurt you," he said irritably. She came, but she curled up as far away as possible.

The night was cold, but he was too tired to notice.

*

22 October 570

The next day there was some sun, and their clothes and even the blanket dried. They walked, and listened nervously, and Dorac found some mushrooms. He dared not delay long enough to fish or hunt.

The longest conversation went:

"What are you going to do when we get to Marod?"

"If we get to Marod. That is not your concern."

A few minutes later, "What could I do in Marod?"

"What did you do at home?"

"I worked in a bakery."

"We have bakeries."

It was a long day. He prayed he was leading them right.

*

23 October 570

Around midday, they came to the River Lither. It was about twenty feet wide, and trees bent over each bank. The water flowed fast, and after all the rain it was higher than he had expected.

"This is the border."

"The border? But isn't there a road, and guards?"

"I am trying to avoid guards. We can get across here. Can you swim?"

She shook her head. *Of course not.*

"You won't have to." He considered. "It's better to keep the food and clothes dry, if we can. You should take off your skirts. At least tuck them up." He took off his boots and most of his clothes, and bundled them together. The wind was cold, but the water would be much worse. The sword he threaded through the satchel buckles. "Give me your cloak. You want to keep it dry. I'll come back."

He would have to make two journeys, one with satchel and sword, and one with all the clothes. And a third for her.

He had known it would be cold. He had known the water was high. Still he gasped. He waded in above his waist, the satchel held over his head, steadying himself with an effort. The river flung itself against him. It was his enemy, more deadly, although less cruel, than Lord Ramos. He struggled across, and then back for the bundle of blanket and clothes. And back again. There was a band of fiery cold across his chest, and a sickness in his stomach. The water roared in his ears, and tugged exhaustingly at him, and he could barely feel his feet.

Melina waited on the shore, her skirts tucked up. She was silently crying with fright. He stood near the bank and looked at her. "Come on. This will get you out of Jaryar. I won't let you drown."

Still she hesitated. "Stay there, then. I am going now." He made as if to turn, and she jumped clumsily in, squealing.

He had to drag her, but he kept his promise. They crawled up the bank, and were in Marod.

"A little further. There should be an old farmhouse." He handed her the blanket, and scooped up the rest of their possessions.

The house was still as he remembered, empty, and almost intact. It had once had two rooms and an attached stable. The partition and half the roof had fallen or been burnt away. "Take off - those - and wring them out, and wrap up. I'll get firewood." He put on a fairly dry shirt and hose, dropped the bundle at her feet and went out.

By the time he came back, the light was fading. Melina had draped her kirtle, or whatever it was, over the rotting bedstead in the corner, and put on his spare shirt and jacket and both cloaks. She'd also cleared the hearth space and moved some of the clutter off the floor. Now she was pacing up and down, clasping and unclasping her hands, trying to keep warm. The wood was damp, but he broke up some of the furniture to help, and they got a blaze going that warmed them a little. He cooked the eggs he had stolen from Sali and Artos. *Praise God, unbroken.* Mixed with fresh mushrooms and more turnip, they almost made a meal.

They sat on opposite sides of the orange glow, and shadows sat behind and hung above them, and walls stood behind the shadows. They looked shyly at each other. The fire made a difference – made it a camp and not just a stopping-place. For the first time he saw her not as a burden or a puzzle, but simply as someone he happened to be travelling with. He tried to ignore the wrongness of a woman wearing his shirt.

Melina said timidly, "Thank you for getting me across the river."

He shrugged.

"So this is Marod?"

"Yes. Much the same as Marithon province. Better weather."

"Why is this building ruined?"

Why are any border houses ruined?

"It's been empty for years. Burnt in a raid. The land was taken by the local Lady."

Melina poked at something at the edge of the fire. "Are we safe now?"

"You may be. I was expecting more trouble getting here. The guards wouldn't want to let Lord Ramos and Lady Igalla through after us, but they might - insist." He thought of the Marodi soldiers at the border, whom he had put in danger.

"You didn't kill them? When I was in the stable?"

"Did you expect me to?"

"I didn't know." She fiddled with the cloak, not looking at him. "Why were you exiled?"

Someone else would tell her if he did not. "A friend of mine murdered three children, and lied to the King that it was me. Because of my long service, I was not hanged."

The fire crackled and flickered.

"Will you be able to find somewhere where people don't know you? Somewhere to hide?"

He took a breath. "I am going back to the capital. I have news for the King."

"Oh - what you asked Lady Igalla? You said something about letters. But if you're an exile - won't the King kill you?"

"Perhaps." Now she was looking at him, and he resented the look.

"Why would you help him? He sent you away!"

"He is still my king," Dorac said angrily. He had been tempted not to go back, and he was ashamed. "I got enough of that crap from your Lord Ramos. I don't need any more."

But suddenly Melina was angry also. "He's not my Lord Ramos! He killed my nephew. Or his men did."

Dorac looked at her. She swallowed. "My sister married young, and had twin boys. The younger one - something went wrong in his birthing, and he wasn't like other children. He didn't understand things, but he was gentle and happy. He laughed a lot. One day, he was five years old, Lord Ramos rode through their village with his soldiers, and Oros was playing in the road and didn't get out of their way. He was told to kneel and beg pardon, and he just laughed, and Lord Ramos told his people to punish him. His father tried to explain – begged – but they went on beating him, all over his body, until he stopped screaming, and Lord Ramos watched. He died two days later."

Dorac was silent.

"So my sister took her husband and the other boy to live in Lefayr, in the south, and maybe the lords there are kinder, I don't know."

She had been staring at the fire, but now her eyes met his.

"I heard that it's different in Marod. In Marod the poor get justice."

"I don't know why you'd think that," said Dorac after a moment. "We try to do justice, but the poor are the poor everywhere. The rich take their pleasures, and make use of them. Marod is no different. We try not to kill children." His mouth tasted sour. "Our Saviour said the poor were blessed. That must be in heaven. I don't see much sign of it on earth."

Melina leaned forward and poked again. She delicately rolled two apples out of the edge of the fire, picked one up in a leaf and passed it over. Soft fluffy flesh was bursting out of the skin. He hadn't noticed her putting them in. "It's hot."

She wasn't wrong, and he burnt his mouth. Still, it was very good. "Thank you."

"Were you born rich or poor?"

"Poor."

"But you became a – a Kingsbrother."

"And now I'm an exile."

"Still, you did. How long will it take us to get to Stonehill?"

"You don't have to come to Stonehill. We took four days the other way. Riding, but not fast. Maybe a week. I want to keep out of sight until then."

"Who was 'we'?"

"That is not your concern - There was a boy. He went home before the border."

"I have some money," she said, "but it's Jaryari. Will any of your people take it?"

"Not if it has King Rajas's head on it. Expect to eat a lot of fish."

"What happened to your back?" she asked suddenly.

He gave his normal answer. "Like most children, I was beaten."

"You were beaten a lot," she said. The sudden pity in her voice defeated him. He got up and walked out of the house.

In bed with Tor, Tor's fingers running gorgeously over his shoulders and down his back – and then stopping – and then hesitantly starting to trace the lines. Horizontal, deep, old; still painful sometimes: all the way down from shoulders to waist. "But what happened to you?"

"My father happened." There were much more interesting things to think about just then. "It doesn't matter."

It had mattered to Tor. Afterwards, he had kissed the scars, and it was this memory, now five years old, that sent Dorac out into the night to deal yet again with old grief, before he could come back and face Melina.

She was hugging her knees and gazing into the flames. Mercifully she said nothing. He banked down the fire, and spread out a cloak, and they lay down again, still not touching.

There was silence.

"A good night to you," he said awkwardly.

"And to you."

*

24–26 October 570

He sat up to find her toasting bread and cheese at the revived fire. This wasn't something he would have thought of. When he fetched water from the river to shave, she stopped him. "If you don't want to be recognised, let it grow."

"You're right," he admitted.

"Yes, sometimes I am," said Melina.

So they set off again. Now they were travelling through land he knew, and along paths rather than through brambles. An absurd and painful pleasure at each familiar hollow tree or oddly shaped cottage. Occasionally they stepped into the undergrowth or hedges to hide from other travellers, but this didn't happen often on his routes. Food was a worry. He was not an expert hunter like Gemara or Kremdar. But that night he managed to seize a lame blackbird, and plucked it. And Melina insisted on cooking it. She did well in the circumstances – as well as even Kai could have done.

The itch of the stubble was bad enough, but on the second

day he could stand the sweat and mud no longer. He led her to a gentle stream with plenty of bushes, and said, "I for one would like to be cleaner. If I leave you here for half an hour, will you be all right?" And evidently she took the hint, for when he returned after a generous half hour, she also was cleaner and tidier – and rather more cheerful. Finally she must be convinced she wasn't going to be raped.

But still she shuddered every time he got too close.

The weather was only a little better than in Marithon. Mostly they walked and slept under gloomy clouds, and they were never quite warm. But one night the sky cleared. They were sitting eating fish and cheese and boiled dandelion leaves, and Melina looked up and said, "A smiling moon."

"What moon?"

"Don't you say that in Marod? The thin moon is smiling, then it becomes the laughing moon, and then the big fat happy drunken moon."

"No." He looked up, and remembered the crescent smiling moon in the Village. He was still not sure if his choice had been the right one.

During the day they didn't talk much, and when they did it was mostly about the journey and what to do next, but the talk they had was amicable. He asked if she had any other relatives in Marithon; still curious as to how easily she had left them all. "My parents are dead. I lived with my brother and his wife. We moved here from -" she gave him an odd look - "a village further north a few years ago. My uncle and aunt were already here. When you first came up to the house, and asked for work, that was my aunt Frall. Sali at The Hanged Man is a friend of hers."

"Ah." He wondered if she were going to ask again if he had killed Sali, but instead she said shyly, "Don't you have brothers or – anyone – in Marod?"

It was fair to answer. He looked away as he said, "I was an only child. I don't remember my mother. I left my father's home when I was fifteen. I've no family except one cousin." *And the King's Thirty.*

"Is your father still alive?"

"I don't know." His voice warned her to ask nothing more. They walked on, and he remembered his father. Remembered lying curled up on the floor night after night, back burning in agony again, praying, "Please God, let him die. Please, God, kill him. Please." The years passed, and God did nothing, and he himself became older and stronger, and the fear grew that one day he would do the killing himself. And that would be an unforgivable sin, and he would burn in hell for eternity.

And then his cousin ran over from his father's farm to say that Lady Luteshi's soldiers were calling for volunteers against Ricossan raiders, and that fifteen was old enough. That day he had done his stones for the first time. Try to join them, and get the worst beating of all if they would not have him – or stay and not try. And he chose, and left, and Araf cursed him as he went, and his real life began.

What was it his father had said? *May you come to an ill end,* or *may you come to be hanged?* He wasn't sure.

*

"Do you think someone was holding back the first letter, that King Rajas never got? To get that lord – Gahran, was it? – in trouble later on?"

"That is not your concern – or mine," he added, softening the rebuke slightly. Melina fell silent, and he thought a little about the events of two years ago. When King Arrion's arm was smashed, and had to be cut off. (Dorac and Gardai Kingsbrother had held him down while the bonesetter sawed: a very bad memory.) He'd had other injuries also, and fever. Stonehill had been tense with dread for months, as he slowly recovered. The border guards were doubled, and the more obnoxious lords and ladies fawned over Prince Jendon, and extra prayers were said in every church and manor house in the country. Perhaps Lord Gahran's prayers had not all been for the King's recovery. Perhaps.

This did not explain the delay.

It was a distraction, to think of this, as they walked on and on through the familiar farmlands and woods, and the beauty of leaves yellow, brown and red. The occasional sunlight, dazzling off little streams. The purple twilights, the gold and pink-clouded sunsets, the slow glory of sunrise.

Once, very drunk, he'd told Tor that his presence was like sunrise. Tor had roared with laughter. Being Tor, he had at once apologised, not wanting to hurt Dorac's feelings or offend him. He could never understand that Dorac wasn't going to be offended by anything he said or did, because that was what love meant.

Or perhaps it was he, Dorac, who did not understand about love.

This was also a distraction. A distraction from the knowledge that he was probably, again, walking towards death.

Even if King Arrion were grateful, he could hardly ignore such a disregard of his sentence. Or could he? Dorac had thought, making his choice, that it was not death he feared. It was going back to face the disbelief and contempt that he had walked away from – and yet still carried with him – on the day of his trial. To be stared at again by everyone he knew, the childkiller - Now he knew that was not all. He had seen too many executions – had ordered too many. He could not face calmly the thought of being hanged from the castle walls, his body left for the flies and crows. *The Hanged Man.*

Melina had blisters, which slowed them down, but this could not be helped. He had to take time fishing, while she gathered nuts and blackberries. Very soon they would have to decide to steal food, as they were running out of bread, and they had nothing to sell.

*

27 October 570

Now they were on the main road north, occasionally passing through villages, when they separated. Dorac would slip round the back, while Melina walked through, filling their water-skins at the well, picking up any stray fruit or vegetables fallen from stalls or baskets, and possibly hearing news. And this was the plan as they came to the village of Queenshouse, a place which thought well of itself. Not one but two alehouses, a name with a legend, and a marketplace. Market had been yesterday, but it seemed as he waited in the shadows at the far end that there was more activity than usual in the street. Several horses were tied outside the nearer alehouse. As he watched, four or five soldiers came clattering out, talking animatedly to the host. He couldn't hear the conversation. Melina was walking slowly past them, not looking at them, and they didn't look at her. Dorac shrank back into the shadows, and she caught up with him.

"There are soldiers," she said, obviously.

"I saw. Did you hear what they were saying?"

"Someone is dead. They were very surprised." She hesitated. "If you're a Kingsbrother, what's a Kingsister?"

Dorac was suddenly cold. "Who is dead?"

"Gemara – I think – Kingsister."

No.

He stared at Melina, feeling as if he had run into a wall.

"I'm sorry," she was saying, but Dorac could not listen. In his mind was blackness. Then a few words slowly arranged themselves into a pattern of obvious truth:

> *Gemara is dead.*
> *And surely*
> *Someone killed her.*
> *And surely*
> *This is connected to Ferrodach.*
> *Therefore*
> *Ferrodach is urgent, and I cannot wait.*

"I am sorry," he said, interrupting Melina. He didn't need the stones. "I have to go now. I have to go to the soldiers. You -" He searched through the satchel for the remaining food, and then changed his mind, took his own water-skin, and handed her everything else. "I'm sorry to leave you like this. If you reach Stonehill, find my brothers Kai or Hassdan of the Southern Six of the Thirty, and say I asked them to help you. Or if you go north to Ondubbi, perhaps my cousin Jaikkad -"

405

"Stop, stop," said Melina. "What are you doing? Who are you talking about?"

"Go to Kai or Hassdan of the Southern Six. God be with you, Melina." He turned away, and walked briskly down the street into the village. Towards the alehouse.

People were turning to look at him. Through the ringing in his head, he was aware of his untidy state and dirty clothes. He heard his name whispered.

One of the soldiers looked up, and then they all did, and were quiet. Five of them, and three he knew, and *one* was- He kept his hands away from his weapon, and stopped a few feet away. Behind him he heard a sword being drawn. So it should be.

He knelt. "My prince," he said.

"M-Master Dorac," said Prince Jendon, after a moment.

That is no longer my name. "I crave of your kindness to tell me," he said as courteously as Hassdan himself, "is it true that Gemara Kingsister is dead?" His voice was hoarse.

"There is a rumour here that she is. No such news had reached Stonehill when we left. But we have b-been to the south and back."

"I know my life is forfeit. I have news for the King. If you will send someone to take me back to Stonehill, I will surrender. I will give whatever pledge you please, I swear to go peaceably, but I must go to Stonehill."

The Prince stared. Then he said, "We were sent to find you. The King has ordered you back."

"Then I surrender." He slowly drew Ramos's sword, and

406

handed it hilt first to the Prince, who grasped it uncertainly.

"And your knife." The voice was hard.

Dorac hesitated. A person must have a knife. It was like demanding his boots. But this was his prince. Slowly he drew it out, but then the other man said, "Do you p-pledge your honour not to try to escape, not to use any weapon against us or any p-person until you stand before the King?"

"Yes."

"You can keep the knife."

"He's a murderer. He has no honour," said the woman next to him.

"He had once. We weren't told to bring him as a prisoner, Garida."

Indeed, it was unclear whether he was a prisoner or not. They gave him a horse, and did not bind him, but they kept his sword, and looked at him suspiciously.

So he rode out of Queenshouse.

After half an hour, one of the soldiers came to ride beside Dorac. Perhaps it was the Prince's kindness, or perhaps his own. He told Dorac all that the inn host had said a passing merchant had said about Gemara. She had gone north with her brother Kremdar, it wasn't clear why. A labourer had found her body in a ditch by the side of the road, covered in a cloak; she'd been stabbed in the throat. Her horse had wandered off or been stolen. *Tara Maid.* That seemed to make it worse. No one knew where Kremdar Kingsbrother was. This was all the news that had reached the city two days ago.

Gemara. In a ditch.

Kremdar killed her. He must have done. What I will do to him -

He took out his knife, and made the ritual slash in the right sleeve for mourning. His hand shook.

Some time later, the Prince rode up. Garida was at his side, looking angry. "We heard you went into Jaryar." Dorac dragged his mind back.

"Yes, my prince."

"And you killed people there," said Garida.

"Yes. Two soldiers."

His face must have shown curiosity. The Prince said, "When we reached the border, the guards said a high Jaryari lady had been looking for you – said you were an escaped m-murderer. She knew your name. The guards t-told her they had not seen you, and wouldn't let her through. I sent someone over to find you in secret - but we g-guessed you would have got back. Without my father's leave. How did you avoid their soldiers?"

"They looked on the road." A thought had occurred to him. "My prince," he said shyly, "you said the King had ordered me back. Did he order you to bring me, or me to come?"

"Both. He was very clear."

"Ah." *So he read my letter,* Dorac thought. He began to feel rather more hopeful of avoiding the hangman's noose. But when this hope failed, oddly, the fear was worse.

He felt guilty about Melina, whom he had abandoned without friends or money in a strange country. He puzzled over why King Arrion had sent his son and heir on such an unimportant, but still dangerous, errand. And he thought of tortures for Kremdar that would have impressed even Lord Ramos.

But most of the time he thought about Gemara.

Before he joined the Thirty, she was already a legend. Strikingly tall and dark, she was said to be cleverer about horses - and about dirty fighting - than anyone in Stonehill. ("Knows exactly where to kick," someone said ruefully.) But Dorac had had little to do with her until, unbelievably, Queen Darisha had named him, and he was branded: the agony that no one talked about afterwards. He became Dorac Queensbrother, brother of Gemara and Stimmon and Taldim and Armi and Lirrin. All dead now, except him.

At first she'd watched him remotely, as she did every new member. It had been Taldim, the kindest woman he'd ever known, who'd helped him with the reading and writing that he now had to learn, to be a magistrate. Gemara had criticised his spelling, and much else.

But she had been kind, in her way. There had been hospitality at the busy but well-run home, where her quiet and cheery husband ran a livery stables. It had taken Dorac time to realise that there were usually women of his own age invited also, and why. He'd had to explain awkwardly to Gemara that there was no point to this.

Some people disapproved of those like him. They were neglecting their God-ordained tasks of populating the world and producing future subjects for the King, purely for their own selfish and unnatural lusts. But Gemara simply said, "I see." For the first time it occurred to him that he might have her and Stimmon (and the King) to thank for the fact that almost no one had worried him about this. Not even years later, when he and Tor were living together in that smoky

409

room near Butchers' Row. Gemara and Habbaroth had welcomed Tor, too, and he remembered Sunday afternoons when the three of them had talked horses so incessantly that Dorac had almost felt left out.

He and Gemara had been sent together in '59 to investigate a disastrous fire in Amachle. Seventeen people had died in one hall, eight of them children. Dorac dug grave after grave, and Gemara listened to the stories, and sifted the evidence, and at last decided it had been accident and not arson. They had ridden away, still stinking of smoke, and at their first stop she had burst into tears.

It was the only time he ever saw her cry. She didn't weep at the funerals of her husband or her youngest grandchild, nor in the long night's vigil for Taldim and the others after the war. Stimmon and Dorac had wept, but not Gemara. Only after the Amachle fire, and he had put an awkward arm around her shoulder, and waited for her to stop, and wondered at the ways of God.

He remembered her words about his behaviour to Hassdan. "I am protecting the King," he'd said stiffly. "You are protecting nothing but your own hate and stupidity. I am ashamed of you, Dorac. Ashamed to call you brother." And Stimmon had added gently, "I have to agree with Gemara." There had been other stinging words over the years, but those were the worst.

And now. "Gemara went to the King," Kai had said. Gemara had returned with the others from Kerrytown. She had been told – as a fact – what he had done. She had been told that the King believed it, and she would have heard Kremdar's version, and she had not even spoken to Dorac, and yet she had believed *him*. Or at least had given him the benefit of some doubt. If he had any future, it was thanks to her, and in this life he would never be able to thank her.

*

They rode, and camped, and he shaved off the irritating stubble, no longer needing to hide. The Prince looked at him sometimes with distaste, and sometimes with curiosity. The other soldiers stared more openly, but all except Garida were civil to him. Now the nights were better than the days. There were only occasional dreams, and these not terrible enough to make him cry in the night, as he thought he had done in Jaryar.

One day they rode along the edge of Wildfowl Lake that he'd passed with Gormad, going the other way. The geese were gone. He rested his eyes on the water. Black and white and sparkling, and even in places brown, at this distance – not blue. Still majestic and calming. He had been so sure, that day, that he would never see it again.

And the city drew nearer.

*

29 October 570

They rode into Stonehill on a sunny cold afternoon, and people crowded the streets to watch. There were a lot of them: the Gathering was about to begin. He stared straight ahead. The eyes again.

And at last he was dismounting in the Castle courtyard. For good or for ill, he was back home. It was so much the same, it made him dizzy. The Prince was talking to people. Garida had put a hand on her sword, and was watching Dorac for signs of treachery. He stood there, absorbing where he was and being stared at.

Fortunately, another group of riders was coming through the gate. They also were dismounting, greeting people, looking around –

411

and one of them was Hassdan. He looked across and saw Dorac, and grinned and waved, and Dorac's heart lifted. With him was the steward from Ferrodach, and several other people, and young Meril.

No, that child was far too small to be Meril.

He looked at the little girl, wondering who she was and what she was doing there. And the little girl followed Hassdan's gaze, and looked up at him.

She looked at him, and she recognised him, and she screamed.

Everyone seemed to stop. They all stared at one or the other, while the child screamed and pointed, and the woman beside her tried to comfort her. The little girl turned away from Dorac to clutch her companion. As she did so she wailed shrilly, "Don't let him! Don't let him! The bad man! Please don't!"

In all the world there was no other sound.

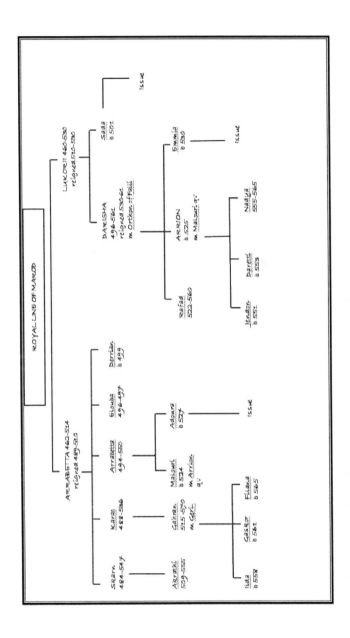

ROYAL LINE OF MAROD

ARRABETTA 462-514
reigned 489-510

LUKORII 460-530
reigned 510-530

Skarn
424-547

Abrakhi
509-555

Ida
b 558

Karat
488-586

Gahrak
515-570
m. Geric

Gasar
b 561

Filora
b 565

Arrabetta
494-550

Maiouri
b 524
m. Arrion
av

Adoura
b 527

ISSUE

Lluvian
496-497

Detrian
b 499

Darisha
496-561
reigned 530-61
m. Orthon of Paiui

Rafad
522-560

Arrion
b 525
m. Maiouri av

Jeradon
b 551

Daveni
b 553

Naira
555-565

Saza
b 501

ISSUE

Emmia
b 530

ISSUE

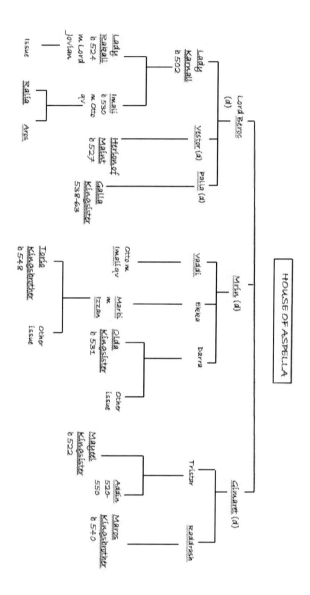

HOUSE OF ASPELLA

Lord Baroc (d)

Lady Karvali b 502
- Lady Rarali b 524 m. Lord Jovian — issue
- Imali b 530 m. Otto qv — Ralia, Ares

Palla (d)
- Vester (d) — Hariom of Malvi b 527
- Galla Kingsister 538-63

Mrin (d)

Ekrea
- Vaddi — Otto m. Imaliqv
- Marti m. Izzin — Toria Kingbrother b 548
- Olda Kingsister b 531 — Other issue

Darra

Gimare (d)

Tristor
- Mayel Kingsister b 522
- Addin 520-550

Raidarish
- Maros Kingbrother b 540

414

Part Three – The Southern

Six

29 October 570

Soumaki Kingsister strode calmly up to the little group, ignoring the wails. She nodded in sibling fashion to Hassdan, and said to the steward, "Hagouna, daughter of Lahni? It is good to see you again. May I present to you Princess Daretti?"

Twisting up from the child, Hagouna curtsied awkwardly to the thin girl standing with Soumaki.

"And this, my princess, is Lady Filana of Ferrodach."

The child had become interested by now, and stopped crying, although she still clung to Hagouna's sleeve.

"Welcome to Stonehill, Lady Filana. My parents have asked me to greet you, and to offer you their protection and hospitality. Come into the Castle, please."

She glanced at Soumaki, who smiled at Filana, and added, "With your friends, of course. There is cake."

"The bad man," Filana whispered.

"We will not let the bad man hurt you," said a new voice. Prince Jendon had walked up to them.

His younger sister glared at his intrusion. "Welcome home, brother," she said crossly. "This is my brother, the Prince." Everyone was already bowing and curtseying around them. Filana put her fingers in her mouth, and stared up at the high faces.

"Shall we go in?" Soumaki suggested.

*

Dorac had not heard this conversation. He saw the Ferrodach people go indoors with Soumaki and the Princess, and then Hassdan came up to him. He was no longer smiling.

"Who was that?"

"That was Lord Gahran's daughter Filana."

"But she died," Dorac said, bewildered.

"The other two died. Apparently she was hiding."

"Hiding in the room?"

"I think so."

"Oh God," said Dorac, and it was a prayer. He shut his eyes so as not to see Hassdan's disbelief as he said, it seemed for the hundredth time, "I did not -"

"I know."

"You can't know. You were not there."

"No, but – we can talk inside."

"Not now." The Prince had followed Hassdan over.

"I am talking to my brother, Your Highness," said Hassdan respectfully.

"Later, perhaps." He waited sternly until Hassdan nodded. Then he looked at Dorac: the look a childkiller would deserve. "For now, he will go in and wait. Garida –"

"I have a message for the King," said Dorac. "I need to deliver it. That's why I came back." He turned to Garida, and let her lead him into the Castle.

He was left in a smallish room, where people normally waited to see the King, the Queen, or the Marshal, Lord Vrenas. So it was appropriate. He knelt and prayed, and then sat down at the table. Out of the window, he could see into the herb garden below, where people were walking, and a few small children were chasing each other among the green and silver bushes. He watched them for a little, and then started to pace up and down. He was still pacing an hour later when Hassdan came in.

*

Hassdan knew he was not bringing the news Dorac would want.

"Brother." He gestured, and they sat at the table. A little over a month before, he had ridden off with the others to risk their lives at Kerrytown. It had been Dorac's turn for dull, safe guard duty.

"I've spoken to the King," he said. "It seems your face frightened the little girl. No one knows yet exactly what she saw. They're going to question her tomorrow, with witnesses, very gently." He eyed his brother's unhopeful face, and put cheerfulness into his own. "Stop looking like a martyr about to be thrown to the lions, or whatever the emperors did to them. Don't tell me you're innocent – I believe you, and so does Soumaki. The King says he can't see you yet, and asks if you will be trusting me with your message."

"Yes." Dorac seemed to collect his thoughts. "Did you know I went into Jaryar?"

"Kai told us."

"I spoke to a Lady Igalla of somewhere." He explained further. Hassdan thought it a curious tale – and also that Dorac had

417

missed part of its significance.

"Two years ago," he said, and their eyes met.

"In the summer, when the King was wounded."

"Yes, it makes sense. Gahran wasn't requesting that King Arrion be killed, he was saying if it was God's will for him to die of his injuries, *he* would be willing - It's still treasonable. Jendon was the heir then as he is now. Perhaps some people would say seventeen was too young to be king. Why did Lady Igalla tell you all this?"

"I was pointing a sword at her."

"I thought so."

"Also, the Jaryari have a spy in the village by the Old Stones. They knew I'd met Kai there."

Hassdan nodded.

Dorac said heavily, "Gemara."

"Is dead."

Silence. Dorac looked down, tracing patterns on the table with his finger. At last he said, "I don't understand about the little girl."

"Nobody does. Why kill the other two, and not her? It certainly is her – everyone recognises her, and she recognises them.

"And Kremdar said you killed her, and he buried three bodies. We dug them up, and there were only two. So that's the first reason I know you're innocent. The second reason is that you ordered food for the children after they should've been dead. You didn't seem sure at your trial, but you told a man called Dav to fetch food for them."

"Yes. Why didn't he say so?"

"Because he wasn't there." Hassdan explained what Dav had done. "We have his statement, and that's the second reason.

"The third reason - is something you said to me and Kai in a tavern several years ago. And the fourth is Gemara. If you've been in Jaryar, you couldn't have killed her.

"By the way, you aren't knowing anything about Arvill's background, are you? Where she came from before she joined the army?"

"She's some kin of Mayeel Kingsister. I know no more than that."

"Is she? How d'you know?"

"Mayeel said so once."

"I will tell Secretary Makkam. Dorac, I'm sorry. We'll get you out, but for the moment you stay here. Is - is there anything you need? The King says you can ask for anything within reason."

Except freedom.

Dorac looked round the room, his new prison, with at least the blessing of a window. "Food. A bath. A blanket." He seemed to think. "Something holy to read. News."

"I will arrange it." Hassdan stood up.

"Wait. Hassdan – if a woman called Melina asks you for aid, please give it to her. She helped me in Jaryar, and I left her in Queenshouse."

Hassdan raised an eyebrow, but nodded. As he was leaving, he added, "Igalla – and her father was Rodas?"

"Yes."

"The Commander of the Army is Rodas, but I didn't know he had any daughters. Well." He hid a smile.

"What did I say in a tavern? " Dorac asked suddenly.

"I'll tell you sometime." And he left, hoping he had given Dorac something to think about other than why Filana had called him a bad man - and why the King had refused to see him.

But he suspected his friend would still have a very bad night.

*

He ordered the requested items, and then reported, as King Arrion had asked, to a busy-looking Secretary Makkam. To his surprise, she seemed most interested in the name Mayeel. Then he went home.

At every alley entrance he passed, he smelt pig or dog or human excrement and urine; every person stank of unwashed skin and damp wool. And there were a lot of people, for the King's Gathering began tomorrow, and every shire in the land was entitled to send in one layman, one laywoman and one cleric. They did not all come, of course, but there were coarse accents from the north, and convoluted oaths from the east, and arguments in plenty with allegedly overcharging innkeepers and stall holders. And country folk gawking: people who had never seen a house of two storeys.

Not that Stonehill did not have plenty of single-storey cottages and hovels, mostly down the more fetid alleys; and the new tenements, four windows high and eight families to a block, were not much better.

The Gathering was not Hassdan's favourite time of year, and he had never been able to understand its purpose, other than to encourage quarrelling, bribery and sycophancy in the presence of the King.

Home.

Soumaki had ridden ahead with news while Hassdan waited at Saint's Rest for Hagouna. And Meril had been put on a cart and carried off to Stonehill, to better medical care – he prayed – than Yalli could provide. It had been a wrench to see her go, wondering how badly she was injured, and whether she would survive the journey.

But *thank God*, Meril's face peering out of the window was the first thing that greeted him as he arrived. She was sitting on a bench with cushions, her feet up, being tended by Alida and their steward. The cuts on her face and arms were healing, her headache was gone, and she was eating well. But she had been strictly forbidden to try to walk or stand, and the foot and ankle still did not appear, to his inexpert eye, to be the right shape.

Alida had occupied her by going over all that she could remember about Ferrodach and Saint's Rest – ostensibly for evidence – but was expecting to resort to lessons and sewing the next day. Hassdan told them both the latest news, and about his two meetings with Dorac – and the ones in between, with Soumaki and the King.

"His Grace seemed a little unlike himself. Tired. Prince Jendon saw him before I did, of course."

30 October 570

The next day he breakfasted early, and walked through the city and up the hill to the Castle. He and Alida had heard the rain lashing down the night before, as they celebrated his return and Meril's survival, and this morning the cobblestones were slippery and shiny, and the alleys off the main streets were made of mud. The thatched eaves of the smaller houses dripped drearily and irritatingly each side of the road.

In the White Hall, the astonishing story of Torio had had to make way for the latest news, and the arrival of the supposedly dead Filana was being gossiped over on all sides. King Arrion, looking paler and less calm than usual, allocated Soumaki to help entertain the child, and Hassdan to guard the Prince. This meant accompanying him and Princess Daretti to Sunday Mass at the Cathedral. The King did not attend, which was unusual, and surely impolitic, especially in the Queen's absence. Idle countryfolk came to the Gathering to see the King. A mere prince made a far less impressive story for their neighbours at home. And back through the drizzle, and so slowly, as the royal family had to give time to be seen and cheered by commoners and visitors, and even talk to some of them.

By the time they returned to eat in the Great Hall, everyone seemed weary and dispirited. Hassdan was concerned about Dorac, and nervous about the enquiry due to take place in a few hours. Nor did he enjoy staring at the ceiling of the Small Chamber after the meal, while Prince Jendon and Ralia whispered to each other. In Jaryar people courted in private, but it was not his place to offer to leave them alone, as they obviously wanted, but did not say.

Then at last the time came. A servant came to call the Prince and the Kingsbrother to Princess Daretti's chamber, to hear what the little girl had to tell.

*

Efforts had clearly been made to reassure the child and make her feel at home. She was sitting, clad in an embroidered jacket and violently clashing rose-pink hose, playing with little bricks with Soumaki's son Shar and the patronising assistance of two much older squires called Gormad and Jamis. She glanced up now and again at Hagouna, and at Dav, who stood by the wall with nothing to do, fidgeting with his fingers. Hagouna was sewing, sitting with the Princess just in front of a curtain dividing the room in half. On the other side of the curtain squeezed the witnesses: the Prince, the Bishop, the Marshal, several of the Thirty, and two secretaries to write it all down.

Hagouna had told the old absurd story of the children who were bewitched to walk on their heads, and then she said, "That's a not-real story, isn't it, love? But you know some stories are real and true? You know your true history that you learned?"

"Ilda says history's boring."

"I know she does. Filana, the Princess and I need you to tell us a story. The real story, that God sees as He looks down on us. The real true story. About what happened to Ilda and Gaskor. No one knows that story but you."

Hassdan and the others behind the curtain heard a silence, and then a muffled whisper.

"What did you say, love?"

"The bad man killed them."

"We need to know about that. We need to know what you know, and what God saw," the Princess said gently. "I promise we will not let the bad man hurt you. I promise. And you need to talk clearly, so I can hear."

(Her brother, listening, made an impatient grimace.)

"You have to be brave. All the Ferrodach children were brave," said Hagouna. "I was there when the two Kingsbrothers came to the house. They took the three of you to a room, didn't they?"

"The playing-and-sitting-room."

"Yes, the room where you played, and Ilda hated to sit."

"She only likes riding and playing outside."

Hassdan felt his heart catch at the "likes". *Lord, have mercy.*

"Yes. But that day you were left in the room. Then what happened?"

All the listeners tensed.

"The bad man came."

"The man you saw yesterday?"

"Yes. He was nasty, with a sword. He said our father was dead. Gaskor said, 'You killed him!' and hit him, and he said something, I don't know what."

"Did he hurt Gaskor?"

"Not then."

"Then what happened? D'you remember?"

"He said he would get us some food, but he never did, and he went away, but Gaskor said he'd come back and kill us too. He was frightened. We wanted to hide." She cried a little.

"Then what, darling?"

424

"We wanted to hide, but there was nowhere for all of us, and Ilda told me to get in the toybox. They took the toys out, and I got in, and then, then, there was a noise, and Gaskor shut the lid, and it was dark, and I was frightened."

"Go on."

"He came back, I heard the door open and shut, and there was some noise, but I couldn't really hear, I was still like a stone, like Ilda said to be, and then after a bit the kind man opened the box, and said, 'It's all right.'"

"Who was the kind man?"

"The other Kingsbrother, with a scar on his face. He was sad. I asked him if the bad man had gone, and he said yes, but Gaskor and Ilda were on the floor - and, and I could see some blood – he called for someone, and a woman came, and he told her the bad man – his name was Dorac – had killed them, and they could save me from him. And she said yes. She let me kiss them, and the kind Kingsbrother took me out, and found Dav, and told him all about it, and Dav took me to the stables."

"And all this is what you remember, and what God saw, looking down from heaven?" asked Hagouna, after a moment.

"Yes, and then Dav took me away."

"When you were in the box," said the Princess, "just one more tiny thing, Filana, did you hear the door open and shut just one time, or two times? Or many?"

There was a pause, with some sniffles. "I don't remember. I only remember it shutting when the bad man came in."

"You're a brave girl. Thank you for helping us."

"What d'you want to do now, darling?" asked Hagouna, through tears. "I know – let's go and count the stairs in that other tower, and then a story."

Behind the curtain, Prince Jendon turned to the secretaries. "Did you manage to write all that?"

Hassdan did not know how long he had been holding his breath. He let it out now.

As he marched along the corridor, determined to see the King, a boy pattered up to him, and said breathily, "Please."

"What is it?"

"Has – has Master Dorac come back?"

*

Dorac was staring unseeingly at the pages of a book called *Patrick of Ap's Commentary on the Gospel of Luke* when Hassdan came in.

"You were the bad man because Kremdar told her you were. Come on. It's not over yet, but it soon will be, and in the meantime you're coming home with me."

"With you?"

"If you give me your pledge not to run away."

So he left the Castle, and walked through the streets to Hassdan's home.

Perhaps to a Jaryari noble – or even a Marodi lord – it would not have seemed a grand place. There were storerooms in the basement, and steps up to the front door. Inside was the largish hall. As well as the usual table, dresser and other furniture, it contained two boards on legs. Alida used them to paint pictures on, Hassdan said. Behind the hall was the kitchen, and beyond that a little garden with a bench, and purple autumn flowers, and their own well. There were stairs outside also, leading to the second floor, where Hassdan and Alida had their chamber at the back, and the steward had a room, and there was a small chapel. Perhaps that was a Jaryari custom. Dorac had never seen a chapel in a townhouse before. And upstairs again for servants' quarters, and more storage, and a nursery if one were ever needed.

Hassdan knew his guest, and allowed him to wander and explore, while a table was set up in the hall. Then they sat down to supper with Alida and the injured Meril, whose foot looked pretty bad to Dorac, and the steward Lilli, and were waited on by a cheerful-looking manservant.

Hassdan did not kiss his wife, or even touch her, although their eyes met constantly and joyously. Perhaps that was also Jaryari manners. And although the house was full, it was orderly and quiet. Dorac was not used to family homes. Especially ones where no one was being shouted at or cursed, and no one was drunk.

After supper, Hassdan sat him down, and explained Filana's account. "And there's going to be a new law, if the Gathering approves it. You can ask for a second trial, and bring new evidence. One of the King's secretaries has worked it all out."

"Oh."

"And that boy Gormad asked if he could come and see you."

Dorac thought. Then he said, "I don't wish to see him."

"He seems a harmless enough lad," said Hassdan, surprised.

"He should forget me as soon as he can."

His brother stared. Then he said quietly, "You still think

you're going to be hanged."

"You tell me that's not going to happen. A new law. But it may. I came back without leave, and Kremdar may have some story. The Ferrodach people will want vengeance. It may happen. And if it does, you must keep Gormad away."

"There is plenty of evidence."

"So you say."

Hassdan said no more, and looked thoughtful.

Dorac also said nothing, and he went on saying nothing for the rest of the evening. That night he was given a pallet upstairs, sharing the steward's room, and he could not sleep.

The moon shone in when he quietly opened the shutter. Since he intended to come back, he did not regard it as breaching his pledge to clamber out of the window, and drop to the street below. It occurred to him that it was a long time since he had climbed out of a bedroom window at night, and for the first time in weeks he took pleasure in a memory.

He tramped the streets of his city for an hour and a half, and he could have done nothing more healing. Barely needing the occasional wall torches to light his way, he explored again the familiar alleys. He disturbed the town cats and dogs, tried not to disturb the various Gathering visitors sleeping in the streets for lack of rooms or money, and dodged the watchmen whose rounds he knew well.

It was a fine cold night. As well as the moon, he could see stars between the roofs. *When I look at Thy heavens, the work of Thy fingers, the moon and the stars which Thou hast established, what are people that Thou art mindful of them?* He remembered quoting that to Tor one night, lying together in a copse outside the city, and Tor saying, "Is that from the Scriptures? You are full of surprises", and that was another good memory.

Getting back up and into the house was more difficult than getting out had been, but he managed it at last, and then he was able to sleep.

31 October 570 (All Hallows' Eve)

Today it was almost November, and chilly, and there was a fire lit in the opposite wall. Alida's painting boards were stacked away, and Alida herself had errands to do and visits to make. Since idleness was a sin, she gave Meril a basket of household linen to mend, and left her to share the hall with the visitor.

Alida had no authority to stop Dorac being idle. He sat in a chair with a book, and said nothing to Meril, who of course said nothing to him. She sewed, and looked guiltily out of the window, and wondered what was happening at the Gathering, and whether her foot was getting better. Master Dorac looked at his book, and got up and wandered into – she supposed – the kitchen and garden, and wandered back. He stared at Alida's paintings on the walls, giving exactly the same amount of attention to each one. Which was a little stupid, because it was obvious that the forest scene with all the animals hiding was the most interesting. The others were all dull pictures of saints' lives. Then he sat down again, and read a little, and dozed a little.

Clumsy and now immobile as she was, Meril dropped several items during the morning, and he picked them up for her, and after the third or fourth time, her gratitude became less hot-faced, and his silence more friendly. When Alida and Lilli returned with their purchases, he poured ale for them all, but still said hardly a word.

Alida gently criticised Meril's work, but thankfully did not tell her to do it again. For a treat, she handed her a board and parchment, and allowed her to draw for a little while. Dorac refused the same privilege with polite dismay. And they all had a bite to eat, and then

430

Alida went out again, and Meril returned to her basket.

Halfway through the afternoon, Dorac got up and pulled the painting board Alida had offered him towards her. "But I have to do the mending."

"The mending has to be done. It matters nothing who does it." Like most people without servants, he could sew well enough, because he'd had to, and when Alida noticed the new arrangement on her return, she only frowned a little.

Meril had no imagination or skill in drawing, but it was better than needlework. And Dorac wandered up behind her, and said, "Stonehill?"

She blushed. It wasn't a pretty picture, only a plan of the streets.

"The river curves more here. And you've left out the soldiers' quarters behind Littleman Street."

And eventually Hassdan returned to say that Master Kai had arrived, with Kremdar as a prisoner, and would be coming to supper. Dorac looked up at the mention of Kremdar, and Meril thought she had never seen so blank a look on anyone's face.

*

Kai had never been so glad to see Stonehill.

His little group had managed to ford the Poto, and had made their slow way back, and on the journey had been caught up by a large party: Mayeel Kingsister, Farili and six more soldiers. Apparently the King had called them to the city. Farili was not actually bound, but it was plain that she did not regard the summons as good news. Kai kept her away from his own prisoner – whom he was having watched obsessively – and felt sorry for her children, left behind confused at Dendarry.

As they rode, Mayeel said suddenly, "Arvill was your lover, then? And Kremdar's, later?"

Kai looked at her with dislike, and grunted.

"I didn't mean any offence, Kai." She rode on a little, away from him, and after that she seemed less hostile but even more silent than usual.

They reported together to the Marshal, and their soldiers were dismissed, and their prisoners removed. It seemed that the King was unwell, and had been unable to attend the Gathering that day. "But I think he will want to see you both. Your letters arrived the day before yesterday." The man carrying their reports had apparently caught up with Kai's original messenger from Pendafor, and the two had come in together.

"What news is there?" he asked.

"I don't know how much it's for me to say, Master Kai. Extraordinary things in your Six." And when Kai heard what had been happening, he had to agree.

So then he went to his cell, as he had done three weeks before with Gormad. He had to wait a long time there, and Kai did not like waiting, pettily annoyed that Mayeel had plainly been called first. But at last he was summoned to the royal bedchamber, where he hadn't been since the King's long recovery, two years earlier. As then, a large room, with a glass window and a shelf of interesting-looking books, and locked chests, and a curtained bed with red and gold hangings. The King was sitting propped on pillows, alert but pale, and with beads of sweat on his forehead. His servant Li sat in a corner. Secretary Makkam stood still and reassuringly by his side, and some physician was fussing around.

"Welcome, brother. I hear you have Kremdar. Good. Read your report." His voice was slightly hoarse.

Kai had made his report as detailed as he could, to make up for the impossibility of interrogating Arvill further, and it took him some time to read it all, gloomily aware of the mistakes it revealed.

At last, "Did you question Kremdar again?"

"No. At least – I asked him to tell me the whole truth of what he and Arvill had done, and why. He wouldn't say, and I hit him. And I thought – if I hit him again I might not stop, and - he probably still wouldn't talk. I thought Your Grace would want him undamaged."

"Yes. Has he said anything?"

"Hardly a word. He just sits, and rides, and obeys. I had him watched day and night." *I was terrified he would do what Arvill did.*

"Go with Makkam, and see if she has any more questions. I'm sorry to be unwelcoming, Kai. These are strange times."

"Your Grace," Kai ventured, "Tommid -"

The last part of his report had been Tommid.

Tommid said Kremdar woke him, and told him to come away from Gemara on a secret mission. He said if ever he (Kremdar) was talking to someone and mentioned King Arrion by name, it was a signal that Tommid was to scream for help. So he talked to Gemara, and he gave the signal, and Tommid screamed - and Kremdar stabbed Gemara in the throat, and she died.

"What about him?"

"Is he a prisoner? He's only a boy."

"You feel sorry for him. You have a kind heart, but he may be guiltier than he's told you. Thirteen is old enough for a lot of wickedness. When his parents come, he can stay with them for the time being, but they'll need to give pledges for his good conduct."

"And – may I speak to Dorac?"

"Yes. Wait," said the King, uncharacteristically indecisive, as Kai bowed. "Don't go yet. Li, fetch them," and while they waited for someone, Makkam handed her master a cup of wine.

Kai moved as directed by a gesture to stand by the top of the bed on one side, with Makkam on the other. Perhaps she knew what or whom they were waiting for, but their eyes only met for a moment. Gardai Kingsbrother was by the door, as Li ushered in Prince Jendon, the Bishop of Stonehill, Mayeel and Farili. And then another guard brought in a biggish man with curly hair, whom Kai faintly recognised.

He thought Makkam tensed as she looked at the newcomer. The man seemed tidy, freshly washed and shaved, and certainly not injured in any way – but he looked very frightened.

Of course. 'My husband is a prisoner in Stonehill.' Ramahdis.

The room was now very full.

Ramahdis and Farili knelt in the centre, close to each other but not daring to exchange looks, rigid and pale. Everyone else looked at them curiously. Kai thought that Gardai and Prince Jendon seemed completely confused, more so even than he was.

The King said to his secretary, "Read the confession." So Makkam read aloud an account given, it seemed, by Ramahdis, of Prince Rafad and his sister Thahdi, who had died giving birth to the Prince's child. And then of how Thahdi's brother and sister-in-law had paid a man called Desor fifty gold pieces to write a document for them. "*We did nothing more*", the document finished.

The King looked at Mayeel, and she passed him another parchment, which he handed to Makkam. She read:

On the second day of January in the year of deliverance 560 Rafad, son of Orthon, prince of this realm, and Thahdi, daughter of Jailib, joined hands and took vows of matrimony in the name of the Father and of the Son and of the Holy Spirit, witnessed by me, Clement, priest of Holy Church.

Kai felt the blood leave his face. There were a few gasps.

"So," said the King. "Marriage lines. Marriage lines that would have made young Gormad the rightful King of Marod. If they'd been genuine. According to what you say now, and to Desor's confession before he was hanged eight years ago, they are not. Mayeel?"

"This Brother Clement was indeed a priest living near Dendarry. I learned that he died in September 560 – but that his mind had been completely confused for at least eighteen months before that."

"Do you wish to maintain," the King asked at last, "that this is a true document? Is this boy indeed my mother's lawful heir?"

"No, Your Grace," and "No," said two voices almost simultaneously.

"He is a good boy," whispered Farili. "Please -"

"A good boy, but a bastard. When were you planning to produce this forgery? When he was old enough to claim the crown? Or when I did something spectacularly stupid or cruel, and you and your friends could argue that I needed to be replaced, like my great-aunt Arrabetta, for the common good?"

Ramahdis said huskily, "It was only a madness, Your Grace, a game, we never intended -"

"Fifty gold pieces is a lot to pay for a game."

"We would never -"

"If you never intended to use it, you would have destroyed it, surely." Silence. "Do you have anything more to say?"

"Please, Your Grace," cried Farili, "don't hurt the children!"

This reminder of the murders at Ferrodach, Kai saw, did not conciliate the King. His hand clenched on the blanket. "Why should I wish to hurt your nephew?" he asked, very coldly. "He is also my nephew. I like him. But as for the other children, I have no especial reason to like them. You will have to trust that I am not a barbarian."

Another silence. The Bishop looked shocked and disdainful, Mayeel impassive, Gardai grim. The Prince shifted his eyes from the culprits to his father, and back again.

The penalty for treason is a most unpleasant death. Kai's stomach crawled.

"Mayeel?" said the King faintly.

"The house was searched. This is the only copy of the document. I have found no trace of any attempt to take action based on it, in the last ten years. No weapons were gathered, no supporters were recruited. Only the people whose names Ramahdis gave you appear to have known anything and they swear they regarded it as a joke, or a folly. Apart from the woman Arvill. Where she learned of it, I do not know."

"Arvill, yes," murmured the King. More strongly, "Bishop Abigail, do you have what I asked?"

"Yes, Your Grace." The Bishop placed on the table a small wooden chest, decorated with gold and pearls. The King gestured, and Ramahdis and Farili stood up. The Bishop opened the box. "A piece of the ship from Erin, and a cloth touched by St Bridget herself," she said reverently. Kai noticed Makkam – indeed, everyone – crossing themselves, and hastily followed their example. "The most sacred relics we have." She closed the box.

"Put your right hands on the reliquary and swear," the King commanded. "The truth or otherwise of these confessions and statements that have been read. Ask God to avenge it if you lie."

The room was very still as the lord and lady of Dendarry swore obediently. Prickles crept up and down Kai's back.

"And now. In the name of yourselves and your heirs, kneel and swear fealty. In the presence -" He paused, and swallowed with some difficulty. He waved away more wine. "In the presence of God and of these saints, and of the Bishop, who is God's shepherd, swear your loyalty. To me. And after me, to my son Jendon, here present, and his lawful heirs. And after them, my daughter Daretti, and her lawful heirs. And after them -" He swallowed again, and again clenched his fist. "To my sister Emmia Kingsister, and her lawful heirs. And so on through the lawful lines of succession."

On behalf of themselves and their bastard nephew and their children, Ramahdis and Farili swore.

"Good. So. If you wish, you may burn the document you forged."

Ramahdis looked up in surprise.

"Burn it. Now," growled Gardai impatiently.

Everyone watched as the parchment was consumed in the fire.

"If you had taken any further action, if you had taken *one more step* towards rebellion, I would be ordering your deaths now. But as it is - I have decided to make my nephew a gift that he'll never know about. Your lives. I will overlook the forgery, and the treason. But those here present know, and will avenge if you break your oath. As will the saints whose names you have invoked.

"And - as to Gormad." Again he swallowed. "He is my nephew, and my children's cousin. I want to treat him as that. You will give him a home, and your care, of course, for as long as he needs it, but you will leave Dendarry to Kammer, or to one or all of the others, as you please. I shall provide for Gormad. And before you go back there, you will tell him the truth. You may omit your conspiracy against the crown. But tell him who he is, and let him decide who he is going to be. Gormad, son of Ramahdis, who is strangely close to the royal house, or Gormad, son of Adam, the prince's bastard."

*

They left the King with his physician and body servant. Ramahdis and Farili were apparently free to go, and they looked around, bewildered. Mayeel bowed curtly to her unwilling hosts and strode away, leaving them staring after her, like lost children after an unloved but reliable tutor. Kai wondered if he should speak to them, but it was Makkam who said, "If you wish to find Gormad at this hour, he's likely to be at weapons training in the back court."

"Thank you," Farili murmured, and through her relief and confusion there was already a returning hint of gracious patronage.

*

"I'm sorry to trouble you further, Master Kai. You must be tired."

Kai was tired, and worried about Dorac and Tommid, and conscious of having been less than fully successful in his mission, and he was also unsettled at seeing the King so ill. He sat wearily at yet another table, in yet another small room, and the secretary read his report again, the report he had scrawled by successive nights' campfires, and he drummed his fingers.

"Arvill," Makkam said at last, in her pleasant sensible voice. "What was she doing? She died. She was determined to die. When did she decide that? What do you think, Master Kai?"

"She seemed quite calm when we left Pendafor," Kai said with an effort. "She asked if she would be executed, but if all she'd done was what she admitted to, it didn't seem likely. If you think she changed her mind - I suppose the change that happened was Kremdar."

"Yes, it must be that. She was afraid that he would be questioned, and what would he tell? You said he told her – or asked her – or warned her – about the killings at Gisren. They cannot have been chance. He must have feared the child was Filana -" She saw the surprise in Kai's face, and said diffidently, "You should ask Master Hassdan about that. Someone ordered a child at Gisren to be killed, and it distressed him, you said. And Arvill must've known about it. Who else knew where they might be? But Master Kremdar did not know." She got up and walked around the room, pressing her fingers to her forehead. Abruptly, and irrelevantly, Kai wondered how long her hair would be, released from the severe secretary's cap. "Perhaps that was what frightened her. If people realised that she had been controlling him, and not the other way around.

"She was the leader in all they did, it seems to me. The story she told you at Pendafor might or might not be true, but it left her, well, half innocent. It looked as if she were defending Kremdar, but it allowed, even encouraged, you – or the King – to suspect him of murder, and her of being his dupe. That sounds a harsh thing to say," she ended almost apologetically.

"No. You're right. She played with him, all the way," said Kai.

"I don't think she was playing. She said, 'I am whatever I have to be.' She was working – but for whom? I think she died because she didn't want to tell us, and perhaps that means that Kremdar doesn't even know. Surely she can't just have feared torture. The King wouldn't -" She flicked a glance at Kai, and he thought again of the man in Broffam.

"She never said anything to you about the Jaryari, or any friends, or any other loyalty?"

"No. But she wouldn't, would she? It's plain that I never knew her at all." He saw Arvill's face, wordlessly, sweetly begging him to make love to her. He felt her arms around him. It had all been lies.

"Thank you, Master Kai." As he got up to go, she said suddenly and awkwardly, "Oh. And – you should know that the King sent a message to Karila, daughter of Ferriol – to explain about, er, the baby."

Karila. "So does the whole bloody city know about that then?" shouted Kai in sudden and unfair fury. Makkam jumped, and there was a shocked silence.

"Shit. I – I crave your pardon, madam. That is good news, and it was good of His Grace to do so, and kind of you to tell me. I am very sorry."

"Please don't distress yourself." She was looking at him, he thought, as if he were a particularly interesting document. Timidly, she said, "I don't wish to offend you, sir, but may I ask an impertinent question?"

"You have not offended me. I was the one who offended. Ask whatever you like."

"Arvill said if you swore to kill her, she would let the boy go. If you had sworn, and she had let him go - would you have done it?"

"I don't know." He shuddered. "I suppose so. I don't know."

"I only thought - it would have been so easy, once the boy was safe, to chain her up and drag her off to Stonehill. You said you never knew her. But she thought she knew you. She gambled everything on being able to trust that you would keep your word."

Kai was silent for a moment. "Thank you," he said quietly, and left.

*

Gormad's parents collected him, and took him away to an inn in the city. They asked him a few questions about his time with Dorac, Kai and Sheru. His father seemed determined to be cheerful but was somehow sad, and his mother was oddly quiet at first but soon returned to her snappish self. And then, "There is something we have to tell you, lad," Ramahdis said with a sigh.

It was a cold damp afternoon, and the inn's backroom was lit with only two candles. For the rest of his life he hated dim crowded rooms. "Something we should have told you long ago."

And so he learned that his parents were not his parents.

441

Dendarry, which he had been so desperate to leave, was not his home. He could go and stay there, but he would only ever be a visitor. His mother and father were his aunt and uncle. His siblings were his cousins.

His real mother had died giving birth to him. His father had been a prince, who had not loved her enough to marry her.

Kammer was not his brother. That was the worst.

*

Kremdar was sitting in a cell with a bench and a bucket, and a little light from a grille in the door. He looked up as the door opened, and looked down again as Hassdan walked in and sat down beside him.

"Brother," Hassdan said. "I won't ask how you are. Listen to me. I need you to listen.

"The little girl Filana is safe. That was what you wanted, wasn't it? You wanted to save her, and she has been saved. Although you could've found easier ways to do it." It was not clear that Kremdar was indeed attending, so Hassdan hit him, not hard, on the side of the head. "Now. Listen. There's going to be a new trial – a new look at Ferrodach. Dorac's trying to prove his innocence. I think he'll succeed, but the King wants to be sure. He is wanting you to confess."

Kremdar slowly said, "I have nothing to confess."

"We both know you have. Anyone who talks to Tommid knows it. You're going to die, anyway," he said gently. "You owe Dorac the truth, I think."

"So that's why you're here, *brother?* To torture me till I confess."

"I don't want there to be any torture."

442

"But there will be. Do you think I'm afraid of that?"

"Yes," said Hassdan. "You are the bravest man I know, but you are afraid.

"*Listen*. You can refuse to tell, and see what King Arrion will do to get the truth. I don't know what he'll do. You can be dragged into the court, after he's done it, and confess, or not. But is that what you want?

"You're not a bad man. Surely you had reasons – decent reasons – for whatever you did. You had reasons that you believed in. This is when you say what you want to say, what you want people to remember. And you do owe it to Dorac, and Gemara. Pay your debts before you die, brother."

He spoke quietly, and with passion. Then he waited, his stomach tensed, and his silent prayers urgent. He waited a long time.

At last Kremdar sighed and said, "When Dorac came out of the room, the three children were alive. When I went in, they were alive. I killed the older two. No one else should be blamed. I am sorry that Dorac suffered for it. And - I killed Gemara. She was trying to stop me from doing what I believed I needed to do. I believed all the time I was doing what was right. I don't expect anyone else to agree. This is the truth, and I will swear it whenever and however you like." He looked up at his brother with the sad noble expression that had always annoyed Hassdan, and now both moved and nauseated him. "Is that enough?"

"It may be." He went and arranged for the statement to be sworn, and took it to the King, and it was thought to be enough.

*

So no one went to torture Kremdar, and he sat on, thinking of as little as possible. He thought occasionally of what was certain to happen to him quite soon, and occasionally, painfully and with confusion, of Arvill.

And not at all – very carefully not at all – of what had happened at Ferrodach on 26 September.

*

Dorac came out of the room, looking sombre. They noticed that his sword was clean, but that proved nothing. He stared at them rather vaguely. "I am going to look through the papers," he said, and left the two alone in the small space. Now they could hear movement and faint voices through the door.

"He didn't do it. You said he wouldn't," said Arvill.

Kremdar sighed. "It would have to be a direct order."

"I'm so sorry, my love," she said, touching his face gently. "I know how hard it is. The hardest thing you've ever done."

"But the most important."

"Yes. Three deaths now; or Marod torn apart like Ricossa is being. Lady Sada is right. The King will understand that she is."

"Yes."

"D'you want me to come in, and -"

"No. I can do this." He kissed her, quickly and fiercely, and walked into the room. His sword was in its sheath, but his right hand was close to his knife.

The children, two of them, looked up at him apprehensively. He was concentrating so hard on the terrible but necessary task that the number registered only remotely, at the back of his mind.

"The other man said food would be brought," said the boy,

444

with the arrogance of a lord's son.

"There will be food soon," Kremdar agreed. He walked calmly up to him, twisted him around, and slit his throat. The blood spurted away.

The girl squeaked. "Be quiet," he ordered, in the voice of authority. It was a trick he'd often used. Common sense should have told Ilda that her only possible chance of survival was noise, yet she obeyed. She shrank against the wall, uttering only a little mewing sound as he came closer. Only when he was a foot away did he realise.

"Where is your sister?"

"I don't know," she whispered, hopelessly, uselessly brave. He pushed her struggling against the wall with one hand, held her head to the side, and killed her quickly with the knife. She slid to the floor, and there was silence.

There was silence. Kremdar looked round, and saw at once there was only one place for the youngest to be. Just a few steps away.

How odd, to have killed people indoors. Battles and executions take place under the sky, in the sight of God.

Such small bodies, and such quiet.

Children.

He was walking across the room, towards the toybox, and there was silence around him, and clamour in his head. *It was necessary. Arvill had told him all the reasons. Terrible but necessary. Ugly. To murder children.*

Why hadn't Dorac done it? It was so much more like Dorac – harsh as he was, the man who mutilated Marrach years ago. Yet everyone still trusted him. The King trusted him. If he had done it, as he should, then I -.

The youngest. The one who looked like Yaina (a little older than Yaina).
In the box.

He could never be forgiven.

He gripped his knife, took a deep breath, and lifted the lid. A frightened tear-stained face looked up at him, so like Yaina's after a nightmare that he heard himself say, "It's all right."

She whispered, "Has the bad man gone?"

"Yes," said Kremdar.

She began to uncurl and sit up, and her eyes widened in confusion. "Don't look, I'm sorry," he said, putting a hand over her eyes. "Arvill!" *If only Dorac had - Why could he not have?*

Arvill came in, and he turned towards her, holding the child close. "He killed them, Arvill. Dorac killed them. But he missed this one. We have to save her, to protect her." He stared at her, willing her to agree, to accept it, even to believe him.

If she believed him, so might other people. If she believed him, it was almost true.

"Dorac killed the children," said Arvill slowly. "How terrible."

"It will be well, sweetling," Kremdar murmured to the child in his arms. "The bad man's gone away."

31 Ooctober 570 (Hallowe'en)

Meril was always glad to see Master Kai, but she had to wait for her turn to be acknowledged. She thought that neither he nor Dorac were entirely dry-eyed when they embraced, but Kai said merely, "So you couldn't stay away?" and Dorac said, "Thank you for bringing the boy back."

"And Kremdar, I hear," said Hassdan.

"He killed Gemara. He's in prison. I don't want to talk about it again tonight, if you would be so kind. How was Jaryar?"

"Foreign. I don't want to talk about that, if you would be so kind."

"What a silent evening we are going to have," commented Hassdan to Meril, lifting her over to a seat at the table.

But, "What happened to you, young Meril?" Kai asked. "That foot looks painful."

Meril's adventures, and the explaining to Kai about Filana and Dav, took most of the meal. The shutters were closed on the dark outside. Meril reflected that it was Hallowe'en, a good night to be indoors, and not alone. The fire crackled, and the candle flames wavered and drove the shadows back, and the room was full and cosy. She could almost forget her injury, and feel truly at home and safe.

Then Lilli asked politely, "Is there news of how the Gathering went today, sir?" and everything began to change.

"People were surprised that the King was not there. It's a bad time for him to be unwell," said Hassdan.

"Yes, a woman was asking about him at the stalls," said Alida.

"Is he improving?"

"He looked very ill this afternoon," said Kai soberly.

"God send him a speedy recovery."

Dorac laid down his knife in what Meril thought was an oddly careful manner. "The King is ill?"

"Yes, he was in bed, perfectly sensible, but tired, and I think in pain. The physicians -"

"And what is anyone doing about this?"

Hassdan looked puzzled. "The physicians are doing whatever they do. There are extra prayers in the Cathedral."

"Praying," said Dorac. "Will that stop poison?"

Meril gasped, and so did everyone else.

"What do you mean? There's no question of poison."

"It's not a question. It's certain. The King is healthy, and not old, and there is no plague in the town. Yet he is suddenly ill."

"People fall ill all the time," said Kai, staring at him.

"There are spies in the Thirty! There are Jaryari spies, and war is coming. They are murdering the King, and we sit here and eat!" He pushed back his plate and stood up, and his eyes met Hassdan's.

"Jaryari spies?" said Hassdan softly, and suddenly Meril was frightened by the way they were looking at each other.

Dorac took a breath. "Ferrodach is not just Kremdar – *you* told me that. Torio betrayed the King and the Thirty, and the King knows this, and must be taking action about it, and the Queen is away. The Queen has gone away to war. Torio and Kremdar have nothing to do with each other, but they have both betrayed us, and they cannot have been acting alone, and the city is full for the Gathering, and now he falls ill. *This is not chance.*"

"Oh dear God," breathed Alida.

Meril saw Hassdan staring at Dorac, and then turning to stare at Kai, and she saw the same look of horrified agreement looking back at him.

"You're right. You must be right. But - has no one else realised? There was no suggestion at the Castle today. There would have been terror."

"I don't believe it," said Kai.

"You do believe it. No one else suspects, because hardly anyone knows what we know. They know Torio was a traitor – they don't know it's connected to Ferrodach."

"Why Torio?"

"Does it matter? The King is dying!" said Dorac.

"Wait. We must think," said Hassdan, desperately. "Think. How could this be done – when was it done – by whom, and why? He didn't look well when we came in the day before yesterday – now he's worse. He was able to attend Council on Thursday. Now he can't go to the Gathering. So it's surely not a poison that works instantly – is it something that someone is feeding him every day?"

Meril shuddered.

"We need to see the Marshal," said Kai.

"Someone close to him, or someone with access – it must be. Do we trust the Marshal? Do we trust anyone?"

This cannot be happening.

"I trust the people in this room," said Dorac. "And Soumaki."

"Yes. Soumaki. And we should talk to Shoran too. He's an

apothecary; isn't his trade to know about poisons?"

"Saysh is our brother," said Kai abruptly.

"None of us knows Saysh well."

"He's been here in Stonehill when none of you have been," said Alida. "He may have information."

"He's the King's choice," said Dorac. "Get Saysh, then, but quickly."

"Yes. Lilli. No one leaves this house without my word. But go and find Soumaki, Shoran and Saysh, if you can. You know Soumaki's home – where does Saysh live? Try his cell."

Pale-faced, Lilli nodded, bowed, and left the room.

Only Meril was still sitting down. Dorac was standing tensely by the fire, staring at Hassdan. Kai was stalking to and fro, fingers rummaging in his hair. Alida quietly cleared the plates away. Hassdan stood with his fingers digging into his forehead. "Surely," he said slowly, "to kill a king is the most terrible crime. Therefore no one would attempt it, attempt it suddenly, without a strong reason."

"Without being afraid."

"Yes – if they were afraid, then they must have known that their plans – whatever their plans are – were being thwarted or discovered. Torio must have been afraid. Perhaps Soumaki can tell us more about him. The King knew more than any of us about what was going on, but what did he do about it? What did he do that made someone so desperate? Who knows what the King was thinking - except the Queen?"

"Prince Jendon?" suggested Alida.

"Secretary Makkam," said Kai.

Like many in the Castle, Makkam was distressed by the King's illness, and after her duties were finished, she went to the Cathedral to join those who were praying for his recovery. Looking over her shoulder as if she feared enemy soldiers (or worse, on All Hallows' Eve) she then made for her room in the tenements on St Paul's Street. There was a man waiting for her outside.

"Secretary Makkam," said Kai. "Can it please you to come with me to Master Hassdan's house now? He needs to talk to you."

"To Master Hassdan's? What matter is this?" But she was already walking back beside him, glancing surreptitiously at his worried amiable face, and wondering aloud. "How did you know where to find me?"

"His wife Alida knows you. She says you talk about pictures sometimes after Mass."

"Oh - is that lady his wife? What does -?"

"Wait until we're there."

"Am I under arrest?" she asked, half-seriously.

"No, of course not. I am sorry," said Kai - and then Makkam felt the thought come to him that perhaps he should indeed arrest her - and she began to be very frightened. She had not imagined it.

They came to the house. It was full of people: Master Hassdan and Alida, and a girl, and Master Dorac looking far more like a murderer than he had done at his trial, and Mistress Soumaki, and a small man who was saying in a strained tone, "You are asking me a question I cannot answer without knowing *what is wrong* with him."

"This is Secretary Makkam," Kai interrupted.

451

"Madam, welcome," said Master Hassdan. "This is an unusual meeting of the Southern Six. Kai tells us that the King is ill. We've all been reporting to you about Ferrodach. Is there any reason why the Ferrodach investigation -"

"Or anything else you know of -"

"Or anything else you know of might have put the King's life in danger?"

"Oh -" Makkam sat down dizzily at the table.

"Wait," said Soumaki. "While you think, my husband needs to talk to Kai."

"Master Kai, you saw the King today. What was his condition?"

"He was in bed. Not well. Makkam was there too. He seemed to be sweating – of course, it was quite warm –"

"Not as warm as that," said Makkam, clenching her fists to hold off panic. "He tended to gasp, as if it was hard to breathe. But he was in full control of himself."

"He was in pain sometimes, I thought."

"Yes. He had wine beside the bed. I poured some for him. Oh God."

"You have a thought," said Dorac suddenly to the child.

Everyone stared at the girl, who said timidly, "You were saying just now, how could anyone poison only him. Medicine is what one person takes, and not anyone else."

"Surely, yes," said Hassdan. "But you take medicine after you are ill, not before. Everyone in the Castle drinks wine."

Dorac said slowly, "When he lost his arm, he told me it still hurt him, although it wasn't there. It still ached and itched. It's possible he takes something to soothe the pain. If somebody knew that -"

"If he is in pain, if he takes something for it, if somebody knew it, if they had access. If, if, if. And somebody close to him. Always back to that. Somebody he trusts. Somebody he trusts absolutely."

"Was he ill yesterday?" the little man asked Makkam.

"I don't see him every day. He seemed well on Wednesday morning, and on Thursday, when he attended Council."

"Could he have been poisoned at Council?" wondered Alida.

"In front of everyone?"

"*Please*. Has he been coughing? Vomiting? Is there a rash?"

"I don't think so -"

"Let me consider." The man turned away, fiddling with his fingers.

"So, Makkam -"

A man ran in, staring at them all. "What's going on? Master Hassdan, Master *Dorac?*"

Hassdan said, "Welcome, brother. This is very strange, but we are wondering – when did you last see the King?"

"I was guarding him at Council on Thursday. The next day I was appointed to watch a suspect's house. I haven't seen him since. What -"

"Explain to Saysh later," said Dorac harshly, and turned to Makkam. "Do you know – does anyone know – any reason why the King's actions might have frightened someone into poisoning him? And who that might be?"

"Fucking hell!" cried Master Saysh.

Everyone was looking at Makkam. She took a deep breath, and said, "Nothing was found out that suggested a plot to kill the King. But whoever was behind the killings at Ferrodach also sent murderers to Gisren. Almost certainly. And the King and Queen asked me -"

"Why you?"

"I was the one who suspected that Torio was trying to read the Ferrodach reports. The King and Queen didn't want to believe ill of one of the Thirty, but they asked me to find connections between certain people. And I had an idea, and I spoke to them more than a week ago – I can't remember, exactly – that the family of Aspella might be involved. It was only a thought of mine; I don't know if they believed it."

"Aspella!"

"The lords of Aspella profited by Gahran's death," said Hassdan, looking over at Mistress Soumaki.

"And everyone had thought that Ralia would be appointed to the Thirty. And if she had been, there would've been one of the Aspella cousins or great-nieces or something in every Six. Ralia, Torio, Mayeel, Olda, Maros. And in the past, Galla in the Southern. It seemed odd."

"Mayeel is as honest as any woman in the kingdom," said Dorac.

"But," Makkam forced herself on, "I could find no connection to Arvill, daughter of Eve, until you came back, sir, and said that she was kin to Mayeel."

"And Arvill was involved if anyone was," said Kai with a grim face.

Hassdan said slowly, "You had a theory, which the King may

or may not have agreed with, that the murders were connected to the lords of Aspella."

"Who are in Aspella, not here," said Soumaki.

"Lady Karnall of Aspella is here," said Hassdan. "She is crippled, and housebound, but she could give commands to others, surely. And Herion of Maint is the Aspella representative on Council."

Saysh said, "But – it was Herion's house on King Tristar Street that I was watching. No one to go in or out without being followed. Day or night."

"Since what time?"

"I was there on Friday, and that wasn't the first day. Not many people know. We were told to be discreet."

"If he's a prisoner in his house and all his servants, then he can't have poisoned the King."

Makkam remembered suddenly. "But he was in the Castle on Thursday. I saw him talking to Lady Sada. It was just before Council started, yet he didn't attend Council. Someone asked, and Lady Sada said he might be late. And he never came."

"Lady Sada!" exclaimed Soumaki.

Saysh said, "That's right. I think that's right."

"His house was guarded, yet he was in the Castle, wandering around when he should have been at Council? What sort of guards are these?" asked Dorac.

Kai said, "Do we truly believe that Herion of Maint -"

The little man who was apparently Mistress Soumaki's husband cleared his throat. "He knows much about poisons. He has a collection."

"A *collection?* How do you know?"

"A few years ago, just after Soumaki was called, he was very friendly – he does business with my mother. He invited me for dinner, and showed me a little cabinet. He said he kept it in the service of the king and the realm, and we discussed poisons and medicines, and he asked me if Soumaki told me any interesting tales about life in the King's Thirty."

Everyone was looking at him. "What did you say?"

"I said Soumaki was too wise to betray the King's secrets, even to me," he said blandly. "I said she knew the old tale of Deb Kingsister, who gossiped too broadly, and was condemned to be crushed to death. People need to remember their history."

"So, then," Hassdan said slowly, after a pause. "The King had some reason to suspect Herion and his family. Herion is related to Torio, did you say, Makkam? Herion's house is guarded, yet he comes to the Castle to do we know not what. Herion collects poisons and asks questions about the King's Thirty."

"And – hell! – his steward had been arrested too," said Saysh. "He's in the Castle still. I can't remember his name."

"Someone must have questioned this steward. We need to know -"

"We need to question *Herion*," said Dorac. "What are we waiting for?"

"Question him?" asked Hassdan lightly.

"Make him talk."

"This is one of the lords of Aspella, and we may be wrong. We have no proof."

"The King is dying, and we cannot wait. We need to get proof tonight."

"Let's go," said Saysh.

"By breaking his fingers." Hassdan was staring at Dorac.

"By any means I have to. I'm going *now*."

"*You*," said Hassdan, "are pledged on oath not to go anywhere without my leave. I am not giving you leave."

The room was full of faces, all tied to each other with invisible cords, and all waiting for Dorac's reaction. Except for Hassdan. He turned and said, "Shoran, what do you think of this sickness?"

Shoran said surprisingly promptly, "It does seem very sudden and isolated to be natural. There are a few poisons it could be. Sleepdust, for instance. If he was being given it every day, not just once - it could be given in wine, it dissolves easily and has not much taste, only a little bitterness. Or perhaps srettin. You are so vague about what's wrong – I would have expected more pain with sleepdust, but there would certainly be weakness, and sweating. If it is that, given day after day, it will kill him if the dosage is not stopped, and if it is, he needs to drink a lot of water or ale, to run the poison out of his body."

Kai asked, "Did Herion have sleepdust and srettin in his collection?"

"I don't remember, but I expect so. It was years ago. I would have noticed, I think, if he had not."

The little girl asked suddenly, "What did he keep his poisons in?"

"There was a wooden box with compartments, so big." He gestured. "With a hunting scene carved on the lid. The poisons were in

457

a little set of beautiful glass jars, with many facets, about this high -"

"Like the one Gahran used at Ferrodach! Yes, Meril! Now. We have a suspicion, and we need proof, without torturing one of the highest people in the land. We need to talk to the steward or to those who questioned him; we need to find out if we can what Herion did at the Castle. If his house was watched, there must've been guards, and their names will be recorded. But we don't know whom to trust. The Marshal – the King's servants – probably they're all innocent, but –"

"The Marshal must be. He has served for years," said Kai.

"Yes. Could we get evidence of the poison – that he had it? What does it look like?"

"A reddish powder."

"We need to get into his house," said Dorac.

*

Half an hour later, they were ready to leave.

Kai voiced what Makkam was feeling, when he said, "Is this truly happening?"

"Save your surprise for later," said Dorac. "We must go now."

"I need a drink," said Kai, and surprisingly added, "In a cup you don't object to losing. People who shout in the street are expected to be drunk." Alida supplied the cup of wine. "Ready."

Hassdan reached for the door, and said suddenly, "May the angels assist us."

"Tonight is Hallowe'en," said Meril.

"Don't say that!" cried Saysh, and Makkam saw Soumaki shudder.

"It makes no difference," said Dorac. "There are evil things abroad every night." He crossed himself, and several of the others did also. Then, leaving the nervous steward and the injured girl behind, the rest went out.

*

Prince Jendon walked slowly out of his father's bedchamber, and into the little anteroom beyond. There was no fire and no window, and the only light came from three candles in a silver holder on a table. Ralia was sitting there, but she jumped up, strode to him and took his hands. Her energy and glowing health contrasted with everything around her. A handful of pearls shone in the cap covering most of her glossy black hair.

"How is he?"

"Ralia," he said, unsurprised. "He is - much the same, I think. Sleeping. Perhaps a little worse."

They sat down. "Is the physician with him still?"

"Yes. He spoke a few minutes ago. He said he didn't know whom to trust."

"Your father said that? But – how strange."

"Yes. And he said he hoped my mother would be back soon." The Prince stared down at their interlinked hands. "How long have you been here?"

"Not long. I ate with your sister, and Lady Filana and her servants. I don't think the Princess realises how ill he is."

"Umm."

Ralia leaned forward, wispy hair escaping her cap to flicker towards his face. "My prince. Whatever needs to be done, you will do. Whatever the kingdom needs you to be, you will be."

"Do you believe so?" he asked, looking directly at her.

There was a knock at the door. The guard whom both had been ignoring leapt to open it.

The room became very full.

*

The little alley led down between the gardens of King Tristar Street and then split to run behind them, left and right. Each garden had a gate opening onto it. Dorac, Alida and Makkam waited down one fork, while Kai strode up the other, trying to look unchallengeable.

"Greetings. A long night."

"Indeed, Master Kai," said the guard shyly, looking up at the clouds.

"Is there anything to report?"

"All quiet, sir. I think they're in bed. They know we're watching them. No one has tried to come out of the back gate."

"I am sent to relieve you, so your boredom is over for tonight. Sleep well, or whatever you wish to do."

"Thank you, sir." As the guard turned the corner, the other three joined Kai. Dorac had smeared his face with soot, to be less easily recognisable, and he and Makkam were both mere shapes in the night. The alley was narrow, and no light shone from houses or cloud-ridden sky. They could barely see the top of the wall above their heads.

The gate was fastened. "Give me a lift." Kai fumbled, but only once, and Dorac was over the wall. He drew back a bolt, and let Alida into the garden with him. "In two hundred," he said, and he and Kai counted softly together to find a rhythm. "One two three -" and then Kai and Makkam left the other two, and walked back towards the street.

"The guard went too easily," Kai grumbled unreasonably in his relief. "He had orders."

"But you're a Kingsbrother. He had to obey *you*," the secretary said – rather snappishly, he thought, but probably she was nervous. She handed him Alida's cup that she had been holding, and he took a swallow, and then poured the rest of the wine down the front of his jacket.

As they rounded the corner into the broad tidy expanse of King Tristar Street, blinking in the light of a wall-torch – and there were other guards further down – Kai burst into song.

> *And we rode all the way*
> *To Derbo and to Avvay.*
> *And we sailed on the sea*
> *To the coasts of Embaddi,*
> *And we flew to the moon*
> *In a –*

"Be quiet!" said Makkam. "Decent people are trying to sleep!" She sounded suitably cross, but she wasn't loud enough.

"Decent people? What decent people? It's not *late* -"

"To the people here it's late. It maybe does not seem so to someone as drunk as you."

"Drunk?" he shouted indignantly. "I am not drunk. I can walk – look – walk in a straight line."

"You are drunk, and behaving like a fool."

Kai blinked upwards, and opened his arms wide in a happy expansive gesture. "Look at all the houses up there. All the shutters. I wager you ten – eleven – silver pieces I can hit that shutter - with this cup."

"No! Don't be absurd! You will disturb -"

The cup hit the wall and smashed. Not loudly enough, but the guards further down had noticed.

"Eleven silvers, please. You are drunk, and you are disturbing the peace. We will be arrested."

"Lemme try again." He had found a loose stone. "Hup!"

Crash. One of the best houses, with glass windows, and they had neglected to close the shutter. There was a shout from within, and also from down the street - and Kai thought he heard a bang from the gardens behind.

"One for me!" he shouted gleefully, and launched another stone. *The joy of breaking things in a good cause,* he thought, but this one only hit the wall.

"Stop it! Stop it now!" Makkam's voice was shrill. "How dare you?"

"What is going on – Master Kai!" The guard stared.

"Yes, I am Kai Kingsbrother, and I am not drunk." He staggered on down the street. "Not in the least."

"You think the name of Kingsbrother gives you licence to destroy property, and bully people, and do anything you like!" He was surprised at the passion, and volume, of Makkam's voice. She was better at this than he had expected. "Everyone to obey you – everyone to believe you – everyone to honour you – and you won't let decent people sleep at night!"

"Stop shouting," somebody called from a nearby house.

Shutters were banging open.

"Decent people don't sleep at night. Decent people have better things to do," said Kai, louder and louder, swaying towards her. "You're beautiful when you're angry, lady – what's your name again?"

"If I get truly offensive, you can hit me", he had said earlier. Instead she shoved him hard in the chest.

"Will somebody call the watch, and arrest this oaf!" she shouted.

"Not now! Not on this beautiful night -"

And then they heard the shouts from the garden.

*

"Wait here," Dorac murmured to Alida, part of his mind continuing to count. In the darkness he couldn't see her nod, but he took silence for agreement. He wished he had Soumaki or Kai with him, rather than either the prim secretary or Hassdan's highbred though amiable wife. However. He walked cautiously towards the house. Rich people with servants had tidy gardens with straight paths, he guessed. He brushed past sweet-smelling bushes, and was aware of the deep quiet.

The house was built narrow. There was a door and a shuttered window. The door wouldn't budge, and he could feel no keyhole. So it was bolted or barred on the inside. He could not break it without a great deal of noise.

He heard himself breathe out, and studied the window with his fingers. A wooden frame holding pane and shutter together. So. He lifted the iron bar he'd brought from Hassdan's, arranged it where he wanted and waited for Kai.

The owner of this house was trying to murder the King. For a pure quiet moment there was nothing in him but hate.

"Try not to kill anyone", Hassdan had said before they left. "Accusation is not guilt", Stimmon had impressed on him fifteen years ago.

Then there was song. There were angry words, and a distant crash. He started work.

The window came out easily enough: too noisy, but Kai was still shouting. He reached through the space he had made, letting in light and cold air. Thank God Herion appeared to keep no dog, and no servants were sleeping in the kitchen. Dorac pictured how the door would probably have been made, and stretched for the bar. An angry jerk, and it slid across, and the door opened. He was able to walk inside, carrying the window still in its frame, and fit it back.

A neat kitchen. He waited for a moment to make himself part of the quiet of the house. And to listen. The only noise was from the street outside.

Move slowly. He propped the outer door open with a jug, to give some light, and stepped out of the kitchen into a narrow passage. It stretched to the front of the house. Opposite him he could dimly see the door Shoran had mentioned.

The darkness settled heavily on his shoulders. He entered the room.

There was no window, and no light except what he had brought with him. An empty fireplace. Shelves of books. A cabinet with a box on it.

There was a chair in front of the fire.

There was a man sitting in the chair.

Still moments passed. Dorac heard regular breathing. *Asleep.* So he turned away to the cabinet, to the box.

His fingers ran over its lid – certainly carved, yes, probably people on horses. *A hunting scene*, Shoran had said. He tried gently to lift the lid, but it was locked. Nevertheless it had to be the one. He looked all round again – he could see no other shapes that matched Shoran's description.

The man in the chair was still asleep.

Dorac eased the box up into his fingers, lifted it and turned. Heavy enough to hold glass bottles. Heavy enough for poison. He shook it very gently, and thought he heard or felt – sensed, somehow – moving objects, rather than documents, inside. *Step slowly to the door.*

He had to choose whether to shift the box to one arm to close the door, and decided not to. No one was in the passage. A gust of cold air swept in from the garden.

He was stepping over the threshold, when he heard the shout.

"What – stop! *Stop!* Astan, Riya! Thieves!"

Dorac kicked the jug from the door, and ran. Footsteps in the house. Alida was at the gate.

"Take it. Go," he said, thrusting the box at her. He shut the gate, and turned, hand moving to where there was still no sword.

The wind had pushed the clouds away. Moonlight shone down on the garden, and on the person at the door. "Guards! Soldiers! We are robbed!"

Two servants pushed past him, and towards Dorac. One sword, one cudgel.

Dorac stood still and said, "Stop. I am here in the name of the

King."

"Kill him!" shouted the man from behind.

"And be hanged for aiding a traitor."

The man and woman had stopped, five paces away. The woman swung her sword.

"They should listen to a house-breaker? Did you kill the guard at the gate?" The man at the door – the man who had been asleep – was Herion of Maint. *Do not think about how high this man is.*

Dorac made his words calm and heavy. "This house is a place of treachery. Why else did the King have you all trapped like rats? Why else was I sent for evidence? Evidence of murder."

"You git, you're lying!" said the woman. But they'd been locked up for days, wondering. She was not as surprised as the people at Ferrodach. And she was not attacking him.

Dorac smiled coldly. He had no reason to say anything more, so he said nothing. Alida must be a street away by now.

"Evidence? A thief's lies. Nobody sent you. Do you know what I can do to your family, your wife and children? Do you know who I am?"

"You are the nephew of Lady Karnall of Aspella. You send murderers to kill children. You have plotted to kill the King. And anyone who helps you is also guilty." He said it as if there were no doubt. If he were wrong, he would die anyway. The servants gaped.

"You're a madman," said the woman.

The gate opened, and her face lifted. "Master Kai!"

Then, "Do you need a sword?" Kai asked Dorac, handing him an unfamiliar blade. "What news?"

"His servants cannot decide whether to kill me or not. I told them the penalty would be death. Now perhaps we should leave."

"Dorac," said Herion slowly. "The exile who slaughtered the Ferrodach children. You were forbidden to return. What are you doing here?"

"I am defending the King from you."

"You're mad." But they looked at each other across the garden, and then Herion said, "No one at Aspella knew anything", and his hand moved to his belt.

"Stop him!" Dorac shouted. He leapt forward, hoping Kai could ward off any swords. He seized Herion's hesitating hand, and twisted roughly. The man cried out, and the knife fell, tinkling. Dorac pushed him down on the ground, and put a knee in his back.

"What are you doing – who are you?"

There were squealing faces in the kitchen too. No one brave or loyal enough to defend their master. But they would value their own lives. He stretched for the knife, and tossed it to one of them. "Master Kai and I are going now. The guard will be replaced. Do not try to leave. If he escapes, or if he dies, everyone in this household will pay the price."

Kai had been holding the two in the garden at swordpoint. Now he said, "And you two good people can go in, and sleep."

They left the garden. "Which of us stands watch?"

"Me. You're not an exile, and can order a replacement from the Castle. Alida took the box. Either to her house or to the Prince, I hope. Where did you get the sword?"

"From the guard at the front. As the secretary says, people

obey Kingsbrothers." As he turned to go, Kai asked, "How – how did you guess he was planning to die?"

"What else could he do, if he's guilty?" *I know what despair is,* he almost said. *I felt him give up.* Kai looked at him thoughtfully before leaving.

Dorac waited in the lane. If Hassdan hadn't been in time, it had been for nothing.

*

Marching uninvited into the Prince's presence at such a delicate time was enough to make Hassdan uncomfortable. Being accompanied by Lord Vrenas, Shoran, and the servant they had found, did not assist him. And Ralia was there, Herion's cousin, which made it, perhaps, much worse. He was conscious of the preposterous dread of which he had told nobody. As soon as Makkam had mentioned Ralia, it had come to him. *Ralia means Prince Jendon.*

"Your Highness," he said with Jaryari formality, and they all bowed or curtsied.

"How is the King?" the Marshal asked.

"He is s-sleeping," Prince Jendon answered. "I trust you are not p-planning to disturb him."

Hassdan exchanged a glance with the Marshal. "My prince, Master Hassdan has come to me with a concern. May we speak to you in private?"

The Prince's face set aggressively. "You have b-brought most of the people. If you mean you do not t-trust my friend, or Aila" (this must be the guard, standing confused by the door), "then say so."

Another glance, and they were obviously irritating him. "Say what you have come to say, and get out."

"Your Highness," said Hassdan, kneeling. "Li here says that the King takes a cup of Aibelli wine each night to ease pain in his arm. The wine is kept for his sole use, in his room."

"And?"

"His illness is sudden. A cask that only he drinks from could have been - tampered with." At the final moment he drew back from the word "poison", but the Prince's face, and Ralia's gasp, told him it was understood.

"You th-think someone has tried to k-kill my father? Who?"

"The most urgent thing is to find out if it is so. Your pardon, Your Highness. My brother Saysh has gone for another cask of the same vintage, to compare. And this is Shoran, son of Drax. He is an apothecary, Soumaki Kingsister's husband, and knows the symptoms of certain poisons. And the remedies. May it please Your Highness, this is urgent."

"There is m-more you are not t-telling me."

"This is madness, Hassdan, surely," Ralia said. "No one would dare to harm the King, or wish to. Why should the Prince believe your tale?"

"I should believe him because he is my parents' b-brother," said the Prince, his voice hard – and young. "But so were Torio, and Dorac, and Kremdar, and at least two of them have betrayed their trust." Abruptly his face seemed to wriggle. "Poison! What do you want?"

"Let Shoran look at him, and talk to the physician. When Saysh brings the wine, compare the two. Many poisons have a taste."

The Prince looked sharply at Shoran, who said in a nervous but composed voice, "Yes, my prince. Sleepdust tastes bitter; empodene gives a smell to the breath; and srettin –"

"Enough." The Prince nodded. "Hassdan, and you, sir, come."

The bedroom smelt of illness, and sweat. The guard, servant and physician looked up at the newcomers in surprise.

King Arrion was asleep. Hassdan was shocked at the glossy sheen to his face as they approached the bed. His breath seemed loud. The Prince halted them with a gesture disconcertingly like his father's, and beckoned Shoran forward. "My prince, who is this?" whispered the physician indignantly.

"Silence."

The others watched. Shoran smelt the King's breath, and touched his forehead. Hassdan said quietly to the servant, "Your friend Li tells me of wine set aside for the King at night."

"Yes, sir, here." He displayed a small cask on trestles in the corner. Hassdan glanced at the Prince, and seeing no denial, removed the bung and poured some wine into a bowl. His heart thudded. He carried it to Shoran, and at that moment they heard the Marshal outside saying, "Master Saysh, you have the wine?"

No one could be kept out. Ralia, the Marshal, Li and the outer guard all rushed in with Saysh, as he carried in a barrel on his shoulder, and set it down in the centre of the floor. His manner was matter-of-fact; only his eyes flicked nervously between Hassdan and Prince Jendon.

The Prince said coolly, "What is this?"

"It is Aibelli wine, '68 vintage, my prince, from the wine seller Grigo on Northwell Street."

"Grigo supplies the King's wine," Li confirmed. "And this should be '68."

"You think that the wine in one of these casks is poisoned, and the other is not? How can we tell?"

Hassdan looked at Shoran. "Er, it could be a natural illness," Shoran said, not very helpfully. "But it could be sleepdust poisoning. A small quantity of sleepdust goes far mixed in wine or water. A little just once won't harm you – some faintness for a few hours perhaps, but a large quantity, or a small one repeated over days, will kill. The taste is very bitter, which is why it has to be diluted."

Prince Jendon looked at Hassdan; then at the barrels. "Give me some, then."

"No!" cried Ralia in horror.

"You are the heir, sir. Please permit me," said Hassdan, and as he was still holding the bowl, no one could have stopped him if they had wanted to. The scent seemed strong. He could not tell if the taste had been bitter or not, but Li promptly handed him a bowl from the new cask, and he swallowed that too. "They are not – not the same."

"Comparing taste is difficult." The strain was clear in the Prince's voice. Breathing rasped from the bed behind them. "You," he said to the Marshal. "You needn't swallow the stuff."

Lord Vrenas tasted both, spitting into the fireplace, and confirmed, "This one is more bitter. I am certain."

"Now you." The gesture was to the guard standing in the background. "Wait. Shut your eyes. Give her the bowls in whatever order you choose."

"The – the first, I think, tasted less pleasant. I *think*, my prince," she said, miserably scared.

"Enough. It is t-true." Prince Jendon turned to Shoran, and Hassdan felt that the rest of them had ceased to exist. "*Is there a remedy?*"

"I don't know how much he has drunk or how often – he must have no more, and instead be given as much watered ale as possible."

"Lord Vrenas. A cask of ale, already opened, from the g-guardroom. And water from the well. Aila, go with him. And th-this." The Prince turned his eyes to the small barrel, from which they all seemed to shrink. "Label it and seal it. But first – c-can we test the stuff? Not on a p-person, b-but an animal?"

Shoran might have answered that, but did not. "Surely we could," said Hassdan.

The Prince turned towards the bed. "Ralia. Would you find my sister?"

"At once, my prince."

"Hassdan, I want a report by m-morning. A full report." His eyes glittered. "And now, leave. All of you."

As he obeyed, Hassdan glanced back, and saw the Prince sit down on the bed, and take his father's hand in his.

It was very late. He ordered the two servants and the other guard to wait in the anteroom, and left with Saysh. Lord Vrenas and Aila were returning with the ale and water.

Had they done enough? *Please God.*

"I am going to the chapel," he said. "And then - I need to find

472

parchment and write." *I'll make two copies, just in case* - "The scriptorium will be long shut, so I'll be in the Great Hall. Can you find how Soumaki is faring with the man Attar, and then if Kai or any of the rest come, send them in?"

Saysh nodded. "Sir. The King – d'you think he will -"

"Pray," said Hassdan grimly.

*

Kai returned his sword to the bewildered guard, and promised that reinforcements would be sent. "Did you see Alida?" he asked Makkam, as they moved away.

"I think I saw her walk down there. She was carrying something."

"Good. I need to go to the Castle. Can you find your way to her home again?"

"Yes, of course. I – I was very rude to you, sir," she said awkwardly.

"And I owe you eleven silver pieces, which I should warn you I have not got."

Makkam grinned at him, transforming her face. "You should worry more about the price of that window you broke."

"Shit! How much does glass cost?"

They both laughed suddenly – and suddenly again stopped laughing, remembering why they were there.

"May God protect the King," she whispered, and he said, "Amen," and left her.

*

Lilli and Meril sat at the table, not speaking much. "Master Hassdan will be able to persuade the Marshal," Meril said once.

"Yes, of course."

What would happen if the King died? Would Prince Jendon believe them – believe Dav – believe Master Dorac? Meril remembered childhood games of fashioning fragile buildings out of twigs, and how often they fell apart at the most frustrating moment. All that had happened in the last month seemed such a structure, and she felt that without the King it could not hold.

And Master Hassdan loved the King. So should they all.

Someone kicked the door, and a voice called, "Lilli!"

Alida stumbled in, her arms full of a beautifully carved chest. "I don't know what happened. They heard him, and I had to go." She shivered suddenly. "Bar the door."

They could not open the box. They could only look at it as it sat on the table, Meril telling herself that it was not evil. But none of them wanted to touch it.

Alida sent Lilli to the Castle with the news, and then fussed around Meril, pouring her drinks and wrapping her in a blanket, and thankfully not telling her to go to sleep. The fire burned low, and she had to light fresh candles. They waited. Secretary Makkam arrived, saying Kai had also gone to the Castle. She and Alida prayed silently for the King (Meril supposed), and tried to make conversation about Alida's pictures.

Another knock. Master Dorac. "Where's Alida? Where's the box?"

All three women were shy of him, and it was Makkam who explained. He nodded, and sat down, and there was silence.

But almost at once more people came - Master Saysh, Lilli and a soldier. The King was still alive. Alida and the box were wanted at the Castle. The Prince seemed to believe them.

So Alida went with them, and Meril, Makkam, Lilli and Dorac sat on.

"I hate waiting!" Meril exclaimed, almost in tears, and blushed as the others looked at her.

*

Prince Jendon, Lord Vrenas, Lady Sada, a meek-looking Shoran and a sleepy Secretary Andros were standing around a table in the Marshal's office as Hassdan was ushered in. It was now very late.

On the table was a wooden box. Next to it, in a little pewter tray, lay a dead mouse.

"Your Highness," said Hassdan, "the King –"

"Is complaining about the quality of the ale. My sister is with him. And your brother Kai."

Lord Vrenas forced the box open with a chisel, and everyone bent forward. And as Shoran had said, there were eleven little bottles in twelve compartments lined with velvet, four rows of three, each bottle labelled cryptically with a single letter. One was marked S, and it contained a few grains of reddish dust.

They were all silent.

Then, "But no empodene," said Shoran.

"Because that was the one that went to Ferrodach."

*

"Please, just one more cup," Princess Daretti was saying, as her brother re-entered.

"How are you, father?"

"Waterlogged. Some new medical treatment." He spoke with an effort, but obediently took another sip from the cup his daughter was holding. Li and the physician Dar looked on anxiously. By the door, Kai Kingsbrother and the guard Aila stared at them all.

"Jendon."

"Father."

"There were a lot of people in here. Before. What -"

"Drink and rest, father. Are you feeling better?"

"I am feeling curious. There were a lot of people in here." As the Prince hesitated, "You are not too old for whipping, young man."

Prince Jendon smiled shakily. "Father. It is th-thought – we think – someone has been f-feeding you sleepdust. In wine."

"Sleepdust! Why am I not dead?"

"Er - it appears that Your Grace is most abstemious in the amounts of wine drunk," the physician said timidly. "The poison was in the cask that stood in that corner."

"Who put it there?"

"I don't know. I am hoping to kn-know more in the morning."

"Vrenas and Hassdan were here. And Ralia. Were they not?"

"Yes. It was Hassdan who came to the Marshal. With his sister and b-brother."

"Ah. Should I drink more?"

"If you can."

The King drank, and murmured, "The Southern Six."

"Yes."

"The question is always whom to trust - I'm very tired. It's late, is it not?"

"After midnight."

"I want Vrenas. Some of you should go and sleep. You should sleep, Jendon. What day is it? You need to attend the Gathering for me."

"I will go and sleep if you f-finish that cup, and rest too."

The King drank again, and stroked his daughter's hand. Then he looked back at his son. "Is there news of your mother?"

*

"I cannot believe it," Saysh told Hassdan and Soumaki, as they sat in the Great Hall. "The fucking idiots said they followed Herion to the Castle door, as they were ordered, and he said to them, 'You are performing a faithful task. I am called to attend Council. I will doubtless greet you on my return', and he went in. And they waited outside until he came out. And he didn't go to Council, so he had two hours to go wherever he liked."

"Because he was Herion of Maint."

"And that's why he wasn't arrested days ago," said Soumaki. "Or so I suppose. His guilt is clear." She handed Saysh the man Attar's confession, which she had read quickly before questioning him further, and had brought to Hassdan.

Attar was still insisting, in the face of all threats, that he knew nothing of any plot to kill the King. If Herion had indeed tried to do that, it seemed he had acted alone. But the confession contained details of much else. The names Arvill, daughter of Eve, and Sil, daughter of Jarri, were frequently mentioned. "Five or six murders, this Sil and her man Rago have committed for him. Including Braf, and the people at Gisren. And yet Herion is only watched, he and Lady Karnall, who knew and approved all that was going on. I don't understand it."

"Don't you?" Hassdan began, but at that moment the Marshal entered.

"Lord Vrenas." Hassdan stood up courteously.

"I have spoken to the King. There seems good hope for his recovery, so Dar and your husband say, madam."

"Thank God."

"The Prince and I have also talked. We are sorry to trouble you. For the time being, one of you four is to guard King Arrion day and night. You have had a long day already, as we all have, and you will require rest, so you'll take four-hour shifts, if it pleases you."

"Four of us?" asked Soumaki, puzzled.

"Yourself, Master Hassdan, Master Kai and Master Saysh. One of you four is to be with the King at all times."

"Me?" said Saysh.

"You are a Kingsbrother of the Southern Six, are you not?"

"Shit, I am!" he said wonderingly, sounding younger than his age.

Hassdan and Soumaki exchanged looks. "You have a report to write."

"Yes. Soumaki, can you relieve Kai when the time comes? I'll have a word with Alida, and finish my report, and then Saysh and I will rest in our cells." He tried to ignore the spinning in his head, and the heaviness of his limbs. The symptoms would go in a few hours, Shoran had said.

478

"When are we going to arrest Herion?" demanded Saysh.

"Not yet," said Lord Vrenas. "The King's orders have not changed."

"Why not?"

"Think about it," said Hassdan. "Think about the power of Aspella."

"But he can't stay in his house forever, can he?"

Hassdan looked at the Marshal, who stared stolidly back.

"What was the King waiting for?" asked Soumaki.

He spoke his guess. "He is waiting for the Queen."

*

Earlier that All Hallows' Eve, Queen Malouri had taken aside the captains under her command, and told them where they were really going, and why. And on the morning of 1 November (while her husband was anxiously watched by his children, and Soumaki succeeded Kai on guard, and Saysh succeeded Soumaki), the soldiers arrived at their destination.

They came to the great house of Aspella, and just as Dorac and Kremdar had done at Ferrodach five weeks earlier, they demanded surrender in the name of the King.

3 November 570

"When I was injured in '68," said King Arrion, "King Rajas saw an opportunity, and wrote to Gahran of Ferrodach. Gahran's reply fell into the hands of Lady Rakall. It was her duty to denounce him, but she did not. It seems that she, her husband, and her mother Lady Karnall thought that if I died, Aspella could win the loyalty of Gahran and Jaryar by supporting them against the rightful heir. She sent messages of support to Gahran, but held back the letter, intending to forward it if I did indeed die. But Gahran thought better of his planned treason, and I recovered.

"And a few weeks ago, Aspella's spies in Haymon told them of raids being planned – news that again they should have passed on. People died because they did not. They were more concerned to 'discover' the letter, having changed the date. They now wanted to destroy Gahran, their rival in the west, who knew that Aspella's loyalty was not perfect. Herion used a secret that they knew to ensure that their agent Arvill was sent to Ferrodach, along with her lover Kremdar Kingsbrother." Hassdan heard shocked gasps. "Aiming to destroy Gahran, as was accomplished. To break up Ferrodach and increase Aspella's holdings in the region, as was accomplished. And to discredit one or more of the Southern Six. So that they would be replaced."

The Great Hall was built for larger gatherings than this. Only four long tables were needed, and these had been arranged to form a rough square, with spaces at the corners. On the western table, in front of the dais, sat the King, still pale and with little appetite, with his son, his daughter and his aunt. (The Queen, God willing, was expected back tomorrow fresh from victory at Aspella. Twenty-seven dead, including Lord Jovian, Lady Karnall's son-in-law, and she and all her close kin under arrest.)

It should have felt intimate and friendly, but it did not. Cold November breezes blew in at the unshuttered windows, and the fire behind the northern table crackled and spat.

The King, his immediate family, twenty-six members of the Thirty, and two secretaries, summoned to what had been called a feast. No one else.

"Lady Karnall already had kin in all the other Sixes, of whom Torio was one. She wanted someone in the Southern. There are few in the land with greater influence, at Stonehill, and in the country, than the Thirty."

The implication was not lost on those present. Murmurs without words wandered through the hall.

"For a long time we had no understanding of Arvill's connection to Aspella, or if she was merely a paid agent. But now we know. Mayeel?"

Mayeel Kingsister stood up in her place, and said steadily, "Arvill, daughter of Eve, was my brother Addin's daughter. He acknowledged her, and several other bastards, when he was dying. I remember meeting her at Aspella when she was a little girl, but her name then was Metta." She sat down again, staring at the table.

"When some of these matters began to come to light – indeed, as soon as Gahran's letter was found – we feared an alliance between Marodi traitors and Jaryar. But there was no such alliance, no grand plot. The Jaryari were doing no more than they usually do.

Indeed, as old King Rajas nears his natural end, most of his court seems to be fully occupied seeking the favour of his heir.

"There is no planned invasion, as far as we can see. Only a rather clumsy, and even petty, conspiracy, arranged with years of the future in mind, to surround the King and Queen with people with a loyalty to someone other than God and the kingdom.

"Clumsy and petty, and not even really well managed. Yet people died. And Gemara and others began to suspect. The Queen and I gathered evidence, and prepared to send out soldiers. The traitors realised that they were almost certainly discovered." He paused. "So Herion chose his gamble. He walked into the Castle, unchallenged because he was Herion of Maint, he made use of knowledge of my habits that someone had innocently given him, and he put sleepdust in my wine."

"Sleepdust!"

Hassdan heard the unease and dread turn to shock.

"Your Grace," cried Mayeel, "Herion tried to poison you?"

"He did. His plan was thwarted by my siblings of the Southern, three nights ago."

The King, looking tired, allowed a pause for the news to be absorbed.

"Your Grace," said Brinnon slowly, "I do not understand what he hoped to gain. If he was already under suspicion, to kill you was lunacy."

"I said it was a gamble."

"But I think I can answer your question," said Prince Jendon. Everyone stared. "With my father dead, I would inherit the throne, I

482

would marry Ralia, Lady Karnall's grand daughter, Herion's cousin. Her friends would destroy any record of the investigation, and she would persuade me to believe no ill of her family. Lady Karnall's heirs would rule Marod after I was dead, and they would have won."

Well! thought Hassdan. And, *when it is something really important, he does not stutter.*

"That at least is what Herion seems to have hoped," agreed King Arrion. "He perhaps overestimated my son's susceptibility."

Then there was a long silence.

"Brothers and sisters, thank you for your attention. I wished to bring you the full facts before the trials begin. It will be - difficult - for the country to believe."

Indeed, thought Hassdan. *The house of Aspella are traitors.* When heralds had announced it in the Castle Square, he had seemed to feel the kingdom shift.

"Some time ago, my aunt warned me." Eyes turned to Lady Sada, sitting very still. "She said the Thirty were important, and they are. The long-term aim, I think, was to destroy the King's Thirty. Hassdan and Kai have told me of people's reaction to the murders at Ferrodach. If this is the way the Thirty behave, no one will trust them, and they will be less useful. The King will in time cease to rely on their connection with the people, or any connection to them. The only advisers he will listen to will be his great and loyal lords and ladies. Like Lady Rakall."

"Your Grace." Mayeel rose again, and spoke with even more deliberation than usual. "You sent troops with the Queen to Aspella. But you sent none of the Western Six, none of the Thirty."

"That's true," muttered several people. *Sending out soldiers without the Thirty. Unheard of.*

The King said quietly, "Torio was my brother. He was reporting to Lady Karnall and to Herion. I could not be certain that others might not be doing the same."

"Others in this room?" asked Brinnon, into the appalled quiet.

"My parents, my wife, and I chose all of you," said the King, and his voice seemed to ache. "I regret none of those choices. But yes. Others in this room."

Maros and Hayn Kingsbrother both jumped up. "Your Grace can trust any of us, any one, to the death!" cried Maros. "You are not doubting my loyalty?"

Many people there had identified by now that he was one of Lady Karnall's kin who had been mentioned. Maros Kingsbrother, Olda Kingsister, Mayeel -

"I do not doubt your loyalty," said the King.

"You should do," said Mayeel, walking out from her place to stand before him. "Your Grace, I - I - I knew of course that Lady Karnall was my first or second cousin. It meant we were highborn, and fortunate. I was taken to Aspella as a child, and it was very grand, and I was told we were all friends or some such. I met other youngsters from around the land, all of us related. We were told stories of the greatness of our ancestors - I had no knowledge of what has been said today, but Herion invited me to dinners now and again, and discussed matters as between family. I cannot say that I have never told him things I should not.

"And - I now realise that Arvill expected, or hoped, that I would help her when she was imprisoned at Dendarry. She made some comment about being treated like kin. She thought I had other loyalties.

"It has been my greatest honour to serve you, and your mother, and the Queen. If you will allow me, I will retire from the Thirty."

She knelt, and many people held their breath.

"You are an honest woman," said the King. No one spoke. "I accept your departure with regret. And now I wish you all good evening. We will not speak of this again, and no one will doubt the loyalty of anyone here."

He walked the length of the room leaning on his son's arm, and left, followed by his daughter and his aunt, and Soumaki Kingsister, whose turn it was.

*

Prince Jendon walked into the Willow Chamber, and bowed. His father was sitting at a table, caressing the noses of his dogs, and looking very tired. He looked up at his heir and smiled, but the Prince did not smile back.

"You can leave us, Soumaki. My son is not going to attack me."

When they were alone, there was a pause. "You're certain of that?" asked the young man. "I don't think Hassdan is."

"Jendon. You are your mother's son, and there is not a treacherous bone in your body. Sit down." As he obeyed, "And why would you conspire with Karnall and Herion for what will be yours soon in any event?"

"Not soon, please God." He stared at his hands. "I - I think I told Ralia about the wine you drank every night. That was me. It didn't seem important."

"Perhaps that was you, or perhaps your Great-aunt Sada told her friend Lady Karnall. She told her a great many things." He sighed. "Lady Karnall, whom I should hang – a frail ancient cripple. What shall I do with her?"

His son had no answer. The King reverted to the previous topic. "He had bribed several of the servants as well; that's how he was able to reach my private rooms."

One of the dogs wandered over to sniff the Prince's fingers. "Good boy, Sidon," he said absently. Then, "That was why you sent me after Dorac, when you c-could have sent anyone else. To get me away from Ralia."

"There were other reasons as well. That was one of them. You surprised several people today, Jendon."

"I know I'm not as cl-clever as you, father," said the Prince, "but I am not so st-stupid as that. It's Daretti who b-believes what everyone tells her. I know why people smile at princes."

The King looked down at the table. "Ralia is easy to admire."

"Yes. And I could not be rude to Lady K-Karnall's granddaughter, and I thought you might choose her to be a Kingsister one day, so she would be my Kingsister p-perhaps, many years from now." He stood up and wandered to the window, his back to his father. "She liked to remind me of tales of p-princes who married beneath them, for love. But I n-noticed that when she m-met anyone beneath her, she was less pure-minded."

"Ah." The King paused. "Is there any risk of a child?"

"No. She would not have risked her v-virtue without good

cause."

"Since you seem to despise her, I hope you would not either - It is not clear that Ralia has committed any crime. I do not think Herion told her what he was planning to do."

"No," the Prince admitted, turning round. "Do not fear, father. When I wed, I will do it for the benefit of Marod, as you did."

"As I did?"

Both dogs jerked at the note in his voice. The King was still weak, and sitting down, yet his son took a step backwards.

"I – I m-meant no offence."

"You have given it. Do you think your grandmother put us in a room together, and said, 'I will hear no arguments. You will marry six months from now, like it or not'?"

"N-no -"

"When you wed," said his father deliberately, "if you are wise, you will wed someone who is of use to the kingdom. As I did. You will wed someone whom you can trust absolutely. As I did. And you will wed someone you are desperately eager to fuck. As I did.

"Have I embarrassed you enough?"

"P-please don't tell mother."

"I will not tell your mother, and you will dance at least once with Ralia at the Christmas dances. And then you can leave her alone."

*

"Makkam," said the King, "I shall never undervalue secretaries again. Thank you. I will think of a reward."

"Your Grace," said Makkam, "I only did my duty."

"Spoken like a Kingsister," he teased. "But there may still be something you want."

"There is nothing, Your Grace."

But of course there was something, she realised as soon as she was alone, and it was something the King couldn't give her. Hassdan and Soumaki and Kai had all presented their reports to her and discussed them in front of her, and she had shared one night of terror and confusion with the Southern Six. And now what she wanted, like so many other women, was for Kai Kingsbrother to notice her existence.

5 November 570

The judges rose to retire, but the King stopped them. "One moment. This is the first time this law has been used. And the next time, the judge whose decision is being scrutinised may not be a king. I charge you to do your duty according to conscience, and before God. Do not be swayed by any earthly fear or consideration."

There was conversation around the edges of the White Hall, but not in the middle. Dorac looked up at the ceiling, or over the heads of the people. Eyes on him again. Sometimes he glanced at the dais. Queen Malouri smiled at him, but the King was looking away. As he had done last time.

It was not long before they came back. Falda Queensister looked nervous, Bishop Abigail dignified, Brinnon intent, as always.

"What is your decision?"

The Bishop cleared her throat. "Your Grace, we have considered carefully all that has been said and sworn. We acknowledge that, the evidence being as it was at the time, you could have come to no other decision. But -" she swallowed – "but in the light of new facts, we unanimously believe that the conviction was wrong, and should be declared void."

He heard a little sigh go round the room.

"Tell *him*," said the King. The three turned round to face Dorac. Their six eyes reminded him of his nightmares in Jaryar. But these eyes were kind.

"Dorac, son of Araf, we declare your conviction void. Go from here quit and free forever." And they stepped away.

Could it be done, just like that? His life put back as it had been?

There was no one between him and the dais.

As Makkam had instructed him, Dorac walked forward and knelt. The King stood.

"When you were last here, I found you guilty. I have never been more happy to be wrong. I took from you lands and gold, horse and armour. I now restore to you Valleroc, and the rest of your wealth. I'm sure we can find Derry." He paused. "And I took from you the name of Kingsbrother, and released you from that companionship. Are you willing to forgive the injustice done to you, and rejoin the Thirty, where there is a place in the Southern Six?"

Makkam had not, as it happened, warned him of this question. He supposed the right answer was, "I am willing", so that was what he said.

"Then welcome back, brother," said King Arrion, raising him up one-handed, and embracing him with a light touch. Queen Malouri held him with more warmth. "I present to you your new brother Saysh." There was some shyness here, on both sides, Dorac thought, but his welcome from Kai, Soumaki and Hassdan made up for that. The King raised his hand and smiled, the heralds pounded the floor with their staves, and everyone raised the ritual cheer.

"Long live the King! Long live the Queen! God save the people!"

Dorac found himself surrounded by folk hugging him, shaking his hand, and telling him noisily they'd always known he was innocent. He felt a little bemused, and for a while was unsure what, or whom, he was looking for.

Gormad had been hanging back, shy for once in the presence of the great. But then abruptly Dorac strode over to him, and picked him up, and swung him around so that other people had to leap out of the way. And it was true what Kai had once said – that Dorac's happiness could light up a room.

*

People drifted away as the afternoon passed, and at last hardly anyone was left but a little knot of the Southern Six – with Meril on crutches, Saysh plainly not sure if he was really part of the group, and Gormad hoping very much that he was.

"Well," said Dorac uncertainly.

"Dorac, this is your night," said Kai. "We will do whatever you like. And that includes going away and leaving you in peace, if you want to be alone."

"Why would I want to be alone? And who else would I want to be with, rather than all of you?" He spoke with such sincerity (and obviously including Gormad and Saysh) that everyone was silenced. Then in a different tone he said, "I'm going to give thanks in the chapel, but I won't be long. After that – The Crimson Cloak is a good place?"

"Yes," said Hassdan. "And I'm paying."

"I should pay. The King said something about returning my gold."

"You haven't got it yet. I'll pay tonight, and you can pay me back if you like."

"Remind me," said Dorac cheerfully. Hassdan walked with him towards the chapel. The others waited, Soumaki sending a message ahead to the tavern.

"Is it far?" asked Meril nervously. This was the first time she had used her crutches, and the cobblestones were daunting.

"I think four men between them can carry you there," Kai said reassuringly.

How can I repay the Lord for all His goodness to me? Dorac thought from the psalms as he knelt before the altar. *I will take the cup of salvation, and call on the name of the Lord.* And then there was another, unexpected, blessing. As he and Hassdan rejoined the others, a guard stepped up to them and said, "Your pardon, Master Dorac – there is a woman asking for you."

Saysh grinned, but all the others looked puzzled.

"*Oh.* Where is she?" The man gestured to a corner of the courtyard, and there she was, cleaner and tidier than before, wearing a different, although still shabby, kirtle, and looking distinctly nervous at the sight of the great folk bearing down on her.

"How did you get here?"

"I came to return this," she said, stumbling in a curtsey, and offering him back the satchel he had left at Queenshouse.

"I gave it to you."

"But it's really yours. And – they said in the street that you're not an exile any more, and all is well. I'm very glad."

"Yes, all is well." He turned to the others, and said, "This is Melina, daughter of -?"

"Freldi."

"Melina, daughter of Freldi. She saved my life in Jaryar, and would never tell me why. This is Hassdan Kingsbrother -"

To Melina's obvious consternation, he introduced them all, and then said, "So where did you sup this afternoon?"

"I -"

"You haven't eaten yet. We're going to a tavern. Come with us."

"I – I can't, Lord Dorac."

Gormad giggled, and Kai cuffed him, hard.

"Not Lord. It would be Master Dorac, if we were being formal. And we're not, so Dorac will do. Why can't you come?"

"Because - you are -"

"We are the rich people who make use of the poor, yes. We are also hungry, and so are you. So come on." He beckoned her with a jerk of the head that reminded Hassdan of King Arrion. "I want to hear how you got to Stonehill."

So Melina came with them, and although some of the party (Gormad) were inclined to resent her presence, others (Hassdan) were distinctly intrigued. They heard her say, "When you left with the soldiers, I went back into the village, and found that everyone was talking about you. So I said we'd been travelling together, and the alehouse keeper gave me a meal in exchange for telling his customers about our adventures. And a woman offered me a lift to the next town, and there I found a silversmith and gave him my money."

"But it was Jaryari money."

"It was still good silver. He gave me enough to pay for a ride here with a merchant I met. I arrived today."

Dorac looked at this newly competent Melina – perhaps she had always been competent away from woods and horses – and wondered a little what she meant by "our adventures". So did the others.

When they arrived at The Crimson Cloak, a smoky room hung with miscellaneous pieces of red cloth in every shade and size, they found that any other customers had been politely asked to leave, and it was theirs alone. Two tables had been pushed together, and their first drink was offered free of charge. Saysh fetched wine, ale, water and cups, and once they were settled they all looked at Dorac.

He stood, raised his cup, and said, "Gemara Kingsister." Everyone drank solemnly, even Melina, who had only the haziest idea who Gemara Kingsister was.

"And," he went on awkwardly, "I can't do this kind of thing, but - I do know what I owe to my friends. Thank you. All of you."

"To friendship," said Kai, helping him out, and they all drank again.

Dorac sat down and said, "Stories."

"You first."

He was not a great storyteller, but this was inevitable.

"I suppose you all know that I went to the Old Stones with young Gormad." (Melina had not known, and she shuddered. Evidently they knew of the Old Stones in Marithon province.) "Then I crossed into Jaryar, calling myself Ettuar, and after a day or two I met Melina, and she kindly sent me to an inn where they wanted someone. The Hanged Man. I suppose I worked there for about ten days."

He stared at his cup for a moment. "The King of Jaryar sent a Lady Igalla and a Lord Ramos and some soldiers to take me to Makkera to serve him, and when I refused they attacked me. Or perhaps I attacked them." He shrugged. "There were six of them, so that was that, but we stayed in the inn for the night, and I managed to get free, and Melina turned up for some reason, and helped me kill or knock them out. I heard some things from Lady Igalla that I thought King Arrion should know, so we came back north."

He paused again. Then he looked directly at Gormad, and said, "We became outlaws for a few days." Gormad almost choked, and Kai laughed, remembering the space behind The Crescent Moon. "You don't want to know all about the journey, but we crossed the country, and forded the River Lither. Less trouble than I expected. At Queenshouse we saw soldiers with Prince Jendon, and heard about Gemara, so I decided to come straight back, and it turned out that I'd been ordered to do that anyway."

"How many were you fighting at once in the inn – six, did you say?" asked Kai, glancing innocently at Gormad. (But Gormad had forgotten that conversation.)

"It was five, and it was one at a time, and I had help."

"So how did you come in?" Soumaki asked Melina, who was sitting between her and Meril, rather than, as might have been expected, beside Dorac.

Melina flushed, but said fairly readily, "I knew L – Master Dorac was working at the inn. I was in the town, and I saw the soldiers and lords from Makkera, and heard them talking about arresting a foreigner. I knew it must be him, so I tried to listen. The woman – Lady Igalla – said something about picking him up without violence if they could, and Lord Ramos said, 'But if we cannot, remember even by his own people's standards this is not a civilised man. There is no need to be gentle.' " She swallowed. "Lord Ramos is a monster, and I couldn't bear – I went home and got what money I had for a bribe or something - and went to the inn. I met the girl who works there on the way, and she said Ettuar had been arrested and tied up, and they were taking him away tomorrow. I tried to talk to the guard outside, but she got suspicious, and asked who I was, and then somebody inside opened the door, and there was a crash, and Master Dorac had knocked Lord Ramos over, and everyone was running at him, so I grabbed one of them, and held on to him until Dorac could knock him out. That was all I was doing.

"So we came away, and you know the rest. The river was terrible. I was sure I was going to drown." She stared at Dorac, and said, "You could have left me there on the other side to cross by myself, or not if I couldn't. You had no need to come back for me."

Dorac stared back, and said nothing.

Everyone else felt the account was incomplete.

"But why?" asked Soumaki.

"She says we have met before, but I do not remember it."

"How can you have met?" They looked curiously at Melina, but she hung her head, and looked away.

"However much you hated this Lord Ramos -"

"Have you ever lived in Marod?"

"I decided she was probably not a spy," Dorac interrupted firmly. "And tonight she is my guest."

It was plain he wanted her left alone. So Hassdan changed the subject by saying, "Well. It's probably a good thing you didn't kill Lady Igalla."

"Why? Who is she?"

He leaned back, savouring the moment. "King Rajas has four children. Igalla is the eldest child of the second – fifth in line to the throne."

"That Lady Igalla?" gasped Melina, in the general hubbub and laughter.

"I suppose you would all have known that," Dorac growled at his siblings.

"I would not," said Kai.

"I would not," said Saysh.

Dorac glared at Soumaki, and said, "The bitch. I made her swear on the holy cross that she was telling me the truth."

"No," said Melina thoughtfully, "you made her swear she was telling the truth about Lord Whoever, and about the soldiers, but not about herself."

"Hmm."

So they moved on. Of course most of them knew most of the stories, in bits and pieces, but it somehow seemed fitting to tell them all. And Melina knew none, and Gormad knew nothing of Meril's and Hassdan's, and Saysh had not heard Kai's. As they talked and listened, they ate, and whoever was talking fell behind in eating, and caught up later, and the food kept coming. Kai told about his adventures at Pendafor and at Dendarry, missing out the treason. Meril told of the ambush (and cried a little for Josper and Anni), and of waking up in the village wondering if she were a prisoner, or would ever walk again, and what had happened to her letter. ("And so you can walk," said Saysh bracingly, but Hassdan looked sombre.) Soumaki let Saysh and Gormad tell about the pursuit of Torio. "We reported to the King, and he sent all of us except the boy to tell the rest of the Western Six," Saysh finished. "Without mentioning Ferrodach."

"And when his mother heard he was dead, she broke down, and told everything she knew," said Soumaki. "Poor woman."

"Poor woman who conspired with Herion and Karnall to murder anyone in the way of their ambition," said Kai.

"What will the King do with them all?" asked Saysh.

Hanging was the normal form of execution in Marod and Jaryar, but other forms were not unknown for the worst crimes. "There was that child-murderer in Derbo they stretched out in the square with hands and feet cut off, and left to bleed to death -"

"In Ricossa they burn murderers alive, don't they?" said Saysh. "At least the worst ones -"

"Kremdar?" said Soumaki soberly.

"He killed another member of the Thirty," said Kai. "The King can't just hang him."

Hassdan said slowly, "Kremdar was a good companion – a brave man – generous – he *was* – and all that will be forgotten. Now he's sitting in a cell, knowing something terrible will be done to him, and that everyone who once admired him despises him. Sometimes I am feeling sorry for him – and then I remember Gemara and the bodies we dug up at Ferrodach, and I stop."

"Did that Arvill make him do it?" asked Gormad.

"No one knows. He won't say. She certainly intended it to happen."

"What I find most horrible," said Kai quietly, "and I know it seems small, is the parchment you and Laida saw. Gahran wrote a letter, at least he wrote something before he died, and Arvill must have destroyed it. A confession, an apology to the King, a last message to his children - no one will ever know what he said."

"That's not the most horrible," said Soumaki, with a bleakness in her voice that made everyone turn to her. "Didn't you read Attar's confession, and Tommid's? After Gahran surrendered the house, Arvill managed to speak to him for a moment. She gave him Herion's empodene, and told him his treason was known and unforgivable. But that she had authority to tell him that the King would spare his children if he saved everyone trouble by killing himself. Otherwise they would die too. And he evidently believed her."

"She told him that, while persuading Kremdar to kill them?"
"Yes."

"How could anyone be so wicked?" Meril asked in a voice that trembled.

"She was a demon, my mother said," Gormad agreed.

"Maybe," said Hassdan. "But - do you want another story? Will everyone excuse a children's story? I've been talking to Mayeel."

"Go on," said Dorac.

"Once there was a little girl," said Hassdan. "Once, and not so long ago. Her name was Metta, and she was under a curse – that her father was not married to her mother." Gormad shuddered, and wondered if anyone had noticed. That story had not been told. Kai also shifted, and Hassdan went on hastily, "This isn't always a terrible curse, but it was for her, because although her father was rich, he refused to agree that she was his daughter, or pay money for her keep. Her mother and grandparents were poor and could not make him, and they were sending Metta out to beg for food on the streets when she was still very young. She was a pretty child, and she found she was skilled at crying whenever she needed people to feel sorry for her, so she did well. But she wished and wished for her luck to change.

"And her wish came true. When he was dying, her father was sorry, and told his secret to a powerful witch. And the witch used her magic to find Metta, and then she used another spell called gold -" – the children looked scornful at the metaphor – "to persuade Metta's mother to let her take Metta away. Metta was taken to a beautiful grand house, like a castle, and for the first time she had plenty to eat, and warm clothes to wear. And the witch bound her with the spells of gratitude and loyalty, more and more tightly.

"When she was nearly grown-up, the witch said to her, 'Metta, you are beautiful and clever. You can choose one of two lives. You can stay here with me, and be my servant. Or I will teach you how to be a witch too, and you can go into the world, and go on magical quests for me and for my kingdom of Aspella.' So that was what Metta chose, and she was renamed Arvill, and taught magic spells. The most important was how to get men to do what she wanted. A powerful spell. And she went out and served the witch for years.

"For very little gain. Although surely she was enjoying some part of it. To make things happen from the shadows, to twist people without their realising it – I think there could be a pleasure in that."

"To destroy people," said Soumaki.

"Yes. At any rate, at some point she must have realised that Lady Karnall was an evil witch, and the quests she was sent on were bad quests. She did terrible things. But the spells on her were strong. She never escaped from them. Perhaps she didn't want to escape. And at last she died, trying to protect the witch and the witch's kingdom from its enemies." He sat back. "Or so I imagine."

"But she was evil," said Gormad grumpily. "And she'll go to hell."

"Don't be insolent," said Dorac. "It depends on how much God values great loyalty, monstrous loyalty, in a bad cause."

The plates were being cleared away, and only drink was left. Melina said suddenly, "What would you have done if the King had ordered you to kill the children?"

A shiver went round the room as every member of the Six applied the question to themselves.

"He would not," said Dorac.

"But if he did -"

"He would not, so the question has no answer."

"Some kings would."

"We don't serve them. We serve King Arrion and Queen Malouri."

"Queen Arrabetta would have," volunteered the prejudiced Gormad.

"Or Darro the Cruel, or a lot of the people in the War of Three Kingdoms," said Kai, who knew some history.

"I'd prefer to think that King Rajas would not give such an order," said Hassdan. "Indeed he never has seemed a bad man, although my parents roused his wrath."

"Did you ever meet him?"

"I was in his presence a few times, when I was a child. He would not have recognised my name, I think."

(Hassdan's background had to be explained to Melina.)

Soumaki said, "Saysh, you've taken the oath the most recently. Doesn't it say 'all lawful commands and honourable tasks'?" and the conversation moved on.

Dorac asked Hassdan, "What did I say in a tavern?"

"What?"

"You said you believed me and not Kremdar because of something I said to you and Kai in a tavern."

"Ah. Yes. Are you certain you want to know? It's not very flattering."

"Less flattering than being a child-killer?"

"Very well. About four years ago, we three were drinking together, and feeling abandoned by love. Someone had refused to marry Kai, and it was when I thought Alida's family would never give their consent, and it was after Tor left you, and before he came back. So we were all thinking deep sad thoughts, but you were the least sorry for yourself. You said you thought people left you because you were too intense."

"Did I?"

"What you actually said," Hassdan continued maliciously, "was 'too intense and too dull'."

"Hmmm."

"Surely, Dorac, you know you were wanting to tell us exactly the route you took from the village in Jaryar to Queenshouse, and where you crossed the river, and why at that particular place. You only had compassion for the children, because you've finally learned that not everyone finds these details as interesting as you do."

"But what," asked Kai hastily, speaking for them all, "does that have to do with Ferrodach?"

Hassdan grew more serious. "I thought – whoever killed the children killed them and lied about it. Why did he lie?"

"So as not to be hanged," said Saysh blankly.

"That might have been your reason, or mine, but not Dorac's or Kremdar's. If they believed in what they were doing, either of them would have shrugged off a little thing like being hanged. There was no possible honour in the lie, spreading doubt among the rest of us. Besides, if they'd said openly, 'I did it, it was terrible, but I thought it best for the realm, as Lady Sada suggested', would they really have been executed? No, I thought he'd lied because once he had done it, he couldn't bear to acknowledge what he'd done. Perhaps not even to himself. Dorac knows everything bad about himself, but Kremdar? He was always looking for praise. I don't remember him ever admitting that he'd made a fool of himself, or telling a story that didn't reflect well on Kremdar Kingsbrother.

"That was how I got him to confess, I think. I told him he must have had a reason, and let him justify himself to the world." He shrugged.

Gormad was trying to understand this, and not succeeding.

Dorac said slowly, "You're right. That wasn't flattering at all, you insolent - treacherous - Jaryari bastard."

Saysh and Melina gasped, but Hassdan said, "You forgave me for being all that long ago," and they clinked cups amicably.

"Most people, Dorac," said Kai, "smile or something to let everyone know when they're making a joke."

"I am not most people. I rely on my companions' intelligence. And now we need some music. I don't sing, Hassdan doesn't sing – Kai? Soumaki?"

"Gormad," said Kai.

By now all had eaten and drunk substantially. So Gormad, to his initial consternation but ultimate pleasure, was made to stand on the table and sing the "Angry Lemon Pudding" song, and then "The Talking Donkey", to great applause. Soumaki sang the whimsical ballad of Barodi who fell in love with a tree. Then it turned out that she and Saysh both knew "The Wolf and the Buttercup", so they performed a duet, Saysh showing surprisingly deft comic characterisation as the wolf.

"Do you sing?" someone asked Melina.

"Not very well, but -" She sang a song called "The Riddler in the Cave". It was perhaps an unwise choice.

"You are the greatest riddle of all," said Saysh when she had finished - and they abruptly remembered the one story that had not been told.

"You see," said Hassdan, "we are finding it strange – much as we love him – to understand why anyone would give up their savings, leave their home, risk their life, to help Dorac. Even if you had met him before, and I surely don't see how you could have."

"But I did. And – I knew he's a good man, and didn't deserve what Lord Ramos would do -"

"I am not a good man," said Dorac, "so plainly she was

confusing me with someone else."

"How can you bear not to know?" asked Kai.

"Everyone has their secrets."

"When a beautiful woman rescues you it's a big secret," said Saysh, to Kai's irritation.

"Did he save your life long ago?" asked Meril.

They were all staring at Melina, and she was unable to hold out. "Ohh!" she exclaimed in frustration. "I'm not his daughter or his long-lost wife, or anything like that. And I'm not a spy. I don't know if he saved my life - I suppose you do want to know?" she asked Dorac.

"I am curious," he said, with commendable restraint.

Gormad and Meril exchanged excited glances, and everyone sat up closer to the table. Melina clasped her hands tightly in her lap and began slowly.

"Well. I was brought up in – or near – the village Lakkeri, close to the border. We had a small farm a few miles from the main village – there were two homesteads and a well. Sometimes when I was a child there were raids from the north, and in between when we went to church our priest would be telling us about the raiders – the savages from Marod who would kill us, and rape us, and burn our crops, and steal our sheep. In those days, I wasn't knowing that we sometimes sent raiders the other way.

"Eight years ago, my mother had died, and I was living with my father and elder brother and younger sister. I was seventeen and my sister was sixteen. One night - the first we knew was seeing the village fields burning. My father and brother rode off to defend them, but we were too young. My brother was hurt that night – he still limps. But we were waiting, hoping and praying they would come back. The raiders must have decided to ride home a different way, and we heard horses and people outside suddenly-"

"Stop." Dorac leaned forward. "That is who you are. I do not want this story told."

There was a general protest. "Why not?" asked Kai.

"Because it is not a story suitable for children."

"We'll send the children home, then," Kai said cheerfully, although he thought Dorac was being unusually scrupulous. Ignoring the reproachful looks of Meril and Gormad, he dragged them out, and gave one of the staff a silver piece to get them safely back. Then he returned, to find that Melina had waited for him. She continued to stare at her hands, and Dorac stared at the floor, as she went on.

"I think they must have been watering their horses at our well. We tried to keep quiet, but then two men pushed into the house. My sister ran up to hit one of them, but he knocked her down, and then got on top of her, and the other one grabbed me -"

Soumaki put a hand on her arm. All the men looked away, except Dorac, who was already looking away.

"He had a knife, and he was tearing my gown, and whispering about making Marodi babies - and then a man and a woman ran in. The man was you. You pulled the men off, and dragged them outside. I wondered if we were going to be raped by twenty men instead of just two, but then the woman came back, and said her captain wanted to know what had happened, and if we were all right. So I told her, and she went out, and I stood in the doorway and watched.

"There were lots of men and some women and horses outside,

and the two were being held by other men, and you were staring at them with your sword drawn, and they looked very frightened. I remember exactly what you said."

She spoke slowly. "You said, 'The penalty for rape is death, so you are fortunate you didn't succeed in committing it. We are not barbarians. *We do not kill children, we do not commit rape, we do not take pleasure in torment.'*

"That's a Marodi saying, isn't it? Then you said to them, 'God expects obedience abroad as well as at home. So. If you never do anything like this again, and tell no lies about tonight, then I will tell no one why this happened, and neither will these soldiers.' And then – I didn't quite see what you did, but the men howled, and there was blood. I think you cut an ear off each of them. And then you said, 'Patch yourselves up quickly, we've lost enough time.' You looked round and saw me watching, and you nodded at me, and said to the woman, 'Guard this house until we leave.' And I asked her, 'Who is that?' and she said, 'Dorac Kingsbrother'. And then you all rode away."

There was a pause, and she looked up at Dorac, and he looked at her.

Hassdan said, "Melina, you do not know how long we have all waited to hear that story. You have made me very happy." He stretched out a hand to her, but she shrank away with the reluctance she had always shown, and which Dorac could now understand.

He said, "I am sorry I didn't remember you. It was dark, and a long time ago. One of those men drowned on the way home – an accident the next day. The other lived a decent life, as far as I know, and died a few weeks past."

"Not mourned by you, I think," said Hassdan.

"No."

"And on his deathbed he called you a self-righteous bastard who would never have killed children," said Kai.

"Mmm."

"And you told nobody. You refused to tell the King," said Soumaki.

"I didn't refuse. He asked, and I told him I'd done what I thought right, and took responsibility. Perhaps he asked Marrach as well. I don't know. We didn't speak of it again."

Melina was adjusting to other people's share in her story. "Is the woman still alive?" she asked.

"Galla Kingsister died in the War from the Sea. Melina, it may have been me who lamed your brother."

"I know. It doesn't matter. You made me feel that people like me could get justice."

"My first captain did that for me," said Dorac, and did not elaborate. Then he asked, "But why didn't you tell me before?"

"You're a fool, Dorac," said Soumaki. "That is just the sort of story a young woman wants to tell a strange man, when she's alone with him in the woods in the middle of the night."

Dorac said, "Oh."

"My father said we should never tell anyone. In case they thought it meant we were too friendly with the enemy. And I never have, and now I am the enemy. I can't go back."

"Oh, you'll get used to the Marodi savages," said Hassdan.

"And if you haven't arranged your lodging yet – and it's

508

getting late – come back with me, and meet my husband and children," said Soumaki.

"Or if you don't like children, my wife can find you a bed. These other three only have cells at the castle."

"And that's where I'm going now," said Dorac, standing up, stumbling and stretching. "And if there's anyone else in my cell, I shall throw them out in the street. But I meant what I said," he added. "It is not a story for children."

"Don't worry," said Kai, remembering Gormad crying on his shoulder for his dead master. "None of us will tell them."

(But it did occur to Kai that Gormad might be worrying about why he had been excluded. He took the boy aside the next day, and told him that in his view the story did not reflect any discredit on Master Dorac. "Of course not," said Gormad.)

Hassdan was settling the account, and Soumaki was telling Melina about her children, and Saysh was standing around absorbing the evening's revelations, and Kai said to Dorac, "Some of the theories about what happened were very offensive."

"To him or to me?"

"Both, but mainly you."

Dorac shrugged.

"And if I were a fanciful man – which I am not – I would say that you saved Marrach's soul, and he saved your life."

"Only God saves souls," said Dorac predictably. "How did he save my life?"

"Would you have died at the Old Stones if Gormad hadn't been there?"

"Gormad and you, Kai. I don't know."

So they all left, and the tavernkeeper simpered, and said it was an honour to host Master Dorac on this night of nights, and all the servants lined sleepily up to bow to them. Dorac managed a reasonably courteous smile, but as soon as they were outside in the abrupt cold, he muttered, "That's ridiculous."

"Why?"

"Hassdan, I went to Ferrodach, and I did not murder anyone. How does that make me a hero?"

"Don't worry," said Hassdan after a moment's thought. "We don't think you did anything heroic. You're right. You did not. You only went on as you always do – doing your duty no matter how difficult, and staying loyal to the King no matter the cost."

"As we all do," said Dorac, missing the point.

Soumaki took Melina home with her. There Shoran had been hoping for some time alone with his wife at last, but he put on a cheerful face and welcomed the unexpected guest, as a man has to do.

Hassdan arrived back to find Meril still telling Alida all about the evening, and complaining about her exclusion. He placated her by explaining that the story concerned attempted rape, which she conceded made it unsuitable for Gormad. Then he was scolded by Alida for the way he'd teased poor Dorac, and the talk went on.

Dorac, Kai and Saysh walked together to the Castle, and they did not say much. Saysh was reflecting on the oath he'd taken a month ago, and a night in a tavern with Gemara and Kremdar, and realising that this day and night were his true initiation into the Southern Six.

Kai was remembering an excruciatingly embarrassing

conversation with Karila, in which she called him "Master Kai" with humble resentment in every sentence, and it was plain that she never wanted to see him again. And he wished he hadn't shouted at Makkam that day, when she had only been trying to help.

Dorac found his way back to his own cell, and there was of course no one there. He sat on the bed and shed a few slightly drunken tears before collapsing into sleep.

Waking the next morning was one of the best moments of his life.

7 November 570

"Kremdar Kingsbrother, I find you guilty of the murders of Ilda, daughter of Geril, and Gaskor, son of Gahran, and of Gemara Kingsister. I find you guilty of kidnapping Filana, daughter of Geril, of unlawfully wounding Morvan, son of Harv, of deserting your post and disobeying your Six's leader, of bearing false witness under oath against Dorac Kingsbrother, and of conspiring to have him wrongly convicted. I find you guilty of adultery with Arvill, daughter of Eve. Also of suborning as your accomplices Braf, son of Arro, and Tommid, son of Lukor, who was your squire, and to whom you owed a duty of moral guidance and care, and of attempting to suborn Dav, son of Andor."

The King paused. "And I find you guilty of breaking your oath to the Thirty and betraying our brotherhood.

"By our new law, I now ask you if you wish to make appeal against your conviction?"

"No," said Kremdar.

The Hall was not quite as full as it had been two days before. Some people did not want to witness what was likely to happen next. But there was still a crowd lining the walls, and all the attention that was not on the King or on Kremdar was on his five siblings ranged on the King's left, as expressionless as they could manage to be.

Kremdar was pushed to his knees. King Arrion took a few steps forward, and spoke almost casually. "My sister Gemara advised me that there was something wrong with the verdict on Ferrodach. And I told her if that were true, the person responsible would beg for a quick death, and be refused. That was before you murdered her.

512

"You have not deigned to give us a reason for killing the children. I might be prepared to accept that you had one that was not wholly vile, and if you had acknowledged the action at once, there might have been room for mercy. But now there is none. Looking back, I can see no such betrayal as this in the history of the Thirty. People have said in the last few weeks that the Southern Six was cursed. It was. You were the curse."

Slowly he said, "Look at me." When Kremdar obeyed, the King continued, "From today, I intend there to be no doubt as to the seriousness of a Kingsbrother's oath." In the silence, "Do you have anything to say?"

Kremdar was very pale, but his voice was almost steady as he said, "No. Your Grace is just. I will accept any death you name, and I will not beg."

"I thought you would not, no matter what was ordered for you. But the sins of the guilty sometimes fall on the innocent. As with Lord Gahran and his children."

He nodded, and two guards pulled in a woman and child. One of them held the woman firmly, while the other placed a chair in the centre, and sat the little girl in it. She looked around in confusion.

Kremdar whispered, "You would not -"

"I will do whatever is needed to preserve the King's Thirty from the likes of you."

The guard standing behind the chair produced two small pieces of wood connected by a twisted wire. The onlookers recognised a garrotte, such as Kremdar had often used. They scarcely breathed. Praja hid her face in her hands.

"Not Yaina!" cried her father. "Yaina is innocent! You can't -"

"Ilda and Gaskor were innocent. 'Traitor's blood.' I have a message to send. You were saying something about not begging, as I am sure Lord Gahran would have begged for his children."

"Please! Your Grace, please! Not Yaina! Oh, God, please!"

"Gag him," said the King, and this was done.

It was then possible to hear Hassdan saying in an appalled voice, "Your Grace, please do not do this."

"There are lessons to be learned here," said the King, looking at his siblings implacably. "This is but just vengeance for the Southern Six. For Gemara."

"But even for a crime like his," Kai dared to say. "Do anything to him, but -"

"Not the child," said Soumaki, and Saysh echoed the words.

"The point is well made, Your Grace," said Dorac calmly. "But if you take it further, you'll frighten her."

There was a soft sigh in the hall.

"Perhaps you're right," said King Arrion. He took Yaina's hand, and gently pushed her back to her mother's arms. Then he turned back to Kremdar. "I see that you still do not understand what all your siblings know. 'We do not kill children, we do not commit rape, we do not take pleasure in torment.'

"I would take very great pleasure in your torment, so I shall have to give you a quick death, after all.

"Take him out, and hang him from the walls at sunset. He can have the time till then to make his peace with his family, and with God. Send him a priest."

"Your Grace," said Praja abruptly, "he doesn't need any time with his *family*." She curtsied to the King, swept her daughter into her arms, and stalked out of the room. Yaina looked back at her father over her mother's shoulder, and he looked at her, until the door closed behind her forever.

*

About an hour later, the King found time to send for Gormad. He entered the Small Chamber alone, very nervously, and knelt. And all the Southern Six were standing by the wall, looking at him.

"You may stand up." King Arrion was also smiling, and that made him more nervous still. Kings do not smile at children. "You've been told that you are my brother's son?"

"Y-yes, Your Grace," he whispered.

"You need to choose whether to be so openly or not. Perhaps a hard choice. You might take counsel from your lord. Whoever that is. So. After all that's happened, do you still want to be a squire?"

His mind showed him Torio, gasping blood, and then dead. There was sick in his mouth. But, "Yes, Your Grace."

"Sheru Kingsister is willing to take you on." He smiled adultly at the face that Gormad couldn't make polite, and went on, "Or would you prefer to go back to the Southern Six?"

"Yes, Your Grace."

"Well, here they are. It is most unorthodox, but I think I shall leave this decision to you."

"To me?"

"Yes. Any of them is willing to have you, so choose, and serve them well."

515

Gormad thought nothing had ever been so unfair. They looked at him in a friendly grown-up way that gave him no help.

"We are all waiting for your word, sir," said Master Hassdan solemnly, making it much worse.

"If you have any sense, boy," said Dorac, "you will choose Kai."

"But I went after you," he said shyly, and knelt. "I will swear my sword to no one else."

Hassdan said afterwards that he would have walked ten miles to see Dorac's face. "You only say that to the King," he said gruffly, but he pulled the boy up, and hugged him hard. "Very well. You may have cause to regret it, but very well."

And the King turned to his siblings, and said, "Good. And now - we all mourn Gemara. She led you well, if strictly. Hassdan, can you lead as well?"

There was a moment's surprise.

"I - I can try, Your Grace."

"Dorac," said the King lazily, "are you willing to serve under a Jaryari brother?"

"In this case," said Dorac, "it would be an honour."

*

Kai said afterwards in the Great Hall that he would have walked, well, at least *five* miles, to see Hassdan's face.

"And Saysh will be a good brother, I think." He grinned at Soumaki. "I confess I did not like him at first. I dined with him, and his conversation was all about his lady, whose name I forget. I wasn't sure she would have liked the way he spoke."

He was surprised when Hassdan laughed, and astonished when Soumaki said, "But you should show the poor man some grace. He was talking to Kai Kingsbrother, after all. He had to boast a little."

"Do I talk like that?"

"No, in fact you're all modesty and discretion. But still you are Kai." She gazed innocently at his suspicious face, and went on, "Kai, whom all the women stare at when he crosses the yard. Kai, who can charm any female out of her smock. Isn't that what they say, Hassdan?"

"Or a nun out of her habit."

"Nobody says that!" protested Kai, very disconcerted.

"Of course," said Hassdan maliciously, "you're the expert in what people say about you behind your back." Afterwards, he said to Soumaki, "You should not have told him. His great charm was that he didn't know."

"He ought to know. He needs to grow up," said Soumaki, not for the first time.

*

The hanging duly took place that afternoon, and there was a gloomy air at supper in the Great Hall. When the meal was over, King Arrion left his place to go over to where the Southern Six were sitting. "Walk with me, brother," he said to Dorac, and they went out together, followed at a few paces by Hayn Kingsbrother and a guard.

King Arrion was silent as he led the way up a stair and along a passage. Dorac said, "I have not yet thanked you."

"Thanked me for what?"

"You changed the law. You changed the bloody law!"

"That was Makkam. She has high thoughts about justice for

517

everyone. You should thank her."

"I will," said Dorac, slightly puzzled.

They came to the Willow Chamber. The King said, "Wait for us outside," to the others, and the two went in.

"You might have trusted me this afternoon," said King Arrion, wandering over to the window, opening the shutters and looking out on the dark. He sounded aggrieved.

"I did trust you, Your Grace."

"You trusted me not to kill her. Hassdan and the others could have trusted me too, I think. But I had spoken to Praja beforehand. She will have told the child it was only a game."

"Perhaps I should," Dorac conceded. "But I still think she was frightened."

"You never liked my little jokes, did you?"

"Not all of them."

After a pause, "Are you going to say it, then?"

"What should I say?"

The King turned and looked at him, and spoke slowly and deliberately.

"You could say: 'Your Grace. With all possible deference and humility - how the hell do you dare talk to *me* about *trust?*'"

There was silence.

"You could say: 'Your Grace. I served you and fought for you and risked my life for you for fifteen years, and never gave you the slightest reason to doubt my loyalty, and as soon as someone told lies about me you believed *them*. You sat in your judgment hall, called me a liar and a murderer, and sent me to die at the Old Stones. Then, when my friends had proved beyond all doubt that I was innocent, and I had returned and saved your life, you graciously allowed me to swear to serve you and risk my life for you for another fifteen years.'

"You could say that."

More silence. Dorac said at last, "There was a trial. There was evidence. You had to listen to the evidence."

"Oh, yes, I listened. I listened to the evidence, telling myself I had to be so just, so impartial, and not let our friendship influence me. So impartial, that I couldn't see what Kremdar and Arvill and Kara were doing to you."

"I didn't make it easy for you. I walked into that room with a drawn sword. What kind of madman does that?"

"Stop making excuses for me. You always do. I should have talked to you, or appointed another judge, or *something*. I'd known you longer than anyone else in that room. I should never have believed for a moment that you would do that, but I did believe it. That is my shame for ever. I even felt guilty, angry, that you had done something so monstrous for my sake. I did believe it, until Gemara told me I was wrong."

Gemara. The conversation stopped for a little time, while they both thought of Gemara, who rarely said a kind word to those she loved, but whose love was none the less fierce for that.

"You begged me to believe you, and I would not."

Dorac said hesitantly, "You are asking if I was angry with you."

"I'm saying you should have been angry! What kind of fucking saint are you that you weren't angry? You were my oldest friend, and I almost hanged you. And I know you. I know there were times when you wished I had."

"Yes."

"I nearly hanged you. And if I had - and discovered the truth afterwards - well, then everyone would have been very distressed, and the Bishop would have led a special Mass for you, and songs might have been written, and what I would have done to Kremdar only God knows, and my wife and family would have tried to console me for the mistake I had made – and all that would have done you no good at all."

"It didn't happen."

"It nearly did." He looked away. "You don't know how nearly."

"You wouldn't call me a saint if you knew what I wanted to do to Kremdar. And you put all that right on Saturday."

"No. On Saturday I did what I could as king, to right an injustice. This is not about being king. This is about you and me. What I did - to my friend."

"Arrion," said Dorac, and few people had ever heard him speak so gently, "if you are asking me to - forgive you - of course I forgive you. It was a mistake. It is well. It is over."

"Over. Thank God."

"Yes. And," he went on rather obscurely, "you read my letter."

Apparently it was not obscure to Arrion, and he laughed roughly. "Yes, your letter. Unusually subtle for you, I thought. 'You will not hear from me again', meaning *Despite what you have done to me, I do not intend to cause you any trouble.* 'I remain your obedient servant and subject', meaning *Although you have taken from me the name of brother and sent me into exile, I refuse to give up my allegiance, and I will return any time you command.* Everyone else wondered why I made it an order."

"Everyone except me."

"Yes. You would've come back from the moon, if I had commanded it."

"What would I be doing in the moon?" asked Dorac.

"I don't know. Isn't there some children's story about people living in the moon? You would have come. You always came when I needed you." He sighed, and then smiled a little. "You remember the first time you came?"

"That was not a command. You made it very clear that it wasn't. I chose."

The memory was still vivid to both of them. The Queen had insisted on her younger son spending some time with a troop of the Kingslands soldiers. And one day they had ridden out together on a routine errand, one a playful young prince, and the other a solemn young soldier. They had done their errand, and had had a rather silly conversation (silly on Arrion's side at least) about orders, giving them, and obeying them, or not - and by the time they rode back, they had both known they would be spending the night together.

That had been twenty-two years ago.

"You never told anyone, did you?"

"No. You?"

"I told Malouri. She has the right to know everything about me. And I told Gemara, a few weeks ago. No one else. I am very glad Karnall and Herion didn't have their grubby hands on that - because you were willing to climb out of windows in the night - and keep part of your life a secret from everyone forever. A hard thing to ask."

"What I remember about that time," said Dorac, "is being happy. Happier than I had ever been."

"And you'd been so very happy before," said the King sarcastically. "So. We were both happy, for a while. And since then we've both been happy with other people. But you are still my oldest friend. And the best, if you are willing."

"Yes," said Dorac. With some embarrassment, but more truth, he went on, "Your Grace, I will be your servant and your subject. And also your friend and your brother. For all my life."

"And all mine."

15 November 570

The white boulders were the same as Gormad remembered. They rode past the graveyard on one side, and the abandoned possessions of the dead on the other, and entered the Village with No Name. Dorac and Gormad rode ahead with two soldiers, and then came the wagon with the guarded prisoner, and Lady Sada and her servant at the back, and more soldiers.

"There is an inn," Dorac turned round to say.

"We do not need an inn."

"It is not yet moonlight, my lady. We might all like to eat. And she might wish to see a priest." He gestured.

"Tcha!"

"It is customary to allow the condemned to make peace with God," said Dorac, and Gormad watched him hold Lady Sada's gaze until she nodded.

So they went back to The Crescent Moon, and two of the soldiers lifted Lady Karnall of Aspella out of her wagon and carried her in. This arrival caused even more interest than their last visit, and the whole village seemed to be crowding after them, but Lady Sada silenced all questions, and banished other guests. The priest was sent for, and Lady Karnall consented to talk to her, but not for very long. They ate, the prisoner guarded at a separate table.

It had been a long quiet four days' ride. The soldiers had talked a little, but not cheerily, and Dorac had drilled Gormad in swordplay, and spoken occasionally to Lady Sada. But whenever Lady Karnall was sitting near, no one said anything.

Gormad had heard one scrap of conversation. Lady Sada, the Warden, had ridden up to the litter and stared at the woman inside. And the woman had stared back. "You can do this, can you?" she said. "We were friends for fifty years."

"Friends. Everything you told me, I believed; every piece of information you gave me, I passed on. I checked nothing. And so innocent people died. Yes, I can do this, and my heart will be glad when you are dead."

Gormad shuddered. He himself had no words with the prisoner. She stared at them all with a look he could not describe, and he seemed to feel her wishing them ill. ("Malignancy" was a word he learned from Makkam later.) Master Hassdan had said she was a witch.

"Is she cursing us?" he dared to ask his master one day.

"Lady Sada and me, perhaps. Probably not you."

"Has anyone cursed you before?"

"I have condemned many people to death. Some of them cursed me before they died. If such things worry you, you're of little use in the Thirty."

And now night had fallen, and thirteen people sat in the inn, with two soldiers outside. One man abruptly started coughing, and could not stop.

"There is nothing to fear," said Lady Sada sternly, and Gormad realised for the first time that he was not the only one who was afraid.

"I have been there before," said Dorac, and stood. "They are carved stones on a hill. Come."

They left the horses at the inn. There was a path behind the village, going upwards. Dorac must have walked it before, the only one, and he took a lantern. Lady Karnall was carried in a litter, with two soldiers behind, and Dorac, Gormad and Lady Sada walked ahead. Lady Sada, who was very old, was slow and panting, leaning on her maid, but she looked grimly determined.

A woman stepped out of the trees, making everyone except Dorac gasp.

"Do you know where you are going, friends?"

"We know."

"Along this road is a circle of ancient stones in a place clear of trees. Step into the circle, and say, 'I have come here to die.' Death will come for you."

She paused, and then said, "And only one can go, the one intending to die."

"No," said Dorac, gesturing towards the litter. "The lady cannot go alone, nor can she step."

"It is the way."

"Not tonight. We are here to escort her, by order of the King." Gormad thought he had never heard anyone speak so quietly and yet so finally. The woman stepped aside.

It was very cold. Gormad tried to cheer himself by imagining how he would tell the story to Meril and Jamis, but they seemed very far away. It was almost too dark to see the path.

Then they were out of the trees, onto a flat space. And the Stones were there, so very big, so very still. They made a kind of circle, surrounding a single stone, smaller than the others, but higher than a man, in the middle.

The litter was laid at the edge. Lady Karnall stared into the ring. She turned her eyes on Lady Sada, a gaze full of hate. "I cannot walk," she said.

Lady Sada gestured to the soldiers, but they shuddered and didn't move. The witch laughed. "I can't do it, then, can I?"

"You can crawl," said Lady Sada harshly. "You were given the choice of any death."

Lady Karnall was still.

Master Dorac bent down and gathered the old lady in his arms. She spat at him, but did not otherwise resist, and he carried her into the circle.

Gormad had thought he could not be more frightened, but he was wrong. The Place to Die. Suppose she said the words *now*, or suppose words weren't needed? But Dorac seemed unconcerned. He laid her down quite gently by the central stone. "May God have mercy on your soul."

He walked back out of the circle, and Gormad breathed again.

Lady Karnall sat on the ground under the moon, and they all looked at her. "Say the words," said Lady Sada. Gormad's back prickled.

"But how do I know – he may not keep his promise," she said, and her voice was suddenly shrill. "He may have killed them all – all my kin, my daughters -"

"You know because my nephew is to be trusted. My nephew whom you tried to murder. You die, Herion dies, Rakall and the others live, and keep most of Aspella. More generous than any of you deserve. That was the agreement. Arrion will keep his side. Say the words."

"You cannot make me." She scrabbled with her hands on the ground, apparently trying to pull herself towards the far side of the circle.

Dorac drew his sword. "You made a bargain with the King, my lady. He sent me to kill you if you break it."

"*You*," she said, her hands still. "The childkiller. They'll always call you that, you know. Nothing King Arrion can do – no new law – will stop people believing that you killed the children at Ferrodach."

Dorac said nothing.

"Say the words."

The old woman looked up at the sky, and sighed. "I have come here to die."

For a moment nothing happened. Then there was a sound like the clear single chime of a bell, but very loud. Gormad blinked. And suddenly there was a figure in the circle next to the crouching woman. It was tall and wrapped all in a white robe, and the glimpse of its face that Gormad saw was white – not like a person, but white like snow. He had never been so cold. *Death will come.*

In its hands the figure held a bowl, and it bent down to offer it to Lady Karnall. "I drink this, I suppose?" she said. The head bowed. She took the bowl, and drank. Death placed a hand on her head, and began to mutter softly, turning to stand between her and the onlookers. They heard a gasping wail that haunted Gormad's nightmares, and saw her slump to the ground.

The figure turned to the watchers, and raised its long white sleeves. "Fare well." Its voice was vague and uninterested, yet commanding.

527

"So," Dorac said, in a voice that was not in the least frightened, and turned away. But he murmured to one of the soldiers, "Hide, and watch to make sure there's no trick."

"What trick could there be?" Gormad ventured, when they were descending the hill, and he had stopped shaking. "How could she trick Death?"

"Death?" said Lady Sada scornfully. "A mummer from the village dressed in white, hiding behind the stone with a bowl of poison."

"Oh -"

"Empodene, probably," Dorac agreed. "Kai was right about this place."

There was no trick. In the morning, her body was lying in the field outside the village. They buried it with the briefest of ceremonies, left the litter in the other field, and rode away.

And far away in Aspella in the west, the trials concluded, and King Arrion kept his word.

Epilogue – Christmas

Gormad was pleased to be back at Stonehill, and to see his friends. He and Dorac had spent a few days at Valleroc, which had not been quite what he had expected. He had been looking for a substantial estate, perhaps not the size of Dendarry, but at least as big as Drumcree, and Valleroc contained barely two villages, a wood and a lake. The hall itself was not much bigger than a good-sized farmhouse. There were hardly any servants, and no modern luxuries.

And Dorac was a boringly serious landlord, and had been very angry at Gormad's total lack of interest in, and attention to, tenants' disputes. "You'll be a lord someday," he said, boxing his squire's ears, "and people will look to you for justice."

This seemed unlikely to Gormad.

Anyway, it was Christmas. And after the midnight procession to the Cathedral with the Christmas light, and the morning Mass and gift-giving, he stood behind the Southern Six's table for the magnificent feast in the Great Hall, and clumsily waited on his master, and in between ate well himself.

Then came the yearly rewards. Two-thirds of the original Ferrodach lands were made over back to Lady Filana, and Emmia Kingsister was ordered to be her guardian and manage her wealth until she came of age. One third of the Aspella lands was distributed to other people. Gormad began to be bored. Mayeel, daughter of Vishara, was named for the second time to the Thirty, this time to the Southern Six, to replace Kremdar. Captain Renatar (*him?*) was called to the Western to replace Torio, and somebody else to the City, to replace Mayeel.

And then, "We have had cause to be grateful to some of our Stonehill children in recent months," said the Queen, and to Gormad's great pleasure she presented jewelled brooches to Meril, daughter of Nilena, and Jamis, son of Raix. Jamis had never been the centre of so much attention in his life, and he looked more awkward than Gormad had ever seen anyone be.

And then –

"Gormad, son of Adam."

When Jamis had been mentioned, he had wondered - but when he heard his name, he froze, and Dorac and Kai had to push him towards the centre of the Hall. He knelt shaking, and stared at the floor, and through buzzing heard the King say, "As squire to two or three different people, and as assistant to the Queen's enquiries, you have done well. Without you, it would have been much harder to uncover the threat which by God's grace has been averted. You are no longer to inherit Dendarry. I am therefore giving you the lands of Maint, forfeited by Herion, son of Vestor, for you and your lawful heirs, to hold directly of the crown of Marod. Will you swear fealty for them? You can say 'I will swear', if you wish," he hinted with a smile, as Gormad looked up in confusion.

"I will swear," he managed to say, and kissed the King's hand, and was handed a long scroll in Latin.

"Be a good lord and a loyal one. Continue to deserve well of me, Gormad. For the credit of Ramahdis and Farili of Dendarry, who brought you up - and of Dorac Kingsbrother your master - and -" the King paused - "for the credit of my late brother, your father."

Behind him, he heard a lot of people gasp. And he realised

with sudden glee that he would have no further trouble with Hanos.

*

After the rewards, Hassdan went home to share Christmas with his wife and Meril. Over the last few weeks, there had much debate with the bonesetters and others, and the time had come for the conversation. As they sat around the table, he nodded to Lilli, who tactfully went out, and then he said, "You know what they are saying about your foot?"

Meril nodded, feeling herself shrink, and the festivities fade. *The foot will never be right*, she had been told. *You will walk, but you'll always limp. You'll ride, but you'll need help to mount.* She would never be able to run, or dance. Or to fight.

"These people may be wrong," said Hassdan. "They often are. You have many years to grow stronger. But it does look as if you will be using a stick for some time."

"I can't be a squire, then," she said, with what courage she could.

"No. But I've been speaking to the secretaries. They think the scriptorium could have uses for you."

"But I'm not good at reading and writing and learning things."

"There are books of maps and charts as well as books of words. And some of the secretaries do other things than read and write. The King and Queen need clever people, Meril. To make plans, perhaps, and in time for other things, I think."

Meril tried to understand this new idea. "Would I live at the Castle?"

"No, you will live here. If you wish. Meril, a Kingsbrother can do very well without a squire. But Alida and I cannot do without you."

"You may be especially needed next summer," murmured Alida, blushing.

"Oh!"

And Hassdan got up and wandered off upstairs, to allow the females space to talk about babies.

*

At a brief ceremony in the chapel later, Kai Kingsbrother made and received the appropriate oaths to and from his new squire. Tommid had been officially absolved of guilt for Gemara's death, but he remained bewildered and in misery. "He needs someone who will be kind to him," the King had said, "and whatever other flaws Kai has, he will always be that."

Very late that evening, less pleasantly for Kai, the Queen beckoned him aside. The dancing was nearly over.

"A merry night, Kai."

"Yes, Your Grace," he said happily.

"And now I am going to spoil it, by making you angry. Makkam is a friend of mine, as is her mother. She suffered a great grief seven years ago. I do not wish her hurt again."

She looked at him with her eyes at their most daunting, and he clearly read the message. *If you wish to make any more bastards, Kai, do not make them with her.*

And she went back into the crowd.

It was only a few dances, and some conversation in between. Kai did indeed feel both insulted and angry, and not for himself alone. A woman like Makkam would not permit anyone to make bastards with her, and would certainly be able to say so for herself. *Makkam Maid-of-*

Ice.

But one could not be angry with the Queen. Over the next few days he considered, and decided that what she meant was that he shouldn't kiss Makkam, daughter of Eve, unless he was also planning to marry her. Marry and settle down, as Soumaki was always urging him to do, and promise to love one woman only for the rest of his life.

And the one woman would have to be prepared to give the rest of her life to a man who had nothing but an old sword, a few debts and (according to Hassdan) an ominous reputation, and who would be at home fewer than half the nights of the year.

He was not at all sure that he was ready for this, but it was something to think about.

So he thought about it.

*

The day after Christmas was the great St Stephen's Day Fair. And the day after that, the King, the Queen and the Prince rode out on an idle expedition called a hunt by courtesy, and Dorac and his squire and a few guards rode with them. As they headed home in the chill of early dark, the King said to his nephew, "Drop back a little. I want to talk to my brother." As the boy obeyed, he asked Dorac, "When did you remember who he was?"

"At first I was feeling too sorry for myself to think of him. When he told me that his father favoured him over the others, I remembered visiting Dendarry with Prince Rafad."

"He's a good lad."

"He is impulsive," said Dorac severely. "And yet it always seems to end well. God must like him."

"Hmm. We have exchanged letters with Jaryar. If Lady Igalla should come visiting us here in Stonehill, you should keep out of her way."

"Is that probable?"

Instead of answering, the King asked, "What can you tell me of her?"

Dorac shrugged. "She is young. Brave. Courteous. Not stupid. She had more - charity than Lord Ramos or his soldiers." He paused thoughtfully, meeting the King's eyes. "A prince could do worse."

"I did not give you leave to speculate about such a matter."

"No, Your Grace. I speculated without leave."

King Arrion smiled. Then he looked up at the looming walls of the city, and said, "I have rewarded many people. I would wish to have rewarded you."

"For not killing Ilda and Gaskor?"

"You saved my life."

"The Southern Six swore an oath to defend the King. That is the purpose of the Thirty. And I have already everything I need."

"There's nothing you want? Few people could say that."

Dorac looked at him, and away. "I'm growing old, and Tor is dead. You can do nothing about either of those things. Valleroc is as much land as I desire. I have enough money." More quietly, "And you have given me a son. Or as close as I'll get to having one."

"Since we are brothers, it's fitting that my nephew should be your son, I suppose. I can truly give you nothing?"

He thought. "Give me leave for a week or two, Your Grace, to go to the north."

"To go home? Why?"

Slowly, "When I came to Stonehill, twenty-three years ago, there were two people in the north I was sorry to leave. Captain Ettuar has been dead for years, but my cousin Jaikkad, I believe, is alive, on his farm with his family. I've seen him twice since I left. He was very proud when your mother named me." He fingered Derry's mane. "You know how rumours go. I don't know what he may have heard since September. I would like to make sure he knows the truth, and he would not be able to read a letter."

"All you want of me is permission to go to your home village, and reassure your cousin that you're not a murderer?"

"Yes. And - there is a Jaryari woman called Melina. We found her a place working in a bakery in the city. I owe her a debt. If you could provide for her, I would be grateful."

"It shall be done. So that is all. It was a good day for Marod, Dorac, when you came to Stonehill."

"Your Grace is kind enough to say so. It was also a good day for me."

They rode home in the frosty dark.

From the Archives of the Stonehill Scriptorium

The fifth statute of King Arrion and Queen Malouri in the year 570 After Landing, regarding the Making of Appeals
(Sometimes called "Makkani's Law")

When a man or a woman has been convicted of a crime for which the penalty is death, exile, mutilation or a fine to the value of five gold pieces or more, before sentence is passed, the judge shall ask the convicted person if he or she wishes to Make Appeal.

If the convicted person so wishes, the judge shall enquire if they have a friend to support them, and if they can pay the price which is one silver piece to the King's treasury.

If these conditions are satisfied, the convicted person shall be sentenced, but sentence shall be delayed. The convicted person shall remain in prison for forty days, and they and their friend shall prepare evidence and argument, but they may not compel any witness who has already given evidence to speak to them against that person's will.

The lord or lady of the place shall appoint three judges to hear the Appeal. One of these shall be a priest of the Holy Church. The other two shall be citizens of good repute of no lesser rank than the convicted person. The judges may not refuse to serve without good reason. The judge and jurors who heard the original trial may not be appointed.

The time of forty days may be lessened by request of the

convicted person, but may not be extended without permission of the King.

At the end of the time, the judges shall question the convicted person, and they and their friend shall present their evidence and arguments. The witnesses in the original trial shall be present if possible, and may be questioned by the judges.

The King's Questioner may take part in the Appeal as he or she thinks fit, in accordance with conscience.

The judges shall consider all the words spoken and evidence presented, and shall decide if the original verdict was correct. If it was so, sentence shall be carried out forthwith, and unquestioned thereafter. If they decide that the Appeal was not merely wrong but worthless, and an insult to God, the guilty person and his or her friend shall both suffer a penalty of twenty lashes. But if they decide, either unanimously or by a majority, that the verdict was false or in error, then they shall declare it Void, and the convicted person shall be declared innocent, and shall go forth quit and free in this matter forever.

No other vengeance may be taken or punishment imposed by anyone on the friend of the convicted person or the witnesses at the original trial, unless perjury is proved. And no blame shall be attached to, or vengeance taken against, the original judge and jurors, for no one is free from error save God alone.

[On the first occasion of use of this law, the appeal of Dorac Kingsbrother, not all the procedures were followed, for obvious reasons. The convicted person did not make his appeal immediately; he did not remain in prison; and the sentence had already been imposed.

The King and Queen and Council waived these provisions in the unique circumstances.

During the next decade, similar laws were introduced in Jaryar, Haymon and Falli.]

ACKNOWLEDGEMENTS

I am forever grateful for the encouragement of those who read on to the end and liked it: Kathy Buchan, Ginny Cooper, Sally Hodges, Clint Redwood, Judith Renton and Eleanor Wallace. Also for the encouragement generally of Fran Beedell, Deirdre Bell, Michael Dunster, Ruth Dunster, Alan Howe, Maura O'Neill, Lindy Todd, Margaret Stone, Andrew Wallace, Ruth Young, my family and the housegroup.

The late Audrey Wallace gave me the diary that started Dorac on his adventures.

A huge thank-you to C.S. Woolley and everyone at Mightier Than the Sword UK Publications, for taking a risk on me. They have been very helpful and supportive throughout the process. And to C.S. Woolley, Stephen Hall and Ian Storer for the artwork and cover design.

Thank you also to Cornerstones Literary Consultancy, especially copy-editor Sarah Quigley and manuscript assessor Dinah Ceely, whose positive report kept me going for a long time.

Thank you to Jono Renton (www.studiorenton.com) for creating my website, Ian Storer (http://scipio6.wixsite.com/scipio-designs) for illustrating it, and Stephen Hall for turning my scrawl into actual maps.

One of the many joys of creating my own continent and history is that I do not need to get facts right. For example, I am aware that my "squires" are not quite like real medieval squires. However, I should acknowledge the assistance of two invaluable, entertaining and very different books in the formation of Ragaris – "The Time-Traveller's Guide to Medieval England" by Ian Mortimer, and "The Tough Guide to Fantasyland" by Diana Wynne Jones. Also, of course, thank you to Wikipedia. I am grateful for the inspiration of Katherine Kurtz, whose Deryni Chronicles gave me the idea that Christendom could be inserted into a fantasy setting.

Jonathan Batchelor answered medical questions, and Gina Hall was helpful about horses. (All mistakes are mine, of course.) I took the liberty of inventing some poisons.

But supremely, for doing nearly all the above, and much much more, thank you Mark.

Fifty years after the murders at Ferrodach -

"Bowing down to be raised
For the Dream, and God's law
-But the sheep, they all wait
For mild peace or grim war."

The Tenth Province of Jaryar

coming soon

The city of Vach-roysh in Haymon is hosting the greatest meeting of the age – electors from all over the country of Jaryar are gathering to choose their next monarch. One of the contenders is a foreigner – the reigning Queen of Marod (King Arrion's great-granddaughter). The other is a young aristocrat with everything to prove, and apparently few scruples.

A dying woman's prophecy may provide guidance and inspiration. Or it may not.

Naive Marodi squire Lida, wealthy Haymonese widow Talinti, and famed Jaryari warrior Errios all think they know what's going on. But the machinations of both sides are more complicated and deadly than any of them have guessed. On the eve of the Council, the King of Marod's servant is poisoned, and an investigation begins. How many more people need to die before the votes are counted?

The Tenth Province of Jaryar brings three nations and their turbulent history to an election like no other; where everyone has a secret, and the wrong choice may mean war.

About the Author

Penelope Wallace has lived in St Andrews, Oxford, Aberdeen and Nottingham. She is a pedantic bibliophile, a sometime lawyer, a not-completely-orthodox Christian, a wishy-washy socialist, a quiet feminist and a compulsive maker of lists. She has practised law in England and Scotland, in the fields of employment, conveyancing, and marine insurance litigation.

Her favourite authors include Jane Austen, Robin Hobb, Agatha Christie, Nancy Mitford, George RR Martin, JRR Tolkien, Marilynne Robinson, JK Rowling and the Anglo-Catholic Victorian Charlotte M Yonge.

She invented a world where the buildings and manners are medieval, but the sexes are equal.

To find out more about Penelope Wallace's work please visit:
www.penelopewallace.com
and
www.mightierthanthesworduk.com
or connect via facebook:
www.facebook.com/swordswithoutmisogyny
or
www.facebook.com/mightierthanthesworduk